THE
ROLEXXX
CLUB

THE ROLEXXX CLUB

A NOVEL

MÉTA SMITH

WARNER BOOKS

NEW YORK   BOSTON

Warner Books
Hachette Book Group USA
1271 Avenue of the Americas
New York, NY 10020

Visit our Web site at www.HachetteBookGroupUSA.com

Printed in the United States of America

First Edition: July 2006
10   9   8   7   6   5   4   3   2   1

Warner Books and the "W" logo are trademarks of Time Warner Inc. Used under license by Hachette Book Group USA, which is not affiliated with Time Warner Inc.

Library of Congress Cataloging-in-Publication Data
Smith, Méta.
   The Rolexxx Club / Méta Smith.—1st ed.
      p.   cm.
   Summary: "A young woman rises from the gritty slums and seedy clubs of Miami to music superstardom, only to discover that nobody's past truly stays buried"—Provided by publisher.
   ISBN-13: 978-0-446-69678-4
   ISBN-10: 0-446-69678-1
   1. Rap musicians—Fiction.   2. Prostitution—Fiction.
3. Nightclubs Florida—Miami—Fiction.   4. Stripteasers
Florida—Miami—Fiction.   I. Title.
PS3619.M5922R66   2006
813'.6—dc22
                                             2005035368

*For my parents, Jesse and Sylvia Smith,
for all the sacrifices they have made for me.*

For my son, Jordan, for changing my life.

*For my best friend, Angela Allen, for encouraging me,
and constantly begging me for more chapters.*

*And to Terrence Henton, my wonderful fiancé,
for loving me like no other.*

ACKNOWLEDGMENTS

I would like to thank my Lord and Savior Jesus Christ for delivering me. Without him, none of this would be possible.

I would like to thank my parents, Jesse and Sylvia Smith, especially my mother, for being my closest friend and confidant, and for always believing in me. Now, what color Jag do you want?

Jordan, my firstborn, Mommy does this all for you. I love you, baby boy!

My sister Kathy and my nephews Troy and Taylor: I love you very much!

Terrence A. Henton, the love of my life and future husband. Miami has brought me lots of great things, but the best thing it ever brought me was you. You're the most amazing man I ever met, and I love you so very much. And love to my new family and friends in Ashtabula, Ohio.

Much love to my family: my grandmother Darlene Charleston, Aunt Eva (thanks for making me your princess), Aunt Dolores (you're wonderful!), my ultra-classy uncles William (Yvonne) and Monroe (Frances). To my super-fun, super-fine, wild, and crazy maternal aunts Cookie, Pat, Gwen, and Dot: I love you to death! Uncle Brother, thank you for always remembering me with jewelry and perfume at the holidays!

Special thanks to my slew of cousins and their families. I don't have room to name you all now, but this is not my last book! But special props to Allison "Gigi" Ellis, for being more of a sister than a cousin and for always encouraging me, and to Danita Smith-Tabron and Jessica Faye Evans for always looking out and being role models. Angie Echols (another role model), Margaret and Lisa, Tasha ("I drank some lead"), Gwen, and Alan for the childhood memories. I will get you all back for exploiting my crybaby ways! Ha-ha! Also, thanks to Kevin for always being there for me when I need you. Joy, thanks for putting me on to Rick James, and Curtis for putting me up on Bruce Lee and the guitar.

Second, third, and fourth cousins, I'd love to name you all but there are so many of you. Don't get mad cuz I don't have that much room. I name you all on my Web site, though.

To my sister from another mother, Angela Allen: I could have never done this without you believing in me for all these years. I love you for being the best friend a girl could ever have, for wearing the same size as me from head to toe, and for having great taste and a fly wardrobe. And I love Mau (I think I threw up in my mouth a little after saying that), and my beautiful nieces Tiera, Dolce, and Sachi.

To my ex-husband, Gregory Randolph Berry: thank you for the gift of Jordan. I will always care and pray for you. Thank you for making my life in Miami very memorable and for everything you sacrificed. To the stepchildren who continued to care long after they didn't have to: Ivy Denise Berry and Gregory Christopher Berry. It wasn't easy for us, but I loved you like my own (still do) and I hope you realize that. Plus, love and respect to all the Berrys and Smiths in Miami and New York.

My girls: Alberia "Tang" Scarbrough, Tyra Martin, Tracey Smith, Valencia Hill: thanks for having my back throughout this and for all the years of true friendship. Love to Shelley

Jackson, Kirsten (Shaft, Parker, and the new baby), and every-body I kicked it with in college.

My boys: Schun Cortez "Serious/Fema57" Johnson, Landry Moore, Marcus (and Mimi) Roseborough (and all them chu'rin), Abnar Farrakhan, Jalal Farrakhan, Imari Havard, Snoopy, Yohance LaCour, Justin Terry, Don Cheatham, An-thony Jones, Anthony Williams, and Steve Leak.

My friends and play cousins that I have lost touch with: Cheri Alou, Fiona Verde, Keiana Peyton Barrett, Staci Col-lins, Danielle and Andrea Jones (Tyrone Jones and Aunt Michelle and Uncle Perry), Lawrence Noble, and Taffy and Taiwan Smith. I suck at keeping in touch, but I love you. Always have and always will.

Special thanks to Fareed "Wolf" Ali for my first grown-up trip to Miami, and for all the love, kindness, and generosity you showed me.

Thanks to the athletes who have been friends (more or less) and shown me insight on "the life"; it was a true education: Rumeal Robinson, Winfield Garnett, Damian "Shug" Gregory, Andre Hastings, Andre Rison, Carey D. Rich, Alton Mont-gomery, Ray Buchanan, Stacey Augmon, and Rod Woodson.

The people who made Miami such a wonderful time in my life: especially Stephanie Marie Jackson for taking me in when I had no where else to go (I will always love you, Sissy!), Heather A. Porter, Serci Cox, Nema Kemar, Kamilla, Jeannie, and Lanka. Thanks to the Miami promoters who made kick-ing it a religion for me: George Dukes, Ingrid Casares, Chris Paciello, Louis Oliver, Jesse Graves, Michael Gardner, Mal-colm Pearson, and Jig. Gracias to the Miami doormen who always showed love and let me in without having to wait for-ever: Mossimo and Reece. The Miami DJs who provided the soundtrack to six years of my life: Radamus, LS One, Khaled, Irie, Tom LaRoc, Tracey Young. The Miami spots I had so much fun in: Chaos, Level, Amnesia/Opium Garden, Penrods/

Nikki Beach Club, BED, Shadow Lounge, the Marlin, the Raleigh, the Clevelander, Mangos, the Cameo/Crobar, and Liquid.

Thank you to my former modeling agents, especially Derwin Jones of Shadez who believed in me, pushed me, was fair, and always paid me on time! Also thank you to Paul Neil, Alliance Talent, Stellar Talent, the Green Agency, and AJ Johnson. Thank you to the photographers who've made me look hot: Dain Burroughs, Albert Ortega, Jim Maxwell, Rich Markese, Lyn Parks, Derrick DeLorenzo Threatt, and Guy Carderelli, for helping me make *Jet* Beauty of the Week. Special thanks to J. Jesses Smith for always giving me plenty of shine, and to Jadakiss and Styles for the most fun I ever had on a video set and the anthem that kept me going, "We Gonna Make It."

A special shout to exotic dancers everywhere. Hope you flip the hustle the way I did! Or better.

Extra special love and thanks to Dion Fearon and Salina Crespo.

Thanks a million to the best hairstylist ever, AJ Johnson, and the staff at Ajés Salon in Chicago for keeping me fly!

Thanks a million to Foxy Brown (Inga Marchand) and Nikki Turner for loving my book and saying so! I wish you much success.

And last, but certainly not least, thanks to the people who made my career happen! You all have made my dreams come true and have my gratitude and loyalty. Marc Gerald of the Agency Group: eternal thanks for taking a chance and signing me on! You're the best! Caroline Greeven of the Agency Group: thank you beyond words for opening and reading my e-mail query and not pressing delete or ignoring it! Thanks to my editor at Warner Books, Jason Pinter, for believing in me straight out the gate. You're awesome! And thanks to Linda Duggins, my publicist and the best in the biz, for hyping me up. You rock!

PROLOGUE

June 2002—Los Angeles

DEZ SMILED FOR THE CAMERAS AS SHE WALKED DOWN THE red carpet of the Kodak Theatre for the awards ceremony. It had been a long journey, but now she'd finally arrived. Her career was on the fast track, and she had the most wanted man in hip-hop by her side. She was young, beautiful, and successful, rap's newest and brightest star. Her first single, featuring a cameo by her labelmate and boyfriend, Bentley, had gone platinum within the initial week of the video airing on BET and MTV. Her debut album, slated to drop the following Tuesday, was being shipped platinum and featured tracks produced by Sparks, the business and creative wunderkind of her label, Titanium Records. There were also tracks by Mannie Fresh of Cash Money, the Neptunes, DJ Quick, Dr. Dre, Kanye West, and, of course, her favorite female, Missy Elliott. The remaining tracks were produced by Dez herself.

Her story had amazed the industry and the media: a model-turned-rapper blessed with not only stunning looks but the creative genius it took to go into a studio with no formal training and produce some of the hottest lyrics and innovative beats the rap world had ever heard. Her style had been described by critics as "Missy meets Tupac." Her single with Bentley appealed to hard-core hip-hop fans as well as the pop audience.

She stopped and pivoted, giving the photographers great face, and they were eating it up. Their lenses devoured her with an insatiable appetite, and she tingled inside as they called out to her, "Dez, over here!" and "This way, Dez!" They were begging just to snap her photo; it was a far cry from the days of cattle calls and auditions, and the long hours of being relegated to the background of a music video. Even when she was the lead girl in a video, walking a runway, or shooting a commercial print gig, the feeling had never compared to this. Yes, she'd arrived, and there could be no denying it.

Bentley was off to the side doing his own thing, talking to Ananda Lewis. Dez flashed a smile at him, mesmerizing him with her exotic eyes. He responded by stepping away from Ananda, grabbing Dez, and pulling her close to him.

"Whoa!" Ananda gesticulated at the spontaneous move and then shook her signature lustrous locks. "We're now being joined by the lovely and talented Dez, the newest artist on Titanium Records. Dez, you look great."

"Thanks, Ananda. You look absolutely fabulous yourself. Is that Cavalli?" Dez inquired about Ananda's outfit.

"It is indeed." Ananda did a little twirl, and Dez grinned. She knew that the art of winning over journalists was to tell them how great they were, treat them like they were a star; make them feel good, and they'll always make you look good. Ananda laughed and then cut right to the chase.

"Now, there's been a lot of controversy swirling around you in the short time you've been on the scene. Would you like to comment on this?" Ananda asked her this in a very caring manner, but Dez figured it was partially because of the stroke and partially because she was just a cool-ass person.

"I'd love to, Ananda. But as a term of the settlement, I can't comment on this case with the media. I *would* like to say that above all of that, I do what I do to touch people, to add to people's lives. If you listen to my music, you'll see that I reveal the most intimate parts of me. So if you want to know about me, listen to what I *can and do say,* not what you hear on the streets. And if and when I can go into more details, you'll be the first one I talk to, Ananda," Desiree answered, fully poised. She was a natural, born to do it.

Ananda moved on to speak to Will and Jada, who, as always, had their children in tow. Dez squeezed Bentley's hand and nodded toward Will and Jada. He winked at her and gave her a quick kiss that made her heart flutter. She had often talked to Bentley about how she loved Jada Pinkett-Smith and how lucky she was to have such a beautiful family.

"Bentley, Dez, this way!" a photographer yelled through the throng of people vying for the perfect shot. They paused and posed. There was a flash so blinding they both responded by rubbing their eyes. Then out of the crowd of paparazzi there were more blinding flashes, accompanied by loud pops and followed by screams. Desiree stood momentarily stunned. A crowd of people stampeded the red carpet, a melee ensuing instantaneously. *Where's Bentley?* was her immediate thought. She attempted to turn and search for him, but her legs wouldn't move. Then her whole body went weak, and she dropped to the ground. Dez put a hand to her abdomen and inspected it through bleary eyes. Her hand was bloody. She'd been shot!

PART 1

MONEY

CHAPTER 1

BIENVENIDOS A MIAMI! WELCOME TO MIAMI. NOT THE Miami that Will Smith rapped about, or the Miami you see in glossy tourist brochures, but the real deal: the Bottom. Don't be fooled by the palm trees and ocean breeze. Miami is no vacation. In order to survive, your game must be tight, and your mind must be right, because if you can't swim with the sharks, you're bound to drown.

Miami is famous for a lot of things, from hurricanes to Cubans. But it is infamous for being crooked. The mere mention of the city brings to mind visions of a white-suited Scarface and detectives wearing pastel T-shirts with loafers, busting grimy drug dealers and gun smugglers. Every city has an underworld, but none as glamorous as Miami's. Only in Miami can a senator sit next to a drug dealer and a movie star in a club, kick it like they've been buddies for years, and no one bats an eye. Only in Miami do drug lords live in huge mansions and serve on boards of nonprofits, while their wives drop their children off at school in Lamborghinis and Ferraris, and everyone acts as if it is all so ordinary.

But for all of the shine, there is a shady side. For every high-powered drug lord living in the lap of luxury, there is a dread in the projects, slanging dime bags of weed and pooches of white, waiting for the time and opportunity to make his mark, to start his own empire or take over someone else's. For every pampered wife and girlfriend, there's one hustling with her man, one working for her man, and two trying to hold it down and send money to be put on his commissary while their man is doing a bid. For every celebrity, there is someone hungrier, grimier, prepared to go just a little bit further than the last to get ahead.

There are three simple rules for "living *la vida local*" in Dade County. Rule number one: trust no one. You will have many friends if you're a part of "the scene," but be forewarned—they aren't real friends. These are the people the O'Jays sang about in "Back Stabbers": "They smile in your face, all the while they tryin' to take your place." Those you trust the most will hurt you the most. Those you keep close want to rob you of your post. If you've got anything worth losing, anything worth fighting for, you will put your faith in no one but the Lord Almighty and yourself.

Rule number two: go for self. Miami ain't the land of philanthropy; that would be Palm Beach. (And those shady motherfuckers are another story altogether.) If you're waiting for your lucky break, your big chance, forget about it. You'll just end up sitting on the dock of Biscayne Bay, wasting time. No one is going to do anything for you unless they are getting something in return, and probably not even then. No one has your back, so if you don't do you, no one else will. It's fucked-up, but that's just the way that it is. People will offer you the sun, moon, and stars, but it all has a price. You're better off doing what you gotta do for yourself, because you will never get something for nothing, no matter how much it seems that way.

Rule number three: the golden rule. This is simple, and it

isn't some "do unto others" crap. It's this: he who has the gold, rules. In Miami, the land of the beautiful people, it's not about looks, it's all about checkbooks. Put bluntly, if you have no cash, you will get no ass. No romance without finance and all that jazz. You've got to pay to play in the M-I-A. Forget English, forget Spanish. The official language of Miami is money. If you don't have any, you'd better find a way to get some, because you have to pay the cost to be the boss. It costs money to floss.

Miami is the most picturesque field of dreams for a player to play on. The weak get caught up in the sidelines or strike out because they aren't focused. They swing too soon or too late and are thrown off by the roar of the crowds. But the true players wait for the perfect pitch and then hit that shit out of the park.

Now, that's what's up. All is fair in South Florida; sportsmanship counts for nada in this town, so play to win. And if you can't stand the heat, then stay the fuck outta Miami, because the mercury is rising, and there's not a drop of rain in sight.

CHAPTER 2

January 1999

THE ROLEXXX IS PROBABLY ONE OF THE MOST FAMOUS black strip clubs in America. Or infamous, take your pick. It has a vibe unlike any other club, that's for sure. Other black strip clubs such as Atlanta's Magic City and Gentleman's Club are known for having the finest women the city has to offer. They're the kind of girls you see in the grocery store, sit next to in class, live next door to, work in an office with, or teach your kids in a classroom; the beautiful sisters you've always wanted to see naked but couldn't.

On the contrary, the Rolexxx is famous for being off the chain. There is no telling what is gonna go down at "the Lex." It's the place that Luke goes to handpick his dancers. It's a club where the dancers can wear sneakers after a certain time; because they're working so hard and making so much dough that they need to rock Air Force Ones and Jordans to stay in the game. The Lex is like a regular strip club on crack. Way the fuck out there.

The clientele ranges from your hardest of hard-core gangsters complete with gold teeth and gats to elderly white men who look like they should be playing with their grandkids somewhere instead of blowing their retirement check at a strip joint. The girls run the gamut from your purest-looking, fresh-faced schoolgirls and businesswomen out to score some easy cash to the shot-out, bullet-wounded, tatted and inked-up, gold-teeth, burgundy hair-weave, house-arrest, anklet-wearing boogers that Chris Rock clowns on.

Dewante Reid, star center for the Miami Suns basketball team, was a regular at the Lex. He was also a regular at the club's main competitor, Coco's. Dewante was a regular at *all* the strip clubs. And when Dewante fell into the spot, he got it crunk. There was nothing in life that Dewante liked more than tits and ass.

For Dewante, whenever the season allowed, it was Monday's at the Rolexxx for "Ho Boxing," the club's female boxing night, and/or Tuesday's at Coco's, where the ghetto fabulous to the fabulously average brother went after the comedy show at the Improv Theater in Coconut Grove. It was doubtful that his wife knew about it, and even if she did, there really wasn't anything she could or would do about it. She had anything and everything a woman could want: a phat mansion, a fat bank account, jewels, gear, and a famous husband. A million women would give their left tit to walk a mile in her shoes. What more could she want?

Dewante didn't care about the tabloids or anything either, because he knew that the only people in the city that would raise an eyebrow would be the women, and probably not even them. As a star, he had carte blanche to do whatever he wanted, just one of the many perks of celebrity. His team was winning, and that's all that people *really* cared about. His endorsements were never in jeopardy because like his childhood idol, Dennis Rodman, he was already known as a bad boy both on and off the court. Any sponsor knew what they were getting before any ink hit a contract. Besides, what red-blooded man didn't like some good old tits and ass, shaking and grinding on your lap for the bargain price of ten bucks a pop?

A new stripper walked around the club asking men if they wanted table dances. At practically every table she approached, the men said yes. She possessed a pair of firm, perky breasts, a tiny waist, and a nice butt. Her large, shapely legs were golden, like she'd been in the sun, as was the rest of her nubile body. But what set this young lady apart from the rest were her eyes. There were plenty of chicks in the Rolexxx with colored contacts in every hue. But this girl's eyes were natural, and seemed to change color from a clear, hazy gray to topaz to deep cognac brown, depending on the angle she stood at or the light she stood under.

As she absentmindedly danced for a short, balding, ordinary-looking man, her chameleon-like eyes were fixated on the VIP section in the back of the club, behind two pool tables, on Dewante Reid. She recognized him the moment he walked in. But as soon as he sat down, some dancer sank her hooks in, and she'd been hemmed up in the corner with him ever since.

The object of Dewante's very special attention was Ginger, a major player in the game. Fuck what you heard, stripping is a game, and Ginger was a championship-ring-wearing MVP. Ginger bounced between Coco's and the Lex when she was in Miami, even though the managers had been tripping on other girls who'd done it lately. And despite the fact that nude table dances were five dollars and topless lap dances were ten, she still managed to clear at least a thousand bucks a night *before* she left the club.

For the right price, and depending on who you were, you could get to know Ginger a little better. Up close and personal. Most men wouldn't make her cut, as she kept her tricking exclusive. After all, she reasoned that there were only five dudes on the court during a basketball game, so she preferred to limit her roster like the NBA. Seven-figure niggas only. She didn't just deal with athletes and entertainers and hustlers she met in the strip clubs either. She was "friends" with businessmen and even a politician. She preferred to deal with men who had a great deal to lose. Their discretion was almost always guaranteed, and they were less likely to nut up and go psycho on her. Those who balked at her price couldn't afford her, and smart ones knew that a night with Ginger was an investment in sensual pleasure; she was worth every penny.

When the mood hit her, she could be found working New York, Vegas, and even Hawaii. There was plenty of money in Miami, but she preferred to explore the world and make money while she did it. Wherever the Super Bowl, NBA Finals, All-Star Game, or Masters Tournament was, so was she. She was a free spirit who followed the gravy train. Have thong, will travel was her motto.

Ginger was elegant. Too upscale for the clubs she worked at when she was in Miami. Sure, she could go work at one of those fancy white clubs like Solid Gold or Pure Platinum. She'd started out at spots like that. But they'd have her on a schedule. At the black clubs Ginger could do as she pleased; she didn't need anyone slowing her flow.

"You fine as hell!" Dewante slurred while running his hand down Ginger's thigh. Ginger stopped him dead in his tracks. She couldn't stand Dewante. Every time she saw him, he was the same: conceited, arrogant, cocksure. Money and fame had definitely gone to his head, and why wouldn't they? He could have any woman he wanted.

"Why you so stuck-up?" he snapped. "You always actin' like you so high-class."

"I *am* high-class. Recognize!" Ginger stared directly into his bloodshot eyes. "Do you want another dance or not?"

"What we at now?" Dewante pulled out his bankroll ostentatiously and peeled a series of bills off.

"I ain't one of these green hos in here. You paid me up front, remember? It was the first time you pulled out your little bankroll and tried to impress me. So you can put it away, because I wasn't trippin then and I ain't now. Now, if you want me to dance another half hour, it'll be another two fifty." Ginger put her hands on her hips. She was only gonna give this clown thirty seconds more to break bread or she was gonna move on with the five hundred of his money she had already acquired.

"How you gonna charge that much for a half hour of your time? Other girls charge by the dance! Your ass ain't do shit but look at yourself in the mirror," he complained.

"Then why was your dick so hard? Why were you moaning and groaning like that? Why were you about to come?" Ginger asked him, suggestively grazing his crotch with her talonlike fingernails.

"These bitches will dance for me for free! You know who I am!" he replied cockily to mask his embarrassment.

Who the fuck he think he is, getting loud on me? Ginger thought. *Let me check this motherfucker right now!*

"Yeah, and what, I'm supposed to get all geeked up or something? Look, I don't care if you get paid to play a fucking game for a living unless you putting some bread in *my* motherfuckin' pockets. This nickel-and-dime-dance bullshit ain't no money. *You* know who I am, and you know how I roll. See me when you're ready to play. Until then, sit your ass on the bench." Ginger spun on her stilettos. Dewante grabbed her wrist and held it tightly.

"You a feisty one, ain't you?" Dewante loosened his grip

a little, "You got attitude, heart." He grinned at her. He loved women who had a little fire. His wife was mousy as hell. She thought she checked him on occasion, but all she was doing in his eyes was nagging.

"Game recognizes game," Ginger replied. She had this nigga right where she wanted him. The tough-girl routine always worked.

"How much, Ginger? What's it gonna take?"

"That depends on what you want." Ginger stepped to him and looked him dead in the eyes. At naturally five feet ten inches, her platform shoes added another seven inches of height, making her an Amazon.

"I want you and another girl to come and party with me," he told her.

"Hmmm. Sounds like my type of party. Let me tell my friend—"

"No!" Dewante cut her off. "I'm gonna pick the girl," he told her.

"Fair enough," she said, not meaning it. She wasn't trying to lick just *any* female.

"Her." He pointed to the new girl with the café au lait complexion. Her extremely curly, dark hair was held back by a black headband and hung to the middle of her back.

"Nice eyes. But I don't know her," Ginger told him, folding her arms. She wished he would have picked one of her friends. Someone who knew how to juice a trick like Dewante for all he was worth. For all she knew, this girl didn't even "date."

"Get to know her," Dewante ordered.

"Okay. I'll see what she says. But if she doesn't want to, who do you want?"

"It's both of you or none of you," he replied.

"What's so special about her? Her body? I don't think so.

Her eyes? I got contacts, nigga!" Ginger frowned. *Who the fuck is this bitch?*

"Are you blind? Y'all look like you could be sisters. It's a fantasy, the two of you together. She looks like an angel, and I *know* you're a demon. It'll be interesting."

Ginger looked over at the girl. She did look an awful lot like her, except younger, and definitely rougher around the edges. Ginger smiled, then opened her mouth as if to speak. She paused for dramatic effect, then answered.

"I want two g's for the night. I'm up and out at 10 a.m. and anything over that is another two g's. Got that? Pay her whatever you want to, but my price is my price. Take it or leave it."

"Handle it." Dewante sat down and rubbed the bulge in his crotch, licking his lips lasciviously. "*Five* g's for the both of you all night." Dewante knew he was making Ginger an offer she couldn't refuse.

"Purse first, ass last. Let's get all the formalities out of the way. Can I get paid?" Ginger wanted to get her cheddar before he had the opportunity to change his mind. Dewante gave her a thick stack of crisp hundred-dollar bills. Ginger thought how stupid Dewante was, rolling with so much cash on hand. It was a surefire way to get jumped. It was also tacky. Carrying so much cash screamed nouveau riche. He obviously wasn't used to having the finer things in life.

But Ginger wasn't stupid. She hauled ass to confront this girl. There was no way she was going to let her say no. Not with all that money on the line. She'd start out low and work the numbers up to $2,500, *if necessary*. This girl would have no choice but to go along by the time Ginger finished spitting her game. Everyone had a price. And from the looks of the girl Dewante had his eye on, hers couldn't be that high. She looked green as hell. The girl disappeared into the dressing room.

Perfect! I'll catch her off guard in the dressing room, Ginger thought, following suit. The girl was buying a snack from the housemother. She quietly sat on a bench, sipping on a ginger ale and fanning herself.

GINGER PRETENDED TO BE REFRESHING HER MAKEUP IN THE mirror, but was checking out the fresh meat's every move.

"Oye!" Ginger called out to her, still preening in the mirror. *"Oye, muñequita!"*

"You talking to me?" The girl looked up, wide-eyed and innocent. She'd heard that aggressive lesbians took advantage of new girls in the dressing room. She'd avoided making eye contact or conversation with anyone, choosing instead to focus on the quest for the almighty dollar.

"Sí. Hablas español?" Ginger asked her if she spoke Spanish.

"Sí, bastante," the girl replied, telling her she spoke enough.

"De dónde eres?" Ginger questioned.

"Nueva Yol. New York, mami. Y tú?" the girl answered, loosening up.

"De aquí. Eres dominicana?" Ginger asked the girl if she was Dominican.

"Yeah, how'd you guess?" The girl looked surprised and reverted back to English.

"I always know my people. I'm Ginger," she said, extending her hand.

"I know. I saw you onstage. You were real good," the girl

complimented her, hoping she wouldn't think that she was flirting. Ginger *had* been good. Before Dewante came in, Ginger had the entire club crowded around the tiny stage. It was like she came alive on the stage. When Ginger danced on the floor, the girl noticed that she didn't dance with very much effort. Mostly, she just wound her hips like a reggae dance-hall girl or whispered in the man's ear. But on the stage she did splits, swung around the pole like an acrobat, and could drop it with the best of the club's dancers.

"Everybody keeps asking me if we're related! But I'm not as pretty as you," the girl admitted. Ginger laughed.

"What's your name, shawty?" Ginger asked her.

"Desire." Desire stuck out her hand. "But my real name is Desiree."

"Cute. My real name is Genevieve," Ginger told her, emphasizing her name with a heavy French accent. "But *everybody* calls me Ginger. They have since I was little. I don't know what the hell my mama was thinking, nicknaming me Ginger. Watching too much *Gilligan's Island,* I guess." Ginger and Desire laughed.

"So you makin' money?" Ginger asked Desire, eyeing her garter. Ginger estimated she had about three hundred dollars. Chump change.

"Yeah!" Desire enthused. "It's pretty good here."

"Wanna make some more?" Ginger asked carefully.

"How?" Desire asked. She wasn't new to dancing. She'd been solicited for sex before but had always resisted. She wasn't trying to get caught up in prostitution. But the thought of more money appealed to her. She could use it. She would at least hear Ginger out. She would probably say no like she always did.

"You like basketball?" Ginger asked.

"Love it," Desire answered, wondering what basketball had to do with anything.

"What about basketball players?"

"Don't know any."

"Well . . . tonight's your lucky night, Desire." Ginger grinned, going in for the kill. She knew it wouldn't take much convincing. A girl like Desire was probably starstruck. She explained to Desire that Dewante Reid had wanted to hook up with her.

"Oh my God! *The* Dewante Reid?" Desire bugged out just as Ginger expected. "He's gonna pay to go out with me?" Desire asked, lowering her voice. Ginger looked at her in amazement. She had to be from out of town *and* fresh out of high school. Either that or straight-up dingy.

"He wants to fuck," Ginger stated bluntly. She didn't have time to waste with this amateur. She was either down or she wasn't.

"Oh! You or me?" Desire asked, catching on.

"He wants to see us together."

"Oh." Desire frowned, crestfallen.

"Look, if you don't get down like that, you can fake it. I'll *pretend* I'm eating you out and let my hair fall all over the place. All you gotta do is moan and wiggle like it feels good. Then we can suck his dick for a while or fuck him or whatever."

Desire sat in thought.

"Shit, you *know* you wanna fuck him! Who doesn't? He's fine as hell! He's paid. You'd fuck him for free if you met him out somewhere else. And he's gonna pay us a grand," Ginger explained.

"I don't know." Desire hesitated. "Couldn't we get in trouble if we got caught?"

"Why would we get caught? Dewante is married! He's not gonna tell anybody. Besides, even if someone found out, the only way we'd get in trouble is if *you* told someone we got paid for it. Otherwise, it's just sex between three consenting adults. Do you plan on telling anyone?" Ginger asked her.

"Well, no," Desire answered.

"So then what's the big deal?"

"I don't know. It just seems wrong," Desire confessed.

"Yeah, okay." Ginger rolled her eyes and stared at Desire in disbelief. "It feels wrong to take a grand for something you would have done for free under different circumstances? You're trippin'! But hey, you can't make nobody wanna make no money." Ginger shrugged and turned to walk away. Desire watched as an easy thousand dollars began to walk away with her.

"Okay," Desire answered quickly. Every time she had been solicited before, she'd say she wanted five hundred dollars, and that was usually the end of the conversation. A grand was a lot of money.

Ginger turned to face Desire and smiled knowingly. She knew that no woman in her right mind would turn down such a deal. At least not one who had the cojones to dance at the Lex. Desire eyed the diamonds on Ginger's fingers and in her ears. She noticed that she wore a diamond tennis bracelet with large clear stones, not diamond chips, which had to cost a fortune. The anklet she wore had baguettes in it. Plus, she *knew* Dewante. Desire guessed that Ginger had plenty of paper. She could probably learn a thing or two from her.

"Cool. Get dressed. You'll roll with me, and I'll fill you in on the details in the car," Ginger ordered. "I'll take care of management for you." Ginger strolled out of the dressing room.

Ginger broke management off with fifty dollars to leave

early and tipped the DJ, then quickly changed her clothes in the dressing room. Within minutes she was leading Desire to her BMW, following Dewante's Porsche out of the parking lot and onto 95 North. In the car they rode in silence until Ginger's voice pierced the night air.

"How old are you . . . Desiree, right?" Ginger asked.

"Call me Dez," she said. "I'm twenty-one."

"Right. Now, how old are you really?" Ginger glanced sideways at Desiree, who was squirming nervously in her seat.

"Eighteen," she admitted.

"So why did you lie?" Ginger queried, full of suspicion.

"I wanted to drink at the club, so I used a fake ID. I'm not a good liar, but what can they say when my driver's license says that I'm twenty-one?" Desiree replied.

"Please. Them niggas at the club don't care. Quietest kept, there's some underage girls working there. For a minute I thought you were one of them," Ginger said.

"Nah, I'm eighteen," Desiree responded quickly.

"Aww, you still got Similac on your breath," Ginger teased.

"How old are *you*?" Desiree asked Ginger.

"Twenty-five," she stated, as if twenty-five were the wisest age on earth.

"You actin' like you *thirty*-five and shit!" Desiree remarked, laughing.

They followed Dewante off the interstate.

"So have you known Dewante long?" Desiree asked Ginger, full of curiosity. She definitely wanted to know more about Ginger after seeing the BMW.

"Kind of. I've seen him at a few clubs I worked at, you know, I've danced for him. And I've seen him at clubs on the beach. He's a real asshole, though."

"Don't tell me that. I'm trying to find me a baller and get

married." Ginger nearly rear-ended Dewante because she took her eyes off the road to look at Desiree like she had lost her mind.

"Damn! What I say?" Desiree gasped with her hand over her heart.

"Please, girl! Them niggas ain't worth all the trouble. You'll see. If you were smart, you'd be trying to get your own money."

"I'm *makin'* my *own* money. I want *they* money!" Desiree hooted, snapping her fingers dramatically.

"Okay. One night with this nigga, and I guarantee you that you won't be trying to fuck with athletes. Or maybe you'll have to learn the hard way. Shit, you might be one of those chicks that can deal with they bullshit."

"You fucked with him before?" Desiree asked, wide-eyed.

"Nah. But they're all the same." Ginger dismissed the question with a wave.

"How so?"

"You'll see. I'm telling you he's an asshole. He's cocky as hell, just like most athletes. Don't go falling in love with his ass if he makes you come and shit," Ginger teased. She liked Desiree. Her naïveté was refreshing, even though she was trying to play so tough. Ha! The girl had blushed when Ginger said "come." Ginger couldn't remember the last time something made her genuinely blush.

"Plus, I heard he was a freak," Ginger added.

Desiree's eyes widened. "What kind of freak?"

"I hear he's into some wild shit. This chick Peaches tricked with him once, and she never gave me the exact details, but she said she thought he went both ways."

"What? I don't believe that!" Desiree shook her head.

"Okay. Think what you want with your young ass! Athletes are always doing shit like that. They call that shit 'the other level.' They get so much pussy thrown at them that they get bored. They probably start out doing threesomes, and then one day they decide to leave the girl out!" Ginger giggled.

"Ewww. That is so nasty. I don't see how niggas do that shit. Or females either, for that matter."

"Oh, come on!"

"Come on what?"

Ginger stared at Desiree in disbelief. "You've *never* been with another woman?"

"Never!" Desiree stated firmly.

"Don't knock it till you try it." Ginger grinned.

Desiree turned up her nose. "What, are you gay or something?"

"Or something."

"What's that supposed to mean?" Desiree folded her arms and shifted her body against the leather seat to look Ginger in the eye.

"It means, if I feel like getting down with a female, that's what I get down with. If I feel like some dick, then I get some dick. Basically, I just like to fuck. I like being naked. I like to party. I want to get married one day and all that shit. But until I decide to settle down, I'm going to have some fun. Besides, no man can eat pussy the way a woman can. A woman knows what feels good to another woman. You'll see." Ginger briefly met Desiree's stare. Desiree averted her eyes. Ginger pulled into the parking lot of the Diplomat Hotel in Hallandale Beach and pulled her convertible 525 into the valet stand behind Dewante's black Porsche.

"When we get in, follow me. Act like you know where you're going. We don't want the hotel staff to think we're tricking. Look like you belong. If anyone stops you, you can say you're staying with your parents," Ginger teased.

"Ha, ha," Desiree replied.

Classy, Desiree mused, looking around. It had to be one of the single most beautiful places she had ever seen. Since she'd arrived in Miami, she had yet to see the sights.

"Give me a sec to get a room," Dewante told them before entering the hotel. Ginger led Desiree to the ladies' room. Desiree had to pee like a Russian racehorse, she was so nervous. She'd never fucked for money before, and now she was about to do it with a hoop star.

When they exited the restrooms, Dewante was by the elevators with the cheesiest grin imaginable spread across his face. They got on the elevator and pushed the button to request their floor. Dewante immediately went to work. He fondled Desiree while showering Ginger with sloppy, wet kisses on the ride up to the top level. Ginger looked at Desiree over Dewante's shoulders and made a crazy face as he mauled at her breasts. She moaned, not to fake ecstasy, but out of disgust from the slimy layer of saliva he left on her skin. Dewante was plastered, and his breath reeked of Hennessy and cigar smoke. He was so tart that Desiree could smell him, even though she was standing an arm's length away.

This is not what I imagined! Desiree thought as Dewante groped clumsily at her. She glanced at the reflection they cast in the elevator's mirrored back wall. Ginger was getting a full blast of his dragon breath as he kissed her dead in the mouth.

When the elevator stopped and the doors opened, Ginger practically shoved Dewante out the car. She gasped a sigh of relief and dramatically took in deep lungfuls of fresh air behind Dewante's back. Desiree tried her hardest to suppress her giggles and found herself relaxing because Ginger seemed so cool.

Once inside the spacious suite, Ginger headed straight for

the minibar. She grabbed two miniature bottles of Absolut, deftly unscrewed the tops, and chugged them down without flinching. Then she grabbed a can of orange juice from the fridge and took a swig. She grabbed a third bottle of vodka and tossed it to Desiree. She motioned for Desiree to drink it. Desiree smelled the strong, clear liquid and made a face.

Drink it, Ginger mouthed to her.

Desiree looked over at Dewante, who was undressing. He was fine as hell and rich too. But she'd only been around him for ten minutes and could see he was a jerk. Desiree hated men who drank too much and got sloppy. She wondered if he acted like such an ass around his wife. When she was a baller's wife, would she have to deal with shit like this? Would her husband stay out all night with women he met in strip clubs? Desiree had thought that she'd feel a real charge when she got the opportunity to sex a celebrity. So far, all she felt was disappointment. She downed the vodka, hoping it would help her get in a partying mood. She was getting a grand for this; she may as well enjoy it.

"Come and get some of this, girl. You know you been dreaming 'bout this moment since the first time you laid eyes on me." Dewante beckoned, curling his finger at Desiree.

"Hey, hey, hey. Not so fast. I thought we were here to party!" Ginger piped up.

Desiree looked at her gratefully. Ginger smiled and tossed Desiree another miniature of Absolut from the bar. She drank this one too, then chased it with orange juice the way she had seen Ginger do. Desiree felt all the blood in her body rush to her head.

"Let's get this party started, right! Let's get this party started quickly, right!" Dewante slurred, flailing his arms around, singing "Set It Off" loudly and off-key. Desiree cracked up.

"What you laughing at, girl?" Dewante asked her.

"You a nigga that should just keep his mouth shut! You actin' like a straight-up nerd and shit." Desiree giggled, feeling the effects of the liquor.

"Come and shut me up!" he challenged, still dancing. He obviously didn't take her comment seriously, which made her laugh harder.

Ginger reached in her pocketbook and pulled out a bag of hydroponic weed and a package of Backwoods cigars. She rolled a fat blunt in no time flat and blazed it up.

"Want some?" She handed the cigar to Desiree.

"Okay," she replied, taking the blunt. The three of them finished off the blunt, no one speaking.

"Do you know who I am?" Dewante asked Desiree, breaking the silence.

"Uh, yeah." She looked at Ginger and rolled her eyes.

"Did you ever think of fucking me? Did you ever dream about it?" he asked her. She had but didn't want to kiss his ass.

"I don't know," Desiree replied like she always did when she didn't want to answer a question.

"Yeah, you look like a fan. You've been dreaming of this," he repeated. Desiree was about sick of Dewante. She walked out onto the balcony and felt the salty air kiss her face. She removed her headband and shook her head, letting her curls blow wildly in the breeze. She looked back at Ginger.

Peeling her blouse from her firm, surgically enhanced breasts, Ginger slunk across the room like a feline, pulling Desiree in from the balcony but leaving the French doors open so the breeze could float in.

"Don't get it twisted. *You've* been dreaming about *this*." Ginger ran her hands over her own breasts, cupping them lightly. Dewante's cock poked at the cotton of his boxer briefs.

Ginger reached behind her back and undid her lacy black bra. She stood before Desiree and removed her shirt. She let her hands travel from Desiree's shoulders to her breasts, where they lingered for a moment before Ginger undid the hooks of Desiree's plain, white, Lycra bra. Desiree shuddered under Ginger's touch. It was like Ginger had little volts of electricity running through her fingertips.

Dewante removed his thick penis from his shorts and began to stroke himself at the sight of them. "Damn," was all Dewante could mutter before pouncing. Ginger grabbed Desiree's hand and ran playfully with her, nimbly escaping his grasp. He charged at them, but they managed to shake him. He couldn't figure out who he wanted to devour more, and he couldn't catch both of them. Dewante stood still momentarily.

"You said you wanted to party. Why rush it?" Ginger asked Dewante. She wanted more time to enjoy Desiree before Dewante butted in. Desiree may have been young and a little rough around the edges, but she did have a certain sexiness about her.

"It's my fantasy," Dewante pouted.

"Believe me, you won't be disappointed," Ginger assured him. "Besides, I heard about you. I know it ain't a party for you unless you have a little candy first." Ginger walked to the table where her purse was sitting. Desiree wondered what Ginger was talking about. Dewante wondered what Ginger had heard about him. Ginger retrieved a vial of white powder and held it up.

Cocaine! Desiree thought to herself, slightly alarmed. She blew trees on occasion and drank, but she'd never tried coke. For one, it was too expensive, but secondly, she'd seen what coke did to women back in her neighborhood in New York. But Ginger certainly didn't look strung out, and Dewante was a superstar. Plus, she was going to need a little something extra to go through with the evening's plans. She decided to play it cool.

Ginger chopped up a line. She bent over and took a heavy snort with a cut-up straw. She stood up and sniffed hard. Then she ran her fingers across her nostrils before rubbing them across her teeth. She felt the residue slightly numb her gums, then tasted the coke sliding down her nasal passages and into her throat. It bugged her out that she could taste something that she had snorted, but it was her favorite part of snorting coke. She knew once she felt the crystals liquefying and dripping down her throat, a beautiful sensation was about to overcome her. Dewante helped himself to a thick line.

"You want?" Ginger offered Desiree.

"I'll try a little," Desiree accepted. What harm could it do? Ginger chopped a thin line for Desiree and handed her the straw.

"Sniff it quick and hard," Ginger ordered. Desiree obliged. She looked at Ginger, then made a face.

Ginger grinned. "You taste it, huh?" Desiree nodded.

"Don't worry. You're gonna love it," Ginger told her. She looked over at Dewante, who was sitting in a chair and enjoying his high.

"I know you want to suck these pretty titties." Ginger lifted her breast with one hand and licked her own nipple. She blew on the dark brown peak, watching it harden and stand at attention.

"You wanna feel this luscious ass?" Ginger undid her pants and let them fall to the floor. She shimmied out of them, then turned around and let him take in her large, round, firm ass, barely covered by a black lace thong. Then she removed Desiree's jeans and ran her hands over her butt. She stood up and stood behind Desiree. Desiree could feel Ginger's hard nipples poking her in the back.

"Relax," she whispered softly in Desiree's ear.

Ginger stuck her index finger in her mouth. "Mmmm," she moaned as she sucked it. She let her moistened finger trail from her mouth to Desiree's nipple. She ran a circle around her dark areolas and squeezed her breasts lightly. Desiree tried to stifle a moan.

"See, it's not so bad," Ginger cooed in Desiree's ear.

Dewante spread his long legs and began to stroke his humongous cock again. The mere sight of it made Desiree forget what a jerk Dewante had been. Desiree was thoroughly excited. Dewante was hung like a horse, and she wanted to ride him like a Ducati. Her attraction to him, his money, in addition to the new sensation of another woman made Desiree's heart pound. Or was it the coke? Desiree wasn't sure.

"Still want to pretend?" Ginger asked Desiree softly. Desiree shook her head no, sheepishly.

Ginger focused her attention on Desiree's lower body, sliding her hand over Desiree's mound, slipping it beneath her thong and moving it in slow circles over her clit. Ginger felt Desiree get wet.

"And I know you want some of this sweet, sweet pussy. You want to feel it get all hot and wet and creamy for you. Feel our tight pussy muscles grip your big, hard dick as you fuck both of us deep." Desiree moaned at Ginger's dirty talk and arched her back in pleasure as Ginger continued to play with her clit. Abruptly, she stopped. Desiree was panting with anticipation.

"Run the tub. And use lots of bubbles," Ginger ordered her.

Ginger strolled to the chair in which Dewante was sitting and replaced his hand with hers. She began to jerk his dick up and down as she kissed his chest. She felt a few drops of precum ooze from the engorged tip of his dick.

"Come on." Ginger led Dewante into the bathroom. Desiree was bent over the tub, swirling the bubble-filled water with her hand. She located the button for the Jacuzzi and switched it on. She looked up to find Dewante and Ginger standing in the doorway, drinking in the sight of her.

"Get in," Dewante commanded. They did so, and lathered and soaped his body, paying special attention to his crotch. Dewante sat like he was king of the world as the bubbles foamed everywhere.

Desiree and Ginger took turns soaping each other slowly while he watched. Ginger took Desiree's face in her hands and kissed her gently at first, then more insistently, probing her mouth with her tongue. Desiree responded, kissing Ginger back, allowing herself to touch another woman; allowing herself to give in to desires she didn't know existed. Most men were rough and clumsy with their touch; Ginger was soft and gentle.

"I'm getting jealous," Dewante said, and then joined their kiss. He nibbled at Desiree's bottom lip before kissing her deeply. Desiree thought she'd explode right then and there. He grabbed Ginger by the hair and kissed her hard. She matched his passion, grabbing his arms and shoulders roughly. Ginger and Desiree kissed Dewante's neck and chest as they fondled him beneath the sudsy water, rubbing their wet, slippery bodies along his. When Dewante began to whimper and arch his hips, Ginger and Desiree led him from the tub back to the bed.

"Look in my bag and see if there's some baby oil in there," Ginger told Desiree. *Only a dancer would just happen to have baby oil in her purse,* Desiree mused, fetching the oil.

Ginger rubbed Dewante's seven-foot-two frame with oil,

using her own flawless body against his skin. "You like that?" she purred in his ear while grinding her hips against him. He shuddered at the sensation of her pubic hairs slipping and sliding across his ass from all the oil.

"Mmmhmm," he agreed.

Ginger flipped him over. He sucked at her breasts briefly as they passed over his mouth and face, smothering him. Dewante moaned as she slid her breasts from his mouth to his dick. She squeezed them together and ran them up and down along his shaft.

Dewante reached for Desiree and began to rub her breasts with oil. He pulled her on top of him and began to eagerly lap at her vagina.

Desiree moaned at the sensation. She'd never had a tongue down there before.

"That's not how you eat pussy," Ginger joked.

"Show me, then," Dewante told her.

Ginger laid Desiree on the bed and spread her legs wide. She parted Desiree's lips and began to taste her. Ginger and Dewante took turns eating her, pausing sporadically to kiss each other. Soon Desiree was writhing and bucking, her screams and moans evidence of her climax.

"See! That's how you do it," Ginger told Dewante.

"Oh! Well, show her how to give me head, since you're such a good teacher, unless she already knows how," Dewante suggested.

"Know how to give head?" Ginger asked Desiree. She offered up a weak no, still spent from the climax. Desiree had had orgasms before, but never as intense as the one she'd just experienced.

Dewante sat on the edge of the bed and eased Desiree to the floor. She and Ginger knelt before him, his cock standing straight up in the air. Ginger took him in her mouth until his entire shaft was engulfed. Desiree tried but gagged a little bit. Ginger guided Desiree's hand and showed her how to caress him while Ginger did all the sucking.

"Lick his balls," Ginger whispered to Desiree. Desiree let her tongue explore his lower body while stroking him.

"That feels so good," he moaned.

Ginger began to moan and groan, then nudged Desiree and gave her a wink. Desiree began moaning and groaning as well, trying hard not to laugh.

"Lick my ass! Lick my ass!" Dewante panted. Desiree gasped, but Dewante didn't notice. Ginger snickered.

Lick it! Ginger mouthed to Desiree. Desiree shook her head violently. She was not about to toss this nigga's salad! Ginger rolled her eyes and grimaced as Desiree held his butt cheeks apart. Dewante enthusiastically threw his legs in the air to give them better access. She licked his butthole quickly, glad they had taken a long bubble bath beforehand.

"More!" he continued to plead.

"Your turn!" Ginger hissed at Desiree. Desiree stuck her tongue out, closed her eyes, and took a lick.

"Stick your finger up my ass!" Dewante begged. Desiree folded her hands across her chest. *Hell no!* she mouthed to Ginger.

"Please, I'm about to come. Stick your fingers up my ass! *Now!*" Desiree didn't budge. Ginger rolled her eyes and did as he asked, inserting her finger.

"Another one! Put two more in!" Ginger obliged, and her eyes nearly bugged out of her head when her additional fingers slid up his ass with no problem; within seconds Dewante began to shake and shiver, climaxing. Ginger moved her head away, and he erupted, his seed landing on his stomach. When it was over, he nonchalantly got up from the bed, put his clothes on, and left without uttering a word.

CHAPTER 3

DESIREE AWOKE FEELING DISORIENTED. FOR THE FIRST NIGHT in ages she hadn't dreamed. She wiped the crust from her eyes and tried to focus. Even through the haze, she could discern that she was in an unfamiliar place. She frowned as she looked around the room, trying to assess where she had been and what she had done. Flashes of bits and pieces of the events from the night before filtered into her head. Her temples were throbbing and she craved an aspirin.

Desiree climbed out of the queen-size bed and padded around the carpeted bedroom decorated in shades of pink, one of her favorite colors, to the small en suite bathroom. She looked in the medicine cabinet and found nothing. She looked in the cabinet underneath the sink and found a bottle of extra-strength Tylenol next to a jumbo box of tampons and a six-pack of toilet paper. Desiree popped two tablets into her mouth and ran the cold water from the faucet. After gulping the pills, she returned to the bedroom.

The room smelled of potpourri and was white-glove clean. The canopy bed and furniture were made of thick, heavy wood and were obviously very expensive. Desiree ran her hands over the furniture's surfaces and looked around, impressed. A picture of Ginger in a crystal frame rested on top of the nightstand. *This must be Ginger's place,* she thought.

She inspected the drawers and found them to be empty aside from a large, high-tech remote control with an LCD screen. After figuring out how to work the remote, she clicked on a TV that sat on an entertainment stand, and absent-mindedly surfed through the channels. She finally settled on a Spanish soap opera, *María la del Barrio,* on Telemundo. Then she thought about her cash. She grabbed her K-Swiss and lifted the blue inner sole to count her money. From the looks of the room, Ginger wasn't hurting for money, but you could never be too sure. She could have gotten all this stuff because she was a thief!

Desiree had $1,327, mostly in hundreds, with a few fifties and twenties thrown in. That in addition to the $3,000 she had managed to stash before she left New York made her feel rich. It was certainly more money than she'd ever had in her life.

"This place is laid out," Desiree said to herself while snuggling under the down comforter on the bed. She was slightly hungover from the night before, and the A.C. was on full blast, but oddly, she felt comfortable and at home.

"I see you're up. You okay?" Ginger was standing in the doorway. Desiree had become so engrossed in the novela she was watching that she hadn't heard her come in.

"Yeah. Good morning," Desiree replied, her voice still scratchy with sleepiness.

"Afternoon." Ginger laughed. "It's five o'clock!"

"Damn!" Desiree hadn't bothered to check the time.

"So how do you feel?"

"All right, I guess. I took some Tylenol. But I still have a little hangover."

"Well, come in the kitchen. I'll make you something to take that away."

Desiree followed Ginger through beautiful rooms and into an immaculate kitchen. There was a steel Sub-Zero refrigerator. Desiree had only seen one on television. The flattop stove looked like one from a cooking show, and Ginger had all kinds of pots and pans and appliances that looked like they belonged in a restaurant rather than in someone's home.

"Your crib is tight!" Desiree complimented her as she took a seat on a stool at the breakfast bar. She watched Ginger intently as she milled about the kitchen, arranging things and rustling through cabinets. Desiree *had* to find out how she could afford such a spread. Dancers made good money, she knew that, but this was the kind of house that belonged to a businessperson or a doctor or lawyer.

"Thanks," Ginger replied modestly. Apparently, she was accustomed to living large. She accepted the compliment as if she lived in a shack, not in a mini-mansion.

"So this is all you?" Desiree asked her, hoping she'd open up a little.

"Yep, it's all me, the fruit of all my labor," Ginger replied with a touch of sarcasm rather than pride. "What about you? Where do you stay?"

"I just got to town, so I checked into this hotel by the airport." Desiree felt inadequate and insecure about her response. Hotel was an overstatement. The crappy room was hot, smelled musty, and was infested with mosquitoes. But it was only twenty-five bucks a night, so Desiree figured it was just as good a place as any to rest her head until she got her shit together. That was until she saw how Ginger was living.

"That's right. You're from New York," Ginger remembered.

"Yeah," Desiree answered dryly. She didn't want to think about New York—too many bad memories.

Ginger didn't take the hint. "Which borough?"

"Queens, the Bronx, Mount Vernon . . . I moved around a lot. You're from here, right?" Desiree changed the subject.

"Yeah, pretty much. I was born in Haiti, but I've been here most of my life. You just here for the Super Bowl, or do you plan to live here?" Ginger asked.

"I'm here to stay. The weather is pretty. Plus, the money seems to be real good here," Desiree said.

"Yeah, it can be. Have you danced anywhere else?" Ginger continued probing Desiree.

"A coupla spots up top. But Giuliani kind of threw a monkey wrench in that. I hear it's not what it used to be." Desiree repeated what she'd heard from other dancers in an attempt to sound sophisticated. They swore that before Giuliani became mayor, money practically fell from the sky.

"Really? I've danced at Score's in Manhattan before. It was *real* good there. I worked at a couple of spots in Jersey too," Ginger said. Desiree imagined Ginger twirling around a pole at the Bada Bing, the strip club from *The Sopranos*.

"Well, I'm sure you make money everywhere you go. Look at you!" Desiree looked at Ginger. She was really beautiful. Her long hair was pulled up into a bun on top of her head, and she was wearing a wife-beater and some cutoff jean shorts, yet she still looked stunning. Without a speck of makeup aside from some clear lip gloss, her high cheekbones, bright eyes, and straight, keen nose needed no further accentuation. Ginger possessed a natural, classic, and fresh beauty.

"Look at *you*!" Ginger replied. "You're just as pretty as I am. And your eyes are natural. I wear contacts."

"Yeah. But your body is better. I'm kind of flat-chested."

Desiree looked miserably at her modest 34A chest. She was definitely not flat-chested, but compared to Ginger, most women would look underdeveloped.

"Buy some tits. I did!" Ginger poked out her 36Ds, then shimmied them.

"Wow. Those are fake?" Desiree had assumed Ginger's endowment was natural.

"Yep. The best five grand I ever spent!" Ginger admitted proudly. She inspected Desiree curiously. "Can I tell you something, Desiree?"

"Yeah, sure."

"Look. You've got a lot of potential. You're really pretty, but you don't play up your features enough. Don't take this the wrong way, but the tomboy look has got to go! I mean, I know you're from New York and all, but there's no reason you should dress so thugged out. That shit ain't gonna fly down here. But with the right clothes and the right makeup, maybe lighten your hair . . . You could be so much prettier. And once you get your game tight, you can make money anywhere. The world could be yours, Desiree. You've just gotta know how to hustle."

"I can hustle. I ask everybody for dances. They just don't like me as much as they like you." Desiree picked at her fingernails self-consciously. The acrylic was chipped, and her thumb and pinkie nails were broken to the nub.

"Not that kind of hustle. The kind of hustle where if there is only one man in the club, you can make him want you, you can turn him into a human ATM. You can make him do whatever you want, whatever you need. It's all a mind game." Ginger pointed at her temple for emphasis. "Real hustle is working smarter, not harder. You're obviously in this game for the money. We're all in this for the money. I don't think that the majority of us dreamed of being strippers when we were little girls. Just having money isn't enough, though; it's what you do with it that counts. By working smarter I mean once you make that money, you gotta flip it. Invest it. Don't blow it all on material shit to floss before you've got any real assets. I bought this house because I knew it would be a good investment. I bought my car for four thousand at an auction; I don't have a car note. Matter of fact, every now and then I buy a car at an auction, fix it up, and sell it. I usually double my money. And I run a Web site that pays my mortgage. See, that's the difference between working for money and making money work for you. I can teach you this stuff if you want to learn. It's not all about college. I didn't learn how to do this in college; I read it in books and went to seminars. You're young. If you start now, by the time you're my age you could be very well off. You could have more than this!" Ginger waved her arm like a game show hostess.

"There you go with that age shit again," Desiree joked nervously to cover the fact that the conversation was slightly over her head. She wouldn't begin to know anything about investing or assets and was surprised to hear Ginger speak like she was some kind of Wall Street big shot. Desiree couldn't imagine doing the kinds of things Ginger described. That was for white people and people with money. Desiree used to think that she was smart but had stopped believing that smarts gave her an edge in life some time ago.

There was another reason Desiree had reservations about what Ginger was telling her. Ginger was practically a stranger, even though they'd been "together." Was Ginger telling her all of this because she was expecting some kind of relationship? Desiree had enjoyed what went down, but she had no intention of becoming a lesbian.

"I'm serious," Ginger stated. She went into the freezer and pulled out a Tupperware container of soup and put it in the microwave. She reached in the dishwasher and pulled out a bowl and a spoon for Desiree to eat with. She poured her a huge glass of Coca-Cola. "Drink this Coke. I know it's kind of flat, but that's how it's supposed to be. It sounds crazy, but I guarantee that it will settle your stomach."

"Can I ask you a question?" Desiree stared at Ginger with her piercing topaz eyes.

"Shoot." Ginger sat on a countertop.

"Why are you being so nice to me? I mean, why do you care? What's in it for you?"

Ginger grinned sheepishly. "I'm not so nice. Here." She reached into her pocket and pulled out a wad of bills.

"What's that for?" Desiree accepted the money but was confused.

"Dewante paid us twenty-five hundred each last night. I kept this and told you he was paying us a g."

"So why are you telling me this now?" Desiree asked her, quickly putting her money in her bra.

"You seem like you need a little help. I can tell you need money, and I can help you. And I don't know if it's because we favor or what. But I feel like I already know you. I guess it's like, if I had a little sister, she'd be a lot like you. Maybe I see a little of myself in you; me from a long time ago. Besides, when you put positive vibes into the universe, that's what you're going to get back." Ginger transferred the soup from the Tupperware container to a bowl and placed it in front of Desiree, who sat at a stool. Desiree didn't know anything about positive vibes and the universe, but whatever Ginger had been doing was obviously working.

"This is so good." Desiree greedily devoured the soup.

"Isn't it? I got that soup last month in St. Thomas. I had them put the soup in this huge-ass container and froze it as soon as I got home. Luckily, the flight was only an hour."

"Wow! It's weird, but I swear my hangover is gone." Desiree wiped her mouth. Ginger refilled her bowl.

"I know. I got real fucked-up when I was there, and one of the locals told me to go to this spot called Walter's and get the island chicken soup, guaranteed to cure a hangover," Ginger told her.

"Damn. There's a whole potato in here."

"There's all kind of shit in there: carrots, celery, and potato and in real pieces, not all smushed up like in a can. It's natural. That's why it works."

Desiree smiled at Ginger. Ginger smiled back. An awkward silence.

"Do you feel weird about last night?" Ginger asked her.

"Yeah," Desiree admitted. "That was some wild shit. I mean, nobody could have told me that a star like Dewante would *pay* to get his ass licked. What is that? Is he gay or what? I mean, he really liked the fingers up his ass and whatnot," Desiree chattered.

"I meant about what happened with us."

Desiree smiled sheepishly. "It was weird. But it was weird in a nice way. I mean, it felt good and everything. But I'm not gay or anything . . ." Desiree's voice trailed off.

"Look, that was business, okay? I don't want you to feel like I expect you to do it again." Ginger smiled, and Desiree breathed a sigh of relief.

"How much are you paying at your spot?" Ginger asked her.

"One seventy-five a week," Desiree answered.

"Well, you can stay here until you figure out what you want to do, where you want to live. I've got plenty of room, as you can see. You can pay me four hundred a month, okay? That's cheaper than a hotel, and you can save up for an apartment." Ginger awaited a response from Desiree.

"Okay. I really could use the help, and this is a great house. It's a whole lot better than my hotel. I promise I'll pay you on time and I'll be clean and I won't get in your way," Desiree rambled. She didn't care that she barely knew Ginger: there was no way she was going to turn the offer down.

Ginger laughed. "Chill, shawty, you at home now,"

Ginger suggested they go get her stuff and then go shopping on the beach.

"Won't the stores be closed?" Desiree asked. It would be after seven or eight o'clock by the time they got dressed and got her stuff.

"Nah. Not on the beach. And the club we're going to doesn't get started till later. We have plenty of time."

"Okay," Desiree agreed. Ginger gave her fresh towels and told her to help herself to anything she needed. Then she gave her a pink Nike shorts suit to wear.

After dressing they left the house and walked toward the Beamer, which was parked in the driveway along with an Explorer.

"The Explorer's yours too, huh?" Desiree inquired.

"Yup."

"So this investment stuff you were talking about earlier, you really think I could do what you did?"

"Sure. Stick with me, kid. You'll be all right," Ginger assured her.

Desiree admired the terra-cotta-colored stucco home with its manicured lawn and perfect landscaping. It was one of the nicest homes Desiree had ever seen. She'd been in a few brownstones back in New York that were pretty tight, but they didn't have the little extras Ginger's house had. Desiree noticed the fruit trees in the yard, as well as the palm trees.

"Is this a golf course?" she asked, her eyes wide with wonder.

"Yeah." Ginger shrugged, like *everyone* lived on a golf course. She chirped the alarm and got in the BMW. She let the top down, and the Florida sun beamed on their skin, even though it was early evening.

"Can I ask you a question?" Desiree asked over the car's stereo as they stopped and started through the traffic on the Palmetto Expressway.

"Sure." Ginger looked at her briefly; her eyes were shielded by a pair of Versace sunglasses.

"What made you start dancing? I mean, you're obviously smart, you know computers and got investments and stuff. Plus, you know guys like Dewante. As pretty as you are, you could be married with a family. Why do this?" Desiree asked her.

Ginger laughed. "Let's not talk about that now." Ginger cranked the stereo louder and sang along in Spanish to a salsa song on the radio that identified itself as "Noventa y Ocho . . . Caliente!"

PACKING DESIREE'S BELONGINGS WAS A SNAP. ALL OF HER things fit easily into the trunk of Ginger's car. All she had was clothes and shoes, and not many of those. After closing up her bill and returning her key to the desk clerk, they headed toward South Beach. Desiree was excited about going shopping with plenty of money in her pocket, something she had never done before.

They went to Metro on Washington and had a ball trying on all the funky clothes. Desiree bought a black sequined halter in the shape of a butterfly and a pair of black boot-cut pants. The outfit accentuated her figure, adding curves to areas where they hadn't seemed to be earlier, and the sparkle of sequins made her eyes shine gray with flecks of green. Ginger bought a supershort denim miniskirt and a sheer shirt. While they browsed the other fashions the store had to offer, Ginger convinced Desiree to try on a blondish wig from the large selection in the back of the store.

"It's final! You *have* to color your hair," the flamboyantly gay salesman told Desiree. "Sandy brown with blond high-lights is so you."

Ginger agreed emphatically and insisted on doing it that night. She whipped out a cell phone and began chatting in Creole.

"Damn, you speak French?" Desiree asked her, impressed.

"That wasn't French, that was Creole, which is French-based. But to answer your question, yeah, I speak French too and, of course, Spanish. I'm Dominican and Haitian." Ginger shrugged her shoulders like her multilingual skills were no big deal. "But anyway, my girl DeeDee can hook you up at the crib. She lives in Carol City, not far from us. She'll roll through around 9:30 to hook us up. So let's grab some shoes from next door and get a move on." Desiree was impressed at how easily Ginger made things happen.

They went next door to Nurielle and bought shoes to match their ensembles. Ginger knew the salesgirl, so she hooked them up with two-for-one Sergio Rossi stilettos. Desiree was ecstatic at the purchase of three-hundred-dollar shoes. She'd never had any quality shoes that weren't sneakers. And as for clothes, she'd owned Lady Enyce and Mecca and Baby Phat and the like, but never foreign de-signers. Now she was going to step into a club on the beach looking like she stepped out of a fashion magazine instead of the *Source*.

"Don't worry about the money you spent," Ginger said. "I can sew. I'm going to bootleg some of their shit for us. Today I just felt like shopping. I figured you'd like it too."

"Like it? I love it! I've only seen clothes like this in videos. But I'm sure glad you can sew. Who knew how much ripped-up T-shirts and old jeans with crystals on them cost?" Desiree replied.

"Yeah, they're buggin' with their prices, but I can't blame them. Tourists spend money like water here. And the reason you've seen clothes like this in videos is because this is where they get a lot of the wardrobe for videos. They shoot one damn near every week here. Matter of fact, you could be in some, I'm sure."

"Me?" Desiree asked, shocked.

"Yeah, you! You could model."

"But I'm kind of short. I'm not white or six feet tall or skinny," Desiree objected.

"Girl, please. You're prettier than all those girls. You look like me, remember?" Ginger teased.

"Well, why don't *you* model? You're tall."

"To make a long story short, I've been there, done that, and don't like it. I'm a control freak, and when you model, you don't have any control over anything."

"I don't see how anyone could not like getting paid to be pretty. I'd do it in a heartbeat."

"Well, you'll have your chance. I know a few people if you're really interested. But shit, you'll surely meet someone who'll claim they can make you a star. I guarantee it. Just be careful. A lot of these so-called agents are full of shit and will get you hooked up in a lot of bullshit," Ginger warned.

"Well, I'll let you help me. I can trust you." Desiree smiled at Ginger.

"Shawty, don't trust anyone. Not here. Sleep with one eye

open. Don't get so caught up in the glitz and glamour of this beach, or it will eat you alive."

"What about you?" Desiree eyed Ginger suspiciously.

"What about me?" Ginger quipped.

"Can I trust you?" Desiree was serious.

"Sometimes *I* don't even trust me," Ginger replied, and headed for her car.

THEY PULLED UP TO GINGER'S HOUSE AT THE SAME TIME AS DeeDee. Desiree took note of DeeDee's hooked-up Acura and crisp denim jumpsuit. Her hair was laid out in a stylish, short cut and dyed a mahogany hue. She sported long acrylic nails with designs and crystals on each finger, and her hands were adorned with gold and platinum rings. DeeDee was iced out and jeweled up, making Desiree wonder how the hell she was gonna do anyone's hair. DeeDee pulled a large aluminum case and a duffel bag out the trunk of her car and teetered on her high-heeled boots toward the house.

"Sak passé?" DeeDee greeted Ginger.

"Ma boulé," Ginger replied in the traditional Creole greeting. "Come on back." Ginger led DeeDee and Desiree to the Florida room at the back of the house. In a corner she had a mini beauty salon, complete with a barber's chair, shampoo bowl, and hair dryer. The station had a huge art deco mirror and contemporary lighting. Desiree's jaw dropped.

"You have a beauty salon in your house?" Desiree asked, shocked.

Ginger laughed. "It's only one station." DeeDee began removing assorted jars, bottles, combs, and brushes from her bag and case.

"You've never been back here?" DeeDee asked.

"Lil' Desiree is just moving in. I'm taking her under my wing," Ginger explained.

"You gonna be on her Web site?" DeeDee inquired as she got to work doing the ladies' hair.

"Nah. Desiree got more potential than that. She's gonna do big things. I can feel it," Ginger answered for Desiree. Desiree couldn't contain her smile at the compliment.

"Y'all going to Groove Jet?" DeeDee asked, snapping her gum as she combed a bleaching solution through Desiree's hair.

"Yeah. You know that's my spot," Ginger told her. She was sitting under a hair dryer, her hair in large curlers.

"I thought you would be working tonight. Ain't Coco's the spot on Tuesdays?" DeeDee asked.

"Yeah, but I needed a little break. I'm taking my little protégée out to the beach with me, let her see how it's done here in the Bottom," Ginger explained. Desiree liked the sound of that: her protégée. No one had ever acted like she had any potential before.

"Well, break her in slow," DeeDee joked, then began to chat with Ginger in Creole.

DeeDee hooked both of them up with Doobie wraps and did Desiree's color within two hours. Desiree was amazed to see Ginger break her off with two hundred dollars for the service.

"Let me give you something," Desiree offered, fishing in her pocket for a hundred-dollar bill, but Ginger refused.

"I'm gonna do your makeup now, okay?" Ginger informed Desiree, pushing her hand away.

Desiree smiled in appreciation and followed Ginger into her bathroom. Ginger pulled a huge aluminum train case containing a ton of cosmetics from a closet in the bathroom suite and motioned to Desiree to sit in the dressing table chair. Ginger arched Desiree's slightly bushy eyebrows and applied makeup to her clear, smooth skin, explaining what she was doing while she did it, so Desiree would be able to re-create the look on her own.

When Desiree finally saw herself in the mirror, her hair full, wavy, and bouncy, and her features highlighted with just the right amount of makeup, she was shocked.

"See what I meant? You were cute before. Now you're *beautiful*," Ginger said. Desiree gave her a great big hug, which caught Ginger completely off guard.

"Thank you, Ginger, for everything!" Desiree spoke with sincerity, her eyes slightly misty. No one had ever taken the time to teach her how to style her hair or put on makeup. No one had ever taken her shopping for pretty and fashionable clothes. It had been so long since anyone cared.

"No problem, shawty." Ginger hugged Desiree back, thinking that Oprah and all those other talk show hosts must feel just like she did when they did makeover shows. Every once in a while, it felt good to do something for someone else, Ginger silently admitted. But she wasn't going to make it a habit.

They got dressed and hopped back into the BMW. Ginger's home looked so beautiful in the moonlight, little footlights illuminating her tile driveway. Desiree felt like she'd been on the go nonstop but was loving every minute of it. In a short twenty-four hours she had found a great place to live, had come up on some funds, had a whole new look and a new best friend. Desiree vowed to herself that she would have a whole new life in Miami, a glamorous life. She had a clean slate. No one knew who she was or where she had been. In Miami she was going to be somebody. It was obvious by the way things were falling into place for her.

WHEN THEY HIT THE STRIP, DESIREE WAS AMAZED AT HOW DIF-
ferent everything looked. Gone was the laid-back casualness
she'd seen earlier that evening. After dark, Miami came
alive. Exotic cars were jammed bumper-to-bumper on the
strip. Women paraded the streets in skimpy fashions. There
was a line outside of every club they passed.

"Usually, it isn't this hectic during the week. But since the
Super Bowl is here, everyone is out and about."

Ginger enlightened Desiree about South Beach. "This is
Washington, where we were earlier. See, there's Metro.
There's a bunch of clubs on this street. There's Cream all the
way down there on Sixth; there's Glam Slam, Prince's old
club, which is closed right now. I think someone is about to
buy it, though, and do something new. There's also Liquid
and the Living Room; Chaos, which is my personal favorite;
and the Cameo Theater. There are more clubs spread out
here and there, like Penrod's and Amnesia. Plus, there's this
new spot called the Bar Room. Oh yeah and Alonzo Mourning's Club Onyx, but I'm not sure if it's open. Just don't go
to Club Cristal. Everyone says it's fun, but it's way too ghetto
in my opinion. You gotta be real careful in joints like that. A
lot of niggas from the club be up in there, so why would you
want to go anyway? You gotta go where the hot shit is. The
tourists that come over from Europe and South America be
havin' major paper. I'm trying to roll like that, so I go where
they go. For example, restaurants are fun, and nice places to
see and be seen. There's a lot to do on the beach. You'll get
to know it well soon enough. Plus, I've got to take you to
Coconut Grove. Oh and Bermuda Bar up in Aventura. Plus,
there are a couple of spots like Baja's, the Chili Pepper,

Manhattan's, Christopher's, and the Brickhouse up in Broward. That's Fort Lauderdale and Pembroke Pines and Hollywood, but you'll see all that soon too." Ginger was pointing left and right, rattling off details like a tour guide.

Desiree's head was swimming with all the information, her pulse racing with excitement. Everyone looked so beautiful and in shape. The people were glamorous and just seemed to have flavor. This was what the hype was all about, South Beach. Desiree could dig it.

"Damn, there seems to be a lot of clubs," Desiree remarked.

"Oh hell yeah! That's what we do in Miami. We kick it. This week is going to be real fun. We're going to work, but we're going to play a little harder. You said you wanted to meet a baller. If it doesn't happen this week, it's never going to happen. I'm gonna school you on how to run these niggas." Ginger headed away from all of the action and made a couple of twists and turns, then left her car with a valet in front of Groove Jet. There was a line, and a big bouncer stood guarding a velvet rope.

"Damn, we've got to wait in line?" Desiree pouted. She was ready to party.

"Ha!" Ginger snorted. "I don't do these kinds of lines. The key is to walk to the front of the line like you *belong* in there. If you act like you belong in line, like you deserve to wait and plead to get in, that's how these people will treat you. Look confident," Ginger instructed. They strolled to the velvet rope. The bouncer did not acknowledge them right away, but when he did, he smiled and asked them to take their IDs out. They went to another doorperson, who glanced at their IDs using a flashlight, then handed them two VIP wristbands.

"We don't have to pay?" Desiree whispered to Ginger.

"Not when you look like us. Don't get me wrong. Sometimes we will definitely have to pay. Shit! Sometimes we'll have to pay out the ass, but it'll be worth it. Just enjoy yourself."

Desiree was amazed at how many people were out kicking it on a weeknight. There was a live band that was playing some funk, accompanied by a DJ who provided an occasional scratch or break beat. It was different than anything Desiree had seen personally, though she was sure that in Manhattan there had to be something similar. After the band finished their set, a new DJ appeared and took over, spinning hip-hop. Desiree and Ginger drank apple martinis and danced until the club closed at 5 a.m.

They repeated the ritual several times that week at other venues. They attended a private party to celebrate the opening of the Bar Room on Thursday, checked out Amnesia on Friday after they'd had drinks at the Marlin, and went party hopping and strip cruising on Saturday.

Rather than work the strip clubs, Desiree and Ginger entertained at a few private parties. Some were held by businessmen, but a couple of them had been for professional athletes. They were always paid one thousand dollars up front for dancing. They made a few hundred more in tips. Then if there were men who wanted special attention, they would provide it with one stipulation: only one man a night. That always started a bidding war for their services, the men's natural competitive instincts kicking in. Men always wanted something that they thought they couldn't have. Desiree wanted to screw all night and collect as much cash as possible, but Ginger explained to her that they weren't some cheap hos to get run up and done up. They didn't, however, mind the exchange of ass for cash, if—and only if—the price was right. They earned a couple thousand a night for a couple hours of work, and a few humps and pumps from a man with money to blow and an ego to feed. They managed to arrange their work and play schedules so that they transitioned seamlessly; the week felt like one giant party. The pinnacle of the week was when they attended the Super Bowl with some fat cat lawyers they'd "entertained." Desiree felt as if she were dreaming, because in one short week her entire life had changed.

Desiree was becoming addicted to the rush she got when a stack of money exchanged hands. It was almost like an aphrodisiac to hear the rustle of bills being counted. Ginger told Desiree what men wanted and what they liked sexually and otherwise, and how to get them to come up off the dough. She taught her where the rich men were, and what to say to them. Ginger seemed to have a different approach for every type of baller: white, black, Latin, young, old, street, corporate, old-money, new-money. Desiree absorbed every bit of information that Ginger gave her like a giant sponge, because Ginger had the goods to back up all her talk. In Desiree's eyes Ginger had made it, and she was going to make it too. Desiree realized that Ginger had been very right about her potential when at the end of the week she realized she'd made over ten thousand dollars.

CHAPTER 4

February 1999

Pack your bags, pickney. We gwan to St. Thomas, mon!" Ginger bubbled in a Miss Cleo, Caribbean accent as she bounded into the house, her arms full of bags. Desiree sat on the couch scribbling furiously in a notebook and eating chips while she bobbed her head to music blaring from a set of headphones. Ginger sat next to her and pulled the headset away from her ear.

"Did you hear me?"

"No."

"What are you doing?" Ginger craned her neck to get a peek at Desiree's notebook.

"Nothing, just doodling," Desiree said, snapping the notebook shut. She turned the headphones off. "What did you say?"

"I said pack your bags because we're going to St. Thomas!"

"We are? When? Why?" Desiree bombarded her with questions, jumping up from her position on the couch, chips spilling everywhere. She'd been to the Dominican Republic, but only once, and that was when she was a little girl. Aside from that, her travels had been limited. Now she was going to the Virgin Islands! She was so glad she'd met Ginger. She'd been living with her for only about a month, but the woman was truly broadening her horizons.

"We can leave tomorrow. The club is paying for our ticket over and our first night's hotel," Ginger explained.

"You mean that there are strip clubs in the Virgin Islands? We're going to work?"

"Of course! Remember I got the soup there that helped cure your hangover?" Ginger was talking a mile a minute.

"Yeah, I remember, but—" Desiree started.

Ginger cut her off. "Why did you think I was over there?" Ginger rolled her eyes toward the heavens and put her hands on her hips.

"Vacation?" Desiree responded.

"More like a working vacation," Ginger clarified.

"Oh. Well, that sounds cool. Tell me about the club." Desiree grabbed Ginger by the hand and pulled her onto the couch. She imagined the club to be lush and tropical, maybe with no ceiling or roof like one of her favorite nightclubs, Amnesia.

"Well, the club looks like shit: concrete floor, wooden benches, a tiny little stage with a pole."

Desiree's bubble burst. It didn't sound like anything to be excited about. "Uh, okay. So do the men have a lot of money?"

"Some do. Most don't. We're not gonna make a g a night."

"Well, if we're not gonna make our paper, why are we going?" Desiree furrowed her brow.

"St. Thomas is pretty," Ginger stated.

"Uh-huh . . ." Desiree waited for a reason to get hyped.

"Plus, I know a couple of fine-ass niggas, they're brothers, and they're gonna take us dancing and shopping and to eat and stuff."

"They got money?" Desiree queried.

"My my my, don't we catch on quickly, little protégée? Slow your roll!" Ginger chuckled at Desiree's gold-digger attitude.

"Well, do they?" Desiree insisted.

"They do all right. St. Thomas is real small, so for there, yeah, they're ballin' out of control. They got a nice-ass crib up in the mountains and you can see the beach. They got some tight little whips too. But, nena, you should see them! Girl, they are fine as hell! Their faces, their skin, their bodies . . . oh my God! I don't think you can begin to understand how fine these niggas are!" Ginger closed her eyes, hugged her body, and shuddered as if the mere thought of their beauty were unbearable.

"Well, damn. Now I really wanna go. I've got to see these niggas. They're brothers, you said?"

"Yeah, I fuck with the older one, but his younger brother is cute to death. You'll like him. Plus, we can lay out on the beach and tan. We can just be beach bums for a while but still make some bread on the side. I need to recharge my batteries, nena. I've been kind of stressing lately."

"Why?" Desiree inquired.

"Just some bullshit." Ginger brushed off the question. "There are spots over there that are so calm and so peaceful, nothing, absolutely nothing, can bother me there. No ghosts can haunt me there. I can be free, totally free, even if it is only temporary." Ginger smiled faintly, her eyes distant. In spirit, Ginger was already lying on the pale white sand, soaking up the St. Thomas sun.

Desiree thought Ginger was the freest person she had ever

known. She had money, clothes, jewelry, a nice car, and everything else a girl could want. On top of that, she was smart and she was beautiful.

"How come you don't feel free now? You've got it all, and you call the shots."

"Then I guess it's true what they say. More money, more problems," Ginger replied, a tear rolling down her cheek. She brushed it away quickly and went into her room.

DESIREE FELL ASLEEP THAT NIGHT RUNNING FROM GHOSTS. IT was a fretful sleep; the sweaty palms of things she couldn't elude kept clawing at her, mauling her with their despair. Distorted images flashed through her head; voices dragged like a record being played on the wrong speed.

"It's all your fault! It's all your fault!" a voice taunted from nowhere, singsongy and teasing like a schoolchild.

"It's not my fault! Not my fault!" Desiree bolted upright in bed, her skin moist with perspiration. It took a long time, but finally, she was able to get back to sleep.

The next morning Ginger was her usual self, focused on paper and not problems. Desiree, however, was a bit unsettled. When Ginger asked her what was wrong, she blamed it on being nervous, so they smoked a fat blunt to calm their flying jitters. They ended up speeding to the airport because they'd gotten too high to concentrate on leaving soon enough to arrive on time. They caught their plane by a hair, arriving just as an attendant was about to close the door to the ramp leading to the aircraft that was taking them to St. Thomas. Desiree had never heard of Presidential Air before, and prayed they weren't some shiesty airline that skimped on safety. Out of breath and disheveled, they flopped into the first seats they came to; the plane was practically empty.

Ginger and Desiree got toasted when the liquor cart came around. They chugged miniature bottles of Jack Daniel's and then sipped on Heinekens while Dez stared out at the cotton-candy clouds that floated in the snow-cone-blue sky. At least the airline didn't skimp on the liquor. The plane hit some turbulence and shook like an earthquake, causing her stomach to lurch. She grabbed the airsickness bag just in case. Ginger looked at her and laughed.

"I don't see how you can't be scared shitless," Desiree moaned, clutching her stomach.

"Girl, I came to America on a raft. It takes more than this to scare me. Besides, I'm not afraid to die. I wanna see what's on the other side anyway," Ginger slurred. "Break on through to the other side! Break on through to the other side!" She sang the Doors classic happily, shaking her hair wildly. Desiree cracked up. Then the plane dipped and dropped a few hundred feet. Ginger threw her arms up in the air like she was on a roller coaster. Desiree threw up in the barf bag.

The plane made a brief stop in St. Croix, landing on a teeny little strip of concrete surrounded on all sides by the lapis-blue Atlantic. Frantic that they would miss the runway and plunge into the ocean, Desiree began to hyperventilate. She was in tears by the time the plane made its way to the Charlotte Amalie airport on St. Thomas.

"I'm never flying again!" she grumbled as they deplaned.

"You'll get used to it, shawty. Death can come at any time, and you're safer in a plane than you are on the street anyway. Besides, if you don't fly, how you gonna get back?" Ginger teased.

"I'll float over on a raft."

"Well, you better make sure you do it from Cuba, because if you come from Haiti, they gonna try to send your ass right back."

RED, THE OWNER OF THE CLUB THEY WERE WORKING AT, MET them at the baggage claim.

"Damn, he's fine," Desiree mumbled under her breath. She took one look at Red, a six-foot stunner with dark, wavy hair and Asian eyes and felt self-conscious. Her hair was a mess, she was sweaty, and she smelled like throw-up. This was not a great way to start a vacation, even if it was a working vacation.

"He's married with like ten kids by fifteen different women, a total waste of time." Ginger rolled her eyes and slipped on her Versace shades. Desiree thought that if Red was half as fine as the dude she was supposed to meet, she was in for a treat.

Red took them to the Windward Passage Hotel and got them settled in. The hotel staff was far from friendly or accommodating. They treated Red with a certain level of detached respect but rolled their eyes and sucked their teeth at Ginger and Desiree. Ginger later explained that the locals hated the strip clubs. The women all thought that the dancers were out to steal their husbands and boyfriends, and some of the men thought American women were lazy or stupid or stuck-up, or at least fronted like they did so as not to make waves with their women. She also warned that they would have to be on their p's and q's, because the women would try and cause them some static.

They took the night off and went to dinner at the Greenhouse Café. A lot of tourists were there, all inebriated, mostly white, dancing off-beat to the ska rhythms a reggae band skanked out on a small stage. They could barely eat in peace; every man in the joint was enthralled and captivated by their beauty. All the food they could consume and all the liquor they could drink were theirs for the taking, compliments of their admirers. Desiree loved the feel of all eyes on her and all the attention she was commanding.

They staggered to their room shortly after 2 a.m., and passed out from too much food and too much drink. Desiree awoke from her semicoma to the sound of insistent pounding in her head. Coming to her senses, she realized the pounding was the housekeeper banging on the door. Before she could respond, a heavyset cleaning woman entered and began tidying up the room. She rustled and bustled and dusted, then stood in between the room's double beds.

"Uh, as you can see, we're still sleeping. No thank you." Ginger spoke without opening her eyes. The woman rolled her eyes and sucked her teeth at them.

"Motherscunt," she muttered through her gritted teeth. Ginger sat straight up in the bed and threw back the covers.

"Did you call me a motherscunt? Well, did you?" Ginger's eyes flashed with anger.

"Good night," the maid answered, as was traditional in St. Thomas no matter what time of the day, and then dragged her bloated body out of their room, making sure to take as long as she wanted.

"You backwards bitch! It's daytime! Say good morning! I swear y'all are so country. I hate this fucking hotel! Y'all always want to start shit. That's okay, though, y'all won't be getting a penny of my money. Motherscunt!" she spat at the woman's flabby backside.

"Yo! What the fuck was that all about? What the hell is a mother skunk or whatever the fuck y'all were saying?" Desiree asked Ginger.

"Basically, that bitch called us a cross between a motherfucker and a cunt. That's their worst insult. It's some old island shit," Ginger fumed. "I'm telling you every time I come to St. Thomas some bitch got to throw shade. It ain't my fault these bitches are fat and ugly. *Some* of the pretty ones be okay. But those fat old ugly hos are the worst! They wish somebody would pay to see them naked. Shit, it's more like somebody would pay them to put their clothes on. I keep telling Red, *don't* put me in the Windward Passage, but he always, *always* does!"

"What you wanna do?" Desiree asked.

"Let me call Red. He gonna pay for tonight and tomorrow somewhere else, and it better not be somewhere fucked-up. He *needs* to put us in an apartment!" Ginger yanked the phone off its cradle and began to dial.

"What the fuck?" She paused, listening to the voice on the other end. "You need to connect me to my number right now. Excuse me? Oh hell no! Y'all are trippin' . . . you know what, fuck you!"

Desiree danced around in front of Ginger, trying to find out what had gone down. Ginger pulled the phone out of the jack and threw it across the room. "Fuck these motherfuckers!"

"Yo, Ginger! Hello?! What just happened here?" Desiree grabbed Ginger, who was pacing angrily back and forth.

"These motherfuckers wouldn't connect my call. They said they had a code of conduct in this establishment, and I do use the word 'establishment' lightly, and that we broke it. They told me that we needed to vacate the premises immediately."

"What did we do?" Desiree's mouth was agape. What the hell had Ginger gotten her into?

"We ain't do shit! Come on and pack your bag. We're outta this shithole."

They dressed quickly and brushed their teeth. Desiree looked around the room to make sure they hadn't left anything behind before they stormed out. Desiree was grateful her suitcase had wheels, because Ginger walked full speed ahead. She marched to the desk and threw the key at the clerk.

"Shove this key up your ass. Fucking hater!" she spat. Her wide-bodied bag knocked over an end table and a display shelf filled with brochures.

"Oops," she sneered, then tossed her hair and left the building.

"What we gonna do now?" Desiree asked.

"Don't worry. I'ma call Derek and Fuzzy."

"Who?"

"Derek and Fuzzy, the brothers I was telling you about."

"Please tell me you're hooking me up with Derek," Desiree remarked.

"Nope, Fuzzy is all yours."

"What kind of bullshit is this, Gin? We've been kicked out the hotel, everybody except drunk-ass tourists acts like we're the fucking devil, now you're trying to set me up with a nigga named Fuzzy? Man, I'm ready to go home."

"Just shut up and watch the bags while I use that pay phone. Gimme some change." Desiree emptied the pockets of her jean shorts and gave Ginger a handful of change. She sat atop a suitcase, folded her arms, and pouted. It was hot as hell, hotter than Miami. Plus, she was getting hungry. It all made her quite irritable.

Ginger returned minutes later, practically skipping.

"They'll be here in five minutes! I called Derek's cell, and they're down the road. Stop acting like a baby and put on some lipstick," Ginger demanded.

"Man, I'm hot. It's too hot for makeup. And I'm hungry," Desiree whined.

"Well, at least put on some clear MAC Lipglass. Your lips are looking a little crusty there," Ginger kidded, but Desiree was in no mood for jokes.

"Yeah, whatever," she remarked dryly, whipping out a tube of Lipglass and slicking some on.

The boom from Derek's Range Rover introduced them before they actually appeared. Ginger's ears immediately perked up, and she smoothed out her top and fluffed her hair. She was grinning ear-to-ear when he rolled down the black-out tinted window. A haze of marijuana smoke emanated from the car, and when it cleared, there were two of the most handsome men Desiree had ever seen in her life.

"Good night, baby." His baritone voice boomed as he swung his car door open. He stood at six feet three inches tall, was the color of Hershey's syrup, with a bald head, dark brown eyes framed by a fringe of dark lashes, and the body of a god.

"Good night, baby," Ginger gushed.

"Oh shit!" Desiree's chin practically touched the concrete. She stared shamelessly as he wrapped his arms around Ginger and gave her a kiss. Then she saw Fuzzy. He was even finer than Derek! Desiree stood mute waiting for Ginger to break free from Derek's embrace.

"Desi, this is Derek," she introduced them after finally releasing her lip-lock.

"A pleasure, Desiree. Ginger's told me all about you." His accent was driving her wild.

"And this is Fuzzy," she said to Desiree. He removed his

shades, nodded, and then replaced them. He began staring out of the passenger window like she wasn't even there. Desiree now wished she had taken the time to put on some makeup.

After I freshen up, he's definitely gonna check for me, Desiree thought, determined to get his attention. *I'm gonna make sure of it.*

Derek and Ginger caught up in the front seat while Desiree and Fuzzy rode in silence in the back. They headed around a few curvy, narrow streets to a dim alley.

"We can get something from Crazy Cal's, and then I'll take you to the guesthouse. I know the owner personally; he's a friend of mine. I'll check you in and pay for it," Derek explained to them, then stopped at a tiny restaurant to get them something to eat. Desiree went in with him so she could see what they had to offer.

"So what you think about Desiree?" Ginger asked Fuzzy in the car. "Ain't she cute? Y'all will like each other."

"Nah, she's not for me," he replied.

"What? She looks like me. I know you don't think that *I'm* ugly." Ginger rolled her neck and frowned up her face.

"Nah, it's not that. She's not ugly. She's pretty. But she's *maaga*."

"What the fuck is *maaga*?"

"Skinny. She looks like a little girl, a baby. I like women. I need my chicken with some meat."

"That's my protégée. Believe me, she's a woman. And she's not skinny at all. I keep telling her about wearing them baggy-ass clothes. I can get her to dress right when we go out, but any other time she insists on that tomboy shit. But her body is tight. Trust me," Ginger said, campaigning for her friend.

Desiree and Derek came back to the Rover with bags of food. Desiree had already dipped in her bag and was munching on some fried fish. Ginger gave Fuzzy an encouraging look, then refocused her energy on Derek. Desiree decided to try to engage Fuzzy in some small talk. So far, he hadn't said a word, and she was dying to know if his voice was as sexy as his brother's.

"So why do they call you Fuzzy?" she asked. He grinned, and Desiree felt her insides grow hot. He faced her, his eyes faintly visible behind the dark lenses of his sunglasses.

"Because the gals them say me goatee feels fuzzy when I'm downtown," he offered suggestively, then chuckled and stroked the dark, smooth hairs of his immaculately groomed goatee. Desiree wondered if he could tell that she was wet from the mere thought of his tongue touching her. Suddenly, she realized why Ginger wasn't stressing about money, or anything else, for that matter. Maybe it was the combination of the flora and salty ocean air, the exotic aromas rising from the street vendors' carts, and Fuzzy's cologne, but she felt intoxicated. It was like Fuzzy had her under some spell and she couldn't break free. She thought of the Miss Cleo commercial, the one with the girl with the burgundy weave claiming, "I think someone put roots on me; what should I do?" She knew what she was gonna do. She was gonna fuck Fuzzy. Even if she didn't make a dime, she was gonna get that dick.

THE FOLLOWING WEEK WAS MISERABLE FOR DESIREE. THE MEN at the club weren't feeling her at all. They all kept claiming she was skinny, even though she had a big ass and terrific legs. She was far from anorexic, but the men acted like she was a dancing skeleton. She managed to scrape up two hundred dollars a night, but after rolling with Ginger she was used to making at least four hundred on her slowest of nights. And to make matters worse, she hadn't seen Fuzzy since they first met. Ginger's days were filled with Derek this and Derek that. Occasionally, Desiree tagged along with them, but after accompanying them to St. John she decided to let them have their privacy. They'd hugged and kissed so much that she only felt worse for being a third wheel. There were other men on the island who tried to holler, but Desiree had her heart set on Fuzzy. Besides, the other men had all been broke compared to Fuzzy.

Tired of seeing Desiree mope, Ginger decided to take action. She phoned Derek and instructed him that he *and* Fuzzy were taking them to the beach at Magen's Bay and there were no ifs, ands, or buts about it. Desiree got angry; she wasn't a charity case. But Ginger insisted that she get cute and game up.

"I know that nigga and I know you. You can get with that. Put on that orange-flowered thong. Show off your shape. Put on some makeup and wear your hair down, not in a ponytail. Come on now. I taught you better," Ginger admonished, sounding more like a mother than a friend.

Desiree did as she was told, taking extra care to emphasize her eyes. If she went swimming, she knew it would all be for nothing, but what the hell, she was willing to do whatever to get with Fuzzy. She wrapped a sarong around her body and waited with Ginger, who shook her head.

"Don't worry, ma. I got this," Desiree told her confidently.

"Okay. The force is strong within you, young Skywalker, but you are not a Jedi yet," Ginger teased. Ginger was a true computer geek; she loved the Star Wars series and *Star Trek* and was always quoting some science fiction shit or other.

"There you go, Poindexter. I'm telling you, it's handled. I

won't be going in to work tonight cuz, um, I'm gonna be tied up with Fuzzy all night long," Desiree predicted.

THE VIEW FROM THE WINDING HILLS OF ST. THOMAS OF THE azure water and pale sand was breathtaking. It was a far cry from the port side of Charlotte Amalie with its shops and restaurants and docked ships. This was nature at its finest. Desiree had hated riding in St. Thomas; the cars drove on the wrong side, they seemed to have no speed limit or traffic laws, and the roads were tiny and usually had a goat or some chickens roaming in them; but now she felt no fear. She felt exhilarated, as if the car could take flight any moment and whisk them off to paradise. Momentarily, she forgot about her obsession with Fuzzy.

They parked the Rover on a small patch of road surrounded by huge coconut palm trees and strolled along the sand of Magens Bay. Desiree stared out at the ocean, playing with her hair as it blew in the wind. She arched her back and allowed her sarong to blow off, knowing Fuzzy had his eye on her. The padded bra of the top made her look curvier and womanly, the thong cut of the bottom accentuated her ass. She looked seductively over her shoulder.

"Come on, Ginny." She reached out for Ginger's hand, and they ran down the beach and off toward the water.

"I peeped that, you know," Ginger told her, referring to her magically disappearing sarong.

"I know," Desiree replied. "I'm gonna ignore his ass. But right about now I know I look too good to ignore. He's used to bitches sweating him, so I'm going to be a challenge."

"Now you're thinking. I know you gonna get up in them pockets, though."

"Oh, I'm gonna get it all. Not cuz I want it so bad, but because that nigga had the nerve to act like he ain't know who I am! You supposed to bow down in the presence of a queen and serve me properly. Now he's gotta get taxed. Shit, he coulda had some free pussy. Fuckin' around calling me skinny, ignoring me and shit," Desiree rambled.

Ginger laughed and splashed water at her. They frolicked in the waves, and when Desiree was satisfied that she was sufficiently wet and had jiggled and bounced and flaunted her body enough to have captured Fuzzy's full attention and desire, she and Ginger tossed the guys a camera and posed seductively, prolonging the tease. They even removed their bikinis and took some nude shots. Desiree could tell by the bulge in Fuzzy's shorts that he was ripe and ready for the picking. But she continued to play it cool.

When they returned to the guesthouse, Fuzzy asked Desiree if he could stay and take her to dinner.

"Sure. You think I need to eat a little more anyway, don't you?"

"So Ginger tell you what I say, eh?" His rich voice caressed her ears, breaking down her defenses.

"Yeah, she did. But she didn't have to say shit. You've been playing me since I got here. I can tell you aren't feeling me." Desiree played innocent. She knew the effect she was finally having on Fuzzy.

"Nah, it's not that. You cover everything up with baggy clothes."

"You could have seen more if you came to Red's," she replied suggestively.

"Well, what about now? Can I see more now?" Fuzzy licked

his lips. Desiree answered his question by slowly peeling off her moist swimsuit. She stood before him nude.

"You got a fat monkey to be a little gal," he said, referring to her genitalia.

"It bites too," she said, giggling. Fuzzy walked over to her and placed his hand gently but firmly on her pussy.

"Owww," he groaned.

Even his groans have an accent, Desiree thought as she threw her head back and surrendered to his touch. Fuzzy stroked her into a frenzy, then pulled his hand away right when she was on the brink of climaxing.

"Lay down," he ordered. Desiree obliged. Fuzzy spread her legs and tasted her.

Desiree and Fuzzy never made it out to dinner. But he feasted on her body until she couldn't move and the bed had crashed through the frame and lay crooked on the floor.

CHAPTER 5

G INGER AND DESIREE ARRIVED AT THE MIAMI LAKES HOME tanned and tired. Desiree and Fuzzy had spent the rest of her stay in St. Thomas together, smoking, fucking, and shopping. Nose wide open, Fuzzy lavished gifts on her from Ralph Lauren and Versace and had copped her a few pieces from a local jeweler. She had a pair of diamond studs, a tennis bracelet, and a Colombian emerald ring. Desiree sprung off the gifts and the dick, sucked and fucked Fuzzy until he couldn't get it up anymore.

"Did you have fun?" Ginger finally asked as she kicked her shoes off at the door, dropped her bags, and flopped on the couch.

"Hell yeah!" Desiree enthused, joining her on the couch. "Got off to a rocky start, but I have no regrets."

"You gonna go back?" Ginger asked.

"Yeah. He's gonna fly me back just to kick it sometime next month, or so he says. If he follows through, I'm game; otherwise, it was cool," Desiree told her.

"I feel you. But I think he likes you. He came up off some major paper."

"I know!" Desiree was excited despite how tired she was.

"You're getting pretty good," Ginger said, complimenting her skills.

"Getting?" Desiree cocked her head back.

"Okay, you're a natural at this shit, Desi. All you had to do was get your confidence up. Now you see what you can do?"

"Yeah," Desiree admitted. "So what we gonna do tonight? It's still early enough for us to take a nap and then go to work, or we can go kick it. What's it gonna be?"

"Damn, girl! Why can't we just chill?" Ginger moaned. She was exhausted and would have enjoyed relaxing and reminiscing about her man in the V.I.

"Cuz we'll get lazy, and one day will turn into a week," Desiree said knowingly. "It's all about the Benjamins, baby. I need that scrilla." Desiree rubbed her fingers together for emphasis.

"Well, shit, I say we kick it. I worked my ass off in St. Thomas. Those concrete floors are murder on the knees. Let's go to Chaos," Ginger suggested.

"Cool. But we're gonna go to work tomorrow. Monday night fights, you know we gonna get cake. Now get a little bit of rest," Desiree ordered, then went to do the same.

DESIREE LOVED SUNDAY NIGHTS ON SOUTH BEACH. THE streets were like a fashion show, and not some local church function, more like the couture shows in New York or Paris. The strip was the real deal. All the big-money designers were being represented: Dolce & Gabbana, Versace, Roberto Cavalli, Chanel, and Chloé. People were rocking thousands of dollars on their backs with no mercy. Desiree was always in awe that on a Sunday, people were out in full force, kicking it like there was no tomorrow.

They rolled through Shadow Lounge briefly for drinks. Desiree absentmindedly flirted with a pro basketball player and locked his number in her newly acquired cell. She was getting over the whole athlete fascination. Ginger had been right: they were almost always more trouble than they were worth. If they weren't total assholes, they were insecure as hell. Plus, she quickly realized that most of them had a long-time girlfriend somewhere and considered her a trick, a fling, a tool to get a nut off. It was easy not to get caught up; she just went straight for the wallets. But a lot of them were cheap as hell. They expected a woman to feel that it was a privilege to fuck with them, and no further payment was really deemed necessary. It was like getting blood from a turnip.

After about an hour or so they went to Chaos. Desiree felt her pulse quicken as she took in the curved, chrome arch sculpture that graced the front entrance. Chaos was the shit! There were plenty of hotboys making their way into the spot. Desiree really liked them. The street hustlers were a different breed than the celebrities. They came up off the ends lovely. It wasn't just about making paper for them, it was about the floss. They always made sure they represented to the fullest, and their girls were well taken care of. Desiree especially liked the New York ones, all hard-core and thugged out. She liked to reduce them to kittens who purred for her with stacks of cash.

They headed straight for the bar.

"Two waters, please," Ginger ordered from the surfer dude bartender. Desiree looked at Ginger like she was crazy.

"I want a cosmo," Desiree ordered. Ginger grabbed the bottled waters with one hand and Desiree's hand with the other.

"Come in the bathroom with me," Ginger ordered, and marched her into the ladies' lounge.

"Don't drink any liquor," she hissed to Desiree in the corner. "Pop this." Ginger slipped Desiree a small pink tablet, then swallowed one of her own.

"What is it?" Desiree asked after she had swallowed it.

"X," Ginger replied.

"Word?"

"Chill, and drink lots of water," Ginger instructed. "And juice. Drink lots of juice. Any juice with vitamin C will enhance your roll."

"My roll?" Desiree asked her quizzically.

Ginger rolled her eyes skyward. "Your high! God, Desiree, sometimes you are so slow!"

Desiree chugged the contents of the water bottle and shrugged. She didn't know what all the hype was about—she didn't feel anything different—but fifteen minutes later she began to feel a little light-headed.

"Look at me." Ginger held Desiree's head and stared at her. "Yeah, you feelin' it. Your pupils are dilated." Ginger laughed as Desiree smiled blankly at her. Her eyes looked especially catlike.

"I love you, Ginny. You're my best friend. You're like a sister to me, and I love you so much!" Desiree grinned wildly. Ginger laughed at her.

"Do you hear that?"

"What? 'Big Pimpin''?" Ginger shrugged her shoulders and began to dance to Jay-Z.

"The music sounds funny. Damn, you're dancing in slow motion!" Desiree pointed at her.

"Why did I give you that pill?" Ginger shook her head and got them both some juice.

"I feel like love!" Desiree chanted as she danced to her

own beat. She looked crazy as hell, but she was cute, so she could get away with looking crazy. Besides, Desiree was far from the only person in the club who was rolling. There were dozens of people whose eyes looked like those of a cat, professing their love to anyone who would listen, grinding their jaws as the effects of MDMA wreaked havoc on their nervous systems.

Desiree felt like every pore in her body was open and the music was sinking into her, replacing the blood in her veins. The bass was controlling her heart, the lights controlling her eyes; Desiree was a slave to the rhythm. She thought she felt cool air blowing through a vent in the ceiling, sending a chill through her body, but everywhere she moved, she swore she felt the breeze, as if it were following her.

"I'm cold. I'm going to the bathroom," Desiree sang as she ground her teeth.

"Mmm 'kay." Ginger smiled at her. She was deep in conversation about nothing with an equally high man at the bar.

"Like I was saying, really, who decided that green means go and red means stop?" Desiree heard Ginger telling him. "Green is the color of money. Money makes the world go round. Red is the color of blood. Blood makes the body go around. Do you realize the whole conspiracy in all of that?"

Desiree went to the bathroom thinking about blood. She could barely stand straight as she crouched over the toilet seat. Even though she was high as hell, she wasn't high enough to put her ass on a public toilet seat. All kinds of shit went on in the bathroom. She could hear the muffled voices of others, but it all sounded like gibberish. She flushed the toilet and straightened her clothes, then placed her ear near the crack in the stall door cautiously.

"Y'all can't fade me! Y'all can't even fade me! I'm covered in the blood of the lamb. Rebuke and yield all of you demons!" Desiree yelled at the patrons as she burst out of the stall. Most of them said nothing; they just looked at her knowingly. Their stares irritated her.

"I see your souls, people. You need to repent the evil of your ways. Jesus is coming back for us, can't you understand that? He still loves us!" Desiree looked pleadingly at the women in the restroom. Most of them were laughing now. But a few people nodded in agreement.

"She might be high or drunk or whatever, but she ain't said anything that wasn't true. Just because I'm in the club don't mean I don't love the Lord," Desiree heard a girl say.

"Thank you! Praise his name!" Desiree clapped her hands together and danced around like she was possessed with the Holy Ghost.

"You're up in here on a Sunday, though," her friend teased her.

"Rebuke and yield. Smite thy tongue. It is Monday now. The cock has crowed on a new day, nonbeliever." Desiree looked into the ceiling, arms akimbo.

"Just say no," the bathroom attendant muttered under her breath.

"I will." Desiree turned to face her.

Does she have supersonic hearing or what? the attendant thought to herself.

"I will say no to the materialism of society! Here. I need not this earthly possession." Desiree handed her a hundred-dollar bill just as Ginger entered the bathroom.

"You're still in here? Oh my God, I've been looking for you for an hour! Have you been in here all this time?" Ginger grabbed Desiree by the shoulders.

"Yes," the bathroom attendant remarked dryly, pocketing the Benjamin discreetly.

"Don't blaspheme, Ginny. Don't use the Lord's name in vain." Desiree looked solemn.

"Uh, okay. Let's go home." Ginger tugged at Desiree gently as they left Chaos through the back door.

CHAPTER 6

*B*ITTER COLD BLANKETED THE BRONX. DESIREE HAD NOWHERE *else to go but home; her friends from functional homes were all eating dinner. Those that weren't were stealing time with their boy-friends. Unfortunately, her mother was already at work on the third shift as an orderly at North Central Bronx Hospital, but her step-father, Ernesto, was home.*

"Where you been, bitch?" he called out to her, not really caring. Desiree ignored him and headed straight for the bathroom. She locked the door behind her and turned the water faucet in the tub as hot as it would go. She attempted to clear her thoughts as she let the near-scalding water pelt her hair and body. She stayed there until the water ran cold. As she headed to her room, Ernesto used his flabby body to block her.

"Move out the way, Nesto!" she told him. Nesto didn't budge. "I don't have the time to play with you! I've got homework!" she snapped. Moving from side to side, she tried to find a way around nasty Nesto. He remained steadfast and began pumping his hips at her lewdly.

"You are such a loser!" Desiree blasted Ernesto with a full dose of uptown attitude, hands on hips, neck rotating in a circle. Nesto responded by attempting to untie her bathrobe. She slapped his

hand away, and he grabbed her by the arm hard and pulled her close.

"Give Daddy a little kiss," he growled through his yellow teeth, and then licked Desiree's neck. She slapped Ernesto with all her might, causing him to drop his ever-present Colt 45 and stagger on his weak, drunken legs.

"Stupid cunt," he muttered as he bent down to recover the can that was frothing and foaming all over the scuffed hardwood floor.

"If you touch me again, I'll kill you!" She glared at him before slamming her bedroom door and locking it. Desiree pulled out the butcher knife she kept beneath her frilly pink bed skirt as protection from prowlers.

"I swear I will kill you if you ever touch me again," she vowed aloud as she inspected the shiny blade of the knife before slipping it under her pillow. Then she kneeled beside the makeshift tabernacle on top of her nightstand. She lit a Blessed Mother candle, a red Jesus candle, and a yellow St. Lazarus candle like she did every night. Then she grabbed the rosary beads her father had given her for her first communion and made novenas.

After her prayers she crossed herself and kissed the picture she kept of her father that she also kept on the nightstand. That always made her feel better. Desiree had faith that God would look out for her and that her father was her guardian angel who'd protect her. After all, when she was a little girl, he told her that he would always protect her, that she could always count on him, and that nothing, not even death, would change that. And the Bible told her that she could always count on Jesus. She had to believe that. It was the only thing that gave her hope.

That night and the night after, Ernesto didn't try anything. Desiree assumed her prayers had been answered. But she still got a nervous feeling when she walked in from school and saw her mother getting ready to leave for work two nights later. Ernesto was parked in front of the television, drinking beer and scratching his crotch. He looked up at Desiree and blew her a kiss. She shuddered with disgust. Desiree didn't know who disgusted her more: Ernesto for being so foul or her mother for acting like he wasn't doing shit.

"Mami, do you have to work the third shift?" Desiree whined as her mother raced about the apartment making sure she had all her belongings. She did this anytime she left the house. If she would have cut down on the blow, Desiree was sure she could have kept her wits about her, but instead she always looked like a geekmonster. Cocaine had her on ninety-miles-an-hour cruise control, 24/7.

"Desi, not now, okay? We've already talked about this so many times. We need the money, and unless I work at night, I can't finish college. You do want me to be a nurse, don't you? You want me to keep making monkey money forever?" Mami replied. She had managed to get herself in community college. Desiree thought for a second that maybe her mother was just using Ernesto until she got her shit together, but then it occurred to her that Ernesto didn't have shit.

"I'll get a job, Mami, since the so-called man of the house won't get one," Desiree offered.

"Desiree, your job is to get a proper education so you don't have to struggle like me. Get a good job with benefits so you won't have to count on a husband or some other man. The good ones never stick around, and, well, the other ones . . ." Mami looked over at the unkempt Ernesto and rolled her eyes. She used those exact words practically every day. Desiree didn't know why her mother didn't practice what she preached.

"I can get a job and still be a doctor when I grow up," Desiree asserted. She needed to stash some money so that as soon as she was old enough to leave home, she'd never have to come back.

"You ain't smart enough to be no doctor," Nesto interjected, slurring. "You'll be lucky if you get knocked up by a doctor!" he belched, and then laughed heartily at his own ignorance.

"You are such a pig! Nobody was even talking to your broke ass anyway!" Desiree sneered. Why did he have to talk to her like that? Why didn't her mother check him?

"Watch how you talk to your father!" Mami snapped. "Show him some respect!"

Desiree cringed. She hated when Mami referred to Ernesto as her father. Her father was gone, and no deadbeat like Ernesto would ever take his place. Her father had been a real man. Having a fucked-up stepfather was worse than having no father at all.

"How you gonna say that, Mami? You not gonna check him? He's not my father! He'll never be half the man my father was!" Desiree yelled. Here her mother was, acting like her real dad had never existed.

"No argument there," Mami remarked dryly. She looked at Ernesto and frowned up in disgust, then grabbed her keys and pocketbook and walked out the door.

She doesn't care, Desiree thought. She doesn't care what happens to me. All she cares about is herself and that punk-ass Ernesto. It was obvious to Desiree that for whatever reasons—love, fear, or loyalty—Mami had made her choice. And it wasn't her sangre, her blood; it was the man who mooched off of her and tried to violate her daughter.

At about 3 a.m. Desiree was awakened by a scratching sound at her bedroom door. Not moving, she squinted, attempting to see through the darkness. The scratching grew louder, and then there was the click of the tumblers in the lock and the turning of the door-knob. Desiree reached for the butcher's knife, found it, and waited in a heightened sense of awareness.

Nesto was clad in only boxer shorts, his flabby chest and back covered by a disgusting layer of hair. His erection poked through the flimsy material of his skid-mark-stained shorts. He crept silently toward Desiree. She appeared to be fast asleep and unsuspecting. He stopped a foot or so away from the bed and bent over to remove his underwear. Desiree took a peek to see him fondling his tiny penis as he approached the bed. When he bent over to remove the comforter from her body with his free hand, Desiree seized the opportunity, springing to life, asking no questions, saying nothing, only plunging the blade of the knife deep into his flabby gut.

She was scared shitless. She gasped for breath as she waited for the body to drop. But it didn't. It wasn't like in the movies when you shot someone or stabbed someone and they died instantly. It was like one of those horror flicks where the killer keeps on coming and coming no matter what you do. Nesto was wounded, but more than that, he was angry. He pimp-slapped Desiree, causing her to fall back on the bed. Ernesto was nude, his overabundant body hair slick with blood and matted to his tanned skin. It was a sight almost too ghastly for her to behold, but there was no way she was going to let this pathetic excuse for a man take her virginity.

Ernesto lunged at her, overcoming her with his body weight. He ripped her underwear off and roughly began to fondle Desiree's privates. All she kept thinking to herself was, Not like this. Her first time was supposed to be with someone that she loved. She even thought she would wait until she was married or at least engaged.

"I'm gonna get you, you little bitch!" he gurgled, blood spewing from his mouth. Desiree was horrified but determined to escape. She squirmed and kicked to no avail. Ernesto wrapped both of his hands around her neck and began to squeeze as he attempted to enter her. She struggled to break free. She felt piercing pain and then light-headedness. She gasped and struggled for breath as Ernesto heaved on top of her.

This can't be happening! Desiree thought. She said Hail Marys and silently begged the Lord to deliver her. She was ready to die, because she really couldn't imagine living through something this awful. Besides, she believed that Jesus wouldn't let her suffer like that. He would take her up to heaven, and that would be the end of her pain. Her mother would be free to start her life again.

Then Ernesto began choking. He tried to breathe, but his breaths were shallow and forced. He stopped moving and slid from Desiree's body onto the floor.

Gasping, she ran out of the room, not stopping until she was out of the door and down a flight of steps, where she banged on the door of the building supervisor, Mr. Lopez.

"Coño! Quién es?" *Mr. Lopez muttered as he stomped to the door. There was the sound of what seemed like a million locks being opened.*

"Mr. Lopez! Soy yo, Desiree! Ayúdame! *Oh God, please help me!" she screamed hysterically while banging on the door.*

Mr. Lopez flung open the door and nearly jumped out of his skin. He clutched his heart and gasped at the sight of Desiree: her hair was all over the place, her nightgown was ripped, and she was drenched in blood. With trembling hands he pulled her into his apartment. He locked the door and then flew into his bedroom, returning in a split second with a cocked and loaded .380 Saturday night special in hand. Mr. Lopez stood cautiously with his back to the door listening for motion, like the cops on TV shows did, then peeked through the peephole. He saw no one and could detect no movement. Mr. Lopez uncocked the gun and placed it in the waistband of his pajama pants.

By this time Desiree was hiccupping and sobbing uncontrollably. Mr. Lopez led her to his prized La-Z-Boy recliner and made her sit down. No one ever sat in his recliner, whose seat cushion was practically molded to the shape of his ass. At first she refused.

"Don't worry about the blood, Desi," *he told her. He sat her down and flipped the lever to lift her feet before going into the kitchen, where he dialed the police; then he called Desiree's mami at the hospital.*

Mr. Lopez poured Desiree a tiny glass of sangria and handed it to her. "Here. Tómalo. *It's the sangria you like to sneak and sip at my domino games when you think we aren't looking. It'll calm your* nerves." She took the glass and gulped down the sweet wine through her sobs.

"What happened, Desiree? Who did this to you? Was it Ernesto?" Mr. Lopez observed the hand prints around her neck. The mention of that pervert's name made Desiree cry even harder. She shook her head as if to say yes, then grimaced in pain, holding her midsection and rocking back and forth.

Mr. Lopez needed no further explanation. He knew Ernesto was a loser, but he had no idea he would stoop so low as to violate a child. Mr. Lopez took the steps two at a time. He walked through the open door and called out to Ernesto.

"Where are you, cabrón?" Lopez demanded. Then he screamed, "Oh my God!" Almost immediately, he was back in the apartment, his normally gleaming tan skin looking gray and dull. He went into the kitchen again and grabbed the bottle of sangria. He poured Desiree another glass, then downed the rest of the bottle himself.

"Please tell me you got to him before he got to you," he pleaded, his eyes full of tears. Desiree just looked down at the floor. Mr. Lopez crossed himself and began to pray reverently, crying the whole time.

Desiree's mami finally arrived at the tiny apartment, which was swarming with detectives and paramedics. She saw the blood covering her daughter and a sheet being pulled over Ernesto's cold, lifeless body. She snapped. She screamed like a banshee, cried uncontrollably, and tried to climb on top of the body on the floor. A cop pried her away from the corpse.

"Your daughter needs you," he told her, leading her toward Desiree. Her mami hugged her, holding her so tightly she thought her ribs would crack.

"I'm sorry, Mami. But he . . . he raped me. He tried to choke me," she sobbed in her mother's arms. Abruptly, her mami held Desiree at arm's length from her body. "This is all your fault!" she told Desiree *as she shook her by the shoulders. "You killed both my husbands! You little bitch, I hate you!" Mami spat in her daughter's face, then slapped her hard. A homicide detective stepped between them.*

"How can you blame me? Ernesto was the pervert. He raped me!" Desiree cried.

"You were always walking around in skimpy little clothes taunting him. You wanted it. You didn't want me to have any happiness. It's bad enough you killed your father, now you've killed Ernesto!" She spat again, trying to hit Desiree. The homicide detective's ears tweaked at the accusations.

"What do you mean I killed Papi? Mami, a drunk driver killed Papi! Remember? He got hit by a car," Desiree raged. "How the hell can you stand there and blame me? I loved my father more than anything. Papi's death was an accident."

"No! He was out getting ice cream for your little spoiled ass. You just had to have chocolate ice cream. Don't you remember? He couldn't tell your ass no, and both of you acted like the sun rose and set on your ass. If you would have eaten what we had in the freezer, he wouldn't have been hit by that car. He would have stayed home. He would be alive!" Desiree's mami screamed. The police, paramedics, and coroner's assistant stood mutely, staring in disbelief.

Desiree felt like all the blood was draining from her body. "No! I was just a little girl, and it was an accident. It's not my fault," she cried.

"That's enough, ma'am. Your daughter has been through a great deal tonight." The detective who'd separated them tried to neutralize the situation.

"It was an accident. I didn't do anything wrong!" Desiree cried, defending herself.

"Oh, and this isn't your fault either, is it?" Mami stated bitterly, pointing at Ernesto's body.

"*Calm down, ma'am,*" the detective told her.

"*I don't have to do shit!*" she screamed on him. "*Fuck you! This is my house!*" she continued, rolling her neck.

"*You're crazy! He raped me! He was always trying to touch me, and I told you. And you never did anything! All you ever gave a fuck about was him, and I know why. You might think I don't know, but I do. It's cuz he keeps you fucked-up off that shit. I don't know how you kept your job, because you're high all the time. You think I didn't hear y'all in there sniffing? You never did anything to help me, you worthless bitch. What kind of mother are you?*" Desiree couldn't hold her feelings in anymore.

"*I hate you, you little murderous bitch! You've fucked up everything, you dumb little cunt!*"

At that moment Desiree stopped loving her mother. It was obvious to her that her mother had stopped loving her long before then, but she'd held on to a tiny shred of hope that if they could just escape the poverty, if they could just get away from the grime of New York and go somewhere nice and clean where they didn't have to worry about bills, everything would be okay. But her mother had crossed a line. Desiree lunged at her. It was useless; there were too many cops there, but her mother got the point. She was out of her daughter's life forever.

"*I'm not your mother anymore! I don't want you anymore! Get out! You killed my husbands! It's all your fault!*"

DESIREE AWAKENED WITH A START. SHE'D SWEATED SO MUCH that her hair was wet and her sheets felt clammy. What the hell was going on inside of her head? The Ecstasy must have brought things to the surface that she had been determined to forget. As far as she was concerned, it was all just some drug-induced nightmare and not a repressed memory. The whole scenario with her mother and Ernesto was a hallucination. But lying to herself didn't make her feel any better.

Her head was throbbing, and her mouth felt so dry that she just held her mouth under the cold water in the bathroom sink until her belly felt filled to capacity.

"The dead has arisen!" Ginger joked when Desiree appeared in the kitchen, her hair skewed all over her head. Desiree only grunted.

"Oh, wait! Let me 'smite my tongue' as you told me so many times last night, Reverend Goodbody! You might think I was blaspheming the resurrection," Ginger hooted.

Desiree winced from the noise. It felt like someone was playing a tom-tom in her head. "I'm never doing X again," she moaned as Ginger brewed some Cuban coffee. Desiree felt the pungent aroma alert her senses as it wafted through the room. "That shit fucks with your head!"

"I'm never *letting* you do X again. You cannot handle your roll!" Ginger admonished her.

"What did I do?" Desiree tried to recollect the events of the previous night but drew a blank. *This must be what a blackout is,* she thought.

"It wasn't what you *did,* it was what you *said*!" Ginger told her. "You were like a preacher, girl. You were quoting scripture and everything. It was wild. It kind of freaked me out, though. You said that God was talking to you, and you talked about angels and stuff. It was deep, like a movie or something. I can't explain it, and don't ask me to repeat it, because I was high myself. But I do remember you saying that you were a direct descendant of Mary Magdalene. And, oh yeah, you talked a lot about the saints, *a whole lot*. You said you were some saint named Christina the Astonishing who floated so she couldn't smell the sin emanating from people. Is that real, or did you make that up? Oh yeah, and you talked about how the saints were, like, willing to die before defiling their bodies with sexual sin and how many of the female saints were victims of rape and attempted rape. It was like the catechism class that wouldn't end!" Ginger shook her head and handed Desiree a tiny demitasse cup filled with dark, thick coffee.

"You're kidding, right?" Desiree gulped the cup's contents like a shot and placed it in front of her for a refill.

"No, girl. You were bugging me the fuck out. You completely ruined my high." Ginger gave her another cup of coffee, which she sipped. "Is your family real religious or something? I don't even think preachers know all the stuff you were spouting."

"I don't have any family, remember?" Desiree's eyes were icy.

"Well, you had one at one time. Did you go to church a lot or something, or Catholic school? Because you really knew what you were talking about. You grabbed my Bible, and you were whipping through pages and everything. Everything you said you backed up with a Bible verse," Ginger recounted.

Desiree shifted in her seat nervously. "I've been to church. I used to be religious, I guess. But then shit happened in my life. I can't say I have much faith anymore," she explained.

"Shit like what?" Ginger inquired.

"Just shit," Desiree snapped. She wanted to open up but couldn't. Ginger had been like a sister to her, but she didn't want to talk about some things with *anyone*.

"Okay. I get the hint." Ginger dropped the subject. "But you know if you ever want to talk, I'm here."

CHAPTER 7

March 1999

"D O YOU THINK I SHOULD GET SOME TITTIES?" DESIREE asked Ginger while they were lying poolside tanning topless.

"Shit yeah, girl, go for it!" Ginger encouraged her.

"How much were yours, five g's, right?" Desiree queried.

"Yeah. But you've got it, and if you don't want to spend it all at once, you can finance them," Ginger explained.

"Yo get the fuck outta here! I can pay for titties in installments?"

"No doubt. You can go to my doctor. She's the best."

"I wouldn't have it any other way."

So Desiree made an appointment for a consultation with Ginger's doctor, a Hispanic woman who assured Desiree that she would look fabulous once the procedure was over. She used a computer program to show Desiree what she looked like now in comparison to what she would look like after. Desiree gawked at the computer-generated image in disbelief. The after picture looked like a woman, a beautiful one at that. It was the body she had always dreamed about.

The night before her surgery, she and Ginger went to fill her prescriptions for antibiotics and painkillers for after the surgery, and also went shopping for a bunch of sports bras, since that would be all she could wear for a few weeks while she was healing. Her stomach rumbled relentlessly; Desiree was not to drink, eat, or smoke for twelve hours before the surgery, but she was too nervous to really think about food.

"You scared?" Ginger asked her.

"Yeah. What if I die?" Desiree panicked.

"Your holy-rolling ass will go straight to heaven," Ginger quipped.

"Don't call me that. It was one incident." Desiree looked fearful. "But for real, what if I die?"

Ginger chuckled. "Chill, you ain't gonna die."

"Okay. Well, what if my titties end up crooked? You know, one nipple pointing one way, the other in the other direction. You've seen those chicks with cockeyed tits!" Desiree giggled.

"Relax, nena. Those heifers had crooked tits to begin with. Besides, mine look great, don't they?" she asked Desiree, who nodded in agreement.

"You're gonna be fine. Trust me," Ginger reassured her.

The next day Ginger drove Desiree to the plastic surgeon's office and dropped her off.

"Aren't you gonna wait with me?" Desiree pleaded.

"Nah. You won't have to wait. Plus, even if you did, you'd drive me crazy. I'm tired of hearing you yap on about them damn tits. Get the water bags put in already," Ginger teased her before pulling off, her hair blowing in the wind. She would pick Desiree up when the center called to tell her that Desiree was in recovery.

Ginger was right: Desiree did not have to wait. She was ushered into a pre-op room immediately, where she was ordered to undress and put on a robe. Shortly thereafter, the doctor came in and gave her two sample implants to stick in her sports bra to double-check that the size she had selected during her consultation was okay. After they were all cleared, the doctor left her to receive her anesthesia.

"Make sure you juice me up good. I don't want to feel a thing. You might want to give me extra, you know. I have a strong system. Oh yeah, my veins are supertiny. You might want to use a butterfly to run my IV," Desiree told the anesthesiologist.

"Hon, I've been doing this for fifteen years. You'll be fine. But I'm gonna knock you out real quick so you can shut up, okay?" He grinned.

Desiree laughed as the anesthesia began to take effect. She was placed in a wheelchair and wheeled into the operating room.

"Have you got them?" Desiree asked a buxom nurse who assisted her onto the operating table.

"We all do. We get a discount. I'm getting my nose done in two weeks," she answered.

"I'm getting lipo next Tuesday," another nurse piped in. And then everything faded to black.

When Desiree awoke, she felt as if an elephant were standing on her chest. She knew her new boobs probably only weighed a couple of pounds, but they felt like two-ton boulders.

"How are you feeling?" The doctor was holding her hand, gently rousing her from her groggy sleep. Desiree looked down at her chest and willed her eyes to focus. She immediately saw the two round mounds stretching her skin beneath the fabric of the bra.

"I love you," Desiree told the doctor, her voice scratchy.

"It's the drugs, honey," the doctor said.

"No, I love you!" Desiree insisted.

"I HATE THAT DOCTOR!" DESIREE WAILED AS THE BEAMER HIT a pothole on the long drive home.

"Don't worry. That Percocet is gonna kick in real soon. You're gonna be in seventh heaven in no time," Ginger said.

"Well, in the meantime, take it easy on the bumps, Ginny," Desiree criticized.

"Cranky, cranky!" Ginger admonished.

Eventually, they made it home and got Desiree in the bed. The painkillers took effect, and she mostly slept for the next three days. On the fourth day much of her pain had subsided. She was able to do normal things, aside from lifting; she just needed special help rising, sitting, and lying down.

"How are you feeling, baby girl?" Ginger asked Desiree gently, before heading into the kitchen to start dinner.

"I'm okay, just a little sore." Desiree shifted uncomfortably on the couch.

"Well, that's to be expected. How are the drugs working?"

"I feel good as hell when I'm up. But mostly, they just make me sleepy."

"Yeah. But you can't do much of anything, so you may as well sleep. Ayo! By the way, who the fuck is Mr. Lopez?" Ginger called out from the kitchen.

Desiree's eyes became wide as saucers. She winced in pain from nearly jumping off the couch at the mention of that name.

"Why would you ask me that?" Desiree inquired. Was

Ginger practicing some kind of voodoo? Desiree had never mentioned him, and she hadn't written anything about him in a notebook or journal.

"You kept calling out to him," Ginger answered.

"Huh? What do you mean?"

"I don't know. I guess you were having a bad dream or something. You kept asking him to help you. I almost woke you up because you were tossing and turning, and I didn't want you to hurt yourself. But I figured the drugs probably had you comatose and seeing shit. We all know how you act on pills, now, don't we?" Ginger teased.

Desiree laughed along, but couldn't help but wonder what else she had been saying in her sleep. Why did she keep dreaming about the past? Desiree made up her mind that as soon as she could manage her pain with Tylenol, she was going off the Percocet. Ginger was right in one aspect: Desiree did not react well to pills. They seemed to counteract her ability to live in denial.

She clicked on the huge television in the living room and flipped to BET to distract herself. Since the surgery, she had a chance to catch up on all the videos she'd been missing due to working or partying. She'd spend hours watching BET and MTV, studying everything about every video she saw. From the time she was really young, she'd catch *Video Soul* and *Rap City*, eyeing not only the entertainers but the gorgeous models in the background. She used to imagine that they lived such glamorous lives. How could they not? They knew all the rappers and singers, they got to wear the fly clothes, go to all the parties.

Desiree had noticed that more and more videos were being shot in Miami. That day, she had seen Trick Daddy and Trina's video for "Naan" and recognized half of the girls in it from the nightclubs and hanging on the beach. She even recognized a few strippers. *I'm just as pretty as any of them. Way prettier. I bet I could be in a video,* Desiree thought, full of ambition. *Shit! I can flow better than these girls too! That new chick Trina is from right here. She used to dance at the Lex too. If she can make it, I can make it.*

"Ginny!" Desiree yelled to Ginger, who was making her famous spaghetti sauce. Desiree was getting hungry from the smell of the meat sautéing with onion, garlic, and green pepper. Ginger came running out holding a spoon dripping with tomato sauce.

"What, girl!" Ginger frowned at Desiree. "You know I'm trying to hook up this sauce."

"I wanna be in videos." Desiree stated her wish simple and plain, as if Ginger could snap her fingers and make it happen. That was how Ginger operated on so many levels, so it didn't seem out of the ordinary.

"Okay." Ginger rolled her eyes.

"I'm serious!" Desiree peeled herself from her position on the couch with a little help from Ginger and followed her into the kitchen. "Everyone is always asking me if I'm a model anyway."

"Oh, I'm sure you'd have no problem doing it, especially now." Ginger motioned toward Desiree's enhanced cleavage. "But are you sure you want to?"

"Sure." Desiree shrugged. "You deal with models for your Web site all the time. Maybe I could work for you." Desiree was eager.

"I don't think so. If you want to model, get an agent. If you want to do porn, fuck with me, because that's the kind of modeling on the Web that my girls deal with." Ginger stirred the bubbling pot of sauce on the stove.

"Well, I'm just trying to get paid!" Desiree didn't care what kind of modeling she did; she just knew that it would be cool for men to open a magazine or turn on the TV and see her looking sexy and tempting.

"Nah, kid. I ain't even gonna put you onto that. You can do better," Ginger said.

"I don't see why not. I dance. I date. You don't have a problem with that. But whenever I ask you to put me down with your business, you say no."

"No, *you* don't have a problem with that. *I* don't think it's what you should be doing, but who am I to knock your hustle? You gotta earn like everyone else. But you're like a little sister to me, and would I want my little sister doing this, any of this? No. I wouldn't want my little sister modeling, because that world can be just as bad as dancing, and in some ways worse. I think you should be making some kind of plans for your future, your education. You're a smart girl, I can tell. You catch on to shit real quickly. So catch this . . ." Ginger's expression became dead serious as she met Desiree's hazel eyes with her green contacts. "This shit doesn't last forever, and even if it did, you'd get tired of it." Ginger stood with her hands on her hips authoritatively. Desiree eyed her and digested what she had been told.

"But hey, you're a grown woman, little sister or not." Ginger returned to her sauce and dismissed the topic.

"Well, I see your point. But if I could model, then I wouldn't have to date or dance or any of that stuff. I could even be a rapper," Desiree added meekly. She'd never shared her poetry and lyrics with anyone. But why should every other girl out there be getting a piece of the pie when she could be out doing the same thing?

"You wanna rap?" Ginger smirked.

"It's not funny. I write shit all the time. I know it's just as good as everyone else's stuff," Desiree defended herself.

"Okay. I'm just surprised, that's all. You write rhymes? Is

that what you're doing when I see you scribbling in your notebook?"

"Well, yeah," Desiree said sheepishly. "Most of the time I just write little stuff, a line or two. But I've got a few songs now. And I think they're pretty good."

"I thought it was your diary or something. I guess I don't really know you, baby girl. Well, if you've got a dream, then go for it. I'm sure you can rap as well as any of these other girls. You're prettier than all of them, that's for sure." Ginger always found a way to encourage Desiree even if she didn't agree with her plans.

"Well, that's why I'm talking to you! What should I do first?" Desiree asked her. "Wait a minute!" Desiree walked out of the kitchen and returned with her notebook and pen.

"You serious, huh?" Ginger giggled. "Okay. Well, what do you want to know? Do you want to model, or do you want to rap?"

"I want to know it all and do it all. I want to be a star."

"Well, first you need to get some really nice pictures. I can hook you up with a couple of photographers who do good work for a good price."

Get pictures taken. Desiree took her time scribbling into her notebook, dotting the "i" in "pictures" with a smiley face.

"Okay, then what?" Desiree looked up as eager as a school-child who just realized she could read.

"God, you are silly. Anyway . . . then you need to find an agent. There are some to definitely stay away from! But there's this new girl out, a black girl, she has an agency that is supposed to be pretty good. She has the hookup when it comes to videos. There's also this guy who I think wants to be an actor too, but he seems to be hooking chicks up on that tip. But you should also send your pictures to the 'white' agencies. They handle real work like for catalogs and stuff.

Not just videos and urban work." Ginger made quotation marks in the air with her fingers as she mentioned urban work.

"Is that just a nice way of saying black stuff?" Desiree asked Ginger, laughing.

"You know this," Ginger replied.

Desiree smiled as she jotted down all of the information. She was beginning to see a clear path for her future, but it wasn't about all the school shit Ginger was always spouting. Teachers had never done shit for her anyway when she did go to school. And most of the shit they taught you didn't help you one bit once you walked outside a classroom door. Ginger could talk about school all she wanted, because she was a brainiac. Desiree didn't mind dancing, but if there was an easier way to get paid and get ahead, she was going to find it and take it.

Within the next two weeks, Desiree felt back to normal, but she had to wait another two weeks before going back to work at the club. The boredom was driving her insane. She had taken a roll of pictures—head shots to get her started—and mailed them to all the agents on a list that Ginger had downloaded from the Internet. But the waiting for a response was driving her insane.

"Let's go sit by the pool," Desiree suggested to Ginger. Sitting in the house watching videos that she should be in was making her angry.

"Cool. I could stand to get a little bit darker." Ginger inspected her already sun-bronzed skin.

"You gonna end up like that lady in *There's Something About Mary*," Desiree joked.

"Nah. Black folks don't get all wrinkly like that," Ginger said, giggling.

Desiree and Ginger sat poolside, sipping a strong pitcher of margaritas made with Patrón and munching on tortilla chips with homemade salsa.

"I wish I could take my top off, but the doctor said no direct sunlight until my checkup. Do you think I'd be okay if I did?" Desiree fiddled with the triangle top of her hot-pink bikini.

"Probably, but leave it on just to be safe. Your tan lines are going to be sexy as hell and make your boobs look bigger," Ginger informed her while spreading carrot oil on her legs.

"I can't wait to go back to work!" Desiree enthused.

"Why? I thought you wanted to be a model and a rapper."

"I do. I just miss the club."

"Don't tell me you actually like working?" Ginger snarled, her upper lip curling up in disgust.

"Don't you?" Desiree looked shocked.

"Fuck no! I like the money, but that's it. Men are pigs!" Ginger flipped her hair and frowned.

"That's right. I keep forgetting you're a carpet muncher," Desiree said, grinning. Ginger flipped her the bird.

"You liked it," Ginger retorted. Desiree responded by returning the flip-off. "Anyway, bitch, I'm saying we have a little cheese. We get props in the clubs. We get little hookups here and there. All that's nice, but don't you ever feel like it's not enough?" Ginger sat up and looked at Desiree.

"All the time! Is there such a thing as enough money, enough stuff, enough hookups?" Desiree looked at Ginger as

if she were insane. Her eyes shone nearly clear in the sunlight.

"You know that's not what I fucking mean!" Ginger
snapped.

"I know. But what you mean is bullshit. Having money is
the best thing that's ever happened to me. You must have
had money all your life to not care about it. Only rich people
think that way." Desiree rolled her eyes and flipped onto her
stomach.

"Look, I came over here from Haiti when I was five years
old. Don't talk to me about being fucking rich. I grew up
thinking that people who could shop at Sears were rich. My
dad walked out on my mom and went back to the Dominican
Republic, and we didn't have shit. He didn't send a chip. My
mother's brother was here in Miami, and if it weren't for him,
we wouldn't have had a damn thing. But we got treated like
shit when we got here. We had to stay in Krome Detention
Center. All the shit we'd heard about America being the land
of the free was bullshit, cuz Krome is just jail for refugees;
now the home of the brave, maybe. I had to be brave; I was
a little girl in a new country who barely spoke the language.
I had to fight off little boys and grown men who were trying
to molest me. And let's just say I didn't always win. When
we were able to move to Miami Shores with my uncle, you
can't imagine the ignorance I had to deal with. People said
we ate cats and did voodoo and had AIDS and all the fucked-
up things that people always say about Haitians. I've been
through shit I wouldn't wish on a dog. But getting money
didn't make me happier." Ginger's eyes reflected pain. Desiree noticed that Ginger had the same spacey look she had
when she told her about the trip to St. Thomas.

"I'm sorry. I didn't know," Desiree apologized.

"Well, how would you have known?" Ginger dismissed the topic with the wave of her hand.

"I guess . . . But can I ask you something?"

"Sure, whatever," was Ginger's response.

"If men always tried to hurt you, why do you dance? Why do you trick?"

"You need to ask yourself that same question." Ginger peered at Desiree over her sunglasses.

"I—I don't know what you mean," Desiree stammered.

"Okay. Play the nut role. But remember, I've not only been around the block, I own a crib on it. Most of us have been raped or abused or molested. Generally, girls who haven't been place higher respect on their bodies and sexuality. They value themselves more. Most strippers are broken people, just trying to find a way to be whole again. Society makes us think that money is the answer, but it isn't."

"Well, maybe when I get to where you are, I can feel that way. But I come from shit too, and I have no intentions of ever going back. I might not have what you have, but I'm a long way from where I was. But believe this: I'm going to make it too, just like you." Desiree's voice contained more than a trace of jealousy, and anger at Ginger for being so intuitive.

"Please, don't ever try to be like me. You think I've made it? Please, bitch, this is nigga rich. You think this quarter-million-dollar house is something? This crib is the size of the *real* rich motherfucker's pool house. You think that you building something with your money by saving it? I didn't get what little I do have by hiding my money in my room. You got what, fifteen, twenty thousand dollars? What do you think you can really do with that?"

Desiree opened her mouth as if to object, but there was nothing she could really say.

"Look, I ain't trying to be all in your pocket, but don't get greedy. The harder you try to hold on to your money, the more it will leave you. Please believe that. You think that money is the solution to everything, but it's not. It's a temporary solution to a few of life's little obstacles. It's like that song you like, that Scarface type of shit by the Lox and Lil' Kim. It's about money, power, and respect. Money is nothing without power," Ginger schooled her.

"Money *is* power," Desiree objected.

"Slow your roll, young grasshopper. Understand this pimping: money is not power. It's how you use it that's powerful. These niggas give us money all the time, and they think they have power over us. What they don't realize is that for all the sweet talk and sex, they're just another dollar sign. Is that power? Now, if we take their money and go shopping, or go and buy some weed, that may give us a little empowerment, but it's only temporary and shallow. But if we take that piece of change and flip it, put it into a business or invest it in our minds, then that's real power."

"I see your point." Desiree nodded, running her fingers through her hair. Why did Ginger seem to have all of the answers? Why did she have it so together? Ginger had been through a similar situation as she herself had, from what Desiree could tell. Maybe it was because Ginger had a mother.

"See, when you have money and power, people respect you—most of the time anyway. Most of the time they don't respect you per se, but they do respect your gangsta. There's a thin line between respect and fear or intimidation. But the respect that's most powerful, the real shit, is the respect that you have for yourself."

"I respect myself," Desiree offered, but it didn't sound convincing, not even to herself.

"Yeah, okay," Ginger remarked dryly. "Can you tell me

honestly that you look at yourself in the mirror and feel a sense of respect for exactly who you are? Are you cool with everything you've done in the past?" Ginger met Desiree's eyes and fixed her stare. "Cuz *I* can't even say that, Desi. I got a lot of shit going on inside that makes me feel like I ain't shit on a regular basis. But I'm finding my way."

"What are you talking about? You've got it going on! Your crib is tight, you have a business, you make money in the clubs, and niggas is all up on your shit. And everyone I see you around respects you, even those assholes at the club."

"You're confusing my confidence with self-respect and with self-esteem. And believe me, I had to work really hard to get that confidence, harder than I ever did to get money. But if I *really* respected myself, I wouldn't still be dancing. Because I know that it's my insecurities that fuel my need to do this. It's my feelings of inadequacy that motivate me to continue to degrade myself, even though I know better, even though from the outside looking in, I *am* better. Because it isn't fun to me anymore. It doesn't feel wrong per se, but it just doesn't feel good. This business will change you."

Desiree said nothing; she just waited for Ginger to continue. It wasn't what she wanted to hear, but Ginger always seemed to make perfect sense. After an awkward silence Desiree spoke.

"You're a good person. You took me in, and I really didn't have anyplace to go. You gave when you didn't have to."

"Desiree, when I met you, the first thing I did was gaffle you out of some money. And if you weren't so cool, I would have just turned your ass out eating your pussy, then thrown your buck-naked ass on the Web long ago. I've done that shit before. And that was the plan with you. Your ass just turned out to be so fucking sweet. It felt like I was trying to take advantage of a little girl or something. It just didn't feel right."

Desiree was shocked by the confession, but no more shocked than Ginger was for making it.

"Wondering if you can trust me now, huh?" Ginger looked smug.

"Kind of, but not really. If you were truly a bad person, you would have never confessed. It's almost like you don't *want* me to trust you, though. You don't want me to get to know the real you."

"You're right, Desi. I told you that *I* don't even trust me. I don't even know the real me. I can only teach you so much, so you're gonna have to know how to play this game on your own."

Ginger was always warning her about this or that. She acted like she knew *everything*. Desiree was beginning to get a bit irritable over Ginger's constant preaching. It was real easy for her to say things like "Don't get greedy." From what she said, Ginger should have understood better than anyone that greed was a matter of self-preservation. Desiree's frustration showed on her face.

"Hey, trust me or don't. Listen or don't. It's your life. Life is a fucking crapshoot anyway really. How you gonna win if you don't play? And how you gonna win big if you don't bet big? But, Desiree, don't get caught up. Don't sell yourself short. I did, but I'm not anymore."

CHAPTER 8

April 1999

A LITTLE OVER A MONTH AFTER THE BREAST AUGMENTATION, Desiree was cleared to return to work and all of her regular activities. Her stitches were removed, and her scar was practically invisible. The doctor ordered her to massage her breasts several times daily to break up any scar tissue and make them soft and natural-looking and -feeling. She hadn't been to work, relying on her stash and favors from men who had no problem catering to her every whim.

Ginger had been helpful as well, cutting back seriously on her work schedule, claiming she was burned-out. Desiree figured that with the money she was bound to make with her new and improved breasts, she was on her way to the top. She would gradually stop dancing as her modeling assignments came in. She would make even more than Ginger.

"Wanna go out?" Ginger asked Desiree while she was squeezing a handful of her new boob.

"Sure. I'm always down to show these bad boys off." Desiree grinned. "I already know what I'm gonna wear."

"Cool. You okay to drive, right?" Ginger asked hesitantly.

"Sure, why?" Desiree was always thrilled to drive the BMW.

"Because I wanna drop this roll, but none for you," Ginger explained.

"I don't want none of that shit no way. Not after what I saw the last time. I don't see why you even deal with that shit. Your brain's got to be fried." Desiree pulled her hair up into a bun on top of her head.

"Well, sometimes I need to escape reality, consequences be damned. Besides, this is a different pill. I wasn't trying to take my chances again with that other shit." Ginger laughed, and the two prepared to hit the town.

They hit up Amnesia for Rocker's Island for some dance-hall reggae under the stars. Desiree loved the open-air-coliseum style of the Amnesia nightclub. Her first time there she gawked at the fact that there was no ceiling. But more than that, she especially loved the bass-heavy riddims that permeated the venue full of winding bodies. Although she wasn't skilled at dancing like a true Jamaican, she didn't hesitate to turn the heads of several men, her enhanced cleavage prominently on display through the plunging neckline of her pale pink top.

"You got any more of those Percocets?" Ginger asked Desiree in the ladies' lounge.

"Yeah, but should you be mixing X and Percocet and weed?" Desiree asked, half warning her.

"Chill, shawty. I know what I'm doing. You're the amateur, not me." Ginger sucked her teeth.

"Whatever." Desiree shrugged as she rummaged through her purse for her prescription bottle. Ginger popped the pill into her mouth and swallowed it dry.

"You okay?" Desiree asked. Ginger liked to party, but lately, it seemed to Desiree that she had been overdoing it.

When she did work, she came home so plastered that Desiree was angry she'd even been allowed to drive. And when she stayed home, she got fucked-up by herself. It was so obvious that Ginger was trying to escape something by getting zooted out of her mind.

"I'm cool." Ginger flashed an artificial smile and bounced out the bathroom, leaving Desiree behind.

Okay. She'll be all right, I guess, Desiree thought as she saw Ginger approach a tall, sexy dread and begin to dance with him.

TWO HOURS LATER DESIREE WAS SITTING ON THE BANQUETTES smoking a fatty with some girls she knew from the Rolexxx. *I wonder where Ginger is,* she thought, scanning the room for her girl.

"Y'all seen Ginger?" Desiree asked China, a thick redbone with Asian eyes.

"Nah, not for a minute. When I did see her, though, she was fucked-up! I ain't never seen her so gone." China slapped her healthy thigh, which was encased in skintight, zebra-print jeans.

"Well, if you see her, tell her to wait for me here. I'm gonna go look for her."

Desiree strolled around the club bopping to the beat, casually gliding by the men who attempted to dance with her. "No, no, no," she sang playfully along with Dawn Penn, her cat eyes narrowed to slits from the cheeba. Then DJ Khaled put on Shelly Thunder, and Desiree got loose. She always loved the song "Kuff" and could chant the lyrics as if she'd penned them herself. Lost in the bass line, Desiree closed her eyes and began winding her hips sensually, imitating the chanting of Shelly Thunder. When she opened her eyes, the same dread who'd been dancing with Ginger was standing before her.

"Not bad." The dread grinned at her.

Desiree grinned back. "That's nothing. I got my own shit."

"Yeah, you look like a star." He stood there smiling, his eyes affixed to her breasts. He snapped out of his trance.

"Your sister is looking for you. But she doesn't feel too good, so she's in the bathroom. You should check on her." He flashed a row of perfect teeth and disappeared into the crowd. Desiree watched him walk away. *Damn, Ginny sure can pick them!* she mused before heading to the bathroom.

"Have you seen my sister? She looks like me, but a little taller?" she inquired of the bathroom attendant.

"Uh, yeah. She's sick. You need to get her out of here and home." The attendant gave Desiree the stankeye and returned to the *Enquirer* that was demanding her undivided attention. Desiree huffed and walked down the row of stalls until she recognized Ginger's shoes. She pushed the door, but it was locked.

"Ginny, open the door! It's me!" Desiree tapped her foot impatiently.

"Mrgrmph," Ginger mumbled from behind the door. From the slight echo of her voice, Desiree could tell that Ginger's head was inside the toilet. She had to be on the verge of death to touch a public toilet seat, let alone sit on the floor with her head in the bowl. *God!* Desiree thought. *What was Ginger's deal lately?*

Desiree was not about to crawl under the door and couldn't climb over the top of the stall. Thinking quickly, she removed a rat-tailed comb from her purse and fiddled with the lock. Desiree heard Ginger retch and heave.

"Oh, don't mind me," Desiree said sarcastically to the attendant, who wasn't offering any assistance. "I'm fine. I'll just keep jimmying the lock while my sister is in there dying!" Finally, she felt the lock give way.

"Ginny!" Desiree gasped. Ginger was sprawled on the floor, her head resting on the toilet seat. There was vomit all over her top and in her hair. Her nose was bleeding slightly. And she was as limp as a rag doll. Desiree grabbed her arm, carefully avoiding the puke. She removed Ginger's T-shirt and threw it in the trash can. She knew Ginger would be pissed, but she wasn't about to carry it or ride all the way home with the smell. Besides, no one would even notice she was just wearing a bra; it was South Beach.

Desiree thought they would never make it home. Blinded by tears, she crept along the expressway, worried that Ginger might die or that the police would pull them over and haul them off to jail. Ginger puked two times, and each time Desiree had to pull over and help her. She'd debated taking her to the hospital but decided against it. The hospital would ask too many questions, and Ginger had probably emptied her system anyway. She just needed a cold shower and some food. Desiree had unfortunately dealt with someone in a similar situation before, her mother having nearly overdosed once. She'd tried to convince Desiree afterward that it was anemia and food poisoning, but Desiree had known better.

At the house Desiree removed Ginger's remaining clothes, then laid her in the tub. Then she cut on the shower full blast, spraying ice-cold water on her to keep her conscious.

"I'm going to die," Ginger said in a low voice as she shivered under the stream.

"You're not gonna die, unless I kill you!" Desiree grunted.

Desiree figured that Ginger would be okay, but was afraid that if she let her go to sleep, she might not ever wake up. Desiree went to her bathroom and took a quick shower and changed into sweats. Then she returned to check on Ginger, who was curled into a ball in the tub, the water pelting her body. Desiree dried and dressed Ginger, then brushed her hair into a bun. All the while she rubbed and massaged Ginger vigorously, to keep her alert.

"You okay, now?" Desiree asked soothingly. The sun streamed into the window, signaling the dawning of a new day.

"Not really," Ginger mumbled.

"Come on. I'll make you some soup. You'll be cool. I told you not to take that Percocet." Desiree stomped into the kitchen and began clanging pots around and slamming the refrigerator and freezer doors. Ginger trudged into the kitchen and sat on a stool. She laid her head on the cool marble of the countertop.

"You could have killed yourself, you know," Desiree fussed.

"You're right," Ginger admitted, her head buried in her hands.

"What? Not Ginny admitting that I actually have some sense? Are you saying I actually *know* something?" Desiree smirked as she ladled hot soup into a bowl.

"You're right, I could have killed myself. And I almost *did* die." Ginger greedily devoured the soup and signaled Desiree to get her something to drink. Desiree obliged, bringing her a glass of orange juice, and noticed that Ginger's hands were shaky. She placed her hand on Ginger's forehead and cheeks. Her skin felt clammy but cool.

"I was on the verge of death. I saw myself from outside my body. I even saw the white light you always hear people talking about. My life passed before me. I saw dead friends and relatives. They were calling out to me, reaching out for me to join them. But God saved me. He told me it wasn't my time. He said I would make a difference in someone's life, so he would spare mine. And now I'm giving my life to him," Ginger said before gulping some of the juice.

"Excuse me?" Desiree's neck snapped back.

"I'm really tired now. I'll tell you all about it later. I need to go pray." Ginger got up and walked to her room, then shut the door.

Desiree stood in the kitchen in shock. *How she just gonna walk off on me like that? What's all this crazy God mess? I take care of her ass till the break of dawn, and I don't even get so much as a thank-you? Whatever, bitch!*

CHAPTER 9

A week later

"YOU READY TO GO TO WORK? YOU HAVEN'T BEEN IN ALL week. I've been balling since I got the twins!" Desiree poked her enhanced bustline forward.

"You go ahead. Have fun." Ginger was stretched out in bed, propped up by dozens of pillows. She had a notebook and the Bible spread across the bed, and her television was tuned to the religious station. Desiree inspected the scene.

"What is going on with you?" Desiree frowned.

"What do you mean?" Ginger tried to look innocent, but the act was wasted.

"I mean, you've changed lately, Ginny. You don't care about making no paper. You don't talk on the phone or go out. And come on, the Bible Network? Are you serious?"

"Look, Desi. I meant what I said that night. I'm done with it all. No more dating, no more dancing. I'm even going to sell my Web sites. I'm going to live righteous from now on. No smoking, no drinking, no sex. Desi, I've been born again." Ginger smiled serenely and grasped Desiree's hands lightly.

"Uh, okay. Let me tell you what happened. You got too

high. You were probably thinking about that time *I* got too high. Your mind just started playing tricks on you, just like mine did; it was the Ecstasy." Desiree shook her head in disbelief.

Ginger locked eyes with her. "No, see, that's where you're wrong. When you got high, everything you said to me was true. My life is so empty that only Jesus can fill it up. It's hard to explain, but I know you know exactly what I mean."

"No, I don't!" Desiree countered. "I was just high. I don't even remember half the shit I said to you that night. And so were you. You were high. That's all. I mean, think about it. You've obviously been doing fine by God. And you're a good person, that's what counts. If God wasn't down with your lifestyle, you wouldn't have succeeded. You wouldn't have all this stuff. You're not just a dancer but a businesswoman. And you would not have taken me in. I was a total stranger. Evil people don't do things like that. You're not empty, and all of this Bible reading and praying isn't going to get you anywhere. Organized religion is set up to control people. You told me that. It's not gonna pay your bills. Next thing you know, you'll be giving all your money to some church!"

"How do you know my success came from God? The devil is a liar. He'll have you thinking good is bad and bad is good. Think about it: does God want me to make money by putting naked women on the Web? I don't believe that and you don't either. That's just the devil trying to scare you, Desi. He wants you to believe that all you will ever be able to do to become wealthy are crooked, shady things. Don't listen to him. You know you hear Jesus whispering to you to come back to him. The devil don't love you. Jesus loves you. Hallelujah!" Ginger clapped her hands together, then closed her eyes in silent prayer. Desiree squirmed uncomfortably. Who was Ginger to all of a sudden try to save her soul?

"Whatever. I, unlike you, don't have a house of my own and a fancy car or businesses. I'm still trying to get there. So I've got to go to work." Desiree was putting an end to all the Jesus talk.

"Go ahead. I'm going to pray for you," Ginger said, opening her eyes. "I know that you will join me. God's gonna bless you so abundantly when you just do what he wants you to do. You're gonna have riches beyond your wildest dreams when you just give your life to him. That's why he brought us together. I'm going to help you. But you will come when you're ready, which will be soon. God won't ignore my prayers." Ginger smiled that moony smile again and went back to reading her Bible.

Ain't this 'bout a bitch? Now she wants to get all religious? Please! Looks like I'm gonna have to find a new crib if she keeps this up, Desiree thought as she grabbed Ginger's car keys and headed to Coco's.

IT WAS TUESDAY NIGHT, AND THE CLUB WAS SURE TO BE PACKED with people coming from the comedy show at the Improv in Coconut Grove. Desiree knew that the guaranteed g she was going to make would take her mind off of Ginger. Besides, if Ginger didn't snap out of her religious fantasy, the money would come in handy when she moved. Desiree felt sad at the thought of moving. For the first time in so long, she'd felt she had a home, a family. Now of all things, God was going to put an end to that. Desiree sighed. This was precisely the reason she wasn't sure she believed in God anymore. If there was a God, he wouldn't have let her life be so fucked-up. He wouldn't have taken away every good thing she'd ever had. Nothing good ever lasted. Why would this be any different?

Desiree ordered a Long Island iced tea spiked with blue curaçao to ease her mind and quickly began to make her paper. It was still relatively early, but Coco's had a nice-sized crowd. By eleven Ginger was the furthest thing from Desiree's mind. Her garter was stuffed full of hundred-dollar bills, and she had a nice little buzz going. She noticed the energy of the club pick up near the door and strolled over to investigate. At the door was Dirty Dan, a rapper, with his usual entourage of five hard-core, Dirty South, pimp types. Desiree had danced for Dan in the past, and he'd always broken her off nicely. She rubbed her hands in anticipation and headed toward their table as they were sitting down.

"What up, Dan?" She grinned at him. She posed and showed off her new rack.

"Damn! Look at you! Your ass been gone what, a month, and done came back with some titties!" he howled in his hoarse southern accent.

"You like?" she asked, sticking her chest in his face.

"I love them shits. You was always fine, but you *that* bitch now!" He grinned at her.

"I was always *that* bitch. You were just sleepin', that's all." Desiree removed her top and started dancing in front of him.

"Shit, you ain't even got to dance. You got all my money tonight." Dan pulled out a knot of bills and handed it to her.

"Thank you, baby," she cooed as she accepted the bills. *That was easy,* she thought. Dan licked his lips at her and narrowed his eyes, which were full of lust.

"Come on, Desire, roll with me. I got some more of that for you," he propositioned, nodding at the money.

"Bet," was all she said. He had forked over what appeared

to be roughly twelve hundred dollars. Desiree had gotten to the point where all she had to do was thumb through a money stack for an accurate count. Desiree could feel her dancing days coming to an end quicker than she had anticipated. And it was without all that religious hoopla that Ginger was carrying on with. All she had done was flash her tits and Dirty Dan had relinquished the ducats with no hesitation. Desiree surmised that Dan was the perfect target to become a full-time sponsor.

Dirty Dan was from Atlanta and spent his time divided between there and Miami. He was a rap veteran, having gotten his start in the late eighties, around the same time as Luther Campbell and the 2 Live Crew. Both rappers had a similar style, but what set Dan apart was the fact that he was extremely handsome—almost *too* handsome. Dark as midnight, Dan had the silky dark hair and keen facial features of an East Indian or an Ethiopian. He was tall, had a nice build, and Desiree estimated him to be in his early forties, though he still looked to be in his late twenties. But once he opened his mouth, it was all over. He had a grill of gold and diamond teeth and the "Duhty Souf" accent to go with them. Dan made Luke sound like Carlton Banks. But his vernacular had earned him millions, which he flipped several times over.

Dan was married; his wife had appeared in many articles chronicling his self-made rags-to-riches story. But Desiree didn't care; it made things easier for her. She'd feel no guilt using him, because he had no business dealing with her in the first place. He should have been at home in Atlanta with his wife and kids, not in a Miami strip club. Dan was perfect. By fucking with Dan as a full-time sponsor, she'd be able to stash some money and be taken care of while she started her modeling career. She knew he would bless her with dough, plus he had the industry connections to make her a star.

Desiree quickly put on her clothes and met Dan in the parking lot. "You want to take your car back or leave it here?" he asked her. "We can go out; we can go to my place. It's whatever you want." He grinned. Desiree wished he would stop smiling, because the gold teeth were truly fucking her up.

"You live in Miramar, right?" she asked him.

"Pembroke Pines. Same thang," he answered.

"Well, I'm in Miami Lakes, which is on the way. Let me drop off Ginger's car, and then I'll ride with you. I want to go to your house," she offered suggestively.

"Shit. It's all good, baby girl."

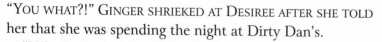

"YOU WHAT?!" GINGER SHRIEKED AT DESIREE AFTER SHE TOLD her that she was spending the night at Dirty Dan's.

"What's the big deal?" Desiree asked as she threw some clothes into an overnight bag.

"He's a smut peddler. He's evil. He's just going to use you, Desiree. He just wants to put you in porn. He doesn't care about you. He's just being nice to you so he can use you and exploit you—"

"And how is that different than how I met *you*? I mean, didn't you admit that was the reason you were nice to me in the beginning? Who the fuck are you to criticize him? Who the fuck are you to act like you're better than him?"

Ginger looked like she had been punched in the gut.

"Yeah, that's what I thought," Desiree spat at her bitterly when she couldn't reply. She tossed the keys to Ginger, her hair over her shoulder, and stormed out of the house.

CHAPTER 10

D AMN!" WAS ALL DESIREE COULD MANAGE TO UTTER ONCE she stepped into the foyer of Dan's palatial home.

"Tight, huh?" Dan grinned prideful with his gleaming gold fronts. "Welcome to the Pleasuredome."

How corny! Desiree thought. What kind of pleasure, other than financial, could Dan offer her? He could probably eat pussy, but at his age what else could he really be capable of?

"Come on." Dan walked into a kitchen that made Ginger's look like it belonged in a tenement. He walked over to a display cooler that showcased fine wines and champagnes and extracted a bottle of Taittinger's Blanc de Blanc rosé champagne.

"Everybody talking about Cris like it's the only champagne around. But this shit is good than a motherfucker," Dan boasted proudly. "We gonna sip some of this," he informed her, leading her out sliding glass doors and into his spacious backyard. The swimming pool was a smaller replica of Hugh Hefner's infamous pool and grotto at the Playboy Mansion.

"This is just like that Playboy shit!" Desiree exclaimed in awe.

"Yeah. You should see the one at my Atlanta crib. I got more land. My shit there is bigger than Hef's!" Dan puffed up his chest and popped the cork off the champagne bottle with a flourish. Foam bubbled out from the mouth, and Dan held the bottle to Desiree's lips. Desiree sipped the foam and licked the mouth of the bottle suggestively, then grabbed the bottle from his grasp. She took a large swig.

"That is good," Desiree commented. Dan reclaimed the bottle and began to guzzle it.

"Strip!" he commanded. "I want to see your fine ass in my hot tub."

Desiree did as she was told. Peeling off her clothing slowly, she maintained eye contact with Dan.

"You are perfect, girl. Them titties set you off. You should be a star, not strippin' in some club."

"You the man, Dan. Make it happen," Desiree countered suggestively.

"You got talent?" Dan quipped.

"Put that bottle down, and I'll show you how much talent I got," Desiree replied, dipping into the bubbly water of the Jacuzzi. Her breasts sat buoyantly above the water. Dan quickly removed his clothes and joined Desiree in the steamy hot tub. Instantly, his hands were all over her.

"Slow your roll!" Desiree teased him as she caressed his erect penis beneath the foaming warm water. "We've got all night."

"Mmm, I like the sound of that," Dan moaned as Desiree took a deep breath and disappeared under the water.

THE NEXT MORNING DAN GREETED DESIREE WITH BREAKFAST in bed.

"What did I do to deserve all this?" she asked him, eyeing the fresh croissants and jam, plate of melon and strawberries, and freshly squeezed orange juice.

"Girl, what didn't you do?" Dan grinned, the morning sun gleaming off his gold teeth. Desiree giggled at the memory. She had pulled out all the stops the night before, because she wanted to ensure that Dan would be thoroughly whipped.

"I still don't know how you gave me head underwater! That water is pretty hot in there. I hope it didn't hurt your beautiful face." Dan brushed her cheek as he set the breakfast tray across Desiree's lap. *Aww, he'd be sweet if he wasn't so country*, Desiree thought.

"It hurt so good," Desiree said. "I just wanted to please you, show you how talented I am." Desiree looked up at him wide-eyed and innocent.

"You got talent, all right!" Dan guffawed.

"Speaking of talent," Desiree segued, gauging his reaction carefully, "you know I can rap, right?"

"Nah, I ain't know. You think you got lyrical skills, huh?" Dan queried.

"Oh, I know I got skills. You saw for yourself I have a very talented tongue." Desiree licked her lips suggestively.

"True dat," Dan agreed, squeezing her breast as she nibbled on a ripe, juicy strawberry.

"I was thinking, maybe you can help me. I mean, you're so smart. Everyone knows you're a brilliant businessman." Desiree stroked his ego before going in for the kill.

"Well, I am intelligence," he replied, nearly causing Desiree to choke.

"Yes, you are. And I was thinking you could take a listen

to some of my rhymes. Give me some feedback. And then maybe—that is, if you think I'm good enough—you could help me get a deal. Or I could just sign to your label." Desiree fed him a bite of her strawberry.

"Tell you what, Desire. I like you, girl. You know I always have. I like you even more, now that I see what a freak you are. So tell you what I'm gonna do. I'm gonna give you a shot. If you can't rhyme, we'll get some folks to help you with that. Cuz one thang's for sho, and two thangs is certain: Don't no bitch in the industry look as good as you. And image is everythang. But there's some conditions to this offer." Dan licked his lips.

"Ooh, Dan, do you mean it?" Desiree selectively ignored his comment about the conditions. Desiree could imagine what they were. And Dan hadn't been half bad in the sack, so she didn't see giving him an occasional blow job or some ass that big of a deal.

"Yeah, I mean it, but hear me out. I want you to be available to me at all times. I know you living with Ginger and everythang, but that's gotta end. I want you to kick it here. But you can't be throwing no monkey wrench in my shit. I got a wife, but she don't come here much. If she does, she ain't gonna say shit cuz she know how I do. I got a couple of other females. But if you play your cards right, you can be my bottom bitch," Dan explained.

"Consider it done," Desiree answered. She felt a twinge of guilt, knowing she was going to just up and leave Ginger, but she was on some old bullshit anyway. As far as Desiree was concerned, Ginger was a big hypocrite, and who could trust a hypocrite? At least Dan was up-front about who he was and what he was about. She'd use him for all he was worth and then get rid of him. Pump and dump.

"YOU'RE MAKING A HUGE MISTAKE, DESI. I WANT YOU TO RE-ALLY reconsider what you're doing," Ginger told Desiree as she loaded the last of her things into a large moving box.

"Look, Ginger, I've got to do what's best for me. I love you like a sister, and I appreciate all the things you've done for me, but I need to move on. You and I are never going to see eye-to-eye on this God business," Desiree stated, devoid of emotion. It was all a front, though: moving out was killing her inside.

"Don't talk like that, Desi. You make it sound so petty by calling it 'this God business.' This is your soul we're talking about," Ginger pleaded.

"Exactly! How many times do I have to go over this with you? It's *my* soul. If I want it to burn in hell, then so be it." Desiree crossed her arms. Ginger crossed herself and clutched a strand of rosary beads.

"Desiree, go to school. You can stay here for free until you finish. Just stop the dancing and the dating and leave Dan alone. He's a married man. He's a pornographer. And before you cut me off telling me what kind of person I used to be, let me tell you that Jesus has wiped my slate clean. Maybe you can't yet, but I know you know how much I love you. You want to rap? Fine, rap. But do things yourself. Put out your own CD. That's how Dan got started. You don't need him. You already have everything you need, and I guarantee you that if you ask God for the words, he'll give you a posi-tive, conscious message to spread through your music. You don't have to settle for being Dirty Dan's concubine. I'll back you. I may not have Dan's millions, but I have the money to do something."

"Look, Ginny, I appreciate the offer, and what you have to say. But you can't force your religion on someone. God knows my heart just like he knows everyone else's. When I'm ready to get religion, he'll be the first to know, not you," Desiree snapped. She carried the box out to the Mercedes C230 that Dan had "given" her, with Ginger on her heels.

"I'm going to continue to pray for your redemption, Desi," Ginger told her, arms akimbo, her head held dramatically toward the heavens.

"Pray for your own redemption, Ginny. That's what this is about. It's all your past dirt coming to the surface to haunt you. You just can't get clean, can you? For all the baptism and the washing of your sins in the blood of the lamb, you just don't feel clean, do you?" Desiree monitored Ginger's expression and realized she'd hit a nerve. She continued. "You want to pray for me, because you think that by bringing me to God, he'll forgive *you*. It doesn't work that way, and you know it. You've got to make amends with God on your own."

"Desi, please . . ." Ginger's eyes reflected not only sincerity but pain. Desiree couldn't continue the tough-girl act. She felt her nose running as her eyes filled with tears. In an unexpected gesture she threw her arms around Ginger and held her tightly.

"I love you, Ginny. You know I do. And I'm not trying to hurt you. But just like you had to find your own way, I have to find mine. Please try and understand. You're the only real friend I've ever had," Desiree sniffed.

"Don't leave. You don't have to go through with this. I promise I'll stop trying to force God on you," Ginger pleaded.

"We both know that's not true. I believe that you really want to change your life. And I've got your back one hundred percent, even if I can't do what you're doing; even though I don't really understand." Desiree loosened her embrace to look Ginger in the eyes. "I left the phone number on your fridge. You can call me, you know."

"I will. Don't you forget about me, you hear, nena? We're *hermanas para siempre*. No man will come between us ever. And, Desi, know that if you ever need me, I don't care when or why, I'm here for you; no questions asked, no I-told-you-so's," Ginger promised.

Desiree wiped her tear-streaked face with the back of her hand and got into the car. She revved the engine and sped out of the driveway, partly because she knew that if she stayed any longer, she just might change her mind. Desiree didn't know what was in store for her. All she knew was that now was not the time for sentiment. Life was tough, always had been; but when one door closed, another one always opened.

PART 2

POWER

CHAPTER 11

August 2001

T HE MIAMI STREETS WERE SO HOT THAT VISIBLE HEAT WAVES rose from the asphalt like steam from a griddle. Desiree's thin white wife beater was moist and slightly transparent from her perspiration, accentuating her full breasts. As she walked, she lifted her long hair on top of her head in an attempt to feel cooler, but it was futile. There was absolutely no breeze.

Desiree frowned, thinking that she would look like a sweaty pig by the time she got to the music video casting. She'd only been outside for a short five minutes, as long as it took to walk from a parking lot two blocks over to the National Hotel on Collins. But the relentless Miami sun had already done its damage. Her long, curly hair felt frizzy and limp, and she was certain that her eye makeup was smeared halfway down her face. Not that it would matter. Desiree could have rolled out of bed and gone to the casting in her PJs and still been the finest woman there.

The record company holding the casting, Titanium Records, was the new shit bumpin' out of car speakers and club

systems all over North America. With over 10 million records sold in the label's short history, it was quickly on its
way to being an urban music legend. It burst onto the scene
like a supernova, hitting the public with a banging album
sprinkled with high-profile cameos, a glossy music video, and
a fashion line all at once. Its star artist, Bentley, had a number 1 hit on the *Billboard* charts and was moving serious
units, according to SoundScan.

At twenty-four Bentley was the biggest thing in hip-hop.
Reminiscent of L.L. back in the day, his pretty boy/thug image
played well with *TRL*'s demographic as well as *106 & Park*'s
audience. He was most recently featured in *People*'s Hottest
25 stars under twenty-five, ranking at an astonishing number
3. Not bad for a guy from the projects whose album had only
been out four months. Blacks, whites, Latinos—it didn't matter. Everybody was feelin' Bentley, especially Desiree. Ever
since she'd seen him on the cover of *XXL,* she'd wanted him,
and it was not like Desiree to get starstruck. She got over that
shit long ago. She made it a rule not to date any more athletes
or entertainers until she made it herself.

Desiree was determined to set the music industry on fire.
She made sure to spend at least a couple of hours a day writing and boning up on her freestyling skills. When she was
with Dirty Dan, she'd written tons of lyrics and filled several
notebooks with raps that she shared with him. She knew he
liked her flow from his expression as he read her raps, and
when she freestyled, his eyes nearly popped out of his head.
And on more than one occasion he used some of her verses,
chalking them up to coincidence when she confronted him.
Every time she threatened to leave him, he'd promised her the
sun, moon, and stars to lure her back in, but nothing of substance ever materialized. Sure, she appeared in some of his
videos and did backup vocals on some of his tracks, but it

became obvious that Dan's idea of making her a star was limited to recording her moaning statements like "Fuck me in the ass really fast, Dirty Dan" and "Ooh, I like it doggy-style" on his tracks. Desiree learned that it wasn't smart to shit where you ate; besides, artists rarely had any power to make real decisions anyway; they were all controlled by something or someone bigger, richer, and more powerful. Dating an entertainer seemed to be an exercise in futility. However, just looking at Bentley gave her a rush. He made her body feel flushed and hot. And now she was going to work with him if things went her way.

Desiree headed straight for the bathroom as a blast of frigid air hit her upon entering the hotel lobby. The casting had only been in session for about an hour, but there were already what appeared to be over a hundred girls there spilling out of a conference room into the bar area.

Even the restroom was crowded as Desiree made an attempt to freshen up. She splashed her face with cool water and gently patted it dry with a hard, crunchy paper towel. She used her fingers to wipe away the eyeliner that had slid from her amber-colored eyes, and then rummaged through her Louis Vuitton baguette for an eyeliner pencil and some MAC Lipglass. Desiree was fortunate that she didn't really need makeup. Her large hazel eyes were framed by naturally long, dark, curly lashes, her honey-colored skin was smooth, even, and clear. Her full, pouty lips were such a deep pink that if she just slicked on some clear gloss, it looked as if she were wearing lipstick. Desiree finished up by putting her hands under the faucet, then running them through her hair. Just a bit of water was enough to banish the frizzies and reactivate her natural curls.

Her wife-beater looked a little wrinkled, so she tied it tightly behind her back in a small knot, making her breasts look enormous and her tight waist even smaller. Desiree turned around to inspect her rear. Her Brazilian-cut jeans dipped dangerously low over her voluptuous ass. Desiree noticed that several of the models in the ladies' lounge were staring at her. They recognized her from her other appearances in music videos, no doubt.

Desiree was a ghetto superstar, or at least that was her rationale. Over the last two years she'd been in over twenty music videos for rappers and R&B singers. She had even made appearances in Kid Rock and Aerosmith videos. She couldn't take all the credit; Dan had introduced her to her manager, and it was her appearance in the music video for his song "Doggy Style" that had first put her face out there. Now as the reigning queen of video, you couldn't tune into BET or MTV without seeing her face. Desiree was in heavy rotation. And lately, Desiree had been getting more work that wasn't video-related, like print ads for urban fashion lines, as well as a hair care ad.

Desiree was smart, and made sure that the more visible she became, the more she charged. She wasn't some cheap video ho, happy to be hobnobbing with the stars. This was a business! She'd met plenty of so-called celebrities in her days as an exotic dancer and during the year that she was with Dan. She considered herself to be on their level. She was a future star, not a groupie. Besides, she was a hustler. She knew the game. She commanded a day rate of two thousand dollars, and sometimes more if they were really big stars, while those cheap chicks were thinking they were doing the damn thang makin' two hundred a day if they were lucky. Strippers made more money than them! Desiree wasn't a supermodel making ten grand a day, but she was a far cry from her humble beginnings, and definitely several steps above the other girls.

Desiree found a way to flip whatever she made, and if she

couldn't flip it, she just stashed it. Now a frugal and savvy businesswoman, Desiree had managed to save a nice little piece of money, have all her bills paid for her, and live a lavish lifestyle by never breaking her cardinal rule learned from Dan: avoid spending your own money at all costs.

Desiree never paid for anything if she could help it. She'd learned early on that was the way celebrities rolled. They walked around like the world owed them a favor; and they could afford to pay for anything, but they were always looking for the hookup. Desiree believed that the first steps to becoming a success were to look the part, walk the walk, and talk the talk. If she surrounded herself with successful people, acted like them, went where they went, and did what they did, she'd soon be where they were.

She'd even acquired quite an impressive array of jewelry, ranging from custom-made pieces designed by Jacob the Jeweler of New York's Diamond Quasar, to baubles from Tiffany and Cartier. Like Marilyn said, diamonds were a girl's best friend. She also had a wardrobe of furs that she only wore when out of town, because it never got cold in Miami. Some of her gear and accessories she got from video sets, but most were gifts from her "friends," the men she "dated" who helped to provide the lifestyle she had grown accustomed to.

She peeped the other girls' reactions before leaving. She adjusted her jewelry, a platinum cross, and positioned her hands so that they would catch the gleam of her platinum and pavé diamond ring. She did it just for spite, so those females wouldn't get it twisted and confuse her with one of them. Who did they think they were fooling with their rhinestones and Austrian crystals anyway?

I got them bitches shook! she thought to herself, grinning. She knew the type of things they would probably say about her when she left. They'd call her stuck-up, or a ho and a slut, and yak about what they'd heard. But Desiree didn't give a fuck. She knew they were just jealous and intimidated. They all wanted to be where she was. But if any of those girls had hopes of dethroning her, they were mistaken. She wasn't just any bitch, she was *that* bitch.

Desiree eyed a skank in a tight purple spandex getup with holes cut out down the sides. Some bitches just didn't have a clue. She gave greetings to some of the other models she knew or had worked with before, but kept it light and casual. She wasn't in the business to make friends. Hell, she wasn't even there to make money. She was there to be a star! Every video was just another step closer to her ultimate goal.

Desiree had a plan. She'd always had plans, but somehow they'd managed to go astray. But she was a smart girl who learned from her mistakes. Her setbacks had been the result of relying too heavily on the grace of others. She'd gone about finding fame and fortune the wrong way—waiting for some man to hook her up. Ginger had tried to warn her. Desiree had been too stubborn to listen, but no more. Men were okay to fuck to pay the bills and buy clothes and the like, but that was it. Real success was going to be the result of her talent.

She was going to parlay her video success into a record deal of her own. She'd just finished a demo that she had actually paid for with her own money. That was an investment in herself that she wanted full control over. A&R reps from indie labels had heard it and offered her deals, but they were not what she was trying to hear. When she came out, she was coming out hard. She wasn't going to be some puppet, or a backdrop to the niggas that had put her down with their label. She'd leave that to Vita and Charli Baltimore. Both girls were beautiful and had skills, but somehow hadn't reached the level of success of some of their less talented male counterparts.

She could keep on modeling if she wasn't going to have any say-so about her career. She knew her product was hot. And once her demo landed in the right hands, she'd be on her way to platinum success. After she was established as a rapper, she planned on tackling movies. Maybe she'd even win an Oscar or something. She was just as pretty as Halle Berry or Salma Hayek. And she was damn sure sexier than Nicole Kidman!

She looked at the wannabes. None of them were talking about anything but auditions and bookings and agents. None of them had shit but were busy trying to impress each other. They were all scratching to be cast, hoping to be seen. They were hungry, but not in the same sense as Desiree. They were all living from job to job, waiting tables or working some other job part-time to make ends meet. Desiree couldn't understand how some girls who had so much potential were so stupid.

Once at a casting she'd heard a hater saying, "She wanted to make it, but she wasn't going to whore herself out doing it." Desiree understood how the girl felt, but she also knew that she was trying to be slick because the girl looked at her when she made the comment. Desiree chose to ignore it. What did her and her friends think modeling was anyway? It was nothing more than legal prostitution. Their agents were the pimps, collecting the bread while the girl did all the work, claiming to be there to "protect" them and their interests. And like pimps, their agents had a ton of other bitches just like them. And as soon as they got too old or too fat, they got kicked to the curb, like raggedy, dried-up whores.

Desiree hated cattle calls. There were just a bunch of girls, all waiting for the opportunity to shake their ass, all gossiping and sizing each other up, being phony as hell. Usually, she wouldn't waste her time and would have her personal manager handle it. Unlike the majority of the girls, Desiree had a manager dedicated to helping her career, who hooked her up constantly with good-paying jobs and always as a lead or a feature.

But this time the buzz was that the artist claimed he wanted as many girls as possible seen, not just the same faces. Usually, a label rep would call agents and have them send the production office head shots and comps of the top girls, but lately, there were more and more cattle calls, and the pay scale was getting lower and lower. The video girl thing was beginning to not be worth the effort.

This time not even her manager had the hookup. And normally, she would just say forget it. But for Bentley, she would make an exception. It was like some ghetto Cinderella story: a handsome prince wants to meet all the available ladies in the land to be by his side—in a video anyway. Desiree didn't let that fade her, though. She knew that Titanium Records could see all the women in Miami, but none had the raw sex appeal she possessed. Her star was just starting to shine.

Desiree watched the girls ahead of her in the line audition. Some of those broads had to be on crack if they believed they had what it took to be in a video. A skinny, pale redhead busted out in a full-on cheerleading routine. She even ended it with a backflip. What the fuck was she thinking? This was a rap video casting, not the auditions for *Bring It On*.

Another girl ripped her dress off and began spasming all over the place in her underwear. She obviously thought she was doing one hell of a sensual striptease, because she kept on grooving after the casting directors screamed out, "Next!" three times. Then they had to call security to escort her out of the hotel. She reeked of liquor as the rent-a-cops dragged her past Desiree. She demanded to know right away if she had been selected, then threatened to key everybody's car. Crazy bitch!

The girl directly in front of Desiree in the line surprised the shit out of everyone by standing on her head, splacking her legs open, and gyrating her hips. It was a move straight out of the shake booty club. After her little freak show she hopped up full of confidence and proudly strutted out of the room like she just *knew* she had a part on lock.

Desiree couldn't have paid for a better time to audition. The clowns before her would only make her look better, if that was possible. And unexpectedly, Bentley and his crew came breezing in, causing a commotion. Looking extra crisp in a Sean John shorts sweat suit, a fresh white T-shirt, and immaculate Jordans, Bentley drew all eyes to himself. The crazy cheerleader shrieked and hounded him for an autograph. How unprofessional! He politely declined, saying he'd have to sign autographs for everyone if he did one, and he was really only stopping by. He gave her a hug and a kiss on the cheek, and any disappointment she may have felt vanished.

Bentley took a seat at the table with the casting directors. His boys nudged each other, taken aback by Desiree's beauty. Desiree made eye contact with Bentley and felt a charge of electricity flow through her veins like a current. Bentley was fine as hell. He stood at six three, with a flawless golden brown complexion, a muscular frame, and a hypnotic smile complete with dimples. And he was tatted up and slightly rugged, just the way she liked her men. Desiree thought to herself how much she wanted to grab ahold of his freshly done cornrows and tongue him down. She felt her nipples harden and licked her lips sensually. Now was not the time for subtlety.

Bentley grinned at her, his straight white teeth sparkling

as bright as the baguettes in the Rolex on his wrist and on the platinum cross dangling from his neck. She dug that he was fly without being overly flashy. Men who were too flossy were usually selfish: they spent all their dough on themselves. Desiree couldn't do shit with a man like that. But Bentley was just her speed.

"I'm Desiree," she stated to the casting directors before handing over a registration sheet and her comp card.

"Turn around, please," a stoic, middle-aged white man demanded. Desiree pivoted slowly, making sure they drank in every inch of her curvaceous body.

A young blond man operated a video camera and a radio simultaneously. He cued up the music, and Bentley's latest release boomed from the speakers. Desiree grooved to the pulsating beat, her body moving fluidly as running water. Desiree was aware of the impact she was making and took full advantage. She shook her hips with sensual power, exuding pure sex appeal.

Judging by the casting directors' faces and by the way Bentley's crew was talking shit among themselves, Desiree *knew* the lead part would be going to her. Bentley gave Desiree a wink, and she thought her heart would explode out of her chest. Desiree wanted to stay and flirt with him, but she didn't want to seem too eager. She had to let him know from jump that simply because he was a star wasn't going to change her game. He'd have to come correct, just like everyone else. She wasn't some green girl with the naïveté to think that she could sleep her way into a video; she was a professional. The casting couch was no myth, but women sleeping their way to the top happened far less often than most people thought.

Desiree left the audition confident and happy. There hadn't been any competition, but she spotted Ysenia Cruz, her sworn rival, coming in as she was on her way out the door.

Ysenia was a bitch! She'd hated Desiree ever since Desiree beat her out to win a bikini contest at the All-Star Café. Petty shit. The prize was only five hundred dollars, but Ysenia acted like it was more like five thousand. Ysenia cut her eyes at her and made a bunch of slick-ass comments under her breath every time she saw her. Desiree wanted to beat her ass, but she knew that Ysenia really wasn't worth it. But if she ever stepped out of line and jumped bad enough to actually say something to her face, Desiree was going to stomp her ass.

But not even Ysenia could spoil Desiree's mood. As far as the video was concerned, it was a wrap. And as far as Bentley was concerned, Desiree could feel that this was the start of something big.

CHAPTER 12

DESIREE HIT THE SHOWER AS SOON AS SHE GOT BACK TO her spacious one-bedroom apartment. She loved living in Surfside because it was perfectly located. She was a short fifteen-minute ride to Aventura Mall, a ten-minute ride to South Beach, and within walking distance of Bal Harbour, the elite shopping center that housed some of the world's most exclusive and expensive shops.

Desiree's crib was hooked up lovely with white custom-made rugs, a plush white leather sectional, and a pink bedroom fit for a queen. She even collected art and had several avant-garde pieces on display. It looked just as good as any apartment in a magazine, and she loved coming home to it. After shacking up with Ginger and then Dan, it felt good to have a place to call her very own.

Desiree switched on the CD player and felt the sounds of Dave Hollister soothe her as they pumped crystal clear through the Bose surround sound system. Desiree went to her bedroom and took off her clothes. She sighed as the air from the cooling vent licked her overheated body. She wanted to roll a spliff, pour a glass of wine, and relax, but didn't have time. Her major sponsor, K.G., was in town, and coming to scoop her in about an hour. She had to be breathtaking when she saw him, because she planned on hitting him up hard. Her birthday was coming up, and she planned on being laced lovely.

Desiree met K.G. over Memorial Day weekend, and he'd been open ever since. He was in his thirties, from Detroit, and paid out the ass. The old-school hustler type, real mellow and smooth, he told her he owned a couple of barbershops, beauty shops, and record stores in Detroit, Lansing, and Flint, Michigan, but Desiree knew that it was all just a front for his main enterprise: hustling. Desiree figured that out quickly because he always claimed to be in town on business. What the hell kind of business did he have to do for a barbershop or record store in Miami that he couldn't do up in Michigan?

Desiree didn't care, though, because K.G. kept her pockets fat. He laced her with jewels and cash and was always a good time. The downside was he was a stone freak, a little too freaky for Desiree's taste. Still, the payoff was worth it. Desiree knew that all men were dogs or freaks or perverts, so she didn't expect much more. She figured if there was such a thing as a nice guy, he probably wouldn't want her anyway.

A guy like K.G. couldn't talk shit about her lifestyle, past or present. K.G. respected her hustle. He was grimy his damned self, so what could he say about her? She wasn't hurting anybody; she was just doing her thing. Some guys had a real hang-up about dating a "video girl." They'd get jealous or accuse them of fucking all the rappers, but K.G. seemed to get off on it. And he was always generous in showing his appreciation. Thanks to K.G. and a few other high rollers, all Desiree ever had to do was dress, rest, and wait for the next modeling job. But lately, that hadn't been enough. She was yearning for something more.

Desiree knew that the video thing wouldn't last forever.

Pretty soon the next hotgirl would be on the scene and someone would put her on. Most girls only worked about two
years if they were lucky before either folks got tired of looking at them or they got tired of being eye candy and moved
on to something else.

Desiree planned on staying in the limelight. All the rappers—Lil' Kim, Foxy, Eve, Trina, even Missy—would have to
bow down and give her props. She planned on a total takeover of the industry: music, films, fashion, the whole gamut.
She was going to be a mogul like P. Diddy or Russell, paid
and powerful.

Within forty-five minutes, she was dressed in a black
Prada sundress with ruffles at the hem and some matching
Prada sandals. For accessories she rocked smoke-colored, rimless Prada sunglasses and a small black Prada purse. Though
Desiree loved high fashion and haute couture, she hated being a walking mannequin. She preferred to mix and match
quality vintage pieces with modern designers for her own
signature, funky style, like she saw all the stars do, or have
her clothes made. But K.G. had bought her the outfit from
the Prada store in Bal Harbour a month before and wanted
to see her in it. So Desiree did what he wanted, because as
long as he was hooking her up, his wish was her command.

K.G. arrived shortly thereafter in a rented Aston Martin
Vanquish from Xotic Cars by the airport. They had all the fly
whips, from Lamborghinis and Ferraris to Porsches and
Hummers, and for the right price you could ride right. Desiree felt a wave of excitement as she got in the car. This was
how she should always roll, she thought. She greeted K.G.
with a juicy kiss and a warm hug. He liked it when she
fawned all over him.

They dined at Smith & Wollensky. Desiree adored sitting
on the restaurant's deck and watching the speedboats and

yachts pass by. The evening air was crisp and cool, a far cry from the mugginess of the day. She sipped on chardonnay and engaged in minor chitchat with K.G. Mostly, he commandeered the conversation, boasting on his mansion in Southfield, his fleet of tricked-out Caddys, and his collection of rainbow-hued Mauri gators. Desiree felt herself both disgusted by his cockiness and arrogance and fascinated with his down-to-earth Midwest style. He was an asshole and the boy next door all at once. But one thing was certain: he knew how to treat a woman.

They cruised the strip until around midnight, riding down Washington and Ocean Avenue Drive, flossing the Aston Martin. Desiree relished all the attention she was receiving, posing and preening like there were cameras rolling. It was obvious that K.G. loved having a trophy like Desiree by his side by the size of the smile plastered on his face the whole time.

When they rolled up to valet parking at one of her favorite spots, Club Level, Desiree was in seventh heaven. Monday nights at Level were always off the chain. The line snaked down Washington, but Desiree and K.G. bypassed it and went straight to the velvet rope. The club's doormen were handpicking people to enter, but welcomed Desiree with open arms and warm smiles. Desiree always brought in big spenders, so practically every doorman at every club on the beach was always happy to see her. They knew they were going to get broken off properly by her escort. Desiree noticed the C-note K.G. discreetly slipped Fabrice, the host, impressed by his confidence and attitude. He was a man who knew he deserved the best and made sure that everyone else knew it too.

Hip-hop pumped through the club, putting Desiree in a partying mood. She made a beeline for the ladies' room

while the VIP hostess led K.G. to their table in the VIP section of the main room. K.G. liked to be in the middle of all
the action, so he preferred that location to the several other
VIP sections in the enormous venue.

Desiree hoped that she wouldn't run into Bentley. It wasn't
that she didn't want to see him; she didn't want him to see
her with the next nigga. Hustlers were one way, but celebrities
and athletes were much different. They had another set of
rules, and Desiree didn't play that game anymore. She lived
and breathed the streets; she didn't have time to fuck with
studio gangsters and bright suit-wearing ballers always com-
peting with her for shine. Those cats couldn't handle a bitch
like her, though she was going to make an exception with
Bentley. He seemed like the real deal, not a faker. They could
be a power couple, but with a Bonnie and Clyde twist. Yeah,
Bentley was a nigga she could ride for.

Desiree arrived at her and K.G.'s table to an ice-cold bottle
of Cristal. Desiree calculated how much money he'd spent on
her so far. At least two to three hundred at dinner, another six
hundred on the bottle, and he'd more than likely buy another
one. Desiree wondered how much money he made. He was
definitely a major player in the dope game, and not some
street corner hustler. Ironically, K.G. was low-profile on the
Miami streets. Usually, the serious hustlers all had a name for
themselves, even the ones from out of town. A few of the girls
she knew who were kicking it with heavyweights in the drug
game had never seen him before he started going out with
Desiree, and didn't know shit about him.

Desiree liked it that way. Keep them bitches guessing at all
times. But Desiree was also guessing. She wondered how much
of his time he devoted to his legal business and how deep was
his connection to the streets. Did he deal directly with a cartel?

Was he hooked up with Colombians or, even worse, Russians? Desiree realized that she didn't really know K.G. at all, but his money spent, so what difference did it make?

"What's on your mind, baby girl?" K.G. interrupted her thoughts over the music, startling her.

She smiled innocently. "Whether or not we're going shopping tomorrow. I saw this really sexy lingerie at La Perla, and I want to model it for you."

K.G. grinned at her. "Nah, baby girl! Remember I told you that after my meeting tomorrow I gotta bounce," he said. Desiree's face fell.

"Don't worry, baby girl. I ain't forget that your birthday is coming up. I'ma break you off, and you can pick that up, as well as some shit to wear in the Virgin Islands. I'm taking you there in a couple of weeks, so clear your calendar. You haven't been there before, have you?"

"Nope," Desiree lied. She was a little disappointed because when she shopped with K.G., it was like having a walking credit line.

"Yeah, get that La Perla, some fly swimsuits, and nothing but sexy shit. I'ma give you your own Platinum card. We gonna do the damn thang." It was music to Desiree's ears. Desiree clinked his champagne glass with hers and took a long gulp. She knew that she should sip the good shit, but she was in the mood to celebrate.

They spent a few hours getting bubbly, getting their groove on, and mingling with some of the other Willies. Level was off the glass! It was filled to capacity with the trendsetters and tastemakers, all dressed in the latest gear, drinking and having a good time. White, black, Latin, and Asian had all come together for the love of hip-hop. There wasn't shit like it anywhere! New York and L.A. clubs closed at 2 a.m., maybe 4.

But in Miami the party don't stop until it's over, whatever time that is. After the clubs close, there's always an after-party, breakfast, or the hotel.

Desiree heard the DJ shout out to Bentley and his crew around 3 a.m., but the crowd was so thick that she couldn't see him. *Good,* she thought. *He probably can't see me either!* Desiree planned on playing it demure with Bentley. She was going to be all whispers and softness like Marilyn Monroe, one of her idols. She'd let a little toughness show through, but only to make sure he stayed interested. No man really wanted a pushover. She wanted to be sweet but not square. A square girl would never be able to snag Bentley.

Looking out at the crowd of revelers, Desiree wondered why no one in Miami had a real job, because if they did, she didn't know how they managed to do it. There was too much temptation, too many good times to be had. Who could kick it like this and then go to some nine-to-five in the morning?

K.G. and Desiree left Level around 4:30 a.m., and Dez thought she spotted Bentley in an upstairs VIP section on their way out, but couldn't be sure. People were still packed like sardines, and Desiree couldn't see that far without her glasses, which she never ever wore.

Desiree and K.G. rode to the News Café on Ocean and picked up a sandwich for him and a fruit plate for her, then headed to K.G.'s luxurious suite at the Delano Hotel. Desiree adored the way the white fabric billowing from the archway flowed in the balmy night breeze. She wouldn't mind an accent like that at her oceanfront mansion after she made it big. She also loved that the hotel had no signage. That's what made it so exclusive and special to her. If you didn't know what the Delano was, you didn't need to be there.

Once in the suite, Desiree nibbled on her fruit while K.G.

took a shower. She had only managed to munch on a few strawberries and pieces of succulent watermelon before K.G. called out asking her to join him. Desiree obliged. K.G.'s penis saluted her as she stepped into the steamy spray, her magnificent body on full display. He kissed her, maneuvering her under the stream of tepid water.

Men always have the water too cold, Desiree mused, frowning and slightly shivering as the water pelted her frame.

"You cold?" he growled as he palmed her breast.

"A little," Desiree admitted.

"Then let me warm you up."

He turned the water up a notch, wincing slightly from the rise in temperature, but if Desiree wanted it hot, he was bringing the fire. He grabbed the miniature bar of soap and used his hands to soap her body. Desiree writhed beneath his touch. K.G. had strong hands, his strokes confident. K.G. nibbled and sucked at her erect nipples until she moaned with pleasure, her body arching instinctively toward him. K.G. worked his way between Desiree's thighs.

Desiree was afraid she would fall. Her body tensed up.

"I got you, baby girl. Just let go. Let go." K.G. held her firmly as he spread her legs apart. Water sloshed and slashed about as he ate her. Desiree had no fear now as she pulled his head closer. She was on the brink of climaxing when K.G. abruptly pulled away.

"You want more?" he asked, staring at her intensely.

"Yes," Desiree groaned.

"Tell me," he ordered as he teased her clit with his tongue.

"I want more! Please! Don't stop!" Desiree bucked her hips, begging K.G. to end the torture.

"In Spanish!" he demanded.

"Ay, papi! Yo quiero! Por favor! Dame más!" she pleaded. K.G.

relented and brought her to a massive orgasm with his tongue. Desiree's body shook and trembled as she screamed in ecstasy. K.G. didn't stop licking until she begged him to stop.

He led her to the bed and bent her over it. Desiree would have loved to get fucked doggy-style long and hard, but she knew that wasn't on K.G.'s agenda. She braced herself and forced out a long breath as he entered her anally. Men always had to go and fuck up a good thing! K.G. rarely lasted more than two minutes, and sometimes went soft from vaginal sex, but he fucked like an animal when he fucked her up the butt.

Desiree tried to disconnect herself from her body and just go through the motions. K.G. was the only person she ever let do her that way, and only after he'd paid her rent for the next year. But Desiree couldn't zone out because K.G. kept talking to her and asking her questions.

"Gimme that ass!" he barked as he plunged deep inside of her. "You gonna give it to me?"

"It's yours!" she responded with fake enthusiasm.

"Tell Daddy you like that dick," he ordered.

"Oooh, I love it!" she squealed for his benefit. But Desiree refused to call any man Daddy. K.G. didn't notice the omission, though. He was too busy getting his rocks off. Desiree moaned and groaned like he was Mr. Marcus, all the while hoping that he would hurry up and finish.

Thankfully, her noises encouraged him, and K.G. was soon shivering from his own climax. Desiree would never understand how a man could get off by doing her in the booty. It made her wonder if K.G. swung both ways. Because Desiree didn't care how thuggish a man was, she believed that men who dug anal sex had a little bit of bitch in them. Why else would they want to sex her like she was another dude?

K.G. removed himself from Desiree's ass and collapsed on the bed beside her. Within no time she heard him snoring, so she eased out of bed and hit the shower once more. This time she ran the water scalding hot, but it would have to burn the flesh right off her bones before it was ever hot enough to make Desiree feel clean.

CHAPTER 13

DESIREE STEPPED OUT OF THE LOBBY OF THE DELANO AND into the heat armed with her very own Platinum American Express card. K.G. told her it was her birthday gift. It came with the warning that she was all his now and that she had no use for other niggas. He also told her he wanted her to start thinking about what she was going to do after she quit modeling. Desiree told him she had no intention of quitting, but decided against telling him her other aspirations. He told her he was going to marry her and naturally she'd have children. Desiree wondered if he was serious, but she had put in work to earn that credit card, and for now she was going to enjoy it. She'd simply cross that marriage bridge if and when she came to it. Still, the situation with K.G. made her a tad bit uneasy. The gesture was extravagant, so it made her wonder what his angle was. He had to have motives.

Maybe he really thought he was in love. That morning he'd managed to fuck her the regular way. He insisted on looking her dead in the eyes the whole time, even when he kissed her. It was like he couldn't get enough of her. He'd told her that he loved her as he came. Desiree ignored the comment, but he told her again as he held her in his arms afterward. He wished her a happy birthday in advance and told her how excited he was about their trip to the V.I., that he had something special for her. He ordered room service and fed her breakfast in bed before cutting out to his "meeting" around 11 a.m.

It had been a long night, and her butt felt raw and dug out. She wondered if she was walking funny or if anyone could tell she'd been fucked up the ass. All she wanted to do was take a long, hot bath, curl into her king-size bed, and sleep. She didn't even have the energy to shop.

Downstairs the doorman stared at her cleavage, encased in the tight Prada dress she had worn the previous evening, as he opened the cab door.

"Do you want it, or is it free?" Desiree quipped as the doorman ignored her outstretched hand holding a five-dollar bill. She was trying to be generous, and this fool was staring at her tits.

"G-gracias," the doorman stammered as he shook out of his stupor to accept his tip. He gave her a pathetic little grin. She contemplated snatching her money out of his grubby little hand. She despised it when men ogled her for free.

Desiree decided to be nice and let him keep the tip; after all, it was almost her birthday. And she considered the week of her birthday "Make Desi Happy Week." The credit card made her happy. She ran her fingers over the embossed letters of her entire name: Desiree Mirabella Torres Jackson. How did he know her whole name when she'd never told it to him? She went by Desiree Jackson, and usually just Desiree or Dez. She thought about it for a moment and then shrugged it off. Mitten Enterprises was printed beneath her name. She wondered what it was but was distracted by the thought of Bentley. She was glad K.G. was gone; that way she'd have nothing standing between her and the man she really wanted. Working with Bentley was going to be the icing on her birthday cake.

Desiree loved the sound of bills being counted. It almost made her wet. There was just never enough! With her freshly French-manicured fingertips, she rifled through the assorted Benjamins and Jacksons she kept in her bedroom safe. Then she placed her jewelry and the credit card in with her stash. Desiree was paranoid about home invasions and robbery, so she never kept valuables out in plain view. She punched in the security code to her alarm system as she always did when she was in the house alone. Then she took a Tylenol PM and went to sleep.

When she woke up, Desiree ordered Chinese food and then checked her two-way pager for new messages. There was one from K.G. telling her he loved her and missed her. There was one from her manager telling her she'd scored the lead in Bentley's music video. *Jackpot!* There was also one from her sometimes friend, sometimes enemy Leilani telling her about a private party. She dialed Leilani.

"What's up, girl! Where you been?" she greeted.

"K.G. came into town for a minute, so I kicked it with him last night. I was tired, so I just slept today," Desiree explained.

"I heard you got the Bentley video. Congratulations!" Leilani offered, cutting her off.

"How'd you hear?" Desiree asked her, surprised.

"I'm working it. I just found out today. One of the P.A.'s pulled out at the last minute."

Leilani and Desiree met a year before on the set of a video. Leilani had once been a popular model and parlayed her connections into several gigs behind the scenes. She said she was going to be a director, but Desiree couldn't picture it happening. She didn't know why anyone would stop being a model to be a nobody, the lowest-paid person on the totem pole. P.A.'s couldn't even make any decisions except for "Should I kiss the right ass cheek or the left one first?" If Leilani was smart, she'd use her looks to find a man to buy her a movie of her own.

Leilani Hong Thomas was definitely not a worker bee. She was spoiled and had never really *had* to work in her life because her parents had money. At twenty-six she could have easily kept modeling because she looked very young. Chinese-Jamaican, with creamy mocha skin, waist-length ebony hair, and deep brown, almond-shaped eyes, Leilani was pure eye candy. But she gave it all up, claiming it was time to move on. She said that she wanted to be respected for her mind. As long as you had a nice pair of tits, no man was going to even notice if you had a mind or not, but Desiree never tried to convince her to keep modeling. She was competition, and stiff competition at that.

"You're really trying to do that directing shit, huh?" Desiree asked. She didn't know why anyone as pretty as Leilani would want to work. All she had to do was find a rich husband. It wouldn't be hard for her. It amazed Desiree that some people who had it so easy always wanted to make things more diffi-cult than they needed to be.

"Yeah, girl. *I* can't shake *my* ass forever. I didn't go to col-lege for nothing." *Now, that's the problem with Leilani,* Desiree thought. *She always has to go and say something slick, like she's better than someone else.*

"Yeah, but you tryin' to shake your ass tonight, ain't you?" Desiree replied sardonically. *Fuck all that bullshit Leilani's spittin'. She ain't ready to stop chilling with the celebrities. She's just trying to cover her motives.* Leilani was as big a gold digger as Desiree. Bigger, if that was possible. But the difference between them was that Leilani was always fronting like she wasn't.

"You know it! Bentley and them are having a party at that new spot, Babylon. I got us on the list," Leilani said.

"Cool," Desiree said nonchalantly. She didn't want to give Leilani the satisfaction of seeing her geeked up about something. Leilani already thought she was the shit, she didn't want her acting any worse. Plus, Desiree hated it when Leilani was more in the loop than she was. It just made her go on and on about how she was being taken seriously as an aspiring director. Right! Like anyone really cared or was paying attention to the way she delivered coffee! Desiree couldn't wait until her career as a rapper took off so she could shut Leilani up, but for the time being she would keep hanging with her and use her connections to meet the right executives and go to the right parties, just in case things with Bentley didn't go according to plan. Desiree liked to be two steps ahead of the game.

"He's a cutie, isn't he?" Desiree changed the subject before Leilani could start bragging about her job.

"Who, Bentley? Yeah. I wouldn't mind hooking up with him. Maybe I'll have a chance at the video."

"Stand in line, girl," Desiree remarked, thinking to herself that Leilani didn't have a shot in hell. She was too little too late. Bentley had already made it crystal clear that he was checking for her. Besides, Bentley was more her speed. Leilani wouldn't know what to do with that. He was too street for her.

"What are you wearing?" Desiree asked as she walked with the cordless phone across her spacious bedroom to her walk-in closet.

"I don't know. I'll call you when I'm on the way, though. Around 11:30," Leilani said before hanging up the phone.

Desiree smiled as she caught a glimpse of herself in the full-length, trifold mirror in her dressing room. Actually, it was just a space in the back of her walk-in, but Desiree swore that when she made it big, her new diva crib would have a dressing room just like all the Hollywood stars had. She located the outfit she'd been saving for a night like tonight, a night when she needed all eyes on her with no exceptions; the most important set of eyes being Bentley's.

She plucked a garment bag off the closet rack and sauntered over to her bed. Unzipping the bag, she revealed a custom-made lightweight leather outfit with a cutout pattern all over it. She'd seen a similar outfit on Beyoncé Knowles on MTV and had to have one. The breast-baring halter and hip-hugging miniskirt were jeweled all over with Swarovski Austrian crystals to accent the design of the cutout pattern. Her Prada shoes set the outfit off just right. The getup had cost her nearly a grand to make, but she considered it an investment. Besides, someone had given her the money anyway. And in order to hook a big fish, one has to use big bait, she reasoned.

"Fuck all those broke bitches that have the nerve to call me a video ho," Desiree said, smirking at her reflection. "They just mad cuz they can't afford wears like this." Desiree stroked the butter-soft leather of her outfit and knew she would be the baddest bitch in the house tonight. "They know they'd have their asses all up in the videos if they could."

Desiree was amazed at the amount of backlash that she received from people about doing videos. People were always saying things about how the model's images degraded and objectified women, but Desiree thought they should lighten up. Men had been degrading and objectifying women long before videos were ever invented, and if videos were to suddenly disappear, she doubted that would change. Anyway, it was just entertainment. Why should she feel bad because men thought she was sexy and that her face and her body in a video could help push record sales over the top? If anything, she should feel bad for boosting someone else's record sales before she boosted her own!

Desiree walked into the bathroom, disrobed, and ran the water for a quick shower. She wanted to hit up her bikini area and underarms with a razor. She hadn't had a wax since she'd last been to the J Sisters in New York for their celebrity favorite: the Brazilian bikini wax.

She shampooed her tawny, bronze-streaked curls carefully, as to not disrupt her extensions. She had gorgeous long hair, but wore pieces because she felt they gave her hair that "perfect" look. Plus, she wasn't going to let a whole bunch of different stylists fuck up her hair. They could do whatever they wanted to her weave. After shampooing she applied a conditioner and let it sit as she washed her body.

Desiree's body was awesome. It was her moneymaker; she felt she owed everything to it. Her magnificent breasts, although implants, were soft, with just enough jiggle. Her surgeon was truly an artist, but she'd had a good canvas to work with. Her skin was the color of butterscotch syrup and tasted just as sweet, she had been told. She received biweekly facials and massages to keep her complexion radiant and smooth. Desiree's complexion was flawless, thanks to her Dominican mother and mahogany-hued African American father. Desiree was glad that even if her parents hadn't given her much else, they'd at least given her their good looks.

Rinsing the soap from her body and the conditioner from her hair, Desiree stepped carefully from the shower and lightly toweled off with a fluffy Egyptian-cotton bath sheet. Her smooth, tanned legs glistened as she spread sesame oil all over her five-six frame. She admired her ass in the mirror.

"Jennifer who?" She laughed, thinking Ms. Lopez had nothing on her backside.

Her eyes shined fiery amber, with flecks of green and gold. The MAC cosmetics she artfully applied only accentuated her dazzling natural beauty.

Leilani arrived shortly after Desiree had finished putting on the final touches, to smoke a blunt before leaving for the club. Leilani might have been irritating, and thought she was all that, but she always had the fire-ass buds, directly from the mountains of Jamaica.

Leilani damn near shit her pants with envy when she caught sight of the glittering and exotic Desiree. The outfit was definitely an eye-catcher.

"Doesn't leave much to the imagination, does it?" Leilani quipped, her soft voice faintly tinged with a Jamaican accent, her roving eyes taking in and critiquing every inch of Desiree. Leilani looked cute in a supershort, tailored white skirt suit with a matching white fedora and white Manolo stilettos. The white of the suit made her skin look like smooth milk choco-late. It was a sexy but classy look.

"Bitch, please. This shit is the hotness." Desiree dismissed the comment with a wave of her hand. Leilani said nothing; she only raised an eyebrow.

"Anyway . . . hat on?" Leilani twirled in a circle. "Or hat off?" She removed the hat, then undid the bun in the back of her head. Her hair cascaded down to her waist, and she shook it out, running her fingers through the length.

"Either way looks cool," Desiree remarked dryly. She could care less how Leilani wore her hair or rocked her brim.

"Yeah, I guess you're right. I look hot either way."

Desiree rolled her eyes. She was ready to get her smoke on, fuck all the bullshit.

"Where's the 'dro?" she asked impatiently.

"Right here." Leilani patted her matching white clutch purse and sat down on Desiree's white leather sofa. "Gimme something to roll on."

Desiree went into her bedroom, then returned with a wooden tray that was painted with the flag of the Dominican Republic. Leilani pulled a small Ziploc bag out of her purse and emptied its contents onto the tray. She took out a Backwoods cigar and used her fingernail to lift the tobacco leaf's edge, then unrolled the cigar. She dumped the tobacco into a paper towel and crumpled it up.

"You got scissors?" Leilani asked. Desiree went into the kitchen and returned with some scissors.

"Why you always gotta make the shit like surgery, Lani? You're Jamaican! You supposed to roll like a pro," she joked.

"I do roll like a pro. I just like my shit neat. Smokes better that way," Leilani replied. "I'm not new to this, I'm true to this, youngster." Leilani rolled the blunt and sealed it.

"Nuke this," she told Desiree, handing her the blunt. "Seven seconds."

"What makes you think that I want to touch a blunt with your wet-ass slob on it?" Desiree asked her, not taking the blunt.

"You gonna smoke it, ain't you?" Leilani rolled her eyes at her. She got up, went to the kitchen, and put the blunt in the microwave herself. Seven seconds later the microwave dinged, and Leilani sparked it. They passed the blunt back and forth, allowing the effects of the herb to take over their bodies.

"Save some of that for the ride over," Desiree told Leilani, and gathered her keys and purse.

They rode the short trip south of Desiree's Surfside apartment to the trendy area of South Beach in Leilani's red convertible BMW roadster. They rode with the top up as they chiefed on the remainder of the lah, vibing to the sounds of

R. Kelly's *TP-2* CD. When the track "The One" came on, Desiree felt like he was singing her theme song. She peeked at her reflection in the side-view mirror and sang softly, "There can only be one me." The herb made her feel like he'd written the song especially for her.

Once Leilani crossed Seventeenth and headed toward the strip, she switched the music to a hard-core dance-hall CD she had brought back from Jamaica on her last visit, and let the top down on the Beamer. As they crept down the congested strip, sound system booming, Desiree and Leilani basked in all the attention that they received. They looked hot, Leilani in all white, Desiree in all black, in the red car. They were the type of women that men thought of when they thought of Miami: exotic, sexy, ready to party.

"You ready?" Leilani asked Desiree as they pulled up to the valet stand of Babylon.

"Let's do this," Desiree replied, putting on a pair of rimless, smoke-colored Chloé glasses accented with Austrian crystals.

They stepped out of the whip on a mission, a modern-day, hip-hop version of Jackie O and Marilyn Monroe.

CHAPTER 14

L EILANI GAVE HER NAME AT THE DOOR, AND THEY WERE IM-
mediately admitted beyond the velvet ropes and into
Babylon. A door hostess gave them all-access wristbands
that would allow them to go into any VIP section of the
club. Leilani *really* had the hookup. Desiree usually only
needed her looks as her VIP pass, but it was cool to watch the
second-rate hotgirls covet her sparkling, silver, iridescent,
plastic bracelet in addition to the ice she sported in the tennis
bracelet on her other wrist.

South Beach's newest and hottest club was filled with
ballers. Babylon was overflowing with athletes, rappers,
singers, and actors who had come out to celebrate Bentley
receiving yet another platinum plaque. Leilani had told Desiree that many of the stars would be making cameos in
Bentley's video. Leilani said the budget was astronomical due
to a lot of special effects that were going to be computer-
generated and edited in.

Outside of industry people, there were the wannabes: the
dudes who wanted to be rappers, the guys who wanted to be
producers, and the gold diggers who wanted to be chosen.
Though Desiree wasn't exactly a star, and had ambitions of

being a rapper, she knew she didn't fall into the wannabe category. Unless you counted the fact that she wanted to be with Bentley.

Desiree squinted and scanned the crowd for a sign of Bentley. He wasn't difficult to spot. All Desiree had to do was find the crowd with the most action. Dressed in a crisp linen top and pants, he was popping open a magnum of champagne. He looked paid and classy, but not in a stiff kind of way. There were a ton of girls trying to get past Bentley's body-guards so they could spit their weak-ass game at him. Desiree figured game would recognize game. She wasn't gonna have to *say* shit.

They made eye contact.

Bentley smiled at her, ignoring a groupie tugging at his arm.

She needs to prepare to step! Desiree thought.

"Let's go over there," Desiree told Leilani, gesturing in Bentley's direction.

"Okay," Leilani agreed.

Desiree licked her lips, then worked her signature pout. Desiree possessed DSLs—dick-sucking lips—and used them to her full advantage. Bentley's eyes narrowed into slits as he checked her out. Desiree strolled slowly, confidently, and deliberately sexy in Bentley's direction. Leilani followed behind her as they approached the already crowded VIP section.

"It's full," a bouncer told them. Desiree gave him a look like he'd obviously lost his mind. Didn't he know who she was?

"Ayo!" Bentley shouted to the burly man in the black suit from across the crowd.

"He's talking to you." Desiree pointed in Bentley's direc-tion. The bouncer turned around.

"Let her in," Bentley commanded. The bouncer unhooked the velvet rope and allowed Desiree to pass, but when Leilani went to enter, he rehooked it.

"Sorry, it's full," he told her.

"I'm with her," she explained, flashing her wristband for added effect.

"It's full," he told her again as Desiree was engulfed by the crowd surrounding Bentley.

"Desi!" Leilani called out to her. Desiree heard her but chose to ignore her.

"Desiree!" she called out again to Desiree's back. "I know that bitch hears me!" Leilani growled as she turned around and headed to the bar. She wasn't going to beg to get in. She'd get her chance to holler at Bentley on the video set. He'd see that she wasn't just a pretty face and would definitely give her some play.

"WASSUP?" BENTLEY REACHED THROUGH THE CROWD AND gently but swiftly pulled Desiree's hand, guiding her to his table.

"Hey," she said, smiling.

"You havin' fun?" he asked her, smiling back, his deep dimples creating comma-shaped gashes in his face.

"Yeah, it's a good way to spend my birthday," Desiree mentioned casually.

"It's your birthday?" Bentley said.

"It is now." Desiree looked at his watch as if she were checking the time. What she was doing was inspecting the stones in the iced-out bezel of his watch.

"No shit. How old are you?"

"Old enough," she answered, blinding him with a dazzling smile. Bentley swore he could smell her perfume even though the club reeked of smoke and sweat.

"Damn, girl, you look good. You smell good too. What is that?" He grinned at her, pulling her closer. He nuzzled the crook of her neck, sending a shock through her system. He was flirting shamelessly. Desiree could sense the static from pissed-off females coming at her from every direction. Bentley was a big fish, and she wasn't wasting any time reeling him in. It wasn't her fault they couldn't compete with her.

"It's from Creeds. I had it custom-blended," she told him, allowing her body to graze suggestively against his. "I like nothing but the best next to my skin." She stared at him with her hypnotic hazels.

"I like the sound of that." Bentley wrapped his arms around her curves. Desiree wanted to tongue him down from head to toe.

"Happy birthday." He stared deeply into her amber eyes. Neither of them could deny the heat between them.

Desiree felt it in her gut. Fuck K.G., fuck all her other sponsors. She had finally caught the big one.

"LET ME GET AN APPLETON RUM AND COKE. NO, MAKE IT A double," Leilani told the bartender as she sulked at the bar. Desiree had the nerve to get new on her, and she wouldn't have gotten into the party without her. The bitch!

This was exactly why she didn't model anymore. The shit was too cutthroat, and for what? To be the background for some nigga makin' all the money, trying to get with some celebrity who isn't doing shit but digging out as many girls as he can before he goes back to his real woman. At least working behind the scenes, all the real money men would take her seriously. She'd be the woman they wanted to marry, not just fuck in hotel rooms and throw a few trinkets to.

Leilani saw Ysenia Cruz at the other end of the bar. She knew security was tight if Ysenia couldn't get in VIP with Bentley. She paid for her drink and tipped the bartender. Leilani didn't mind paying for her own drinks. At least that way she could enjoy them in peace instead of being stuck with some loser who thought she owed him her evening because he had spent a lousy eight bucks.

Ysenia headed toward Leilani. Leilani knew that Ysenia couldn't stand Desiree, and she wasn't feeling too keen on her at the moment either. A bitch session brewed.

"What's up, mama?" Ysenia greeted her with a fake smile and hug.

"Hey, lady," Leilani greeted her back, equally phony.

"Who you here with?" Ysenia asked, like she didn't know the answer.

"I was here with Desiree, but she's up there all in Bentley's ass," Leilani remarked sourly.

"Hmph. So that's how she got the lead, huh?" Ysenia's voice dripped with accusation.

"Nah, he didn't have anything to do with picking the girls," Leilani replied. She was mad, but she wasn't about to go talking shit about Desiree with Ysenia.

"Whatever! Bentley shows up to watch her audition, then she gets the lead. You think that's coincidence? I mean, come on! Desiree *is* a ho," Ysenia said.

Leilani didn't argue. The last thing she felt like talking about was Desiree. "You been up to VIP?" she asked, changing the subject.

"Yeah, girl, I was up there earlier before it got so crowded.

It was too hot, and there were too many groupies," Ysenia explained.

Leilani was really pissed now. Would everyone but her get to kick it high post and sip champagne with Bentley? She frowned. "So what's he like?" she asked, her jealousy showing.

"Kind of stuck-up. He knows he's all that. He might be gay, though," Ysenia said.

"Why you say that?" Leilani asked with a raised eyebrow.

"Because he didn't even *try* to holler. It was like I was invisible," was Ysenia's cocky answer. Leilani thought to herself that Ysenia was even more vain and conceited than Desiree.

Speaking of Desiree, Leilani peeped the VIP section, curious as to what she was up to.

"Well, he's definitely not gay," Leilani told Ysenia, pointing toward Desiree and Bentley hugged up and looking extra cozy.

Ysenia dropped her martini glass, causing her bright pink cosmopolitan to splash Leilani's white suit, as she caught Desiree and Bentley sharing what looked like a very passionate kiss.

"Son of a bitch!" Leilani shrieked. Could the evening get any worse?

"Sorry." Ysenia giggled, obviously not sorry at all.

A FEW HOURS AND A FEW MAGNUMS OF CRISTAL LATER, BENTLEY and Desiree snuck off for a little private time in the backseat of his trademark black Bentley Arnage. Once he'd kissed her, she knew there would be no use in playing it demure. She was going to fuck the hell out of Bentley, and she was going to put it on him so good that he'd never even think about the next bitch.

Desiree shivered as he kissed her neck and slid his hand beneath her top. She arched her back and allowed her hand to travel from his chest to his crotch to inspect the package.

Damn, he is the big one! Desiree mused.

"You want that?" He groaned seductively as she caressed his bulge.

"Mmm-hmm," Dez purred. "But I want it the right way." She kissed him sweetly on the lips and smiled at him. Then she slithered down his body like a snake and began to tease the tip of his penis with her warm tongue. Bentley moaned and arched his hips to meet her mouth. Desiree continued to tease him.

"I don't want to be just another bitch to you. I wanna be *that* bitch." She gave his shaft a lick and watched his dick grow even longer and harder.

"Shit, as far as I'm concerned, you *are* that bitch," he managed to utter as she slowly, torturously slipped more and more of his throbbing cock between her lips.

"I wanna be the *only* bitch," she whispered, her breath warm on his dick.

"You can be that," he told her.

She replied by engulfing his entire penis until he was deep within her throat. Her mouth felt like warm velvet caressing him. Desiree flicked the tip of his dick with her tongue.

"You could say that shit to all the females you meet. Are you gaming me? I'll stop if you are. And I know you want this." Desiree had him right where she wanted him. Once Desiree had a man in her mouth, he was helpless to resist her. She'd perfected her oral skills as a way to avoid sex with men she really didn't want to sleep with, but still get their money.

"Never that, ma! Never that!" Bentley whimpered helplessly as Desiree worked her jaws back and forth. It was only a matter of time before he was climaxing in her mouth.

"Damn, girl. You are the shit!" Bentley exclaimed after he'd regained his composure.

Desiree looked at him innocently, as if she hadn't just given him head in the car, and swallowed. Forever the ingenue, she was artful at looking incredibly sexy yet demure at the same time. "I hope that's not all you got for me. I mean, I really hope you ate your Wheaties and took your vitamins, because I am not done with you yet."

"Well, then, let's get to the telly cuz I'm not done with you either," he replied, and started the engine of the Arnage.

LEILANI STORMED FROM THE BATHROOM ANGRILY. NOW SHE knew why Desiree couldn't stand Ysenia; she was just a big hater. But at the moment, she couldn't stand either one of them. She was seriously pissed off. Ysenia had ruined her outfit, Desiree had ruined her evening, and to top it off, she was nowhere to be found. Bentley was no longer in the VIP section, though the party in his honor was still going strong.

It wasn't Chinese arithmetic for Leilani to put one and one together. Desiree was obviously with Bentley, God only knew where, doing God only knew what. She could have at least said good-bye or sent her a page so she wouldn't spend her evening searching for her. Leilani felt like if you came together, you should leave together unless you specifically told your crew otherwise.

There were a lot of crazy men in Miami who would love the chance to slip a girl a Mickey and take advantage of her. Females had to stick together. This would be the last time she looked out for Desiree's selfish ass. She knew that Desiree was a little younger than she, but immaturity was one thing and rudeness was another.

"Who knows how Desiree was raised! She doesn't have any home training! Desiree was just hating because she was afraid that Bentley would check for me," Leilani said aloud to no one.

But how come Desiree always came up on the ballers? Leilani knew she was pretty, and *she* was all-natural. To top it off, she had a promising career in film. She had beauty and brains, but unfortunately, men in Miami, at least the men with money that she met, preferred their women on the stupid side. She'd learned not to count on them a long time ago because she wasn't going to dumb down for anyone. Was it too much for her to find a man who wanted the total package and not just a bimbo?

"Well, can I?" a voice boomed from beside her. It belonged to a handsome, clean-cut man.

"I'm sorry. Can you what?" Leilani asked, puzzled.

"I said you look like you could use a drink. Can I get you one?"

Leilani sized him up. He was very attractive and looked familiar, but she couldn't recall where she recognized him from. The Audemars Piguet watch must have cost him over one hundred large easily, but aside from it, he wore no other jewelry. Some girls might think he was broke because he had no ice, but Leilani knew he was just conservative. Her eyes dropped to his shoes. They were from Prada's newest collection and weren't even available in stores. She'd seen them in an issue of *Maxim*. His linen outfit, though casual, was of top quality and excellent cut. It hung off his athletic frame like it was made just for him.

"So do I pass?" he joked, calling her out on her inspection. He twirled in a circle and hit a *GQ* pose.

"Yes." Leilani giggled, her anger fading.

"Yes, I pass, or yes, I can get you a drink?"

"Yes to both," she said, flirting.

He looked into Leilani's almond-shaped eyes and flashed a row of perfectly straight white teeth. His skin was a beautiful smooth butter pecan, and he appeared to be of Hispanic descent. Leilani felt her heart do a little pitty-pat. He wasn't just attractive, he was fine as hell! Where did she know him from?

"I'm Leilani." She extended her hand and shook his. It was soft, and he had a fresh manicure.

"It's nice to meet you, Leilani. You are beautiful. Your accent is so sexy! Can I ask what you are?"

"Can you tell me your name first?" The remark came out a little harsher than intended, but having been called so many names growing up due to her biracial background, sometimes she was a little bit defensive. Leilani softened the remark with a mischievous smile.

"My bad. I'm Sparks. I guess I'm used to people recognizing me," he told her.

Then Leilani remembered where she recognized him from. He was the CEO of Bentley's label, Titanium Records. Sparks was Bentley's older brother and one of hip-hop's hottest producers, commanding upwards of $200,000 a track. He even had remixes for Mary J. Blige and Madonna under his belt. He was one of the most talked-about people in the industry. Leilani felt stupid for not recognizing him at once, even though he was low-key and behind-the-scenes.

"Duh, my bad." Leilani rolled her eyes.

"Nah, it's cool. It's real cool." He was sick of women throw-

ing themselves at him trying to come up, so Leilani's ignorance was refreshing.

"I'm just kind of in another world right now," she explained. "But to answer your question, I'm Jamaican. And
before you ask, yes, someone in my family is Chinese—my
mother." Leilani ran down the evening's events to Sparks,
but didn't let on that she had wanted to meet Bentley. She
played the "concerned friend" role like she was worried about
Desiree.

"Your girl is cool. She's in good hands. She and Bentley left
a little while ago; he hit me on the two-way," Sparks reassured
her.

"Oh, okay," Leilani replied. She felt the previous envy begin
to disappear and focused her attention on Sparks. He was
older than Bentley and had more money; he was the brains of
the entire operation. Leilani smiled at the irony of it all. Desiree was the queen of the sack chasers and frowned on Leilani
because she wanted to be known for something other than
her looks. And Desiree had no problem shitting on her in
order to get to Bentley. Yet Leilani was the one that had come
up on the money man, not Desiree.

"You know, we're working together in a few days on Bentley's shoot. I'm a production assistant." Leilani sipped her
rum and Coke, then twirled the straw suggestively. She
wanted to be taken seriously, but that didn't mean she didn't
want to be seen as sexy.

"Damn. You look like you should be modeling in it! You are
so fine," Sparks enthused.

"Gee, thanks," Leilani responded dryly. Was that all he
could come up with? She looked like a model?

"I meant it as a compliment. But I'm glad you're not a
model," Sparks came back quickly.

"What's wrong with models? I used to be one," she said.

She wanted to see just where his head was at so she would know exactly how to play him.

"Nothing. Models are cool, but you gotta admit that a lot of them's mental ain't tight. I'm just trying to say that I'm glad to see that you have a brain to go with your beauty. You seem like the total package, you know. You got a nice style, you carry yourself well, you're pretty, and you're smart. You got to have a man. Ain't no way a dime like you could be single." Sparks grinned at her. Leilani dug his smile. Plus, she always loved a compliment.

"Yeah, I am, as a matter of fact," she replied. He was definitely showing interest and claimed to appreciate a smart woman. This was too good to be true.

"Cool. Then I hope you don't mind mixing a little pleasure with business. I mean, I hope I don't have to wait until the video to see you again." Sparks ran his hand over his closely cropped curls.

"I think that can be arranged." Leilani grinned, glad that the night was starting to turn around.

DESIREE RUBBED BENTLEY'S HARD-ON AS THEY DROVE THE FEW short blocks from Babylon to the Loews Hotel. Desiree adored the Loews; it was so plush. It would be the perfect place for her to put it on Bentley. She couldn't believe he was hard again so soon after the blow job she'd given him. She could tell from his stamina that they were a perfect sexual match.

"Girl, you gonna make me crash my whip. You makin' me feel so good!" he groaned as he nearly rear-ended a yellow cab at a stoplight.

Desiree leaned over and let her breasts brush against his arm as she kissed him on the cheek and let her tongue trail down his neck.

"I want to feel you inside of me," she breathed into his ear, and then stopped to nibble briefly on his earlobe as she continued her ministrations to his throbbing crotch. Bentley abruptly put the car in park, grabbed two handfuls of her hair, and kissed her forcefully. The light changed colors and cars honked and blew, but she and Bentley continued to grope at each other until Desiree finally broke free and gasped for breath.

"Get a room!" a frustrated motorist shouted as he swerved around the car. A carload of teenage girls recognized Bentley and shouted, "We love you!" which made them laugh as they sped off down Collins Avenue.

Moments later they were in the Jacuzzi tub of Bentley's suite with a bottle of Cristal. They took turns pouring the bubbly, golden liquid over each other and licking it up, then engaged in an hour of unprotected, animalistic sex. Desiree was on such a high from the combination of Cristal and Bentley that she didn't bother to protest when Bentley climaxed deep inside of her. Hell, she even hoped she'd conceive, because a baby by a baller of Bentley's stature meant financial security for life.

Bentley kissed Desiree on the forehead and held her as he fell into a deep sleep. *It couldn't be more perfect,* Desiree mused contentedly. She snuggled closer to Bentley, smiling as she closed her eyes, her dreams filled with visions of cribs, car seats, and cash.

CHAPTER 15

DESIREE AWOKE THE NEXT MORNING THOROUGHLY SATI-
ated. It was like she was still dreaming, waking up next
to Bentley. Or better yet, it was a dream come true. Desiree
watched Bentley as he slumbered. He was so adorable; he
looked innocent, the way Desiree imagined he did when he
was a child. But he was all man, and Desiree wanted to experience more of him.

Reaching across the bed and beneath the tangled sheet, she
massaged him until he was rock-hard and throbbing. Deftly,
she repositioned herself so that she was between his legs, and
proceeded to give him another phenomenal blow job. She felt
his body stiffen and immediately stopped. He wasn't about
to get off that easy; she had needs to satisfy.

Desiree straddled him, inching down his elongated shaft
until she felt his hardness deep within her. She ground her
hips against him, drenching him with her wetness. She worked
her muscles like a vise as she rode him until they both cried
out in pleasure and climaxed together.

"Shit! What a way to start the day!" Bentley grinned, wip-
ing away the beads of perspiration that had formed across his
forehead.

She smiled back. "Good morning, papi."

They looked into each other's eyes, grinning; no other words were necessary. They had a chemistry that was beyond words. They'd both had plenty of sex, but none so explosive or so intense. Bentley kissed her eyelids and forehead and squeezed her tightly. He felt completely at ease, like he could let his guard down with Desiree. And he knew it wasn't the sex that had him open. It was her. She was special. He couldn't pinpoint what it was, but he knew she had something rare, that "it" factor that made her stand out in a crowd.

"Can I order room service? I'm starving," Desiree inquired, snuggling closer to him.

"You can have whatever you want. I'm gonna go down the hall and holler at Sparks. See what I gotta do today. I hope you ain't got no plans for your birthday, because you're mine today."

"I'm all yours," she replied with a mischievous twinkle in her eyes. She lay back languidly on the bed, allowing him full view of her body.

"I like the sound of that," he said as he reluctantly got out of bed and pulled on a pair of shorts. He gave Desiree a peck.

"Order me some cheese eggs, grits, steak, and some hash browns," he added on his way out the door.

"What do you want to drink?" she called after him, but he'd already gone.

After putting in his order, plus a platter of buttermilk pancakes, a fruit plate, assorted juices, and coffee, she flicked on the TV. As usual there was nothing on. Desiree hated television unless she was on it. She heard her two-way vibrating from inside her tiny handbag and quickly retrieved it to check her messages before Bentley returned. *Happy birthday, baby! I love you, I miss you, where are you?* the LCD screen read, followed by K.G.'s signature. *You don't want to know*, she thought. Deciding to ignore his page, she headed to the bathroom to take a shower.

Bentley returned as she stepped out. "Damn, you fine!" He shook his head at her.

"Nah, that's you," she kidded him. "I ordered the food. It should be here any minute," she said as she wrapped a towel around herself.

Bentley yanked the towel away. "I wanna look at you. You're so beautiful."

For the first time in a long time, Desiree blushed. Because for the first time in a long time, it felt like she was loved. K.G. claimed to love her, but it just wasn't the same; she didn't love him. But she felt like she was in love with Bentley. He was everything she'd ever dreamed of. Desiree wrapped her arms around him and gave him a big kiss.

"*You're* beautiful," she told him, smiling. She knew that it was some corny shit to say, but she meant it, and it just kind of slipped out. There was something about Bentley that made her feel like she could really be herself. She felt like she could trust him, even though she'd just met him. They embraced and shared yet another kiss. Usually, Desiree avoided kissing. It was way too personal and intimate. She kissed K.G., but he took care of her, so that was different.

"We'll never leave this room if you keep that up," he said, breaking free from her.

"My bad, what do you have to do today?" she asked him. She wondered if this was what it felt like to be married to Bentley.

"We gotta head out to this radio interview at 99Jams around noon, but then we're free for the day. We can Jet Ski and shit later. Maybe rent some scooters, whatever you want to do."

"Cool. But, baby, what am I going to wear? It's not like I can wear this outfit all day," she said, motioning toward the leather skirt and top that lay in a heap on the floor. "Should I go home and get a change of clothes?" She knew damn well she didn't want to go home for clothes; she wanted *new* ones.

"You can go pick something up right quick if you can do it in an hour. I know how ladies are when they shop. You and your girl can go together, but don't get lost."

"Me and my girl?" Desiree was confused.

"Yeah, your girl, what's her name? Leilani. The Jamaican one that looks Chinese. She's in the room chillin' with Sparks."

"What?" Desiree was shocked. Leilani was chillin' with Sparks? The man was touted as the next Russell Simmons! Leilani always had to try and one-up her. She was such a hater!

"Yeah, ain't that a trip? Sparks don't never hook up with nobody. He's a loner and shit, old nerdy-ass nigga. That's my brother and I love him, but he's strange. He thinks on a whole other level. I was starting to wonder if my brother was gay and shit!" he said, laughing.

Desiree laughed along, but she didn't think that shit was funny at all. "Yeah, that's a trip."

Desiree quickly slipped on her clothes and shoes from the night before. She stood before Bentley, hand extended to receive the money for shopping.

"Sparks is gonna give your girl a credit card. That's how we shop. We write a lot of shit off as business expenses for taxes and shit like that."

"Oh, okay. Well, I'll see you in an hour." Desiree was getting sick of the credit card shit. What ever happened to cold hard cash? She kissed him again, then headed toward Sparks's room double time. She didn't want Bentley to see the anger brewing inside of her. Leilani was trying to ease in on her territory, and the lioness that she was, she didn't like it one bit.

When Desiree got to the room, she found Leilani and Sparks with arms around each other, kissing and whispering and looking all googly-eyed. Something was terribly wrong with that picture. Leilani was wearing the stained white suit from the night before. Desiree cleared her throat loudly. Leilani giggled and turned around holding up an American Express Black card. *Oh hell no! That's the shit you have to be invited to get! How did she come up on that?* Desiree fumed internally. *She probably don't even know what that shit is!* Desiree was rumbling inside like a volcano as she coveted the credit card.

"Let's go shopping!" Leilani squealed, her eyes twinkling. She ran up to Desiree like a schoolgirl and threw her arm around her shoulder.

"I promise we'll be back in an hour, Johnny!" She blew Sparks a kiss, and he caught it in the air. Desiree swore she must have stepped into some kind of parallel universe. What was this shit? Who the fuck was Johnny? And why were they catching and throwing invisible kisses like they were in the fucking third grade? As soon as they were out of earshot, Desiree confronted Leilani.

"Yo, what the fuck is going on, Leilani?" she snapped, yanking Leilani's arm from her shoulder.

"What's the matter, Dez?" Leilani asked, eyes innocent.

"What's the matter, Dez?" Desiree mocked her. "What are you doing here with Sparks?"

"The same thing *you're* doing with Bentley. Why are you bugging out?"

"You always talking all that shit about being respected for your brain. Talking down on me cuz I still model and cuz I let niggas take care of me. You always actin' like I'm a gold digger, but if I am, so are you."

"First of all, maybe that's your low self-esteem talking, because I never look down on you, or anybody else, for that matter."

"Whatever!" Desiree threw her palm up to Leilani's face.

"Maybe you feel bad about how you're living, and that's just your guilty conscience talking. But for your information, me and Johnny didn't do anything last night except for talk and kiss, after you disappeared without even bothering to say good night. After you straight up igged me to go sweat Bentley. So don't even trip."

"You're just trying to be me," Desiree fumed.

"Be you? Don't even get me started on why that statement is wrong on so many levels."

"Oh, come on! You wish you still had this body, getting a little thick there, aren't we? You wish you were still in front of the camera, not behind it. You wish a star like Bentley wanted you." Dez glared at Leilani, her eyes nearly black with anger.

"From what I hear, Bentley wants someone new in every town. But he especially wants his girl back in New York. Why don't you ask your boy about that?"

"Fuck you, Lani. You just hatin'. You're just tryin' to get me shook. Don't worry about me and Bentley."

"And you don't worry about me and Sparks." Leilani shook her head and started to walk away. Suddenly, she turned on her heels to face Desiree. "And why should I hate on you? I thought we were friends, but you proved me dead wrong last night when you were acting flaw. And as far as Bentley being a star, you're right, he is a big star. But Sparks signs Bentley's checks. Marinate on that, little girl." Leilani strode off ahead of her.

"Yeah, whatever," Desiree replied. There was really no other

answer she could come up with. Sparks *was* the CEO of Titanium Records. Bentley was fine, he had money, he had fame
and maybe even a girlfriend, if there was any truth to what
Leilani had said. Sparks had both those things—money and
fame—plus an additional one: power. Sure, Bentley possessed
power onstage and in videos: his image sold records, products,
and a lifestyle. But Sparks had the power to make things happen, to control an empire and even the media and entertainment industries. It was becoming more obvious every day that
"pop culture" and "hip-hop culture" were merging. Sparks
had control. And he wanted Leilani. Something was definitely
wrong with that picture.

Desiree and Leilani shopped in silence at Follies on Lin-
coln Road. Leilani opted for a nondescript sundress that was
neither very casual nor very dressy. Desiree thought it was
something a schoolteacher would wear. Who was she trying
to fool? Dez decided on a short, strapless denim minidress
that looked extra sexy with her stilettos. They purchased the
gear on the AmEx card and put their old clothes in shopping
bags. Then they hot-tailed it back to the Loews.

Desiree wanted to confront Bentley, to find out if he had
a girl back in New York, someone who had history with him
and possibly even his heart. She wanted desperately to know
if she was just some ass to him—an expensive piece of ass,
but a piece of ass no less. He couldn't be playing her, could
he? As much as she wanted to interrogate him, she held her
tongue because she knew that there was a time, a place, and
a way to find out everything she wanted to know. Besides,
Leilani just wanted to get under her skin, and if she caused
a scene or initiated some drama, she'd just be letting Leilani
win. So instead she changed her game plan. She acted like
everything was cool and enjoyed the time she was spending
with Bentley to the fullest. She snuggled close to him on the

ride over to the radio station and made sure to laugh and giggle a lot, just to work Leilani's nerves.

Desiree loved every minute that she was at 99Jams. The DJ interviewing Bentley made a fuss about her being in the studio, almost as big a fuss as he made over Bentley.

"You girls have been calling all day for a chance to holler at your boy Bentley. Well, I got a surprise for all you fellas out there. Here with Bentley we've got the beautiful Desiree Jackson. Now, for those of you who don't know the name, I am sure you know the face and the body. You've seen her in a ton of music videos. Desiree, tell the listeners who you've worked with," the DJ asked her after he had finished getting the meat of the interview from Bentley as he was preparing to take phone calls from listeners.

"Wow, I've worked with practically everyone. My latest project was P. Diddy's newest joint. I was the lead girl. But I've done some stuff with all kinds of artists from Ricky Martin to Aerosmith. Tomorrow I'll be shooting with Bentley. I'm really excited!" she gushed, just to let Bentley know she wasn't trying to steal his shine.

"True dat, it's sure to be a hit. You're working with the best in the biz. And then what are you up to? More videos? Have you thought about exploring other career avenues?" He grinned at her while ogling her cleavage.

Sensing the timing was right, she told him, Bentley, Sparks, Leilani, and all of South Florida that she was going to continue modeling.

"But my main focus is going to be my music. I've got a really hot demo, so I'll be shopping that and looking for the best deal." She smiled at her good fortune. Her statement had the desired impact: the DJ had allowed her to hype herself up for the whole city to hear, Sparks and Bentley raised curious eyebrows, and Leilani fumed silently in the corner. Desiree would show her that she wasn't the only one with a talent beyond looking good. As far as she was concerned, Leilani had challenged her, and Desiree never stepped down from a challenge.

"FLOW!" SPARKS ORDERED. HE AND DESIREE WERE SEATED IN the parking lot of 99Jams in the Hummer he had rented. After the interview he grabbed her by the hand and led her there, leaving a surprised Leilani and Bentley behind.

"Now?"

"Flow right now!" Sparks made eye contact to let her know he was serious. He was the one that had selected Desiree for the video in the first place. Bentley wanted her, no doubt. But Sparks had the final word. He sensed that besides her looks, she had something special. Desiree was nervous, but she knew he meant business. Sparks's reputation as an eccentric but shrewd businessman preceded him. And his millions were the proof of the pudding. She cleared her throat, took a deep breath, and spit the lyrics of her "Down to Ride," a hard-core song about her devotion to the streets and to her man. Sparks sat expressionless. Desiree couldn't tell if he loved her skills or thought she was wack. He put on a CD with an instrumental track and instructed her to freestyle. She did so. After a few bars he cut the track. He sat there in silence, Desiree anticipating his next words as if her life depended on it. Her life *did* depend on it.

"What you call yourself?" he finally said.

"Dez. Nothing fancy, just Dez," she replied. She wasn't about to be Lil' this, Sexy that, or Lady such and such. That wasn't her. She hoped he would offer her a deal, but really hoped he wasn't about to make her a clone of the females already in the industry, or some model-chick rapper. She *was* a model-chick, but at heart she was still a tomboy.

"I like that," he said, stroking his goatee. "You want a deal?" he asked her, practically reading her thoughts.

"Hell yeah!" Desiree didn't bother to hide her enthusiasm.

"Cool. Welcome to the fam."

And just like that, every dream she'd ever had was realized.

"WHAT THE FUCK IS GOING ON?" LEILANI ASKED BENTLEY AFTER watching Sparks and Desiree exit the studio in a rush.

Bentley shook his head. "I have no fucking idea. With my brother you never can tell."

"I bet he's reading her up and down. I mean, did you see the way that she tried to take over your interview? Desiree always has to be the center of attention," Leilani said, hoping to create a rift between Bentley and Dez.

"Nah, she was cool. She handled that shit well. That shit was kind of smart."

"You've got to be kidding." Leilani frowned and crossed her arms. "Don't you feel used? Like maybe the only reason she's hollering at you is because she wants to get put on?"

Bentley eyed Leilani suspiciously. "What are you trying to say? Aren't you supposed to be her girl?"

"That's exactly my point. I *know* Desiree. She's an opportunist. I'd be careful, Bentley."

"Yeah, well, I can handle myself. And I could say the same thing about you. Hooking up with my brother can't hurt *you,* now, can it?"

"I'm not even like that," Leilani countered.

"Yeah, but how would we know that? I'm giving Desiree a chance, like Sparks is giving you a chance," Bentley replied.

Leilani didn't have a response. She just tossed her hair and fumbled in her purse for a piece of gum. She snapped on it angrily, taking out all her frustration on the cinnamon-flavored stick. As far as she was now concerned, Bentley and Desiree deserved each other. They were equally shallow, all fluff and no substance. Bentley had to be an idiot if he couldn't see through Desiree; either that or pussy-whipped or both. Her only consolation was the hope that Sparks had seen through her and was putting her in check.

Desiree and Sparks came back into the studio laughing. Sparks told her he had to say bye to the general manager of the station and handle some business and disappeared into an office with an administrative assistant. She spotted Leilani and Bentley stepping off an elevator.

Leilani confronted her almost immediately. "What happened?" Desiree ignored her.

"Baby, you'll never guess what happened." Desiree snaked her arms around Bentley's waist and gave him a kiss.

He grinned at her. "So tell me."

"Sparks offered me a deal."

"He what?" Bentley and Leilani shouted in unison.

Desiree felt Bentley's body stiffen, and she took three steps back. She looked at Leilani and Bentley. "Uh, how about a congratulations? I've been working hard at this. And I have skills," she said, defending herself.

"Nah, baby. That's not it. I trust my brother's judgment. But we supposed to be partners. He could have at least consulted with me."

"You don't want me on your label?" Desiree pouted.

"Listen to me. If Sparks thinks you got skills, you got skills. It's a business thing. It's not personal," Bentley explained.

Whatever! It didn't matter, because she had a deal, so Desiree just nodded in agreement. Leilani had already heard enough of her business. She'd approach the topic later, if at all. Sparks joined them.

"Sparks, let me talk to you for a minute," Bentley said. "Desiree, Leilani, why don't y'all go wait in the car? We'll be right out." Bentley tossed the keys at Desiree, not giving them much of a choice.

"Dude, why would you offer her a deal without talking to me first?" Bentley asked his brother as soon as the ladies were out of earshot.

"Man, you made it clear a long time ago that you wanted to perform and you would leave the business end to me. Your girl got mad skills," Sparks explained.

"That's just it, man. You know how I roll, man. I'm not one to be tied down. I gotta be able to do my thing. What if I want to hit some groupie after a show? If she's always around, there's going to be some trouble. I don't need that kind of fucking drama."

"But you like her, man, don't you? You ain't gonna care about seeing her."

"Yeah, I like her. That's not the point. The point is we both know that it ain't smart to shit where you eat."

"I feel you, man. But you can handle that shit. I ain't sayin' you got to marry her ass. She might just surprise you and pull a switch once she blows up. She might decide to sample some of her own groupies," Sparks teased his younger sibling. Bentley made a face.

"But this is a business, and she's money in the bank," Sparks went on. "She's fine as hell, *and* she can flow. She ain't no Amil, we ain't gotta write her rhymes. She looks better than Foxy, she's sexier than Kim, and she's rawer than Eve. She got more ass than Trina, plus she's got the titties to match, *and* she freestyles. Man, she's gonna be large."

"That's cool. But what am I supposed to do when I want to get some new pussy?" Bentley questioned. "You know and I know that it ain't no pussy like new pussy."

"Nigga, you got game. Plus, she's gonna be so busy she won't have time to be all up in your face. I'll see to that. Besides, y'all ain't about to be Kim and Big. You gonna do your thang, and she's gonna do hers. I know what the fuck I'm doing."

"Aight, then," Bentley replied reluctantly. "But respect me, brother. I'm not a little boy anymore, I'm a man. And I've put just as much into this label as you have, dog. Respect me, man. Ya heard?"

"I feel you, nigga." Sparks gave Bentley a pound, and they headed to the Hummer.

"DO YOU HAVE CRACK IN YOUR CUNT OR WHAT?" LEILANI snarled in the Hummer.

"What is your fucking problem, bitch?" Desiree asked her, knowing full well what her problem was.

"Oh, so you're a rapper now?" Leilani responded sourly.

"You're the one constantly talking down on me about shaking my ass in videos, acting like I'm stupid. Well, now I got something because of my talent, and you hating. I do have talent, you know!"

"You still used your ass to get what you wanted. If you weren't fucking with Bentley, Sparks never would have given you the time of day."

"That's cool. You know that's not true, but even if it was true, it would have been someone else if it wasn't Sparks. Believe that," Dez replied, full of confidence. "This ain't my first deal offer, just the best."

"I wouldn't be shocked if you sucked Sparks's dick to get your deal. Nobody saw what y'all were doing out there."

"Feeling threatened?" Dez suggested.

"By a whore like you? Never!" Leilani retorted defiantly.

"You need to watch your fucking mouth before I punch you in that shit, bitch. Don't get it twisted. Keep fucking around and trying me. See if you're working tomorrow."

"Fuck you, Desiree," Leilani spat. She had no idea what the big deal was about Dez, but she for one was getting sick of all the hype.

"You probably want to." Desiree glared at Leilani, her eyes a vibrant green. She decided right then and there that Leilani had one more time to say something slick, one more time to jump bad, and she was going to give her the beat-down of a lifetime.

WHEN HE AND BENTLEY FINALLY GOT IN THE HUMMER, SPARKS suggested they go get something to eat and discuss the changes that would need to be made at the video shoot, so they rolled out to Monty's on the Beach for stone crabs while listening to Desiree's demo on the CD player. Desiree could tell by the expression on Leilani's and Bentley's faces that her shit was hot.

"We can't have you be like another one of the models in this video. I know you got cast in the lead and shit, but un- less you want people to think you're a puppet, you're going to have to take one for the team," Sparks told them while pounding a stone crab claw with a wooden mallet.

"I hear you," Desiree agreed, though she had really been looking forward to her role. She picked nervously over a shrimp Caesar salad.

"But what I have in mind is you doing an a cappella free-style at the beginning and end of the video. When we edit, we can give the audience a teaser to your first release. What do you think, B?"

Bentley was busy grubbing on a steak and lobster combo. "I trust you, Sparks. That shit could be real hot if we do it right. Everybody will be trying to hear what my baby got to say." Bentley squeezed Desiree's thigh, and she felt a chill run down her spine.

Sparks turned to Leilani. "Lani, you know that Hype and me are directing this. But you wanna be second A.D.?"

"Of course. Are you kidding?" Leilani nearly spilled her water at the news.

"Cool. It'll be your responsibility to make sure that Desiree looks her very best. Make sure her lighting is real good to emphasize her beauty. And why don't you call the stylist and make sure that she has some shit that really stands out? Not too sexy, because we want people to hear her, but sexy enough so that they won't be able to take their eyes off of her. The number is in my two-way." Leilani was happy about the pro-motion, but couldn't believe that she was going to have to cater to Desiree. It was like she was Desiree's do-girl.

Desiree smiled smugly and sipped on a glass of iced tea. *Your title may have changed, but you're still a P.A.*, she thought.

"Sure, Johnny," Leilani agreed, and went to work. It was official. She *hated* Desiree.

Sparks got on his cell with his lawyers and had them draw up a simple three-album deal for Desiree. He assured her that he wouldn't dick her when it came to her points and royalties, but just in case, Desiree told him that she'd have her own lawyer look over the paperwork. Desiree had many corporate connections from her days as a dancer and had learned a thing or two about the industry while she was with Dan. She decided that she would always have someone strictly in her corner to protect her interests, even though she'd have to pay a pretty penny of her own money to do so.

Desiree thought about how proud Ginger would be if she knew the direction her life was about to go in. *Maybe*. Ginger was so caught up in her religion that she thought everything was evil. Desiree missed her sister-friend but resisted the urge to call. That was a lifetime ago, and Ginger probably wouldn't talk to her anyway. Chicks like Leilani and Ysenia thought they were so smart and had their shit so together, but they were ignorant peasants compared to Ginger. Desiree figured she'd never have a real friend again once her face was really out there. Everyone would just want a piece of her fame.

Desiree needed to go back to her house to get ready for the shoot the next day. Bentley insisted on coming with her, which Desiree didn't mind at all. At least he wouldn't be out with some other female, and she'd be able to get to the bottom of Leilani's allegations. They stopped off at a small market near her apartment so she could pick up a few things, and arrived at her place as the sunset was streaking the sky in crimson gashes.

"It's so fucking pretty here." Bentley admired the lush courtyard surrounding the swimming pool that was in the center of Desiree's complex. "Your crib looks like Melrose Place," he teased.

"Yeah, I know. That's what I love about it." Desiree laughed, knowing it sounded goofy.

Desiree fixed Bentley a drink from the liquor cart in her

living room and encouraged him to relax and get comfortable while she changed clothes. She adjourned to her room to take a quick shower and changed into a pink Baby Phat sweat suit. Desiree examined herself in the mirror. She wanted to look good for Bentley, but she didn't want it to seem like she was trying too hard. She decided to swoop her damp hair into a high ponytail and slick on some soft pink Lipglass and call it a day.

Desiree smiled at her reflection. Was she glowing? She certainly felt like it. Her thoughts were interrupted by a loud buzzing noise, which she identified as her pager. She checked the screen: *Where are you? Call me. I love you.* K.G. again? She'd give him some story later, but for now she was going to focus on Bentley. She turned the pager to silent, as well as her cell phone, so there'd be no further interruptions, then headed to the kitchen to prepare dinner.

Bentley watched in awe as Desiree chopped plantains, seasoned chicken, and boiled rice like it was second nature.

"Did your mom teach you how to cook?" he asked.

"Yeah. She's dead, though," she lied. Desiree knew that saying her mom was dead usually kept people from asking too many questions because it made them uncomfortable. Besides, it wasn't a total lie. Her mother was dead to her.

"Mine too. Both my parents are dead. It's just me and Sparks."

"I know what that's like. I'm an orphan too. I'm sorry." Desiree gave him a warm smile.

"Me too." He smiled back.

Desiree heaped piles of food on his plate but had no appetite herself. Beaming with pride, she watched as he ate every bite. She knew that the way to a man's heart was through his stomach, and once he was good and comfortable, she'd pry him for information.

"Damn, girl, you can burn! This was so good." He smacked his lips as he pushed his plate away.

"You liked it?" she asked as she cleared the table.

"Hell yeah! You're a keeper. You're fine as hell, and you can cook. Plus, you can flow. Shit, you perfect," he said.

"You say that to your girl up top too? Is she a keeper?" Desiree smiled at him seductively and used her Marilyn Monroe voice to make sure it came out soft and not accusatory.

"Ain't got no girl up top. I did for a minute, though, but that's dead," he explained.

"And buried?"

"Nothing but a skeleton," he joked back.

"Well, keep that skeleton out of your closet, okay baby? I told you I don't like to share. And I don't like to be lied to." She looked at him with doe eyes. Who could hurt someone with a face like that? But beneath all the innocence of her whispers and smiles, Desiree knew that *she* had plenty of skeletons she never intended to let out. And she lied so well she forgot when she was doing it.

"Let's get this straight, okay, because we're gonna be together a lot," Bentley said. "Business is business, us is us. You gonna hear a lot of shit about me doing this and that, the press is gonna have me linked up with this one and the next one. But it's about me and you. Like my boy Common said, 'It don't take a whole day for me to recognize sunshine.' I knew you were gonna be mine when I saw you in a video. I just had no idea then that you would be as bomb as you are. Like I said, baby, you're perfect."

"Okay. I believe you, baby," Desiree told him, and she did.

Later on that night they made love, slow and tender. It was a far cry from the unbridled passion they had before. Desiree showered him with kisses as she clung to him.

"Do you love me, baby?" he asked, catching her off guard as they lay tangled in each other's arms.

She laughed nervously. "What would make you ask me that?"

"Just answer the question," Bentley persisted.

"Yes. I never loved anybody before. But I love you," she admitted, her voice cracking.

"I love you too, baby girl. It's not just because you're pretty and shit either. You're smart. I can tell you been through a lot, but now you're on top. I recognize that. I respect that. You're like me. This shit is crazy as hell, but I love you. I been in love with you from the moment I laid eyes on you."

Desiree had been waiting for so long to hear those words from someone she felt the same way about. K.G. and all her other sponsors were in love with an image. They didn't care about her, who she was inside. They just wanted her to shut up and look pretty. Someone had finally seen her, the tomboy, the outcast; they'd seen past the Desiree she built, and they loved the Desiree she was. At least as much of the real her as she would reveal. She didn't bother to stop the tears from rolling down her face.

CHAPTER 16

DESIREE COMMANDED THE MODELS' TRAILER AS IF SHE WERE the Queen of Sheba. It had been too late to get her own trailer; Desiree suspected that was Leilani's doing but let that shit go because she intended to let everyone on the set know that she was no longer just a model. She was a fucking artist! As soon as she stepped aboard, she ordered that all the models head toward the back of the trailer or wait outside because she was going to need the front half for herself. She demanded extra-special treatment and was in full diva mode.

She insisted that the best stylist immediately drop what she was doing and take care of her. That was not a problem. But then she required that her curls be blown straight and flat-ironed, a job that was going to take nearly an hour. Dez didn't care. Bentley had said she could have the world, and she was starting the takeover right then and there.

After all, there was a model on the set with hair like hers, and she refused to go on camera looking like someone else, especially some girl who was clearly beneath her. She had a record deal; she was supposed to stand out, not blend in with the other girls. When the stylist radioed Leilani to complain,

Bentley grabbed her walkie-talkie and insisted that Desiree have what she wanted. If the video ran behind, so be it. Dez was his girl and a new artist; she had an image to uphold.

Desiree knew that Leilani was probably ready to shit her pants. She probably thought that since she had fucked her way into the assistant director's chair (because she definitely didn't believe that shit about her and Sparks not doing it), she'd be able to control her. Leilani thought she had been the one to come up, that she was the one who was making strides in the industry. Wrong!

Next, Desiree insulted the makeup artist so badly that she walked off the set. It took nearly an hour to calm her down, but she refused to work on Desiree unless she could "rearrange that bitch's face." Desiree was unfazed. It wasn't her fault that the makeup artist didn't know what she was doing. Desiree knew exactly what colors looked right on her, and she wasn't going to let some amateur make her look like a clown in her debut as an artist. Once again Leilani was called to squash the beef. Reluctantly, she went into the model's trailer.

"What's the problem, Dez?"

"That silly-ass makeup artist is the problem. She tried to put C6 foundation on me. I know my MAC. I'm clearly an NC45. I just went on and did the shit myself. At least one of us knows what we're doing. She would have ruined the whole shoot," Desiree told her crossly.

"Okay, Dez, I feel you. But you can't go around insulting people. She's union. You don't want to start trouble for Bentley, do you?" she asked, her voice dripping with sarcasm.

"No. But I'm an artist now. *Talent,* as y'all call it. I deserve to look as good as I can. Anyway, I'm helping you out." Desiree inspected her makeup job in the mirror. She'd done an excellent job without a makeup artist.

"Helping me?" Leilani looked offended.

"You don't want to waste film, do you? You don't want your big break to go from sugar to shit, do you? You don't want to look like an amateur in front of Sparks, do you? It's your job to make sure I look good. We may be a little behind, but at least you won't have to dump any footage. At least you won't look like a novice who couldn't even manage to make sure the makeup artist could handle her responsibilities." Leilani and Desiree locked eyes.

"Fine, Desiree. Have it your way. Just know this. The diva attitude isn't going to get you very far. You've got a deal, but you ain't even recorded a single yet. You haven't even done a cameo. You're not a star yet. You're still just a video girl; it's not going to be an easy image for you to shake. Please believe it." Leilani stormed out of the trailer.

"Hater!" Dez mumbled under her breath.

BENTLEY AND HIS ENTOURAGE PASSED A BLUNT STUFFED WITH hydro around the trailer as they waited to be prepped for the video shoot. The smoke created a visible haze in the luxurious RV. Fresh, the company's stylist, coughed as he entered the vehicle, fanning and swatting the air around him.

"Y'all gonna have the gear smelling all fucked up! Crack a window or something!" he sputtered while rushing over to the rack that held the shoot's wardrobe. The crew cracked up laughing.

"Nigga, it's a video! Motherfuckas can't *smell* shit!" Bentley joked.

Sparks stepped onto the bus.

"Damn! How can y'all breathe out this motherfucka?!"

He grimaced as the pungent odor of chronic hit his nostrils. His eyes zeroed in on an empty cigar box. "I know your ass ain't been smoking out of my Cohibas!" Sparks snapped.

"Yo, man. I'll get you some more," Bentley promised.

"Dude, them shits is contraband. Do you know what I paid for those? They illegal! Yo' ass is gonna swim to Cuba right fucking now and get me some more 'gars! Fuck Castro's ass!" Sparks exploded, heading for Bentley. Several of his homeboys held him back, laughing the whole time.

"See, what I tell y'all motherfuckas? I told y'all his ass was gonna squawk like a bitch," Bentley roared. "Nigga, I got your shit right here." He grinned and pulled a small stash of Cohibas from his pocket and returned them to their box.

"They better not be all dried up and broken neither!" Sparks sulked, arranging his clothes. Bentley, always the practical joker, continued to laugh.

There was a knock at the door. Sparks opened it, and instantly, his scowl turned into a smile. There Leilani stood, casual but pretty in navy-blue yoga pants, a white tank top with skinny straps that bared her midriff, her waist-length hair pulled into a ponytail that spilled out the back of a Yankees cap. She held a clipboard, and attached to her hip was a walkie-talkie.

"Hey, pretty lady," he greeted her.

"Hey, Johnny. Can I talk to you for a second?" she asked him. "In private?"

"Sure."

They exited the trailer and stood near a craft-service truck.

"First, before you tell me anything, give me a kiss." Sparks nibbled on Leilani's lower lip until she thought she would pass out.

Leilani finally pushed him away. "That's enough, baby,"

she admonished him. "I've gotta talk to you about *Dez*." Leilani spat Desiree's moniker with contempt.

"What about her?"

"She's buggin'. She's acting like the sun rises and sets on her ass, and it's causing the crew a lot of stress."

"Look, she's got a lot of pressure on her. She's been in a lot of videos, but never as anything but a model. The transition is gonna be rough on her, and she's probably nervous."

"Ha!" Leilani cackled.

"Come on. Relax. Everything's gonna be cool. You'll see. Besides, that's your friend. If anyone can help her, it's you."

"Hmm," Leilani replied, holding her tongue.

"That *is* your friend, right?" Sparks looked into Leilani's eyes with confusion.

"She's just been trippin' since she met your brother. She's acting real new."

"Y'all will be all right." *Women are so petty!* he thought to himself, slightly amused. Sparks bussed her cheek and left her standing there holding the clipboard and a powder keg of anger inside.

"BE CAREFUL IN THERE!" LEILANI WARNED YSENIA AS THEY crossed paths. Ysenia was on her way into the trailer. Leilani had promoted Ysenia to the lead role that had been Desiree's in order to provoke her. But considering how the day was going so far, she was beginning to wonder if that had been such a good idea. Desiree was already being impossible; when she caught wind of Ysenia, she was likely to have a conniption.

"Let me guess," Ysenia said. "Desiree?"

"You got it, mami." Leilani put her hands on her hips.

"I can see her now. She's walking her fat ass around the trailer like she's goddamned Jennifer Lopez just because she fucks with Bentley. And what is this I'm hearing? Now the bitch is supposed to have a record deal?" Ysenia didn't bother to mask her envy.

"Yeah, can you believe it? But, girl, he'll use her up and throw her away. I guarantee it. That's what you do with trash!"

Ysenia raised her eyebrows in surprise. "Damn. You still mad at her?"

"You don't know the half of it. She's gotten worse since the party. And now that she's supposedly the next big thing, she is really feeling herself. She's acting like someone died and made her queen over some new dick, and we've been cool for almost two years!"

"I still can't believe how overnight her ass got a record deal and her and Bentley are what, a couple now?" Ysenia ran her hands through her hair.

"They claim they're in love! I heard them telling each other they love each other!"

"Oh, get real. That's game, and Desiree is falling for it. I always thought she was smarter than that, but I guess I was wrong! Shit, I bet you Bentley wouldn't fuck with her ass if he knew how she really is!" she seethed. Ysenia was furious that he could have overlooked her the night of the platinum party to kick it with a skank like Desiree.

Leilani raised an eyebrow at the comment.

"Come on. Don't act like you haven't heard!" Ysenia cackled.

"She's not that bad. Don't believe everything you hear." Leilani defended Desiree out of habit, not sincerity. She was mad at Desiree, but she also hadn't forgotten how Ysenia had ruined her suit. That shit was unforgivable. Now Ysenia thought they were friends or something, but she was just a pawn. Besides, Ysenia was no saint. Leilani had heard a tale or two about her.

"Don't be naive," Ysenia replied patronizingly.

"I'm not naive. Men do the same shit she does all the time. I'm not saying she's an angel. I'm pissed as hell at the bitch. I just don't think she's done all the things people say she has. I would know. I'm probably the closest person to her; at least I was before all this recent shit," Leilani explained.

Ysenia shook her head in disbelief. "Trust me, Leilani, she's done it all and then some." Ysenia smacked her lips and continued. "It's like the Geto Boys said, you gotta let a ho be a ho. Say what you want, but someone ought to tell Bentley he can't turn that trick into a housewife. He sure can't turn her into no rapper." Ysenia rolled her eyes and sucked her teeth. Leilani rolled her eyes too, but not in response to Ysenia's comment. It was in response to Ysenia's over-the-top actions, the drama that she seemed to add to everything she said and everything she did.

"I'm not even in that. That shit is a nightmare." Leilani couldn't decide who irritated her more, but she knew she wanted to drop the subject of Desiree altogether. Somehow things always went back to her. Leilani was directing a video, and all people were focusing on was Desiree. Most of them hadn't even heard her flow. It just went to show how blind people were, how they would buy just about anything if it was packaged nicely enough.

"Ooh and I see you doing your thang, Miss Director! Look at you, chica. And if I'm not mistaken, I see you've got you a man too." Ysenia went on a fishing expedition, anxious for a tidbit of gossip. She was in a very provocative mood, it was obvious. She was the type of woman always caught up in some form of drama. She thought it was cute. She also thought it was "acting black," blinded by the gum-snapping, neck-rolling, wig-snatching, loudmouthed hoochies she saw on *Jerry Springer* and *Jenny Jones.*

"We're just friends," Leilani said, blushing. She wasn't about to tell Ysenia all of her business. Besides, she didn't want the reputation that Desiree had.

"Oh. Well, all I have to say is that Desiree better not fuck with me. I'm not like all these other chicks here. I will put that ho in her place!"

"Yeah, well, I gotta go. I've got work to do," Leilani cut her off. She'd had enough of Desiree *and* Ysenia.

Ysenia watched Leilani walk away. She folded her arms. *Leilani is green as hell. She ain't never gonna make it in the industry. Hmph! I should blow Desiree's ass right out of the water. She doesn't know what to do with a nigga like Bentley. That nigga is sleepin' on me. I could make him happy, not a ho like Desiree. And I think I'm going to have to just take that man for myself!* she thought spitefully, the wheels in her mind busy at work concocting a scheme.

"DESIREE, YOU LOOK PERFECT. WE NEED YOU ON THE SET," Leilani told Desiree firmly as soon as she was inside the trailer. "How long on the models?" she continued, not giving Desiree the chance to object.

"Just some powder and we're ready to roll," answered a frazzled makeup artist.

"Ladies, you all look fabulous. My stylists and makeup artists, you all have done a wonderful job. I just want you to

know that everyone really appreciates the work you've done."
Leilani offered the staff a grateful smile, which somewhat
eased the tension in the small, hot trailer. But she had a feeling in her gut that the worst was yet to come.

A large section of Virginia Key Beach was cordoned off for
the shoot. Bodies milled about adjusting lights, reflectors,
and cameras for the master shot that would account for the
majority of the video and some of Dez's scenes. The models
found their way to the set and awaited direction from Sparks
and Leilani. They stood around chatting and adjusting their
skimpy costumes.

Bentley and his entourage made it onto the set, and Desiree instantly joined Bentley. Hype Williams, one of Desiree's
favorite directors, instructed her. "All right, Dez, before we
start shooting the master scene, we want to get some footage
of you and Bentley freestyling with each other," Hype said.
"We're gonna do some with audio and some with no audio.
Just vibe off each other and make it raw and hard-core, all
right?" Hype had been the first to congratulate her on her
deal and promised to direct her first solo video.

Desiree and Bentley did their takes as the crew and cast
stood transfixed. As dynamic as their chemistry was behind
closed doors, it was just as hot when they rapped. Anyone
who had thought that Desiree was just a pretty face, with
her boyfriend writing all of her rhymes, was shown proof of
the contrary. Hype, Leilani, and Sparks took a look at some
of the footage they shot. The grin on Hype's face said it all.
Desiree had that "it" factor that all stars possessed. He had
the crew make some adjustments to the reflectors and the
position of the lights, then proceeded to the master shot.
Ysenia took this as an opportunity to start some shit.

"Sorry, mami, but I need to cut in here, just doing my job."
Ysenia grabbed Bentley by the hand and gave it a squeeze.

Desiree immediately stepped to Ysenia. "Bitch, don't fuck with me."

"I don't know what you're talking about," Ysenia said, grinning.

"Baby, why don't you go relax, okay?" Bentley told Dez, letting go of Ysenia's hand and taking Dez's in his. "This won't take long. I love you," he told her softly before kissing her, but not so softly that Ysenia didn't hear. Ysenia nearly gagged on her envy.

"I love you too," Dez replied loudly, then rolled her eyes at Ysenia and stormed off to the trailer. At least she would have it all to herself, since everyone else was on the set. She decided to freshen up, reapply her sunscreen, and take a little nap. It was over ninety degrees, and she could feel her skin beginning to tingle, although she wasn't so sure that it was from the sun.

They broke for lunch around noon, about seven hours into what was sure to be a very long day. Desiree exited the trailer as the models from the shoot were coming in. Ysenia bumped into her hard, then stood back with her hands on her hips.

"I don't know what your fucking beef is, but you need to check yourself. You don't wanna see me," Dez warned, her cat eyes narrowed into slits.

"Whatever. You don't wanna see me, bitch."

"Bitch? I got your bitch right here." Desiree lunged at Ysenia but didn't have much room to maneuver. A few of the other models stepped between them.

"You must be forgetting who I am, bitch. Your ass is done," Desiree growled, and stormed off.

She contemplated going to Hype and having Ysenia booted from the video, but took a deep breath and decided to go for a walk on the beach. She'd work on some lyrics and relax for an hour while everyone else was too busy eating to disturb her. She had to get her mind right and stay focused. Ysenia had no power over her. She was a nobody.

YSENIA WAITED PATIENTLY AS SHE SAT IN HER RANGE ROVER, the air-conditioning on full blast. She bobbed her head to the P. Diddy CD playing in the sound system. She was a major fan of Diddy's, as well as a frequent face at the lavish parties he often held when he was in town. Ysenia lit a roach and inhaled deeply, being careful not to muss her lipstick. It wouldn't do to ruin her makeup, because at the rate things were going, Desiree was going to do her best to prevent anyone else from getting any shine. But she had something for that bitch.

Ysenia peeped a Camry with tinted windows and sitting-on chrome pull into the parking lot. She extinguished the joint. The Camry pulled up next to her, and the driver's side window rolled down. The boom of Miami bass music blared into the otherwise silent lot. A handsome, athletically built young man grinned at her, flashing a row of gold teeth.

"Nigga, turn that shit down!" she screamed at her younger brother, Junior. He turned the volume down. "You are so tacky, nigga!" she snarled, sucking her teeth at him.

"Whatever, Ysenia, damn!" he said, sulking. Junior was nineteen and wild, and though he considered himself a grown man, Ysenia always treated him like a child. Yet she was only five years older than him. She took care of him, though, so he mostly put up with her bitching and nagging. Plus, she had tons of fine friends. It was better than living with their parents, who were so old-fashioned.

"You got the tape?" she asked, rubbing her hands to-gether.

"Yeah, I got it." Junior opened the glove compartment and pulled out a black VHS tape with a neon-peach-colored label on it. "What you want with this anyway?" he asked, hesitating before he handed it over.

"That's my business! Just chill and let me do my thing." She waved him off. He had served his purpose.

"Whatever," Junior replied absentmindedly while inspecting his own reflection in the rearview mirror. He looked up at her. "I'ma come on the set with you all right," he said matter-of-factly.

"No, you're not. I'm working, this ain't a club."

"I'm just fucking with you. Do your thang, girl." He flashed his grill again and pulled out of the lot. He really didn't care what Ysenia was up to. He knew she would buy his clothes, keep his pockets tight, and keep a roof over his head, and how she did it didn't matter. He made sure no grimy niggas fucked her over in return and looked out for her. It wouldn't do to have his meal ticket feeding someone else.

Ysenia shook her head and chuckled at her brother as his car disappeared around a corner. She loved him to death, so she stayed on his case to keep him out of trouble. She knew spoiling him and taking care of him wasn't the smartest thing to do, but she wasn't going to let him get caught up in the hustling game. Besides, her parents had practically disowned him because he wouldn't act like some preppy white boy. But Ysenia had better things to do than sit around laughing at Junior. She was a woman on a mission.

Ysenia returned to the set and walked straight to Bentley's trailer. She didn't even bother knocking, she just barged in. Bentley was chilling with two of his friends, about to spark an L.

"Bentley, I have to tell you something." Ysenia spoke slowly and carefully. She didn't want to have to reveal her hand in front of Bentley's crew. It wouldn't have the same impact.

"Is that right?" Bentley asked flirtatiously. His heart was enraptured by Desiree, but Ysenia *was* fine.

"Yeah," Ysenia continued, strutting toward him. "This won't take but a second, guys, excuse us." She tossed her dark blond wavy hair. Fuck it, she was gonna take charge of the situation. She grabbed Bentley by the hand and pulled him to the bathroom of the trailer, shutting the door behind them. The bathroom was small, and they were forced to stand body-to-body. Ysenia was exactly as tall as Bentley and looked him directly in the eye.

"You know what, Bentley? You seem like a classy guy; like you deserve nothing but the best," she murmured, leaning toward him and letting her body rub against his seductively. She deftly slipped the tape into his hand. "Peep this flick and think about whether what you're working with now is the very best, and then holler at me. Do it now," she continued in a throaty voice. "Don't hesitate."

Bentley looked at the tape and then at Ysenia and grinned.

"It must be good," he remarked, then licked his lips. Ysenia felt herself get wet. Bentley was so sexy.

"That depends on what you call good." Ysenia grinned back at Bentley, then kissed him on the cheek. She didn't want to appear desperate; she just wanted Bentley to know that she was interested. Ysenia was confident that Bentley would come to her on his own. "Get at me," she breathed into his ear, and then exited the bathroom.

All eyes were firmly planted on Ysenia's backside as she sashayed out the trailer. She threw a little wiggle into her stroll because she knew they were all looking.

"Yo, what was that all about?" Scoop, one of Bentley's

homeys, asked, admiring Ysenia's ass, which was tightly encased in hot pants, as she left the trailer.

"Yo, man, I don't even know," Bentley responded, looking
confused. "She just gave me this tape and told me to get at
her."

"Put that shit in, kid!" Jazzy, his other crony, jumped up
and motioned to the VCR. "It's probably some old freaky
shit. You know how them video hos are!" he continued.

"But nah, man, that chick is like a *real* model. I've seen
her in a bunch of magazines and shit. She's probably seen
that Dez got put on, and now she's trying to get a record
deal too or something," Scoop argued.

"That don't mean nothing! Shit! 'Real models' are freaks
too. I'd say like ninety percent of them are hos. They are the
ones that are all off into that dyke shit and group sex. It's
because they're so used to everybody looking at them and
wearing skimpy clothes and stuff. I'm telling you. I bet she's
on that tape buck ass naked, man. Play that shit!" Jazzy
spoke as if he were an expert on the topic of models, but
truth be told, were he not a part of Bentley's entourage,
there wasn't a model alive who'd give him the time of day.

"Well, *now* I gotta play it! Man, spark up that L and let's
peep this," Bentley said as he popped the tape into the VCR
and settled on the edge of his seat.

The credits rolled, flashing the logo of a small but well-
known Atlanta-based company called Peach Records. They all
knew of the company's founder, Dirty Dan, a lower-budget
version of Luke, who was also a pioneer in bass music, as well
as a champion of free speech. It was obvious that in many
ways he modeled himself after Luther Campbell. Known for
his explicit and by some standards obscene lyrics and stage
shows, Dirty Dan had amassed a street following by recording
catchy call-and-response party anthems with infectious hooks.

He had also gained his fair share of infamy for his many arrests on obscenity charges. Bentley and the entourage waited with bated breath for the tape to start rolling, because they knew there was bound to be some freaky shit on it. Dirty Dan was a man who liked to push the envelope.

Dan had broadened the scope of his business, venturing into adult videos featuring a wildly popular reality-based series called Sinful Strippers, in which he toured the strip clubs of America and abroad and taped the wildest and raunchiest exotic dancers around. This particular tape was titled *Sinful Strippers in Mexico: What Happens in Cancún Stays in Cancún!* The footage was shot Memorial Day weekend of 1999 during the festivities of Black Beach Weekend.

"I knew it was some freak shit!" Jazzy said with a smirk.

"Damn, is she in a porno?" Bentley asked of no one in particular.

"I guess Jazzy was right," Scoop admitted, shaking his head. "Shit, let's see what this freak got!"

Dirty Dan stood with a microphone on a small makeshift stage erected in the middle of a sandy white beach. Bentley fast-forwarded the tape. "I ain't trying to hear that country, 'Bama-ass nigga stutter and stammer," he cracked.

"Ayo, stop that shit. You gonna pass it up, man," Jazzy said eagerly.

Half a dozen young women in T-shirts and thongs joined Dan on the stage. One by one the girls were doused with buckets of water until their T-shirts were drenched and transparent. The last contestant on the stage grabbed her T-shirt and ripped it off with a flourish, exposing a large pair of undulating breasts. That last contestant was Desiree.

"Damn! Ain't that your girl?" Scoop said, all hyped up.

Bentley said nothing, but silenced Scoop with a motion of his hand. He leaned forward and stroked his goatee, eyeing the screen intently. He continued to watch in silence as the contestants followed Desiree's lead and all stripped down to their skimpy G-strings. The girls gyrated about the stage, inciting the crowd with their blatantly sexual moves. Throngs of men salivated and groped at the young women, who began to touch each other suggestively. Piles and piles of crumpled bills began to build up around the stage. Dan collected the cash in a plastic grocery bag.

"Do you wanna see more?" he yelled into the mic to the horny crowd of men. They replied with a deafening roar.

"Then flash that cash, brothers!" Dan screamed. "And remember . . . what happens in Cancún stays in Cancún!"

The dancers, led by Desiree, removed their thongs. Desiree opened her legs far apart and then swooped to the ground in a crouching position. Her waxed pubic area gaped open, exposing her inner lips for the whole world to see.

Scoop and Jazzy looked at Bentley, who remained expressionless. He didn't bat an eyelash when Desiree began to stroke herself, tossing her head back in ecstasy. One dancer began to lick and suck at Desiree's nipples. The crowd went bananas. More cash collected on the stage. Dan continued stuffing the money in the bag, which was now bulging.

Another dancer replaced Desiree's hand with her face, going down on her with reckless abandon. Desiree's hips bucked wildly as the girls all licked, sucked, and fingered any body part within reach. Dan filled a second plastic bag as the orgy continued. Bentley shut off the tape.

"Out," was all he said. Scoop and Jazzy didn't need to hear anything more and immediately left Bentley alone in the trailer.

He sank back into the plush seats, covered his face with his hands, and inhaled deeply.

Damn, he thought. *What the fuck have I gotten myself into?*

CHAPTER 17

DESIREE CAME BACK FROM HER STROLL FEELING REFRESHED and ready to tackle anything, even Leilani and Ysenia. The ocean was one of the things she loved most about Miami. It always made her feel connected to something. All of her ancestors had lived near the Atlantic. Her family in the Dominican Republic, even her African ancestors, whoever and wherever they were, were probably looking at that same water. For once, thinking about her family and where she came from didn't make her feel sad or angry. She had a new family now. Bentley and Sparks, Titanium Records, were her fam. She was their first lady, their princess, and their Queen Bee all in one. She decided to see what Bentley was up to before she had her makeup touched up.

"Hey, baby," she cooed. She kissed him, but his lips were unresponsive.

"What's the matter?" she asked him. She hoped he hadn't heard about her minor scrape with Ysenia and started tripping. Bentley didn't say anything; he just grabbed the remote, punched rewind, and then pushed play. Desiree sucked in her breath as if she'd been punched in the gut. That was how it felt to see the tape.

"Where did you get that? Who gave that to you?" she demanded.

"What happens in Cancún stays in Cancún?" he spat at her, his voice full of sarcasm. "Obviously not."

"I can explain." Desiree's mouth felt like the Sahara. Her throat was burning.

"I don't really want to hear it."

"Can I just talk to you?" she begged. Dez reached for his hand, her eyes pleading.

"Don't touch me, Dez." Bentley dodged her like she had leprosy.

This can't be happening, she thought in a panic. *What did you think? That it would disappear? That he'd never find out? You're so stupid! You aren't good for shit! How could you think anything good would ever happen to you? You're nothing!* She shook her head violently.

"That was a mistake from a long time ago," she began.

"It was two years ago," he said. "I hardly consider that a long time."

"I was young."

"Yeah, right. What, twenty-one, twenty-two? That's old enough to know what you're doing. You ain't shit but a freak. Be a woman and own up to that shit."

"No. I was younger than that." Dez choked on her words as she began to cry. She felt the bile rising in her stomach. She resisted the urge to heave.

"Please." He looked at her with contempt. "And spare me the tears. You're a good fucking actress, I'll give you that."

"You've gotta let me explain. Hear my side of the story. I was a little girl." Bentley was headed toward the door. She couldn't let him walk out of her life. She couldn't let her dreams blow up in her face.

Tell him the truth, she thought. *If he really loves you, he'll understand.* His hand was on the knob. *He's leaving you. They'll always leave you. No man in his right mind would want to stay with you. You're dirty!* Sucia!

"I was only sixteen!" she blurted. Bentley froze. He turned around to face her.

"What?"

"I said I was only sixteen."

"You really expect me to believe you're what, eighteen or nineteen?"

"I'm eighteen. I turned eighteen on my birthday yester-day."

"Get the fuck outta here. I done heard it all now."

"B will you please just sit down and let me explain? I know it looks bad, really bad. And I'm ashamed and sorry that I ever did it. But I honestly just didn't know any bet-ter. I'm a different person now, and it's partly because of you. You and Sparks gave me a reason to believe in myself. You gave me a shot. Don't take that away from me. You said you could tell that I'd been through some shit, and that you respected me. Let me tell you what it is. If you wanna walk after you hear me out, then okay. But please don't go until you hear me. I love you. Please?" Desiree had no pride left. She knelt on the dirty floor of the trailer, her makeup streaked, her hair standing all over her head. He sat down.

"You've got two minutes," Bentley informed her, totally devoid of any emotion.

Desiree felt her heart sink. At precisely that moment she knew that Bentley had been full of shit the whole time. All that talk about respecting her gangsta. When it came time for him to ride, he didn't even have the patience to hear her out. How the hell could she begin to explain, in two minutes, how she ended up in a porn tape at such a tender age? She'd been played, she of all people, the master of games. Desiree felt a fury unlike any other building within her.

"Well, if that's all I have then fuck it. My whole name takes damn near two minutes to say. So fuck it, be that way. As long as I have my deal, that's all that really matters. I don't have to fucking grovel for you," Desiree spat, half meaning it. "All I want to know is who gave you the fucking tape? If it had been any other time, things would be different. But somebody here is deliberately trying to fuck me and I want to know who it is!"

"Does it matter? Does that change the fact that you a ho?" Bentley's eyes were daggers. The comment made Desiree cringe inside; she was so angry she balled up her fists until her knuckles were white. The way she was feeling, the situation could get much uglier very quickly.

"Fuck you! Fuck you, you bitch ass motherfucker!" Desiree shouted at him, and this time she really meant it. Then it hit her like a ton of bricks. *Leilani!* She had clearly been coveting Dez's post. How could she not be jealous? If she could get her out of the way, Leilani would be free to milk Sparks *and* Bentley for any and everything she could. She wouldn't be surprised if Leilani had tried to kick it to Bentley, even though she was acting like it was all about Sparks. Who else would want to see her fail? Who else would go to such great lengths to make her look bad? In a fury she ran out the trailer, leaving Bentley behind. She was out for blood. It was real personal now.

Desiree ran all over the set like a madwoman in search of Leilani. She found her sitting on a stool, munching on a plate of crudités. She looked beat, but not as beat as she was going to after Desiree got through with her. Swift and silent as a ninja, Desiree grabbed Leilani's ponytail and threw her to the ground, knocking over the stool.

"You fucking bitch. You couldn't stand to see me get ahead, could you?" Desiree snarled at the astonished Leilani as she tried to stand. Desiree administered a swift kick to Leilani's rib cage with her stiletto-heeled, calf-length boots. Leilani winced in pain and dropped back to the ground.

"Dez. Please, stop. Why are you doing this?" Leilani begged, holding her midsection. A trail of blood dribbled from her lip. A small crowd gathered to observe the disturbance, but no one bothered to stop it.

"Bitch, you know why!" Desiree sat on top of Leilani and pimp-slapped her. Then she slapped her again. She balled her fist up tightly and prepared to clock her, but was prevented from doing so by Sparks, who had come to Leilani's aid. Leilani lay on the ground crying and holding her face as Desiree struggled to release herself from Sparks's iron grip. Bentley came running up to them out of breath.

"Dez, chill!" He grabbed her by the shoulders and shook her hard. "It wasn't Leilani," he screamed at her.

"What?" Desiree was confused, breathing heavily, her breasts heaving up and down

"It wasn't her. Leilani didn't give me the tape," Bentley explained.

"What tape?" Leilani asked, bewildered, as she put a hand to her mouth. Her saliva was thick with mucus and blood, and her bottom lip was split. Sparks knelt beside her and cradled her in his arms.

"We need to talk, the four of us, in private. Now!" Bentley barked and dragged a kicking and screaming Desiree back to his trailer. Sparks and Leilani looked at each other, both at a loss for words, confused about exactly what was going on.

"You okay, baby?" Sparks asked Leilani gently as he held her.

"I guess so," she sniffed, shaking with fear and confusion. Leilani felt a wave of embarrassment wash over her as the entire cast and crew of the video stared at the scene.

"Come on, boo. Let's find out what the hell is going on." Sparks scooped Leilani up and led her, limping, to Bentley's trailer.

Sparks turned the latch on the flimsy lock of the trailer door and then methodically went around the trailer shutting all the windows. He pushed a button that automatically released metal shutters that covered all the windows, including the windshield. He cranked on the AC full blast and sat in the swiveling passenger's seat.

"What the fuck is going on?" he asked, exasperated. Bentley and Dez eyed each other. He shook his head at her, then buried his face in his hands. Dez cleared her throat.

"Somebody gave Bentley a tape that has me on it doing some things that I'm not proud of. I thought it was Leilani, since she's been giving me so much grief lately. That's why I kicked your ass. My bad." Desiree glared at Leilani, then felt a twinge of guilt. She looked down at her nails, rather than at Leilani's bruised and bloodied face. *She had it coming,* she thought, to ease her conscience.

"Well, what the fuck is on the tape?" Leilani barked through swollen lips. Dez's guilt disappeared instantly. She gave Leilani the stankeye.

"Why don't you see for yourself? Sparks, why don't you take a look at your *superstar*. Now maybe you'll talk to me before you go signing folks on the spot," Bentley snarled sarcastically, walking over to the television and switching on the tape. Leilani and Sparks watched in a combination of shock and horror before Desiree cut off the set angrily. She felt like a sideshow freak on display.

"What Bentley is conveniently leaving out is that I was

only sixteen when I made the tape. Are you satisfied? You've humiliated me, okay?" Desiree glared at Bentley.

"Wait a minute. That tape can't be *that* old," Leilani pondered aloud.

"How old *are* you, Dez?" Sparks asked.

"Eighteen," she answered. "I turned eighteen yesterday."

"You can't be eighteen. I know you. I've seen your ID, your place. You were my friend," Leilani said in disbelief, holding her lip.

"Dez, you are full of shit. Sparks, please give the bitch the boot," Bentley hissed angrily. Dez rolled her eyes.

"Look, I'm, I mean, I was a runaway. I left home when I was sixteen and met Dan not long after I got to Miami. I was living with a woman named Ginger, but then she got all religious and tried to control my life, so when Dan offered me a new life, I took it. He said he cared about me and that he was going to make me a star. I trusted him because I was young and hungry. After about a year, I realized that he wasn't going to get my career off the ground unless it was as a porn star, so I broke it off. That was about a year ago. Now here we are."

The three of them were silent for several moments.

Leilani was the first to speak up. "Why did you run away?"

"I don't want to say. Does it really matter? Life was fucked-up where I was, so I left." Desiree's eyes were nearly black with anger. Leilani was still trying to be all in her mix.

"Are you telling the truth now? I mean, are you legal?" Sparks asked, stroking his goatee.

"Yes, I am. I don't have anything that shows my real age. Why would I? But I'm sure you can verify it. I turned eighteen yesterday."

"I'm just asking because if you weren't, your deal wouldn't be legally binding," Sparks replied.

"Well, I am. So you can't get rid of me that easy." Dez rolled her eyes and neck.

"If I wanted to get rid of you, I could. There's always a loophole, Dez, remember that. But I don't want to get rid of you." Sparks looked at her and grinned.

Dez, Leilani, and Bentley screamed in unison, "What?!"

"Baby, look how much trouble she's caused," Leilani whined. "Look what she did to my face! You mean you want her to stay?"

"She can't possibly be reppin' our label!" Bentley countered.

Dez stood mute, in total disbelief.

"Dez has skills out of this world. You name one female out there that can outflow her. If I toss her aside because of the tape, someone else will sign her," Sparks explained, which made Dez smile.

"But what about our reputation? We worked hard as hell to build this label. You gonna give her a chance to destroy it?" Bentley was heated.

"Dez ain't gonna destroy the label. She's gonna take us to a new level. Eve used to strip, and so did Trina. It's not a big deal," Sparks explained. Bentley opened his mouth to object. Sparks cut him off. "Hear me out. That tape is illegal. She was a minor. It's child pornography. With or without us, Dez, you're about to come into a lot of money," Sparks continued.

"Sue Dan? This isn't totally his fault. I lied to him," Desiree interjected.

"How much money have you seen from doing that tape? Not shit. But that nigga's seen plenty. You were a little girl, a runaway. He shouldn't be allowed to profit off a child, I'm sorry. Wrong is wrong. We've got a legal department and a P.R. department, and that's what we pay them for—and very well, I might add. The tape is illegal to own, illegal to buy, and illegal to sell. Anyone who posts it on the Internet can get sued or go to jail. Child pornography is no joke. Dan don't want that kind of trouble. He'll offer you a nice settlement for your pain and suffering," Sparks finished.

"This shit won't die," Bentley protested.

"Bentley, you just do what you do, and let me handle the legalities." Sparks stood and put his arm around Dez. "Dez, you family now, period. Family don't turn its back on family. We're gonna handle this together. When you're ready to talk, I'm here to listen. I can only imagine what life has been like for you." Sparks gave her a reassuring smile.

"This is bullshit," Leilani huffed.

"Yo, chill, babe," Sparks told Leilani.

"She's right, this is bullshit," Bentley cosigned for Leilani.

"I'm gonna handle this. Don't worry, Dez. We gonna take a break. Get yourself together," Sparks said to Dez, but she wasn't hearing it.

"I want to know who did this to me. Bentley won't tell me who gave him the tape. It's gotta be somebody on the set. Whoever it is, they're probably laughing their ass off at me. How can I work like that?" Dez said, playing on Sparks's sympathy.

"Bentley, who gave you the tape? This shit is gonna cost us money. Who are you protecting?" Sparks asked, beginning to get irritated.

"I'm not protecting anybody. I just wanted to hear what Dez had to say for herself before she went off and tried to handle some personal shit between her and that chick; the lead girl, Ysenia," Bentley responded defensively.

"Bet. I got something for that bitch," Dez huffed, ready to go kick Ysenia's ass.

"Me too," Sparks interjected gruffly. "Leilani, go tell her

that her services are no longer required. Then call her agent and explain what happened so we don't have any bullshit. Tell them Ysenia will get paid, but she's got to leave the set immediately."

"What?" Leilani asked in shock.

"She's the troublemaker. This shit is costing us time, money, and most of all, difficulty within my family. Why? Probably because she wants to fuck my brother. Don't nobody have time for that shit. This is a business. After you handle that, meet with me and Hype. We need to decide what to do about the video; whether or not we're going to scrap the footage, bump up one of the other extras, and start over, or whether to change the concept. We still have another day of shooting, but we can't afford to get behind. Will an hour be enough time for you to get it together, Dez?" Sparks asked her.

"Yeah, as long as that bitch is gone," Dez replied smugly.

"Leilani, send makeup over here. Dez, try and get along with her. Bentley, we'll move you to another trailer or something. She needs this space more than you do. Come on, man. Let me holla at you." Sparks was clearly in control of the situation. He led Bentley out of the trailer.

Dez and Leilani glared at each other before Leilani exited the trailer as well.

That bitch know she don't want none of this! Dez thought to herself. Then she flopped onto a chair and breathed a sigh of relief. She had no idea what the future held for her, but she knew that things couldn't get any worse. After all, Sparks had assured her that her deal remained intact and that she was entitled to some dough. Things could only get better, couldn't they?

PART 3

RESPECT

CHAPTER 18

The aftermath—September 2001

L EILANI SAT AT THE VANITY MIRROR IN HER SOUTH BEACH apartment, studying her face in the mirror. Dez had clocked her good. The bruises were fading, though, and were barely visible thanks to a generous application of Dermablend cover stick and MAC foundation. But Leilani knew they were there, and that pissed her off. She attempted to cover her face with her hair, but only succeeded in looking utterly foolish. Frustrated, she threw her comb across the room. Angry tears spilled from her eyes. This had to be a joke. Any minute now, Leilani expected a camera crew to come crashing into the room to tell her that she was on television and everything that had transpired was an awful joke. Desiree could *not* be on her way to superstardom! It was ridiculous!

From what Leilani could see, Dez had no real education and had done no real hard work. She just popped on the scene as a model and blew up. She hadn't even begun to pay the dues that Leilani had paid to get to where she had gotten as a model. It simply wasn't fair, and she had to think of a way to level the playing field.

I can't believe that bitch hit me! If she hadn't snuck me, I would have stuck her ass! Leilani thought. *Ysenia puts her business on blast and causes all that trouble, and all she gets is fired. Dez kicks my ass, and I have to work for her to make her look good! This makes no sense at all!* Leilani frowned and paced about her apartment.

"Sparks ain't shit!" she said aloud. "I can see that now. He'd put her before me again if he had the chance, all because she's on his label. It's always about pussy and money with these niggas. Shit, her flow ain't all that. Okay, she's nice, but damn, why does shit have to always work out for her? Why does she get all the breaks? She ain't nothing but a ho." Leilani was furious and holding a full-on conversation with herself.

"Well, not this time. Somehow Dez is gonna be out of the Titanium Records family, and I'm going to be *in* as the true first lady, the boss's wife! Shit! Dez is like a roach, though. She'll manage to find some way to stick around. But it's all good. She will bow down. I'll see to it," Leilani swore.

"She has zero class. She's all sex. Why can't they see through that? What's she got that I haven't got besides fake boobs and a porno tape? Ha! Well, I can think of one thing that I have that she doesn't, and that's the top dog, Sparks. I'll do whatever it takes to make sure that man stays mine. I'll even get knocked up if I have to." Leilani grinned deviously as she patted her pancake-flat stomach. She arched her back and stuck her belly way out to see what she'd look like with child. "That's more Dez's style, but drastic times call for drastic measures," Leilani stated with disdain.

"Hell, I did not go to college, I did not give up modeling to become Dez's do-girl. These sacrifices are going to pay off one way or another! But Sparks is the key! Right now he's my life. There's nothing more important than winning his heart and his trust. I've just got to fight fire with fire, starting immediately. Shit! Once I hit Sparks with the poom poom, it's a wrap, baby." Leilani grinned with satisfaction. She knew what she had to do.

EVERY DAY SPARKS WONDERED WHY HE WAS EVEN IN THE MUSIC industry. He hated the attention it brought and all the drama it entailed. Everyone was grimy; they were all out for self. He had to deal with A&R reps and his other staff, producers, distributors, the media, and his artists. What was the payoff, fame? Fame was overrated. Sure, there was money. But what good was money unless there was someone special for him to share it with? He'd gotten over the initial hype of buying extravagant gifts for himself, friends, and family. He'd secured investments in his future; he owned stocks, bonds, and real estate. But it all still felt empty.

He'd done the groupie thing. But he never derived much pleasure from using women and throwing them away. He remembered how happy his parents had been when they were alive, and he wanted something like that. Sparks wanted a family. Bentley had been so young when their folks died. Sparks surmised that Bentley tried to replace his longing for a mother figure with all the different women he bedded. Sparks was happy when his brother seemed to be willing to slow down and give love a chance with Dez.

At first Sparks believed that he'd met someone special that he could share not only his fortune with but his dreams and even the hard times. He thought both he and his brother had lucked up and found the women of their dreams. But Dez and Bentley's relationship now seemed dead, and there was something unsettling about Leilani. She was beautiful, she was smart, and she had a bright future ahead of her. But Leilani was cold. Everything about her seemed calculated; she was totally devoid of passion. She also seemed to lack a heart. When he'd tried to discuss Dez's situation with her, Leilani just called Dez nasty names and pressured him to drop her from the label.

Leilani had even gone so far as to accuse Sparks and Dez of having an affair, and if there was one thing Sparks couldn't stand, it was an insecure woman. Leilani claimed that the reason Sparks was giving Dez a chance was that he had feelings for her. He'd told her that the whole idea was nonsense. He and Bentley were brothers, and he would never date the same woman his brother had dated. But was Leilani that far off the mark? The truth of the matter was that he was, in fact, feeling Dez. She was the total package. She was beautiful, talented, and street-smart. She was confident and she had fire. And because he got to spend so much time with her, he discovered that Dez was a sweet and compassionate person. She just hid behind her tough-girl image. But what difference did it make if he was feeling her or not? Dez was off-limits. Or was she?

BENTLEY COULDN'T BELIEVE WHAT HAD HAPPENED. FOR THE first time, he felt love for a female, but just as he had already known, bitches weren't shit. He thought that Dez was special, that if "the one" existed, she was it. But he was wrong.

How was she different from any other groupie besides the fact that she could flow? She'd whored herself out for the whole world to see, and made that country, 'Bama-ass Dirty Dan a fortune in the process.

Bentley couldn't refute the fact that he still had love in his heart for Dez. But his head was telling him to cut the bitch loose. When word got out, if he was linked to her, he'd be the laughing stock of the industry. He'd look like a trick and a sucker.

"How the fuck does Sparks think that this can possibly be good for business?" Bentley wondered aloud. "This ain't gonna cause shit but drama."

But there were still so many unanswered questions he had. How did Dez get away with lying about her age for so long? Why did she run away? What was the nature of her relationship with Dan? Dez had tried to explain, but he wouldn't listen; he had his pride. All she was going to do was spit some game to him. He knew he definitely couldn't trust her, so what difference could it make, what she had to say? It would probably be all lies.

But all Bentley could seem to focus on were her angelic face, her sweet lips, the sound of her moans when they made love, and her soft, warm body. He could still recall the way she called his name. How was he supposed to pretend that she was never in his life? And what were his other options? The thought of his future without her seemed empty, like it was lacking something.

Focus! He had to stay focused! He just had to forget about Dez. But how? She was his labelmate; he'd have to see her. Bentley hoped to God that the old saying about time healing all wounds was true, because he was hurting and he couldn't see an end in sight.

FOR DEZ THE NIGHTMARISH PART OF THE VIDEO HAD ENDED, but her life was still like a bad dream. Surprisingly, things on the set had turned out okay after the videotape fiasco. There had been a few changes in wardrobe and location, and the concept of the video was changed. Sparks and Hype had decided to give it a rawer, edgier vibe and forgo the cliché models and bottles theme that had been oversaturating the airwaves in practically every rap video. They scrapped most of the celebrity cameos, opting instead for footage of the real Miami streets—Liberty City, Overtown, Carol City. The result was a unique video that focused on Dez's and Bentley's lyrical skills and Hype's famous special effects. Adding to the hardcore vibe of the video was the tension between her and Bentley. Their freestyle battle was phenomenal and very personal but had generated such positive feedback from test audiences that Sparks decided to release the results as a remix.

But the battle didn't do anything to help matters between Dez and Bentley. He avoided her at all costs and didn't speak to her when they did happen to cross paths. Dez offered futilely to sit down and explain the chain of events that led to her making the tape. But his attitude was that she'd had her chance; why would he listen to her after she'd had ample time to concoct some kind of story to arouse his sympathy?

K.G. paged her incessantly, but he was the last person she felt like talking to. In a brief conversation with him she had told him about her record deal and that the relationship was over. But he didn't believe her. He told her that she was going through a phase and that if she needed time, he would give it to her. He told her that he was confident that she'd hate the music industry; therefore, he'd let her explore her options and he'd be there for her when she inevitably "came home to Daddy." It was the most blatant form of denial she'd ever seen.

After their talk she ignored the messages, often deleting them without reading them. He was starting to freak her out a little; most men would have gotten the hint. They'd had a thing, now it was over, couldn't he understand that? She'd never told him that she loved him. He'd spent an awful lot of money on her, but that was the nature of the game. Besides, he had plenty of money; the chips he'd laced her with wouldn't kill him.

She had even cut up the American Express card and phoned them to cancel her account. He'd served his purpose; there was really no reason in juicing him any further. Besides, she was an emerging star. Fashion labels and jewelers would hunt her down to wear their clothes and jewelry. She wouldn't need a man to take her on a shopping spree.

Dez tried to focus on her work instead of her pain, but it was hard. Though she was extremely busy, she couldn't get Bentley out of her mind. Within days of shooting the video, she was off to New York to begin working on her album and publicize the remix with Bentley. She was staying with Sparks at his home in the Hamptons, where he had a complete state-of-the-art home studio and a helicopter pad. It made everything she'd previously thought of as the hotness pale in comparison. Dez had hoped she would be staying in the city, where she could really take a bite out of the Big Apple, but Sparks wasn't hearing it. He insisted on total dedication to the project and didn't want her distracted by the nightlife or his brother.

Sparks also wanted to make sure that they capitalized on the controversy that had started to swirl around the label. He'd already orchestrated several brief, carefully staged casual appearances at a few nightclubs and restaurants, which had generated a lot of buzz in the media. Initially, Sparks had tried to keep the news of the Cancún tape as muted as possible, but Ysenia had other ideas.

When Sparks, Dez, and Dan began mediation about a settlement regarding the tape and word leaked out to the press, Ysenia really had a field day. She claimed to have heard through the grapevine Dez's true age, and stated that she only showed Bentley the tape to help Dez and not harm her. Ysenia was crafty, though, Sparks had to admit. She'd obviously hired a lawyer who was coaching her on how to dance across the fine line of defamation of character and exploitation of a minor. As long as Ysenia phrased her wording just so, it was difficult to do much to stop her from talking about Dez, and Ysenia was a master at manipulating words. Ysenia was very careful to separate her opinion from actual fact, and spoke only about Dez the adult, although technically, the only time Ysenia had had contact with Dez as an adult was at the video shooting.

Was Dez really a porn star? Was she sleeping with both brothers? Where had she come from? What was she really about? Inquiring minds wanted to know. The rumor mill was spinning out of control, and the media were in a frenzy. Sparks knew that if he let Dez roam the streets of New York alone, it was like sending out a sheep amongst the wolves. He didn't want her to be cornered anywhere by overzealous journalists or paparazzi without her having first undergone the proper media training. Sparks knew that Dez wasn't ready for that scenario.

Sparks assured Dez that under his watchful eye everything would work itself out. He knew that the only bad press was no press and insisted that all the hype would make buyers more curious if Dez could just bite the bullet and deal with it. But that didn't give Dez any comfort. Ysenia was laughing all the way to the bank, *and* she'd totally fucked up Dez's relationship with Bentley. What kind of vindication would she ever receive? Sparks said that Dez's success was the best revenge, but Dez wanted Ysenia to pay in spades.

Sparks had become like a big brother to her, and for that she was grateful. But there was a gaping hole where her heart used to be, and his friendship simply couldn't fill it. Still, he tried. He couldn't help but notice the sadness in her pretty brown eyes; he felt helpless to do anything, and it frustrated him. The more time he spent with Dez, the more he could see that she was truly a good person. Beyond her hard core and aloofness, when he got to the real Dez, he saw that she was energetic and funny. He realized that people never got around to seeing it, because they were always after her for something. So she'd built walls around her heart to protect herself. He'd stayed up many a night wondering what had happened to her; she'd obviously been hurt, and he was determined to find out what her real story was.

One night while they were recording in the studio, Dez couldn't concentrate. She flubbed her lines, and even forgot some of them, even though she had written them herself.

"Dez, come out here," Sparks said over the intercom that piped into the soundproof booth of the recording studio. Tired and frustrated, she removed her headphones, set them on a stool, and joined Sparks at the mixing console.

"Yo! What the fuck is the matter, Dez?" he interrogated her. "You're so off today. Is the shit with my brother still bothering you? It's been over a month."

"Yeah," she admitted softly. "He acts like he doesn't even know me. And he said he loved me. I thought that love meant giving people chances. I guess I fell for the okeydoke. He never cared about me. He won't even give me a chance to explain how I came to make that tape." Dez fought hard to prevent the tears that were welling in her eyes from falling.

"Look, Dez, that's my brother. I know he had love for you. Y'all had just met, but I saw how he felt about you. The problem was that you both had problems before you could build a foundation. He still cares, trust me. But he's not that mature. Me, on the other hand, I'm Mr. Maturity," Sparks kidded, making a funny face and smoothing out his School House Rock T-shirt. Dez managed to crack a tiny smile. "Why don't you tell me? I'm a good listener. Telling someone will help," Sparks finished, taking her hand in his.

"I don't know," she started.

"We fam, right?" Sparks asked her, staring deep into her eyes. *Damn, she is so beautiful. My brother is a fool,* he thought, then felt guilty for thinking it. He pulled out a cigar and began rolling a blunt in an effort to distract himself from his thoughts.

"Of course, Sparks. But it's a really long story. And it's so fucked-up. Right about now you're the only friend I've got. If I tell you, I might lose you. I couldn't bear that," Dez confided. She grabbed a bottle of cognac from a nearby table and poured herself a stiff drink.

"You won't lose me. I'm from Harlem. I've seen it all and done it all. I swear I won't think any differently of you. Do you trust me?"

"Yeah."

"Then tell me. Maybe I can help. Maybe I can get Bentley to listen to you, or help you explain things," he offered.

"No!" she responded vehemently. "This stays between me and you. Swear to me," Dez said, panicked.

"I put it on everything. I'll take whatever you tell me to the grave. Here, blaze this, and relax." Sparks handed her the blunt and she lit it, inhaling deeply.

"Okay, here goes . . . It's not like I thought the shit would never come back to haunt me. I knew that it would eventually, because what's done in the dark will always come to light. And Lord knows I had it coming because karma is a mother-fucker. But then again, isn't karma just a bunch of bullshit? I mean, think of all the babies that die every day that never did anything to anyone. Did they have it coming to them? Did they deserve the bad things that happened to them?" Dez rambled.

"Stop stalling, Dez. I'm not judging you, remember?" Sparks said firmly.

"Okay, okay. People have all these ideas in their head about me, who I am, what I'm about. The truth is that no-body knows me cuz I barely know my own damn self. No one can say shit to me unless they been through what I've been through. Nobody else could begin to even understand. I didn't ask for the cards that I was dealt. I only played the game the best way that I knew how. I cheated a lot, too, but I had to do what I had to do to stay in the game, to stay alive. I couldn't just quit. I wasn't some suburban girl who could call on mommy and daddy whenever I got in a pinch. I can't control where I was born and how I grew up. Because if I could, I would have chosen some fly shit, not the bullshit I had to live through."

"Let me give you some advice, Dez," Sparks interrupted. "Don't bend over. You don't have to apologize with me or with anyone else for who you are. Fearlessly be yourself. If other people can't see how special you are, if they can't see past what you've been through to who you are now, then it's their fault. Not yours. You've gotta stop giving folks a dis-claimer. It's like giving them permission to judge you." He smiled at her. Dez felt her heart flutter a bit. He was so cute, just like his brother. And he seemed to truly care for her, but then again, so had his brother. The painful memory made her tense up. Instinctively, Sparks sensed this.

"Look, Dez. Why don't you tell me about who you are? Who were you before you ran away from home?" Sparks prodded gently.

"Well," Desiree started cautiously, "I was a good girl. I got good grades, stayed out of trouble. I had friends, but mostly, I kind of stuck to myself. My homelife was really fucked-up. My mother was Dominican. My dad was African American. They met when my mother was in high school, right after her graduation they got married, and a few months later I came along." Desiree began to feel herself loosen up, but was uncertain if it was due to Sparks's caring nature or the cognac.

"My mother's family had a fit, because my mom could have gone to community college right away, then maybe gotten a scholarship to a four-year school. She was real smart. But she had to put that all on hold," Dez explained.

"Do you feel like the reason she didn't go to school was your fault?" Sparks asked.

"Sometimes . . . sometimes I feel like the world would be better off if I hadn't been born. Mami wanted to become a doctor, she used to say so all the time, but couldn't on account of having me. She used to always talk about how far along in school she would be if I hadn't been born."

"I'm glad you were born." Sparks smiled. Desiree smiled back.

"So was my papi. I was Papi's pride and joy. Papi was a hustler if there ever was one. He did whatever he had to do to provide for me and Mami. It's not like I remember it all, but you know, people talk. They say he used to do petty shit like snatch chains and steal cars, but then his best friend got killed in a robbery and he just put the shit down. Just like that. And dig this, he became a garbageman!" Dez laughed.

"He used to stink to high heaven every time he came home. I was only like seven when he died, but I do remember that smell just like it was yesterday. It fucks me up because I can't walk past a Dumpster without missing my papi." Dez smiled at the memory.

"Yo, garbagemen make good money!" Sparks kidded. "Plus, they get first dibs on all the good stuff people throw away. I used to watch *Roc*."

"You so crazy!" Dez giggled, then continued with a sigh. "Yeah, Roc was cheap, but Papi was generous. If I asked for a dollar for some ice cream, he'd break me off with five instead. He always told me that anything I ever needed in life, he would provide. I would never have to count on any man but him for anything until I got married. He constantly told me how pretty I was and lavished me with toys, stuffed animals, dolls, and other trinkets. He was the first man to spoil me, and I knew how to work it. He set the standard for every man I ever thought about seriously in my life."

"Your father sounds like he was a good man," Sparks said.

"Yeah, he was a good man. But one night he took a walk to the little corner store and a car ran him down and kept on going. It turns out the driver was high off PCP and thought he was in a rocket ship and shit. He crashed a few blocks down the street. He ended up in a wheelchair and in jail, but fuck it, the damage was already done. My father was dead, and my moms was only like twenty-five then and had never worked. All of a sudden she's got to hold it down for herself and me."

"I'm sorry," Sparks said.

"It's okay. The one thing that gives me comfort about Papi's death is that he made his peace with the Lord when he was alive. My family was really religious. My papi and I used to go to church all the time. On Wednesday nights we would go to Bible study at his church in Harlem, a Baptist church. The kind of church that had a choir so strong that you thought they would blow the roof off the church when they sang. Then sometimes he came with me and Mami to mass, because Mami was Catholic and she made me go to confession and get baptized a Catholic and everything. Papi didn't care, as long as I knew about the Lord and how good he was. He taught me how to pray and what it meant to be saved. I was really young, but those are things about Papi I can never forget. I tried to so many times. From the time I left home, I tried to erase every bit of scripture I'd ever heard from my head. When I lost Papi, I lost my faith. But like I've heard some folks say, if you train a child up in the right path, he won't stray from it. Or something like that. Anyway, my papi was saved, so I know that he is in heaven." Sparks said nothing; he only smiled encouragingly, so Dez continued her story.

"If he was alive, maybe my life would be totally different. Maybe I'd be a doctor, or even a teacher or something. Maybe Mami would have had a chance to be a better parent. My dad had a few benefits with his job, so we had a little something to live off for a while. But I think it just got to be too much for Mami. She couldn't keep up the note on our little crib in Queens. So she swallowed her pride, and we went to my grandparents' for a minute, but that didn't really work out. My mom was different after all that shit happened. She only cared about kicking it. She was always in the streets with her friends, fucking with this nigga and that nigga. Not taking care of me and shit. My grandma got real sick, and my grandfather said my mother had to change her ways or bounce, so she bounced. She left me with them and did her thing, even though her parents were old and sick. She didn't even care about me. Finally, when my grandparents were both in the hospital, my mother came back and got me. It was only because she didn't have a choice, though. They both died soon after that. That was the last time I can actually remember feeling loved and loving someone in return no matter what. I thank God that I had my dad and my grandparents, even if it wasn't for that long."

"That's a good way to look at it, Dez. You were blessed to have them. But I know you can't help but think about all the things you didn't have. Mothers are important to daughters. They teach them how to be women," Sparks reasoned.

"Yeah, but it's a good thing I learned from her how *not* to be instead of how to be."

"So things didn't go so well when she came back?" Sparks asked.

"Nah. When Mami came back, she had a job and a fiancé named Ernesto. Ernesto wasn't shit. He just mooched off of her. He didn't work, at least not a real job, he drank like a fish, he was fat and sloppy and disgusting. I don't know what she saw in him. At least I didn't for a while, but when you grow up in New York, you learn fast. It didn't take me too long—maybe I was like eleven—to figure out that my mother was on that shit. She was sniffing coke, and guess who was giving it to her? Ernesto. He was a do-boy for his brother Lou, who was running things uptown, so he always had a stash available."

"Dominican Lou?"

"Yeah, you know about him?" Dez asked.

"Uh, yeah, I heard of him," Sparks stammered. Dominican Lou had been one of the most feared drug lords uptown during the late eighties and early nineties. Everyone had heard of him.

"Well, indirectly, he's the source of my problems."

"I guess so," Sparks said, but he didn't necessarily agree with her logic.

"I know that no one *made* her sniff coke," Dez replied, nearly reading his mind. "And if Ernesto and Lou weren't slanging, she'd have gotten it from somewhere else. But still. He's got some kind of accountability," Dez stated, vexed. "She was just all the way out there. It got to the point where he could control her with that shit, heart, body, and mind. He treated her like shit. He was always telling her she wasn't shit, and occasionally, he'd kick her ass. She just took it. She never complained, she never stood up for herself. It was like she liked it."

"Your mom probably didn't like it. Some women just aren't strong enough to leave. I'm not taking her side or anything. Don't get me wrong. But to understand your life, you've gotta understand all the sides. You feel me?" Sparks looked at her with compassion.

"I understand what you're saying. But how could she choose him over me?"

"It wasn't her. It was the coke."

"How could she choose coke over me? Didn't she realize what she was doing? Didn't she care?"

"I'm sure she did. Anyone would be a fool not to care about you." Sparks looked at her with soft eyes. An awkward silence.

"Anyway, Ernesto eventually started in on me. I was like eight or nine when he started talking to me crazy. He used to call me the abortion that got away, and say shit like I should have been in a rubber or swallowed or in a tissue instead of born. He constantly told me I wasn't shit, that I wasn't gonna be shit. Then when I was eleven, I started to develop. I still looked like a little girl, but I was starting to get breasts, and my ass started plumping up, and that's when Ernesto started touching me. To make a long story short, my mother ended up in jail, and I ended up in foster care."

"Damn." Sparks shook his head in disbelief. "Your step-father molested you?"

"Yeah," Desiree sniffed.

"That's not your fault, you know." Sparks wished silently that he could find the asshole and show him what real abuse was.

"Yeah, but my mother blamed me."

"But you know she wasn't right. It wasn't your fault. He was the grown up. He was supposed to know better!" Sparks yelled, trying to convince her.

"I guess you're right," Dez admitted.

"Damn straight I'm right." Sparks began to calm down a little. "But what happened to your stepfather?"

Dez hesitated. "I can trust you, right?" she asked, her hazel eyes filled with worry.

"Of course," Sparks reassured her.

"I killed him. One night shit got really ugly. He raped me and damn near killed me. Somehow I managed to kill him instead. It was self-defense. I just wanted him to stop." Dez poured herself a shot of cognac and gulped it down quickly. She grimaced at the aftertaste.

"Serves the bastard right! He's in hell now where he be-longs," Sparks said, but he knew his words would never soothe the wounded little girl still inside of Dez. Simultane-ously, he also was impressed by the fact that she was no doubt a rider, a survivor. She was fine enough and smart enough to be wifey material, *and* she definitely had thug appeal. Despite her troubled past, Sparks saw Dez as the perfect woman.

"Come here." Sparks reached out for Dez. Meekly, she scooted her chair toward him. Too ashamed to face him, she stared at her feet. Sparks placed his arm around her shoulder, and Dez allowed herself to surrender. She buried her face in the crook of his arm. Sparks cradled her and let her sob softly while he stroked her hair. Dez looked up at him, her face swollen and puffy.

"Do you think less of me now?" she asked him.

"No, not at all. I think more of you now," Sparks told her, kissing her on the forehead. Dez looked up at Sparks and wiped her tear-streaked face.

"I guess I look pretty terrible." She laughed halfheartedly.

"Nah. You're beautiful, Dez," he told her. In that moment Sparks knew he'd crossed the line. He couldn't hold back what he was feeling any longer.

"Dez, you're one of the most beautiful women in the world. That's why I chose you for the video."

"You?" Dez was surprised.

"Yeah. I made the casting decision. Me and B used to see you in the videos, and we'd always talk about how fine you were and how we were gonna get you in one of our videos. We even used to joke about which one of us would get with you."

Dez's face dropped at that revelation. "So what, you all just assumed I'd naturally get with one of you? Y'all thought I was a typical video ho, huh?" she asked him with attitude.

"No. That's not what I meant. I meant that we both saw something special in you. The difference is I'm willing to accept you the way that you are. Dez, I'm willing to *love* you the way that you are." Sparks stared into her eyes. "Is Bentley?"

Dez was astounded.

"Bentley doesn't appreciate you. He's not really down for you, Dez." Sparks held Dez slightly away from himself, bent down, and kissed her.

Dez broke their embrace. "Y'all are brothers!" she protested.

"I love you, Dez. Let me love you. Forget about what

everyone will think or say. Me and B will always be broth-ers. Our being together can't change that. Let me give you everything that you deserve, everything you ever dreamed of. Let me love you, baby," he murmured softly as he kissed her gently. Dez felt herself becoming light-headed. Sparks was so fine and powerful. It was he, not Bentley, who had made her dreams come true. She owed him whatever he wanted; he was making her a star.

Besides, he had a point. Bentley didn't appreciate her. He'd talked such a good game, and at the first sign of trouble he had bounced. Sparks saw her talent, and now he knew about her history and still wanted her. When would she have an opportunity like this again, to know that someone knew her, her issues, and yet still wanted to love her? More than the fame and the glory, Dez realized that more than anything, what she wanted was to be loved.

Dez found herself surrendering to his embrace and the urgency of his tongue when he slipped it into her mouth. Her clothing along with Sparks's quickly ended up in a heap on the floor of the studio. Sparks interrupted their passion as he cued a track on the mixing board. Then he carefully lifted her up and carried her into the sound booth. A sensual melody filled the room commingled with the sighs and moans of making love.

"I love you, Dez!" Sparks shouted as he climaxed deep within her.

"Ooh, I love you too, Bentley." She sighed and shivered with pleasure. Immediately, she felt like an asshole and burst into tears. "I am so sorry. I don't know what to say," she said as she felt him shrivel like a prune.

"There's nothing to say except I guess it's true when they say you can't help who you fall in love with." Sparks looked crestfallen as he began to put on his clothes.

Tears fell down Dez's face. How could she be so stupid? She was rebounding from Bentley, and Sparks was family. Now she had gone and fucked up the only relationship in her life that she could count on. And she'd told him her deepest, darkest secret.

"Baby girl, don't cry," Sparks cooed. "It was wrong of me to come at you like this when you were vulnerable. I feel more fucked-up than you do. Sex isn't what you need, Dez. It's love. And I love you. So I'm willing to let this go however you want it to go. We can pretend it didn't happen, or we can try to move on from this and maybe try and build something real. Don't try to decide now and don't feel bad, baby. Let's just get some sleep and start again fresh tomorrow."

Sparks's words didn't make Dez feel any better. She felt dirty. No matter what she revealed to a man, no matter how honest or how phony she was, they were all after only one thing. She thought that things would change once she made some money, but her money problems had been long gone and still men only seemed to want to use her. She had a little power now. She had, after all, been able to use what she'd had—good looks, a few dollars, and a whole lot of dreams— to get what she wanted: a record deal. Yet she wanted more.

Dez finally understood what Ginger had been trying to tell her a couple of years ago. It wasn't enough to be able to walk into a store and have the ability to buy whatever her heart desired. It wasn't enough to be able to incite the desires of men and motivate them to provide for her. It even wasn't enough to have fans eagerly awaiting her words. Dez wanted to be able to walk the streets with her head held high, despite any scandal or controversy and without the aid of a publicist or media trainer. She yearned to have people look up to her, not because she was a star, but because they believed that she was smart and could be a catalyst for positive change. She wanted to be able to look in the mirror and not feel dirty or tainted or inferior simply because her circumstances growing up had been less than ideal. She wanted to feel clean. Dez wanted respect.

CHAPTER 19

THE NEXT DAY AND FOR WEEKS AFTERWARD, SPARKS AND Dez went about their business status quo. It was if their tryst had never taken place. There were no awkward silences, no tension between them. Dez was glad because she couldn't bear to lose her new "big brother" and didn't want her career to be a casualty of the war on her emotions. Besides, working on the album and promoting the single had them too busy to let the incident stand in the way of business.

Still, Dez couldn't deny that she had feelings for Sparks, because he was everything that Bentley was and then some. Yet her feelings for Bentley were just as strong as when they'd first met. How was this possible? Dez began to wonder if she had the capacity to be faithful. She'd had every intention of being true to Bentley, but she couldn't get past the hurdle of revealing herself to him. The fact that she had entrusted the story of her past to Sparks had to mean something, didn't it? Maybe it was just that she'd had the opportunity to get to know Sparks a little before revealing her story to him.

Whatever it was, Dez hoped that her feelings of being torn would subside quickly. Her stomach seemed like it was constantly in a knot, and her appetite was unpredictable; at times she could eat a horse, at others she could barely finish a salad. And she was drinking and smoking weed way too much. Sparks chalked it up to being a part of the "creative process," but Dez was always afraid that she was genetically disposed to addictive behavior, and found herself fearing the worst: that she'd turn out just like her mother. But her fear wasn't bad enough to make her stop, and that scared her even more. Her personal life was out of control.

Her career was a dream. The sales of the single were excellent; it debuted at number 1, and after a mere week on the charts, it was certified platinum. The controversy surrounding Dez's history with Dan, and Ysenia's big mouth, had only served to fuel the demand for the product, just as Sparks had predicted. Fortunately, an injunction had been filed barring any further sales of the Sinful Strippers tape. It was snatched from the shelves immediately, and Sparks had a team of cybersurfing interns alerting lawyers to file suits against the myriad Web sites claiming to have the tape available for download. Sparks warned her that they wouldn't be able to catch everyone—people who already owned the tape, for example, would probably pass it around—but with felony charges of child pornography associated with owning the tape, those numbers would remain small.

What irritated Dez the most were the people who seemed to crawl out the woodwork who claimed to have known her or been her friend. If they had been such good friends, why hadn't they helped her? She hadn't even met most of the people who surfaced! As far as she was concerned, aside from Sparks, she'd only ever had one true friend, and that was Ginger. Sometimes Dez half expected Ginger to pop up on television and share their story, but in the nearly three months since she'd gotten her deal she hadn't. Dez knew that Ginger had no way of knowing where she was living;

she hadn't spoken to her since before she moved out of Dan's place. But Ginger was resourceful if anything, so she could find Dez if she wanted to. *Maybe she doesn't want to find me,* Dez often thought to herself. *Maybe she's ashamed of me. Or maybe I just need to call her. Her number is probably still the same.*

THE WEEKS TURNED INTO MONTHS, AND THE HOLIDAYS CAME and went. Dez thought she would die. Every time she turned on the television or the radio, there was talk about family and togetherness, but she felt so alone. Bentley stopped by on Christmas briefly, but ignored her as usual. And for the first time in years, Dez stayed in on New Year's Eve. She and Sparks drank a magnum of Cristal to themselves and ended up making love in front of the fireplace. Dez knew that it was wrong, that she and Sparks could never be more than friends, and that her actions were selfish. But she couldn't stand the feeling of not having anyone at the holidays. And deep down inside she believed that Sparks knew the truth but that he didn't want to feel alone any more than she did. Then the Super Bowl rolled around. Dez thought about how the Super Bowl just three years before had been the beginning of her life as a hotgirl. She missed Ginger.

Desiree should have been on top of the world. Her career was greater than she ever imagined; she and Bentley were slated to perform at the NBA All-Star Game in Philadelphia. For once, she'd be in the presence of the NBA's most talented athletes, and she would be on their level. They wouldn't be able to look at her as just some stripper. They'd have to give her respect. The only butt-shaking she would be doing this

All-Star Weekend would be during her performance at half-time.

She figured that since she and Bentley would have to work together, she'd have a way to get close to him again. Maybe she would be able to resolve what was left of their issues and mend their shattered relationship.

No such luck. Bentley ignored her the whole time they prepared for the performance. There were to be all kinds of special effects and pyrotechnics, and Dez was excited yet nervous. She'd never performed in front of more people than could fit inside of a strip club or on a video set. Now there were going to be tens of thousands of people in attendance and millions watching on television.

The entire Titanium Records crew—artists, dancers, and staff—arrived in Philadelphia by private jet. Dez for once had no fear of flying. There was everything she could possibly need to soothe her nerves aboard the aircraft. She indulged in the Rémy Martin Louis XIII, potent marijuana, and a full-body Swedish massage during the one-hour flight.

By the time they checked into the Sheraton Society Hill Hotel, Dez was amped and ready for action. *Fuck Bentley,* she thought. *I'll show his ass!* There was so much business to be taken care of that Dez thought she'd never get to enjoy Philly's nightlife. Sparks kept her roster full with promotional appearances. There were meet-and-greets, autograph signings, and a photo shoot scheduled with none other than Dewante Reid, a favorite to win the MVP Award.

Dez nearly choked when Sparks told her that she'd be shooting a suggestive layout for the *Source* with Dewante. The shoot would consist of Dez in Dewante's jersey and a shirtless Dewante. There would also be an interview where Dez would ask the questions and he would answer, and then they would switch places.

"Houston, we have a problem," Dez hissed at Sparks through clenched teeth when they arrived at the gymnasium where the shoot would be staged.

"What?" Sparks asked. "Everything is going great!"

"No, it isn't. Why didn't you tell me that this shoot was with Dewante?"

"I wanted it to be a surprise. I know how the ladies love Dewante."

"Not all of us," Dez replied curtly.

Sparks arched an eyebrow. "You know him?"

"Intimately," Dez revealed.

"Well, get over it. This is business," Sparks barked, not even attempting to mask his jealousy.

Dez ignored Sparks's attitude and got to the point. "What if he brings up our past? It was a real freaky scene." Dez was concerned only about her image, not about Sparks and his bruised ego.

"Yeah, well, I've come to expect that from you, Dez," he spat.

"Fuck you, Sparks! You and your brother are two of a kind. I'll handle this shit my way!" Dez turned on her heels and stormed off.

"WELL, WELL, WELL, DESIRE. SO WE MEET AGAIN." DEWANTE grinned that megawatt smile.

"The name is Dez. And I don't recall having ever met you." Dez extended her hand and shook Dewante's.

"How soon we forget. I've met you and a young lady named Ginger before. Remember her?" Dewante smirked.

Dez smirked back. "Actually, now that you mention it, I do. I lived with her briefly, when I was sixteen." If Dewante wanted to play hardball, she was down.

"Sixteen?" Dewante looked confused.

"Yeah, see, I'm only eighteen," Dez explained.

"That's bullshit. I thought that all the mess with Dirty Dan was just media hype. You know, stir up a little controversy, sell a few more albums."

"Oh, no hype. So if you want to pay like Dirty Dan had to pay, be my guest. Bring up the fact that we've known each other in the biblical sense. I'll be forced to mention our little tryst in vivid detail. Child pornography is one thing, but statutory rape is another."

"Ain't nobody gonna trip off that. You were the fast-tailed ho in the Rolexxx," Dewante countered. "I'm a star. You think people are gonna care about me doing it with a lying teenage groupie?"

"Still like it up the ass, Dewante? Because maybe your fans and wife would love to hear all about that from this lying teenage groupie. As a matter of fact, let me call Ginger, she's in town," Dez lied. "I could have her come to the shoot and tell the *Source* her side of the story." Dez smiled triumphantly as she threatened him. Running into Dewante made her feel a lot better than she thought it would. Who had the power now?

"We cool, Dez. Let's just handle this business, because I'm a very busy man." Dewante walked away in a hurry.

"Sure. No problem," Dez called after him, barely able to control her laughter.

DEWANTE WAS A PERFECT GENTLEMAN FOR THE REMAINDER OF the shoot, and although he was an asshole, Dez had to admit to herself that Dewante was fine and the resulting photos were bound to be the sickness. She'd gain an even bigger fan base, and she got to give Dewante a taste of his own medicine, so all in all it was a good experience.

The All-Star Game, however, was not. Bentley flirted with every groupie that looked his way, and he put it on extra when Dez was looking, which was most of the time. She was not lacking from male attention; every baller in the league tried to holler. But Dez wasn't interested.

By the time they performed, Dez was ready to kill Bentley. Right before they took the stage he kissed a girl, an ugly one at that, dead in the mouth, and right in Dez's face. She pretended to be unfazed, but the pain cut through her like a knife.

The crowds went crazy when Bentley flowed. Girls screamed, and every head in the house bobbed to the beat. But the most amazing thing happened when Dez made her entrance. Seated atop a candy-pink Harley-Davidson, she roared onto the stage as the music to her upcoming single, "Down to Ride," played. The audience went wild. Dez forgot all about Dewante and all about Bentley as she gave her all to her performance. Dez had to scream her lines in order to be heard over the deafening crowd.

After giving them a teaser, she and Bentley performed their collaboration. Balloons and confetti dropped from the ceiling as sparks shot into the air and explosions went off on the stage. It was the best performance NBA audiences had ever seen at an All-Star Game, and even the most critical sports announcers had nothing negative to say.

Backstage, Sparks scooped Dez into his arms and twirled her in a circle.

"You were the shit, mami!" he exclaimed, kissing her on the cheek. "I'm sorry I was jealous," he whispered as he set her to her feet.

"Thanks, Sparky!" She smiled, using her special nickname for him to show him that all was forgiven.

"Baby brother, another great performance, as usual." Sparks gave Bentley a pound.

"No doubt. What did you expect?" he answered nonchalantly as he joined the groupie from earlier and disappeared.

"You okay?" Sparks asked Dez. He knew that Bentley's dig had to have hurt her.

"Never better," Dez answered, feigning ambivalence. "Wanna go celebrate?" she asked him with a wink.

"You ain't said shit but a word," Sparks replied as they headed back to the hotel.

CHAPTER 20

April 2002

IT WAS LATE, NEARLY 4 A.M., AS DEZ DUG INTO HER OVERSIZE suede Coach Hobo bag, a gift from Sparks, and pulled out her two-way pager. There were four messages from K.G. This was getting ridiculous. First thing in the morning she would call him and really straighten things out. Apparently, he hadn't understood that she was serious during their previous conversation. She'd be firm yet gentle. What they'd had was over. Putting K.G. to the back of her mind, she scrolled through the pager's address book until she came across the phone number she had been searching for.

Please be the right number, Dez prayed silently as she dialed it with shaky fingers.

"Hello?" A sleepy voice breathed into the phone on the other end.

"Ginny?" Dez asked hopefully.

"Praise God, Desi, is that you?" Ginger's voiced perked up.

"Yeah. It's me," Dez replied softly.

"I've been praying for you to call. I sensed somehow that you needed me. Is everything okay?"

"Still praying, huh?" Dez kidded.

"All day, every day. My motto is PUSH. Pray until something happens," Ginger answered. "But stop trying to change the subject, Desi. Something's wrong, isn't it?"

"Yeah, but . . ." Dez hesitated.

"But you're afraid to tell me what's wrong because you think I'm going to start preaching. Or, worse, you think I'll come at you with some 'I told you so' stuff," Ginger predicted.

"Well, are you?"

"Of course not. We have plenty of time for that later." Ginger laughed. "For now, why don't you just tell me what's the matter? When I told you that I would always be there for you, I meant that. I'm just so glad that you called me. It's been, what, almost three years."

"Yeah, it has been. I really meant to call, Ginny. But I had no idea what to say to you. You were right about so many things. I'm sorry."

"Stop apologizing already. I didn't *want* to be right about a lot of stuff." There was a silence. "Anyway, I saw you on a billboard *and* during the All-Star Game. You're a real rapper now, huh? I'm so proud of you. You are very talented, nena. I had no idea." Dez began to sob softly on the other end of the receiver.

"Are you gonna tell me what's wrong, or am I going to have to come over there? You still at Dan's?" Ginger asked.

"Oh no. I want you to come over, only I'm in New York. Can you get on a plane? I'll have a ticket waiting for you at the airport. JetBlue, okay? Can you come tomorrow?" Dez pleaded.

"Yeah, sure I'll come. Some things change, and some things don't. I'm still always ready to travel. Are you going to be okay until I get there?" Ginger asked, her voice filled with concern. "You're not sick or hurt or anything, are you?"

"Not really. It's an emotional and spiritual matter."

"And you called me? I'm flattered. You know I'll be there!"

"Good. Cuz you're my only true friend. You're the only person that I can trust," Dez admitted.

"I'm glad you feel you can trust me, because you really can. So much has changed in my life, but we'll get into all of this tomorrow," Ginger told her. "Well, all I can say is that you'll be in my prayers until we meet. In the meantime, say a prayer for yourself. Please. That's the end of my sermon for now."

"Okay," Dez said. "I'll call you in a few hours with your flight info. Just be ready to go in the early afternoon."

"I'll see you later today, Desi," Ginger assured her.

"Okay, Ginny, get back to sleep. See you soon."

ROUGHLY TWELVE HOURS LATER, DEZ PICKED UP GINGER AT JFK in a chauffeur-driven Lexus truck. Her jaw had nearly dropped to the ground when she met Ginger at the baggage claim. Ginger's hair was cropped short in a face-flattering style. Gone were the colored contacts and skimpy clothes. Ginger looked elegant and sophisticated in a brown pantsuit and crisp pink shirt, accented with pearl jewelry. She looked like a businesswoman or schoolteacher.

"No, I'm not a schoolteacher, unless you count Sunday school," Ginger quipped when Dez commented on her change in appearance.

"You do not teach Sunday school!" Dez shrieked.

Ginger smiled. "I sure do."

"Right. Next you'll be telling me that you're going to be a preacher or something." Dez rolled her eyes.

"Well . . . ," she started.

"Get the fuck outta here!" Dez howled. "Oops, my bad. I didn't mean to curse," she apologized as they retrieved her bags and headed to the Lexus truck.

"Stop trippin'. I'm not as bad as I was when I first got saved. Act normal, and I promise that I will too. I've learned to live in the world, but not of it," Ginger explained.

"Cool. But you're gonna be a preacher?" Dez shook her head.

"Well. I had contemplated joining a convent." Ginger raised an eyebrow at Dez.

"Get the fuck outta here!" Dez yelled again, then covered her mouth.

"Yeah. But I'm not going to do it. I was raised a Catholic, but now I'm attending a Baptist church. It just gives me a different feeling, you know?" Ginger gave Desiree's hand a squeeze. Dez looked down and noticed a stunning two-carat pear–shaped diamond set in a thick platinum band.

"What the hell?" Dez lifted Ginger's hand. Ginger smiled mischievously.

"I guess I'm going to just have to settle for being a preach-er's wife." Ginger wiggled her fingers in front of Dez.

"You're married?" Dez asked in disbelief.

"Not yet. In about three months. You better be in my wed-ding, but we'll go into that later."

"Who? When? How did this happen?"

"Well, after I had that experience and found the Lord, for a while I drifted from church to church, trying to find a place to call my spiritual home. That's when I went to discernment weekends and retreats at different convents and checked out some seminaries and theological schools and stuff. But none of it was speaking to me. You know I couldn't give up all my stuff. That might have been cool for Mase, but he didn't work as hard as I did to get what I had. I knew that some of it was wrong, how I got it, but still!" *Yeah*, Desiree thought, *she's still the same old Ginger!*

"I'm striving to be like Jesus, but I'm not there yet. I sold the Web sites for a hefty profit, then I went to the Dominican Republic and Haiti for a while to get in touch with my roots and find my center. I figured if I couldn't get rid of all the things that 'dirty money' had bought, I could at least do some good with the new proceeds. I needed to get to the heart of who I was as a person. I found my father and confronted him. He had a new family that knew nothing about me. It wasn't pleasant, but we came to a sort of understanding, and it helped me to vanquish some of the ghosts I had been dealing with. I got rid of a lot of the anger. I donated a lot of my clothes and technical help to the poor people in Port-au-Prince. I just went on a spiritual journey, you know? I met my fiancé while working with some orphans in Haiti. He's a doctor and a minister, and he was working on a mission. I don't know, we just hit it off."

"Damn. That must have been . . . interesting." Dez looked at Ginger in amazement. She had always known that Ginger had a good heart, she'd just been hiding it. She spoke up on it. "I always knew you were a good person, Ginny. You deserve a good man who's going to treat you right."

"Yeah, well, I'm glad you thought I was a good person and deserved love, but there were times when I didn't. But that's enough about me. We've got time for that talk later. I'll be glad to share any of my experiences with you then. Tell me where *you're* at, Desi. Are you wondering if you're a good person? Are you looking back at how far you've come and at what price? Are you wondering if it was all worth it? Do you feel like you've sacrificed too much of yourself and now there's nothing left? Or what's left—hell, you don't even know who that person is?" Ginger looked Dez squarely in the eyes.

"Oh my God, Ginny, yes! How do you know?" Dez sniffled and started to tear up. Ginger had read her to a T.

"I was going through the same thing when you came to live with me. Girl, don't worry. We're gonna work everything out. Now, let's relax and eat a little something. I'm starving, aren't you?" Ginger tossed her arm around Dez's shoulder.

Dez felt herself relax as the Lexus pulled into the gate of Sparks's home. Ginger would help her. They'd have dinner, perhaps some wine if Ginger still indulged, and chat like old times. Dez wondered how much Ginger had heard about the tape and her case against Dan. Dez knew she had to come clean and reveal to Ginger her true age, and she was hoping that Ginger could forgive her for the lies. But since Ginger was "born again," Dez didn't anticipate any problems with that. Christianity was based on forgiveness.

Sparks had left Dez a note stating that he had to fly to Virginia for a few days on business, but to call him if she got bored and wanted to go out so that he could make arrangements. Dez was glad he was gone; she could reunite with Ginger in peace.

"You finally made it, huh, girlfriend? His crib makes mine look like the projects!" Ginger quipped after settling in and joining Dez on the patio.

Desiree had prepared her signature arroz con pollo and plantains along with black beans. Ginger bowed her head and said grace over the food. Without seeking approval, she held Dez's hand as she prayed. For once, Dez didn't mind

Ginger's spirituality. She felt so lost that anything was bound to help.

"I see you can still only cook one meal," Ginger chided as she lifted her head and prepared to dig into the steaming-hot plate of food.

"I see you're still a smart-ass," Dez joked back.

"Well, hey, God made me this way. You got beef, take it up with him."

"Or *her*," Dez replied. They shared a laugh, happy to be with each other again. They ate in relative silence, engaging in minor chitchat now and then. When they were done, Dez cleared the plates and straightened up the kitchen a little.

"You mean to tell me that with all this big house, Sparks ain't got no maid? I see why he got you staying here with him, he got you cleaning up!" Ginger laughed as she helped Dez load the dishwasher.

"That's not why Sparks has me here," Dez said softly, looking at her feet.

Ginger took Dez by the hand and led her to the kitchen table. "Okay, spill it. I've been really patient with you, but you can't avoid things any longer. Whatever it is that's bugging you, tell me right now," Ginger said firmly.

"Okay." Dez sighed. "You still drink, or no?" Dez asked.

"A little. But if it's like *that*, I do believe I'll take a glass of champagne," Ginger remarked. Dez extracted a chilled bottle of Veuve Clicquot from the refrigerator, popped the cork, and poured them both a crystal flute of the bubbly liquid.

"Okay, first things first," Ginger said. "How did all of this happen? The last time we spoke, you'd moved in with Dan. Then you fell off and I didn't hear from you. Then all of a sudden you're a big star and I see you everywhere! So did Dan help you like he said he would?"

"Fuck no! Dan was a big waste of time. I spent all my time writing lyrics, only for Dan to brush them aside, and when I finally did get into the studio, all I did was sing the bullshit chorus with a bunch of other females. My parts usually consisted of me screaming shit like 'Do it to me doggy-style' or 'You like the way I shake my ass? I know you wanna spank that ass.' Straight garbage. It didn't take me long to realize that even if Dan put me on, I wasn't going to go lead, let alone platinum. But the way I saw it, I would milk him for everything that I could," Dez explained. "But Dan put me in my first video. Thank God it kind of bombed. It was so cheesy and embarrassing! Nobody ever mentions seeing me in it anyway, and I don't put it on my résumé. Anyway, he introduced me to my manager. It just blew up overnight from there. My manager got me some better gigs, and pretty soon I realized, hey, I don't need Dan. So I moved out of Dan's place and used his money to get my own spot. He didn't seem to care too much. He probably went out and replaced me that night. But Dan caused me more trouble than you could begin to imagine."

"Yeah, girl, I *can* imagine. I've known Dan a long time. He's not a bad person, but all he really cares about is money. But from what I saw, you were too talented to be hooked up with him anyway. At least it ended on a good note. A fair exchange is no robbery. You all used each other until it just didn't work anymore. And I'm glad it didn't work and that all you did was that one cheesy video."

"Well, not exactly," Dez said.

"Uh-oh! What does that mean?" Ginger queried suspiciously.

"You really haven't heard?" Dez replied.

"Heard what?"

"I can't believe you haven't. It's been all over the tabloids and gossip shows. Where have you been?" Dez shook her head.

"I don't buy that crap. And I don't watch too much TV. The only reason I found out you were rapping was because I read about it in *Sister 2 Sister.* I read it because they talk about a lot of gospel artists," Ginger explained.

"Well, I guess Jamie Foster Brown hasn't gotten around to this yet. I'm sure she will, though." Dez frowned.

"Okay, just tell me what it is already. Besides, she seems very fair. I know she'll get your side of the story. But will I? I mean, dag, Dez, spill it already!" Ginger said, crossing her arms in frustration.

"When I was with Dan, we went to Cancún for Memorial Day. I was kind of high, we partied really hard that weekend, and I let Dan talk me into making a videotape."

"Oh, who would want to see you and that old motherfu— oops, I mean old *man* getting it on?" Ginger caught the curse word before it spilled out of her mouth.

"Not that kind of tape. It was a Sinful Strippers tape," Dez explained.

"You mean that bootleg Girls Gone Wild series? Is he still doing that?"

"That's it."

"Let me guess, the tape has come back to bite you on the butt."

"Well, yeah, but um, you might need another drink on this." Dez refilled Ginger's glass.

"Go ahead," Ginger said tentatively.

"It was a girl-on-girl tape," Dez admitted sheepishly.

"And somebody let it leak," Ginger finished.

"Uh-huh. You have no idea just how badly it leaked. This girl Ysenia let Bentley see it on the set of a video. She was jealous because I had beaten her out of the lead role. Then

I hooked up with Bentley and got my deal and well, you can put two and two together. She couldn't stand it because she wanted him and I had him. See, me and Bentley were in love or something like that until he saw the tape. Now he won't forgive me." Trouble clouded Dez's face.

"Dang! Haters don't stop, do they? But if y'all are meant to be, Bentley will forgive you. You've probably got to give him some time. That was a messed-up way for him to hear about that. But if *I* found true love, believe me, you will too. I told my man about *everything*. And he still loves me. If Bentley can't forgive you, he's not for you. Because if my man could forgive me, and Christ could forgive the world all our sins, Bentley can forgive you for something you did before you even met him."

"Well, Ginny, that's not all. I have a confession to make to you," Dez said, fiddling with her nails.

"Go ahead," Ginger said as she sipped her champagne.

"When I made that tape, when I lived with you, I was only sixteen years old." Dez braced herself for the fallout.

Ginger sputtered and choked on her champagne. "Get the fuck outta here. Excuse me, Lord, but I had a cussword coming to me. Sixteen, Desi?" Ginger stared at Dez in disbelief.

"Yeah," she admitted.

"I knew it!" Ginger hopped up from the table clapping her hands.

"Huh?" Dez was confused.

"I knew there was something. My instincts are rarely wrong. You never looked eighteen, but you were kind of mature, so I ignored my gut. You had a tight vocabulary, you were smart, and so I never really questioned you. But there were times, I can't explain it, I just knew. You were too naive, too untainted. That explains it." Ginger took her seat, gulped the champagne down, and poured herself another glass.

"Are you mad at me?" Dez asked her friend.

"Let's see . . . am I mad that I committed several felonies dealing with you? There's the lewd behavior, the contributing to the delinquency of a minor, and who knows what else? Am I mad? Well . . . nah. It's better that you met me instead of Dan or some other guy first. I know I wasn't the best 'guardian,' but you're a lot better off having lived with me first than some pimp, I'm sure of it."

Dez breathed a sigh of relief. "You don't know how glad I am to hear you say that. I didn't know if you'd forgive me for lying."

"Hold up. You think I'm gonna let you off the hook that easy, you got another thought coming."

"What do you mean?" Dez felt her heart pounding.

"I need to know how you got to me. I can only imagine. Runaway?" Ginger asked intuitively.

"Yeah," Dez admitted. She had no idea how many times she was going to have to tell the story of her life. At least it got easier every time.

"I can only imagine what you ran away from. I know you had to be abused or something," Ginger guessed.

"How did you know that?" Dez looked shocked. Could everyone tell what she had been through? Was she wearing some sign on her head that screamed sexual abuse survivor?

"Desi, I hate to break it to you, but most of us have been. By most of us, I mean women in general. A woman is sexually assaulted every two minutes."

"Are you serious?" Dez had never heard that statistic before.

"You know I research my stuff. The Justice Department came up with that number. Those are the people who tell. Think about how many don't tell and suffer in silence. I've been doing a lot of volunteer work lately. You'd never guess what goes on in the world. It's so sad. But dancers especially have high numbers of women who are survivors of rape, incest, you name it. It isn't caused by the profession as much as we seek that profession because of what has happened to us. We have low self-esteem. We always say that it's the other way around and that we have to have all this confidence to strip. But we couldn't have placed very much value on our bodies if we thought a peek was only worth a ten-spot here, a dub there. We learned from the abuse to disconnect our bodies from ourselves. We used our bodies as a tool to get what we wanted or needed, instead of connecting them as a part of us. We objectified ourselves."

"You were abused too, right? I kind of remember you hinting at that a long time ago." Dez wished she'd confided in Ginger ages ago. All this time she had felt so isolated, so alone. She didn't think that anyone could really understand her pain. She always thought that she had done something wrong.

"Yeah, Dez, me too. When I came over from Haiti, we had to stay at the Krome Detention Center. Our living conditions were shit in Krome. I was a refugee that hardly spoke any English. We were overcrowded, there was never any private space, and not all the refugees that were there with us were good people. A lot of bad shit happened to me." Ginger looked as if she were in mourning for her childhood. "Things that no little girl should have to endure."

"But you said you were only five when you came here," Dez interjected.

"Yes, I was." Ginger silenced Dez with a look that spoke volumes. Age was everything to a pedophile. Dez shuddered at the thought of the horrors that her friend had gone through. Dez understood why Ginger was so tough, but also why she never wanted to be poor, and why she wanted respect so badly. They were the same as her own reasons. She also understood why Ginger had at one time preferred women sexually. Dez could admit to herself that sex with women seemed emotionally and physically safer. Dez and Ginger's bond of sisterhood, although born of pain, was official. They both wanted the same thing: to not feel like a freak, an outsider. They wanted a sense of normalcy, and both had gone after the common denominator of the people who seemed to have it all: money.

Dez broke down and told Ginger the story of her mother and father and Ernesto. By the time she finished, they were both in tears.

"How on earth did you get to Miami?" Ginger asked in awe. "You were only a baby!"

"Well, when I was fourteen, I ended up in a girls' home called Morristown. It was a nice place to live, as far as places like that go, but I was done. I wanted out, and I was gonna get it, no matter what I had to do. I had it all planned out. I'd heard through the grapevine that Mr. Lopez, the neighbor that helped me, had moved to Miami to live with his daughter. He'd offered to adopt me or be my guardian when all that shit went down, but the state wouldn't allow it because there was no woman in the house. So that's where I was headed. I'd decided that they would be my family. Marisol, that's Mr. Lopez's daughter, had just had a baby. I thought I could help her out, maybe even live with her. I didn't know where she lived exactly, but I figured that I would cross that bridge when I got to it. I wasn't worried about them saying yes because I knew they would never have the heart to send me back to a foster home, if I could just make it there. They would get lawyers and work it all out. I was going to get my GED, then go to college early. Then I'd get a good job and be set to live my life happily ever after. With that goal in mind, I was willing to do whatever I had to do in order to get out of Morristown as soon as possible.

"It wasn't that things were so bad in the foster home. For one, it was in Mount Vernon, a much nicer neighborhood than where I'd been living. There were homes with grass in the surrounding area instead of wall-to-wall concrete like the Bronx. The other girls were decent, and there weren't any perverts or creeps around trying to hurt us, but the way I saw it, I had already experienced the worst that life had to offer. In my mind no one could hurt me any more than I had been, so I was pretty fearless. As far as I was concerned, I was on my own, a renegade, or, better yet, an outlaw like Tupac. Just like his lyrics, it was me against the world. I used to listen to Pac's CD every single day. That shit and my dreams were the fuel that kept me going when nothing else could."

"Don't I know it! You used to play the heck out of 'All Eyez on Me.' Drove me half crazy! So he's why you wanted to rap, huh?" Ginger asked.

"Yeah, I could relate to him. Plus, writing and rapping were easier than therapy. I hated the counseling sessions I was required to go to with a passion. I felt betrayed, because I went into it thinking that these people really wanted to help me. But it was so impersonal. They didn't care about my feelings, they just only about statistics so that they could keep that money flowing. It was like they were trying to provoke me or make me crazy or something. They always managed to make things worse. It's like they weren't satisfied to just let me forget about my life. They had to keep dredging shit up time and time again, and I just wanted to forget. So mostly, I sat there with this blank expression on my face, and the whole time inside my head, I was flowin'."

"You shouldn't try to forget, Dez. You can't run from the truth," Ginger told her.

"Yeah, I know that now," Dez admitted. "But at that time I just wanted to escape. Most of the time I ditched school and went to the library. It was safe, warm, and there were usually field trip groups that I could blend into or stacks I could get lost in. I'd read all day. I read the classics like *Catcher in the Rye* and *The Great Gatsby*. I read *True to the Game* and E. Lynn Harris. I read *The Coldest Winter Ever* like twenty times. Reading was the only thing I had that could take me away from it all. That and writing.

"But eventually, that wasn't enough. I wanted out for real, but I knew I wasn't going anywhere without money. I had no clue how I was going to get it, but I figured that anything that I needed to know, a vet at the home named Tasha could tell me. She was seventeen and had lived at the home since she was thirteen. Tasha knew the ins and outs of the home and the neighborhood, so she was the residents' hookup on gear, liquor, weed, and anything else a girl would need to get her hands on. Little did I know just *how* thorough Tasha was with her shit.

"She told me she and this other girl, Shelle, worked at this strip club, Sue's Rendezvous. They had things all worked out with the guards and managers and stuff. Tasha said she could hook me up with a fake birth certificate so I could get a real ID. Then I could work at the club. They always seemed to have plenty of money. I wanted out, and Tasha was offering me the way. I figured, what harm would it do? I'd just do it long enough to save up for a few months' rent on a place in Miami till I found the Lopezes, maybe get a car, and pay for college. I figured six months max and I'd be ready to roll. In my eyes it was a do-or-die situation. Once I turned eighteen, Morristown was going to turn me out to the streets with not a pot to piss in or a window to throw it out. I had to start thinking about my future because it was clear to me that no one else was."

"What was it like, being so young?" Ginger asked Dez. "You had to be scared. It must have been awful for you. I remember how disgusted I was when I first started dancing."

"At first I felt degraded. It was embarrassing to be half naked in front of strange men. They said some of the nastiest, foulest shit I'd ever heard in my life. I couldn't believe that there were bigger pigs in the world than Ernesto. They would lick their crusty lips, leer at me, and touch themselves. And, of course, they tried to touch me. It thoroughly disgusted me. But when I got my first taste of money, it was like crack. I was addicted, and there was no going back. Gone was the disgust and shame. Suddenly, nothing I did felt too low, as long as I got my high in the end, my dough. But there was something else. There was the rush of power I felt when a man stared at me, longing to touch me, and both of us knowing that he couldn't without paying the consequences. These men could have chosen any other woman in the club to dance for them, but they chose me. They could be out spending money on their wives, girlfriends, or even on themselves. But they chose to give it to me, all because of an illusion. It was a game to me, playing pretend. I pretended to be interested in their weak conversation. I laughed at their corny jokes and told them how cute and smart they were. Sometimes I was a total bitch. It didn't matter. It was like they couldn't help themselves. In the end I always got paid."

"But Dewante was your first trick, wasn't he?" Ginger asked.

"Yeah, but I would have had sex with him for free. Now, imagine what *that* would have done to me! I'd be scarred for life. I used to have a huge crush on him. I'd have been ruined when I found out that this guy I thought was the business liked it in the butt. Besides, if it hadn't been for that trick, I wouldn't have met you. And I don't know where I would have been if I hadn't met you. I mean, honestly, think of how low-budget I would have been!" Dez laughed.

"I feel like I was a bad influence." Ginger looked filled with guilt.

"Don't. You didn't make me do anything. It wasn't my first situation like that, where I was faced with temptation. If anything, that whole episode went down because the price just happened to be right. Money can tempt even the strongest of people. Greed is natural, even if it is wrong. Come on, twenty-five hundred dollars? Who wouldn't go there?"

"I guess you're right," Ginger said. "So you came to Miami looking for Mr. Lopez."

"Yeah. One Sunday morning, after I had been stripping for nearly four months, me, Tasha, and Shelle were sitting in the TV room watching football. The camera scanned the crowd and stopped on a group of wives chilling in the stands watching their men ball. The commentator remarked on how lovely they all were, and I agreed, but they weren't any prettier than me. I eyed their perfect hairdos, their artfully made-up faces, their fancy fur coats, and their blinding diamonds. The shot only lasted a few seconds, but for me it was an eternity. It was like I saw my destiny laid out ahead of me.

"I was going to end up with a man like the football players I saw on TV. That's why I wanted a baller so bad. Fuck bumping and grinding for perverts in strip clubs. I'd never have to struggle again. My man would pamper me and spoil me, and maybe someday I'd have children of my own. Everyone would respect me and envy me. I pictured a fancy house with a swimming pool and gardens and a maid to cook and clean for me. My kids would know nothing but the best, never suffering. If I married a guy like that instead of linking up with some loser like Ernesto, I could be a good mom, a good woman.

"When they happened to mention that the Super Bowl was in Miami, I saw it as providence. Tasha and Shelle told me some girls from Sue's were gonna dance at the Rolexxx. So I came up with the plan to make money and find Mr. Lopez. Instead I found you. I just packed my stuff a little bit at a time and either took it to the club or stashed it in my locker at school, since I wasn't keeping any books in there, and I bounced," Dez concluded.

"Girl, you are so blessed you can't even see it. But I can. Anything could have happened to you! Your little fast behind probably should have been dead. But now you're a success. You should be proud of yourself."

"But I've done so many things that I'm not proud of. Besides the tape, I slept with Sparks. Here I am, supposedly in love, and I can't keep my legs closed for the man's brother," Dez confided.

"How the hell did that happen?"

"Well, you know how it goes. I was feeling all vulnerable and sad over Bentley, and Sparks was there to listen. One thing led to another . . ."

"And you let him hit it."

"You got it."

"But it was a one-time thing, right?" Ginger asked.

"Not exactly. There was the first time, there was New Year's Eve, there was All-Star Weekend . . ." Dez rattled off their encounters.

"Well, when was the last time it happened?" Ginger wanted to know.

"Right before I invited you out here," Dez admitted.

"You're kidding, right?" Ginger inquired. Dez shook her head.

"No wonder he left town. Obviously, dude's head is messed up. Desi, you gotta slow your roll. If you want Bentley, you have to commit to that, but if you want Sparks, you need to admit to that."

"Well, that's not all. Sparks had been kicking it with my so-called friend Leilani. She used to model with me, and then she moved to behind the scenes. She's always been kind of a hater, but aside from you, she was the only person I ever really let into my life in Miami. We had been beefing really ugly over Bentley, and when I got my deal, she started acting really funky. She was a production assistant on the video, then she got bumped up to assistant director by Sparks. We kind of clashed on the set, so when Bentley confronted me about the tape, I just knew she was the one who had set me up, and I kicked her ass."

"No, you didn't!" Ginger doubled over in laughter.

Dez smirked. "Yeah, I did. Real bad."

"You oughta be 'shamed! So what's the deal with her now?" Ginger asked, still chuckling.

"I don't know. Sparks said she was cool, but he wasn't feeling her, he was feeling me."

"You believe that?" Ginger became serious

"Of course! Why wouldn't he? I am me, after all," Dez joked.

"You better be careful. Hell hath no fury like a woman scorned," Ginger warned her young friend.

"I ain't worried about her. I'm worried about K.G., my old sponsor." Dez realized that her life was an even more tangled mess than she'd first thought. Bentley, Sparks, Leilani, K.G.— all of them were pissed at her for some reason or other.

"Why? What's up with him?"

"He's been paging me off the hook. He's starting to get a little scary. I tried to end it, but he keeps saying shit like I can't escape him. It's been like five months! I told him that it was over, I needed to focus on my career, I couldn't give him what he needed, he deserved more than me, it wasn't him it was me, blah blah blah."

"Why not tell the truth, Dez? Lies have already gotten you into so much trouble," Ginger advised.

"What? Tell him I never felt anything for him, that I played him and used him for his loot? Ginny, he's a street-type nigga. You gotta be real careful with them, you know what I mean?"

"Oh yeah. I feel you. So what are you gonna do?"

"He claims to be giving me some space. But eventually, I may have to get a restraining order."

"Let's hope it doesn't get to that. He isn't saying he's going to hurt you or anything, is he?"

"No, but I still get this funny feeling." Dez couldn't articulate it, but something didn't sit right with her and K.G.

"Well, relax, girl. It sounds like K.G. is the least of your worries. He's miles away. What about the here and now? What are you gonna do about this brother situation?" Ginger figured that Dez needed to deal with what was on her plate and not worry about what was for dessert.

"I have no idea. I dig Sparks, I really do, but in more of a big brother kind of way. My heart belongs to Bentley. I can't explain it. It was like love at first sight. He's who I want. What I feel for Sparks is more like a crush or gratitude."

"Is this going to affect your career? There could be some fallout if Sparks decides to confess to his brother. Or what if he starts forcing you to keep doing it? He could blackmail you. He knows all your business, plus he signs your checks."

"I don't know. Sparks is cool, plus he doesn't want to hurt

his brother. I'm pretty sure that he'll keep his mouth shut. I still love Bentley. So I'm going to make sure that what happened before, never happens again. I've got to make this work out. I'm not ready to give up on Bentley."

They were interrupted by the intercom alerting them a visitor was on the premises.

"I wonder who that can be," Dez pondered aloud. "I'm not expecting anyone. And no one ever comes all the way out here unannounced."

"Only one way to find out!" Ginger instructed her. "Answer the door. I'm nosy!"

Ginger followed Dez into the foyer to look at the closed-circuit TV that monitored the house. *It couldn't be!*

"It can't be!" Dez exclaimed.

"Who is it?" Ginger peered at the monitor.

"It's Bentley!"

CHAPTER 21

S PARKS WAS CONSUMED WITH GUILT. HE HAD MIXED BUSI- ness and pleasure as well as betrayed his brother. He knew he'd crossed a line that never should have been crossed, but he couldn't resist Dez. Now he was falling in love with her! He knew she didn't feel the same. It was obvi- ous that she was still hung up on Bentley. What did he ex- pect? He had known that what his brother and Dez had shared was real. He knew his brother. And he never wanted to hurt him, but he couldn't help but covet such a prized possession as Dez. He'd only wanted to experience her love for himself, even if it wasn't real. Besides, Bentley was too young to give Dez what she needed. He was still into getting with groupies. Sparks could provide her with a home, a ca- reer, a sense of stability, more love than she had ever known, and he could buy her the world.

He was interrupted from his thoughts of Dez by the ring- ing of his cell phone.

"Hello?" he answered.

"Baby, it's me, Lani. I haven't heard from you in a few days. Is everything all right?" Leilani asked sweetly on the other end.

"Hey, Leilani. I've just been really busy. Me and Dez have been in the studio 24/7, trying to get this album out. And the announcement for the nominees of the BET Awards came out today. Bentley and Dez are up for Best Rap Collabo."

"So soon? The song and video have only been out a couple of months!" Leilani exclaimed.

"Yeah, can you believe it? It just made the cutoff. The awards are in June in Cali," he informed her.

The BET Awards! Leilani thought. *He better take me! L.A. is just where I need to be to network with the real Hollywood players.*

"There you go, leaving me again. I'm never gonna get any time to spend with you. As it is, I already have to share you with Dez! I'm not good at sharing," Leilani pouted, hoping he'd catch the hint and suggest that they spend time together in L.A.

"Uh, yeah. Well, you know . . . business is business," Sparks stammered. He liked Leilani, but he knew in his heart that she wasn't the one for him. She was far too jealous of Dez, although she had good reason. But moreover, he wasn't stupid: he knew a sack chaser when he saw one. Leilani put on an excellent front, but her true colors were starting to show. She was always name-dropping and hinting at things she wanted him to buy for her or do for her. She also put on airs, trying to impress him, instead of being herself. She just didn't get the fact that he would have given her far more than she could have ever schemed out of him. Dez was up-front and honest about what she expected, and he could respect her for that. And she was real, faults and all. It was just one of the reasons why he felt so strongly about her.

Why can't I stop thinking about Dez? Sparks mused.

"Well, where are you?" Leilani said, snapping him out of his daydream.

"Virginia. Had to holler at Missy about some tracks," he

explained, silently debating whether he should just end their fling now and get it over with.

"Think you can make it down here? Just for a day or two?" Leilani pleaded. She'd whip some good loving on him, and then it would be the BET Awards for her.

"Yeah, I think I can manage that. I've got something I want to talk to you about anyway," Sparks told her. Leilani felt a rush of excitement. Sparks was probably going to make their relationship more "official." Leilani began to plan what she was going to wear to the ceremony.

"Okay. Well, I'll call you with the details a little bit later. I've gotta run," Sparks finished.

"Okay, honey. I'll see you soon." Leilani hung up the phone, satisfied and confident.

That settles it, Sparks thought. *I'm gonna break it off with Leilani. If I can't have Dez, I don't want anyone.*

"IT'S BENTLEY!" DEZ EXCLAIMED. "WHAT SHOULD I DO?" SHE squawked, running around the foyer like a chicken with its head cut off.

"Go upstairs, fix your hair, and put on some makeup. I'll handle Bentley," Ginger instructed. Dez hesitated.

"Girl, what little game you got, you got from me! You love Bentley, right? You want your man back, right?" Ginger asked her with her hands on her hips.

"Hell yeah!" Dez declared.

"Well, then, get your butt upstairs. I'll buzz him in. Don't come downstairs until I tell you to."

Dez took the steps three at a time, nearly tripping when she got to the top. She ran with haste to her bedroom.

Ginger looked in the mirror by the door after pressing the buzzer that opened the gate. She fluffed her hair, smoothed her clothes, and answered the door with a Martha Stewart smile.

"Why, you must be Bentley." She grasped his hand and shook it firmly before gently pulling him inside.

"The one and only. But I haven't had the pleasure of meeting you. Are you a friend of my brother's?" He grinned at her flirtatiously. Although Ginger was much more conservative-looking, she was still a dimepiece.

"No. I'm Ginger. I'm Dez's sister." Bentley's smile faded immediately.

"Where's my brother?" Bentley asked impatiently, his tone ice-cold.

"Your brother is out of town, but there's no reason to be funky with me, Bentley. I haven't done anything to you." Ginger looked Bentley squarely in the eyes. It would take more than some pretty boy with an attitude to intimidate her.

"Yo, I'll be back when he comes home," he announced, and turned to leave.

"Huh-uh. You're coming in the kitchen, and you're gonna sit down and talk to me," Ginger commanded. Bentley looked at her, but before he could object, Ginger was dragging him to the kitchen table.

"You got a lotta balls to be ordering me around in my brother's house," he snarled.

"Yeah, so what's your point?" Ginger threw his attitude back in his face. *Lord, please don't let this boy make me forget I'm saved!*

"Yeah, you Dez's sister, all right!" Bentley laughed, softening.

"Well, yeah, I guess I am. You hungry?" Ginger asked him.

"A little."

"Cool. I'll fix you a plate. Want some sweet tea?" she asked him pleasantly. Men were so simple. A little food in their bellies made them putty in a woman's hands.

"Yeah, thanks." Bentley began to relax a little.

"So my sister told me what happened between you two," Ginger informed him as she set his plate in front of him.

"Yeah?" he answered nonchalantly.

"Want to hear a story?" Ginger asked him brightly.

"What?"

"Well, Dez and I aren't blood sisters. I took Dez in when she was sixteen. It was when she first got to Miami," Ginger explained.

"You lie just as good as her," Bentley replied sourly. "You had me fooled. Y'all do look alike, but y'all ain't real sisters."

Ginger silenced him with an intense look. "You know just as well as I do that family ain't just about blood. So chill and listen to the story. Desi and I are sisters in the strongest sense of the word. We go back a while. When she came to me, I didn't know she was a runaway or anything, let me just say that. But it probably wouldn't have mattered to me anyway. I used to be a different woman. Back then I was a dancer, and Desi and I stripped together. A lot of the things she was involved in were due to my influence."

"So?" Bentley seemed unaffected. Ginger knew he'd be a tough nut to crack, but she was convinced that she could be a bridge between him and Dez.

"So you can't hold her responsible for everything that happened. Some of it was my fault. Now, like I said, I didn't know she was a kid. If anyone should be mad at her, it should be me, because I committed countless felonies dealing with her. Things I could have gone to jail for. She lied to me big-time. I had her on the beach and drinking and clubbing. Desi was green as hell when I met her. I knew Desiree, not Dez. I *know* her, you feel me? I know Desi is a good girl, a smart girl, a talented girl. In many ways I saved Desi's life. Her life hasn't been easy. She ran away from a foster home she was put in after her stepfather raped and tried to kill her. I'm sure you didn't know that."

"No." Bentley pushed his food around on his plate.

"Well, that's the truth. She's been to hell and back, and she might have made some mistakes along the way, but she's sorry. Dez didn't have any guidance at all growing up. She had to find her way on her own. Even you had your brother. She had no one for a long time until she met me. But let me get to the point and tell you something about her. If you let her walk out of your life, you'll be sorry. She's special. In many ways she saved *my* life, and for that I am eternally grateful." Ginger looked at him with tear-filled eyes.

"I don't mean to sound cold, but what does this have to do with me?" Bentley asked her.

"Look, I'm just trying to show you that Dez is not the horrible person you want to make her out to be. When we lived together, I was really messed up. I knew that the Lord had something better planned for me, but I had no idea what it was or how to do it. I was feeling like a failure. I drank, smoke, and did whatever drugs I could get my hands on to try and forget my pain. See, me and Desi are the same. Our pain comes from the same source, and we're motivated by the same things. We didn't have families. We didn't have homes. I had more of a stable family and homelife than her, and I was a refugee. We both survived horrible sexual abuse. And I don't rely on that as a cop-out. It explains a lot, but it doesn't excuse everything, for me or for her. Because once you know better, you should do better, which is so much easier said than done. But I understand her. You would too if you tried."

"Your little theory sounds good, but everyone has choices. Dez made some fucked-up ones," Bentley said.

"Yes, but everyone also makes mistakes, even you. I used to feel the same way. When I first got saved, I was so judgmental of people who didn't live the way I thought they should. Especially Dez."

"So why did you change your mind?"

"Because I realized that I was wrong. You know, one night I got really high. I almost OD'd, but Desi took care of me. That night I gave my heart to Jesus. And it wasn't easy for Desi. I wanted her to change her life just like I was planning to change mine. I must have seemed like the biggest hypocrite. I turned her out, and then I wanted to save her. It messed with her head. She was just a baby, you know. She decided she couldn't live with me anymore, and that's when she got involved with Dan."

"That's her fault. You didn't make her leave."

"No. But I wasn't accepting her for who she was. That's what love is. Accepting someone as is. I tried to change her, when only God and the person doing the changing can do that. I forced her hand. I promised to help her become a model, and I let her down. I tried to push my dreams onto her, but instead of telling her where I came from, and sharing my experience, I came at her telling her what she *had* to do. No one responds well to that, and you know it. You almost tore my head off when I ordered you around. I hardly know you, imagine how I did Desi." Thinking about how Ginger came in telling him what he had to do without explaining who she was made Bentley chuckle.

"Look, I'm not gonna preach to you. But I will tell you this. After I got out of that life, I met a wonderful man that I'm going to marry." Ginger wiggled her ring finger at him. "It was hard, but I told him my past. He loves me. He's willing to accept me for who I am now, and not reject me for the things that I've done. And trust me, what Dez has done pales in comparison to my escapades. If you love Desi, you'll do the same. You'll at least talk to her."

"Maybe," he said slowly, mulling it over.

"Look, I'm living proof that people can change," Ginger said. Bentley sat silently digesting what Ginger had told him.

"Are you a Christian, Bentley?" Ginger asked him, interrupting his thoughts.

"No doubt."

"What's the best thing Jesus did for us?" She quizzed him like he was one of her Sunday school pupils.

"He died for us," Bentley answered smugly.

"Very good. And what did that accomplish?"

"You know," Bentley said, avoiding the question. "What are you, some kind of Sunday school teacher?"

"Yes"—Ginger grinned—"I am. And I'll be marrying a minister in three months. What is your point?"

"You went from the strip club to Sunday school?"

"Yeah! Look, it's like I told you, people change. But this ain't all about me. To answer the question, when Jesus died, we were forgiven all our sins." Ginger raised an eyebrow.

"Well, I ain't Jesus!" Bentley remarked sardonically.

"No. You most certainly are not. And it's a good thing you aren't. We might still be hell-bound if we had to count on you for forgiveness. Now, if God can forgive the whole world for committing sins far greater than anything Desi's ever even thought of, can't you forgive her? Are you better than Jesus?" Ginger put the pressure on.

"Okay, I get your point. I'll *talk* to her. But I'm not making any promises. It's just crazy seeing her all the time and not speaking. It could be bad for business."

"Right, business," Ginger said sarcastically. She could see right through Bentley. He wasn't a bad guy; he was just young and full of pride. "You do love her, don't you? If you don't, don't waste your time or hers. Let her go." Ginger couldn't help being protective; she didn't want to see Dez hurt any more.

"Yeah, I love her," Bentley admitted.

"Can't help it, can you?" Ginger rubbed his arm in a matronly fashion.

"Nah. There's just something about her . . ."

"I know. You were lucky enough to meet the real Desi. Now, be smart enough not to let her walk away," Ginger related wisely.

Bentley smiled at her. "You're something else, you know that?" He cocked his head and looked at Ginger curiously. How was it that some woman he'd never seen was able to get him to talk to Dez when no one, not even Dez herself, could? Bentley chalked it up to her sincerity. Ginger seemed as real as they came. Despite all the God talk, she seemed to be accepting and nonjudgmental, unlike most religious people he knew. It didn't hurt that she was fine too.

Ginger laughed. "That's what they say."

"Is Dez home?" Bentley inquired. "I got something to tell her."

"Yeah, she's here." Ginger stayed planted in her seat but yelled at the top of her lungs for Dez to come downstairs. She looked at Bentley and laughed again.

"You can take the girl out of the ghetto, but you can't take the ghetto out of the girl." Ginger grinned and shrugged her shoulders.

Dez came bounding down the steps in a sports bra and yoga pants. She wanted to look sexy, but she also wanted it to look like she wasn't trying. Ginger winked at her when she appeared in the kitchen.

"Bentley. This is a surprise," Dez lied, feigning shock.

"Hey, babe," he said, smiling at her.

Babe! He called me babe again! Dez's heart leapt with joy. She had no idea what Ginger had said to Bentley, but she could sense that whatever it was had helped.

Bentley stood and crossed the floor to where Dez stood. Her heart was palpitating wildly. "I was here to talk to Sparks, but this has everything to do with you." He grabbed her hand and smiled.

"What?" Dez could barely utter a syllable. Ginger sat silently spectating from the sideline.

"I've been nominated for several BET Awards," he began cockily.

"That's great!" Dez replied enthusiastically. She'd been so busy with Ginger that she'd forgotten about the nominations announcement. She still saw Bentley as her man and couldn't help supporting his efforts. She wanted so badly to give him a congratulatory kiss.

"And one of them is for the song with you! We've been nominated for Best Rap Collabo for the remix!" Bentley announced.

"Oh my God!" Dez shrieked. "You've got to be kidding! We're nominated for a BET Award?" Dez did a little dance and jumped up and down. Ginger hopped up from her chair and hugged Dez with all her might.

"Oh, Desi! I'm so happy for you! You deserve it. I know you're going to win!" Ginger cried.

"You know, without you, I wouldn't be here," Dez responded.

"All that matters is that you're here," Ginger answered modestly. "Congratulations, Bentley!" Ginger gave Bentley a big hug and a kiss on the cheek. "Talk to her," she whispered in his ear before joining their hands and leaving the kitchen with a mischievous smile on her face.

Bentley looked into Dez's feline eyes and couldn't believe that he'd allowed himself to remain angry with her for so long. She was so beautiful and so sweet.

"Bentley, I'm sorry," she began.

He interrupted her apology with a kiss. "Dez, we've got a lot to work out. But I do want to work it out. I love you," he murmured in her ear, stroking her hair as he held her tightly.

"I love you too," she whispered back. Then she cast her eyes toward the ceiling and silently mouthed an amen for all her granted blessings.

LEILANI STOOD AT THE DELTA AIR LINES GATE AT MIAMI INTERnational Airport, eagerly awaiting Sparks's arrival. He was one of the last people to exit the plane. He looked exhausted, but Leilani figured that one of her special massages would get his juices flowing. But when she greeted him, she couldn't help but notice that there was absolutely no passion in his kiss.

"What's wrong, Sparky?" she asked him, fearful of his answer. In the few short months they had been seeing each other, Leilani had grown attached to Sparks. At first she had mainly been interested in who he was and what he could do for her. However, she felt no shame about that, because at least what she felt *now* was real. It was hard for a woman to make it in the entertainment industry, and it's not like he was interested in her only for her mind. He wanted a trophy, and she provided that service for him. The way she saw it, one hand washed the other. But now she had feelings for him, strong ones. She couldn't imagine her life without Sparks. She thought about him all day and dreamed about him all night. Who would she find better than him? He was the epitome of a man, the pinnacle, a true catch.

"Can we go somewhere and talk?" he asked her. He hated when she called him Sparky. That name only sounded right coming from Dez's lips. He was going to cut to the chase, then check into a hotel, handle some business, and head back to New York.

"Aren't you staying with me?" she asked.

"I don't think that's such a good idea," he said softly.

Leilani stopped walking, dropped his hand, and stood in front of him. "Hold up. What's the deal? Before, you couldn't get enough of me. Now you don't even want to stay with me?" she asked him, getting slightly loud.

"Can we just go grab a bite to eat and talk about this?" Sparks didn't want to draw too much attention to himself. He preferred to keep a low profile.

"I had a feeling something was wrong! Are you going to dump me?" she asked, bypassing the bullshit. This caught Sparks off guard. He'd planned a speech to give her over dinner. He was confident that she would handle the situation like a lady, but he could see that he had overestimated her.

"You're fucking dumping me, aren't you? I could tell something was up from that tired-ass kiss you gave me. Plus, you haven't been calling me like usual. I knew it!" Leilani screamed. Several people began to point and whisper.

"Lower your voice, Leilani, please. I said we need to talk, but here is not the place," he said evenly.

"Don't tell me what the place is. The place is where I make it! You're dumping me, and I want to know why. Does it have something to do with that bitch Dez? She got to you, didn't she? You all have been fucking, haven't you?" she asked, jealousy dripping from her lips.

"Relax, Leilani. Let's get my bag and get out of here!" Sparks was willing to say or do anything to get her out of the airport and somewhere with more privacy. It was obvious that a restaurant wasn't going to work either. "Let's just go to your house."

"So you're not dumping me?" Leilani looked hopeful. Not answering her, Sparks kissed her on the cheek and walked around her toward baggage claim. *Crazy broad!* he thought.

Thankfully, his baggage arrived in a short time, and soon they were in Leilani's convertible and on their way to her apartment. They rode in silence, Leilani staring out the window pensively as she whipped her tiny car through the Miami streets. Her almond eyes were narrowed to slits, and her expression was hostile, but when she noticed Sparks looking at her, she gave him a big smile.

As soon as they were across the threshold of Leilani's apartment, she pounced. She smothered Sparks with kisses, clawing at his clothes and grinding her pelvis against his. She snaked her hand down to his crotch to get him nice and hard, but something was drastically wrong. His penis was totally limp.

"Okay, nigga. You need to explain some shit!" she barked, pushing him away.

"Leilani, calm down."

"I will not fucking calm down, motherfucker. Are you a fag or something? A batty boy? Did you meet someone else? What? What's the deal? It's got to be something because there is no way you could not want this!" Leilani said, running her hands across her body.

"Look, Leilani. I like you, but I think you're better off with someone else. We aren't gonna work out." Sparks decided to come right out with it. Leilani would be mad, but she'd get over it. She was a beautiful girl, she'd meet someone new.

"Fuck you!" she spat. "That's bullshit. There's only one reason why a nigga flips the script all of a sudden, and that's because he's fucking somebody else. Who are you fucking?" Leilani's Jamaican accent appeared out of nowhere, thick as molasses.

"I'm outta here." *This is too much drama!* Sparks thought, picking up his cell phone to call a cab. Leilani snatched it and hurled it at the wall, smashing it into myriad pieces.

"I hate you!" Leilani shrieked. Then she began to rant in patois, spewing forth expletives like a geyser. It was bumba-clot this, batty boy that, and rasclot the other. Sparks observed her tirade, unsure of what to do next. He could try and calm her down, but that probably wouldn't work. Leilani was liable to haul off and hit him or, worse, try to really hurt him. Then he'd go to jail, because he'd surely kill her crazy ass. He didn't want to put his label or artists' careers in jeopardy. A scandal surrounding Dez was one thing, but a scandal surrounding him was another story altogether. Sparks's thoughts were interrupted by a shoe hitting him squarely upside the head.

"What the fuck?" Sparks had to stop himself from choking the life out of Leilani. Not an easy task. "Yo, I'm up outta here." Sparks grabbed his bag, shoved Leilani out of the way, and made his escape. He didn't care if he had to walk all the way back to New York; he just knew he wasn't going to spend another minute in Leilani's presence.

Luckily, Leilani resided in South Beach, so he walked to the Loews. He was a puddle of sweat thanks to the South Florida sun, but it didn't matter. He took a shower and ordered from room service, glad he'd broken off the relationship before things had gotten any more serious. He'd heard that Jamaican girls weren't to be tangled with, and now he knew exactly why. Leilani had transformed into a madwoman! But Sparks knew Leilani's tantrum was fueled by a little more than island blood. Regardless of whether or not her accusations were justified, Leilani was clearly not balanced.

When Sparks heard a knock on the door, he assumed it was room service.

"Come on in," he yelled from the bed while flicking channels on the TV. Police stormed his suite after the bellman let them in.

"Jonathan Baker?" a butch female officer questioned.

"Yeah?" Sparks answered, puzzled and alarmed.

"You are under arrest for assault," she replied gruffly.

"Assault of whom?" he asked, already knowing the answer.

"One Leilani Hong Thomas," she informed him before slapping handcuffs around his wrists.

IN THE DARKNESS OF HER BEDROOM, DEZ COULD FEEL EVERY CUT of Bentley's muscular body as she caressed him.

"I've missed you so much," she breathed into his ear.

"I've missed you too, baby girl." Bentley grabbed her face in his hands and kissed her deeply. Dez felt her insides melt and her head spin. Quickly, she removed her clothing before dropping to her knees to fiddle with Bentley's belt buckle.

"No, baby. Not tonight," Bentley told her before scooping her into his arms and placing her on the bed. Before Dez had a chance to object, he was between her legs, softly licking the center of her womanhood. Dez threw her head back and allowed herself to enjoy the sensations washing over her body. He pleased her with his tongue until she was quivering, begging him to enter her.

When he did, Dez wrapped her legs tightly around him, putting all the passion she had inside into making love to him until he climaxed, shuddering and holding her tightly as he called her name.

They awoke the next morning to Ginger banging on the door.

"It's open!" Dez muttered, her face buried in the pillow.

"Turn on the TV now! MTV!" Ginger commanded. Dez did what she was told. MTV News flashed a picture of Sparks across the screen.

"Turn the volume up," Ginger ordered. "Bentley, wake up! You need to look at this. You need to call your brother." Ginger pointed at the screen.

The VJ broke the story of Sparks's arrest in Miami, showing footage of a past interview with Sparks, along with a tearful Leilani walking out of the police station escorted by a lawyer.

"What the fuck?" Bentley asked, rubbing his eyes.

"Bentley, your brother was arrested!" Ginger exclaimed.

"What?" Bentley snapped to life. "For what?"

"For assault," Ginger relayed.

"Of who?" Dez asked, knowing but not believing the answer and thinking that assault seemed totally out of Sparks's character, though she'd put nothing past Leilani.

"Your girl Leilani." Ginger shook her head and gave Dez a cautionary look. Dez felt her stomach lurch. What the hell had happened? Did Sparks tell Leilani about their tryst? She had to know.

"Bentley . . . ," Dez began with fear in her eyes and a

trembling voice. She was afraid for both Bentley and herself, and the future of Titanium Records.

"I'm on it. Don't worry, baby girl. Everything is cool," Bentley reassured Dez with confidence. But no one watching the broadcast was totally sure of that.

CHAPTER 22

GINNY, I KNOW THAT YOU HAVE A MAN AND A LIFE AND ALL, but do you think that you could stay a few more days?" Dez pleaded with her friend, her eyes childlike.

They were in the kitchen, where Ginger was fixing a snack for them. Ginger wasn't scheduled to return to Miami for another day, but Desiree sensed that she was going to need her friend's shoulder to lean on for longer than that. The arrest had shaken her to the core because she wasn't sure whether or not Sparks and Leilani's altercation was related to her.

Bentley had left the house in a rush, his cell phone attached to his ear. He kissed her and told her that he loved her before he left, but Desiree felt like he was walking out of her life for good again. She hated feeling so insecure, but she couldn't seem to help it. She had already lost him once and barely had him back. She was afraid that their reunion had been a dream and that any minute she would wake up and discover that he in fact did hate her and had not forgiven her at all. Everything was so up in the air, so out of control. There was simply no telling what the day would bring, and that scared her.

"Sure, I can stay," Ginger agreed. "My man understands; we talk every day. I can stay as long as you need me to."

"Well, it won't be that long. I just need you to stay while we deal with this drama with Sparks and Leilani. I don't really want to be alone right now."

"Girl, I understand. This has got to have been quite an emotional roller coaster for you."

"Yeah. It's just one thing after another."

"So what's up with your girl?" Ginger asked, referring to Leilani. "What do you think happened?"

"I can't call it. Leilani has a hot temper, but Sparks is very mild-mannered. He's a laid-back, cool type of motherfucker. My bad, Ginger. I can't stop cursing," Dez apologized, and Ginger brushed it off with a wave. "Maybe things got a little too heated. I just can't imagine Sparks beating up any woman, though. Not like Leilani claimed he did. I'm just scared she found out about me and Sparks or something," Dez continued.

"Well, we'll know soon enough. When is Bentley's flight supposed to get to Miami?" Ginger inquired.

"The lawyer said by the time Bentley got to Miami, Sparks would already be out. He doesn't have a record, so arranging for bail is gonna be standard. He's gonna meet Bentley at the airport, and then they're going to come back here," Dez explained.

"Sparks isn't going to have to stay in Miami until the case is heard?" Ginger asked.

"I thought about that, and I asked Bentley. He said that the lawyer assured him he had it all under control. Famous last words, right?" Desiree smacked her lips in disgust. She had a general distaste for lawyers. She'd met a few in her day, especially since the business with the tape. She saw how manipulative and calculating they could be, and she couldn't trust any of them, not even her own personal attorney, who'd looked over her record deal.

"I'm sure Sparks has an excellent team. And maybe you should have a little faith yourself. They are handling a lot of your business, you know," Ginger told her.

"I guess you're right." Desiree sighed, still divided on the issue. "But lawyers get paid very well to lie. They'll probably say anything to justify how much they're charging!"

"Well, Sparks has the truth on his side. At least, from everything you've told me about him, he seems to. Good always prevails," Ginger said optimistically.

"Does it?" Dez retorted sardonically.

"Sure it does. Don't you believe that?" Ginger seemed shocked.

"Sometimes . . . but not always."

"Well, it does," Ginger said with finality. "Anyway," she said, changing the subject, "how is Sparks gonna feel about a stranger in his house while he's going through all of this?"

"He'll be cool. You're family." Dez smiled, and Ginger smiled back.

"Dez, are you scared?" Ginger asked, catching Dez off guard.

"Yeah," Dez answered.

"You shouldn't be. I'm here for you, you know this. But where do you think that I'm getting my strength from? I mean, it has to be coming from somewhere, right?" she asked candidly.

"You're just strong, Ginger," Dez reasoned.

"Yes, I am, but why?" Ginger raised an eyebrow.

Dez shrugged. "I don't know." Some people were just tougher than others, she thought to herself.

"Sure you do," Ginger told her. "It's from God." Dez said nothing.

"Desi, when you're faced with trouble, you've got to lean on God. You've got to humble yourself and admit that you don't have all the answers. You have to ask him to show you a way."

"Okay. And so then God just shows you the way? I mean, I'm not trying to act funny, but I pray. I really do. I still don't understand half the things that are going on around me. What's up with that? Where is God when I really need him?" Dez asked.

"Everything isn't for you to understand right now. You have to be still to hear his voice. And don't look at it like you're testing God to see if he has an answer. He does. *You* don't. You have to be open to hear the answer. Be still and just trust in him. Believe in something that you can't really see or hear. You know he's there. That's what faith is. Besides, if he weren't there, you'd be dead, wouldn't you? If he weren't there, you wouldn't be here."

Desiree hesitated. "I guess."

"There ain't no guess to it, Desi. You either believe or you don't. You can't straddle the fence on this one. This is your salvation!" Ginger said, a serious expression on her face. Desiree picked at her fingernails.

"I need to ask you a question, Desiree. It's the most important question you will ever have to answer," Ginger stated dramatically.

"Go on," Dez replied.

"Are you saved, Desiree? Is Jesus Christ your Lord and personal savior?"

"I guess so," Dez answered. She knew what it *meant* to be saved. She thought she was, before Ernesto and the foster home and the strip clubs. But when she really thought about it, Jesus hadn't seemed to save her from much.

Ginger stared directly into her eyes. "Have you ever asked him to forgive all of your sins? Have you told him that you believe that he died on the cross so that you would be saved from hell? Do you believe that no matter what, you're going to heaven?"

"Well, yes, I did ask him to forgive my sins. I do it every day. And I know that what he did at Calvary, dying for us, is supposed to save us."

"Why do I sense that there's a 'but' coming?"

"But me go to heaven automatically? I doubt it. But then again, maybe you're right. I've already been through hell," Desiree added.

"This is serious," Ginger said. "If you've asked Jesus to come into your heart, to forgive you your sins; if you believe in what Jesus did for us and that he's your savior, then you're saved. Now, you've got to make an effort to live a righteous life. You can't just go around doing whatever you want and go 'Oh but I'm saved.' There are rules to life. They're in the Bible. But God already knows where you're going to fall short. And he's already forgiven you. Look, I know that this is a lot to digest right now, but think on it, okay? I mean, really think about what it means to have faith."

"Okay," Dez agreed. "I'll think about it. But I don't think that I'll ever see things the way that you do. I don't think I'll ever have as much faith as you."

"Oh, I'm pretty positive you will," Ginger stated matter-of-factly.

"How can you be so sure?"

"Duh! Faith, Desiree, faith." Ginger rolled her eyes at Dez, making her crack up.

DEZ AND GINGER SPENT THE DAY IN MANHATTAN AS A DIS-traction, stopping in some of the fancy stores and boutiques that lined Madison Avenue. Prices were mad steep for just about everything, but Dez indulged her friend and herself in two outfits from Lacoste.

"Pretty conservative, huh? You couldn't have told me that we'd be rocking twin sets and plaid pants a few years ago!" Ginger giggled.

"I know that's right. But this is cute in a Palm Beach kind of way. Besides, I can wear this when I want to be low-key. No one would ever recognize me in this getup," Dez said, laughing.

"Yeah, but you look classy. Plus, you'd be surprised how funky you can make that outfit look with the right accessories. You know, a Kangol, some funky shoes, and a unique bag. I bet if anyone saw you, you'd start a trend."

"Don't make a sucker's bet, Ginger!" Dez teased, and they burst into laughter, leaving the store with their booty in two large shopping bags. They had a late lunch at Tavern on the Green before making the long trek back to the Hamptons. The day had been an excellent diversion from the current situation.

"You know, I've been thinking about all the things you told me. You know, about having faith and everything. Ginger, you've been right. I need to trust in the Lord a whole lot more. It's like this song they used to sing in my dad's church, 'Noways Tired.' There's a line in there that says . . ."

" 'I don't believe he brought me this far to leave me,' " they said in unison.

"You're right, Desi. He didn't bring you this far to leave you. And now he's going to take you even farther."

"I've also decided that when the heat blows over, maybe after the BET Awards, I'm going to share my story," Dez said. "There are some legal issues that will need to be sorted out, of course. But I'm ready to fess up. There are probably so many girls out there, just like me, just like us, who think that they're all alone. They think that no one understands, and no one cares. Maybe if they know that I survived, and I made it, they'll find a way too. I'm not saying I have all the answers, but I think I'll be able to make a difference."

"Oh, Desi! I think that's a wonderful idea. If I can help you in any way, you know that I will. I'll even volunteer my future husband's help! He can't say no to me," Ginger joked. "But I know he wouldn't want to say no." She looked at her engagement ring.

"I can't wait to meet this man. He sounds like a helluva fella," Dez said.

"You'll have a chance soon," Ginger told her. "His schedule is hectic, but he'll make the time to meet you. I know he's dying to. I used to talk about you all the time. He used to pray with me, that somehow you'd find me."

"I've got an idea!" Dez said, snapping her fingers. "Why don't you guys come to L.A. for the BET Awards? My treat, of course."

"Are you serious?" Ginger asked, wide-eyed. Dez nodded enthusiastically. "Well, then, heck yeah! Consider it a date!"

Ginger and Dez had barely been home for two minutes before the doorbell rang.

"I wonder who that is," Dez said, visibly on edge. "Like I said the last time, no one ever comes by unannounced. And they have to get buzzed into the gate."

"Not this again, Dez. Dang! There's only one way to find out: answer the door."

"It's probably Bentley and Sparks. Maybe Sparks forgot his key or something. It *is* about time that they arrived. They probably just punched in the access code and came on in."

"Gosh! Stop jaw-jacking already. Oh, forget it! I'll get the door. You've been so jumpy," Ginger exclaimed, and opened the door.

Leilani stood on the doorstep, her hands on her hips. "Who the fuck are you?" she said contemptuously.

"Excuse me? I should be asking you the same question. How did you get in?" Ginger retorted. Leilani and Ginger, both over six feet in heels, stood face-to-face.

"Where is Sparks?" Leilani demanded, attempting to push her way into the mansion.

"Oh hell no! Are you Leilani?" Ginger clapped her hand over her mouth in astonishment.

"Ginny, who's at the door?" Dez stepped into the foyer and stopped dead in her tracks. "What are you doing here? How'd you get to New York so fast? Oh, you're crazy as hell! I see I'm gonna have to kick your ass again!" Dez started toward Leilani.

Leilani pulled a switchblade from behind her back and wielded it menacingly. "Oh, I'm ready for you this time, bitch!" she said. Dez and Ginger both stepped back hastily.

"Are you Sparks's new bitch, his flavor of the month?" Leilani asked Ginger, and stormed her way into the house.

"That's my sister," Dez answered. "Leave her out of this."

"You're probably trying to set her up with Sparks," Leilani said accusingly.

"I'm engaged to a doctor in Miami. I don't want your

man," Ginger answered softly in an attempt to calm her down.

"Hmmm, well, maybe Dez wants my man. She always was a greedy bitch. Always had to be the center of attention! Bentley wasn't enough for you, huh? You just had to have my man too, didn't you? You never could stand to see me get ahead," Leilani screeched maniacally.

"That's not true. Nothing has ever happened between me and Sparks. It's strictly business, you know that," Dez lied.

"It's strictly business, you know that," Leilani mocked. "You think I'm stupid. But I'm not. You are."

"Leilani," Ginger pleaded, grasping Dez's hand. "Think about what you're doing. No man is worth all this."

"Ha! Sparks is. And if I can't have him, you two sure as hell won't," Leilani threatened.

"Leilani, you already have Sparks," Dez began.

"*Had.* I *had* Sparks. He dumped me for no apparent reason! Which means only one thing: you got to him. And now you're going to pay," Leilani warned.

This bitch done lost her mind! Dez thought. *I had no idea she was this much of a nut job.*

Leilani continued to hold the two at knifepoint.

"I tried. God knows that I tried to do everything in my power to make that man happy, everything. I was more than a woman. Then out of nowhere, bam! He says he isn't feeling this. It isn't working. Well, I'm tired of getting the short end of the stick! I'm tired of busting my ass to be the best, only to get shoved to the background! That shit is over!" Leilani barked.

"Leilani! What the hell are you doing here?" Sparks bellowed from the doorway. He and Bentley had arrived and let themselves in to see Leilani holding Ginger and Dez at knife-point.

"Now, is that any way to greet your woman?" Leilani cooed, her personality switching 180 degrees.

"Why do you have a knife? Leilani, what are you doing?" Sparks asked cautiously.

"Oh, this little thing? I'll put it away. I was just teasing them, baby. I came here to talk to you, to apologize for what went down in Miami. But they wouldn't let me in. I know we can work out whatever is wrong."

"How did you find my house? I never gave you this address," Sparks said, inching his way toward her.

"It wasn't easy. You're a tricky one, aren't you? But nothing can stand in the way of true love. Once I found out where you lived, I hid in the bushes and waited for those two hos to come home. I ran in the gate behind their car. Smart, huh?" Leilani grinned, satisfied with herself.

"Put the knife down," Sparks ordered.

"Not until you agree to talk with me. Tell me you still love me," Leilani begged. "Tell me we can work it out."

Bentley, Dez, and Ginger stood frozen, their mouths agape.

"Girl, you know I still love you. I was just trippin'. I had a lot on my mind. I'm sorry." Sparks played along to appease her.

"I knew it! Oh, I love you so much, baby." Leilani tossed the knife aside and ran to Sparks. She held him tightly and smothered him with kisses. Sparks grabbed her and wrestled her hands behind her back. He shoved her out the front door and locked it. Dez ran into the kitchen and called the police while Leilani banged on the door.

"Oh my God!" Ginger placed her hand over her heart.

"Are you okay?" Bentley asked her.

"Yeah, just a little bugged out is all," Ginger responded.

"You must be Ginger, Dez's sister. Bentley told me all about you." Sparks extended his hand, and Ginger shook it.

"I wish that we had met under more pleasant circumstances," she said, smiling.

"I wish that we'd met before you got engaged," Sparks quipped.

"Bentley told you, huh?"

"Yeah." He grinned back flirtatiously. "As you can see, my luck with women sucks."

"I just got off the phone with the police. They'll be here shortly," Dez interrupted, returning to the foyer.

Leilani was still banging on the door, demanding to be let in.

"She can't get off the property unless she hops the gate," Sparks told them.

"Well, at least now you can have the charges against you dropped. It's obvious that she's a stalker. She needs some serious help," Ginger told him.

"That's true. But I feel sorry for her," Sparks admitted.

"You were going to feel even sorrier for her if she didn't have that knife. She was about to get the smack-down all over again!" Dez piped in.

The police arrived and hauled Leilani off the premises. Sparks decided not to press charges. He just wanted the matter to be done with.

"I don't think that's such a good idea, dude. That bitch is sick. She might come back," Bentley warned him.

"She won't come back," Sparks replied, and hoped to God he was right.

CHAPTER 23

June 2002—Los Angeles

DEZ WAS ACCUSTOMED TO BEING PAMPERED, BUT HER EX-perience before the BET Awards was bar none the most indulgent experience of her life. She'd spent the week working hard on her performance piece with Bentley. In addition to their collaboration and her performance of "Down to Ride," she was going to introduce a few of her new songs in the form of a medley. There were also the press junkets, interviews, and meet-and-greets that came with the territory. The whole pre-awards process had been hectic. Sparks and Bentley insisted that she be totally relaxed and look her absolute best, so it was arranged for Dez to not have to lift a finger the day of the ceremony.

First, an aesthetician arrived at her suite at the Château Marmont to give her a facial and body scrub with glycolic acid so that her skin would be radiant. Then she received a ninety-minute head-to-toe Asian massage, complete with warm stones being placed on all her "chakras." The attendant informed Dez that the placement of the stones would open her body up to positive energy. Dez figured that she needed all the positive energy she could get. She was so nervous, and it was hard to believe how much had happened in just under a year.

She took a break for a snack and reflected on her journey to the realization of a dream that no one had believed was possible, not even her. She finally understood that it was by God's grace that she was able to come so far. She used to believe that it was because she was pretty and because she was slick that she had been able to remain on top. But where did her looks and her "game" come from? Dez chose to believe that they were gifts from God. She realized he hadn't given her any more troubles than she could bear, even though it had felt that way many times. Everything he'd brought her to, he'd brought her through.

She used to think that God put her in the ghetto and had her overcome so many obstacles because he despised her. He couldn't have cared; otherwise, life would have been good instead of so hard. Now she knew that God put her right where he needed her to be to do whatever it was he intended for her to do. She had survived the concrete jungle of New York, rising above the millions of nameless, faceless people to make something out of herself in a tiny little city near the Atlantic Ocean.

Dez was grateful. She could have died that night with Ernesto. And since then, she'd found herself in many situations that could have gotten ugly. But somehow she always survived. It wasn't her looks or her game, it was a blessing.

"You better get it all out now. Because once I make up that pretty face of yours, you had better not ruin all of my hard work!" a pretty young makeup artist who resembled Halle Berry kidded her. Dez looked up startled. She hadn't even realized that she was crying.

"My bad." Dez wiped her face with her forehand and smiled.

"Don't apologize. It's cool. I'll make sure to hook you up, but try and be careful. I know it's hard, though. If this were all happening to me, I'd probably be so happy that I'd be in tears too," the makeup artist, Kennedy, stated. She patted Dez's hand. "Congratulations! You deserve all of this."

"I do?" Dez asked, surprised a total stranger would say such a thing.

"Sure. Some of these artists can be so evil! I've been peeping your style all day. You've been really friendly and gracious to everyone. We understand that performers and celebrities can get nervous before a big night like this. But some of them go a little overboard."

"Well, I've been there and done that. You wouldn't have said that I was friendly and gracious if you'd met me last year. Maybe not even last month!" Dez admitted.

"Well, what happened? Why the big change?"

"Jesus. My sister helped me find him again," Dez answered with a smile.

Kennedy smiled back. "Amen. I knew you deserved this, girl! You'd be surprised at how many stars are atheists or believe in crazy cult religions and the like. It's been a while since I worked with a fellow Christian."

Dez noticed that Kennedy was wearing a beautiful cross around her neck. It made her feel good to be respected by another Christian. Dez knew her lyrics weren't exactly clean or religious, but she knew her heart was good, and she was trying to be a better person. Apparently, it hadn't gone unnoticed.

Forty-five minutes later Dez inspected her face in the mirror, visibly pleased.

"You did an excellent job!" Dez complimented Kennedy. "Honestly, I've had my makeup done by a million different folks, but this is the very best!"

"Well, it helps when the canvas is beautiful to begin with," Kennedy replied, lifting Dez's face and sprinkling her with shimmery powder that gave her a golden glow.

There was a knock at the suite door.

"Can you get that?" Dez asked Kennedy. "I need to use the bathroom."

"Sure, no problem," Kennedy agreed, while Dez slipped into the bathroom.

Dez turned on the water, quickly folded a towel, placed it next to the commode, and kneeled on it gingerly. She felt her stomach lurch and the bile rise as she heaved into the toilet. It was the third time in two days she'd vomited, and she knew in her gut that it was more than just the jitters. Her period was more than two months late, her breasts were extremely tender, and she couldn't seem to stop spitting. She'd even picked up a few pounds and was always exhausted. Dez flushed the toilet and carefully wiped her mouth. After checking herself out in the mirror, she decided that she looked fine and went to slip on her clothes.

Whose baby is it? a nagging voice inside her head asked. She shook the thought away. No doubt it was Bentley's baby.

"Dez, these came for you! Aren't they beautiful?" Kennedy presented Dez with a huge bouquet of exquisite calla lilies.

"Oh my God! They're fabulous! Calla lilies are my favorite. But no one knows that except for my sister, Ginger. They must be from her. But I wish they were from Bentley." Dez knew she shouldn't share her personal business with a virtual stranger, but everyone knew that she and Bentley were an item. Dez plucked the card from the bouquet.

Congratulations! Here's to the future. I love you! Bentley.

A huge smile spread across Dez's face.

"Judging by that grin, those flowers are from your man. That ain't a sister smile," Kennedy quipped.

"Yeah, they're from my baby," Dez replied.

"You're a lucky woman," Kennedy said.

I sure hope so! Dez thought. If the baby was Sparks's and not Bentley's, her life would be in shambles again! Dez couldn't figure out how she kept getting into such messes, but with God on her side, she knew that she would find her way out.

"You better get a move on, Dez!" Kennedy told her. "It's almost time for you to leave."

Dez quickly slipped into the custom-made gown designed by Donatella Versace. It was gold, sequined, and supershort, yet managed to be sexy and classy at once. Dez twirled in the mirror; she felt just like a fairy-tale princess. She had it all: good looks, a great career, recognition, and the man she loved. And now she was going to be a mommy. It reminded her of the day that she, Tasha, and Shelle saw the football players' wives back in Morristown. She'd come far. Everything she had dreamed was now a reality. What could be better?

Dez's stylist, hairdresser, and Kennedy carefully packed everything that she'd need for the ceremony: hairpieces, makeup, and her performance outfit and shoes. They were going ahead of her in a separate car, while Dez, Bentley, Sparks, Scoop, and Jazzy piled into a bulletproof stretch Hummer to dazzle the red carpet. Ginger and her fiancé were not going to attend the ceremony—Ginger's man hadn't been able to get away in time to catch an early flight—but they were meeting them at the Titanium Records after-party. Dez wanted her sister there, but late was better than never. Besides, they wouldn't have been able to have any fun, since she was performing with Bentley, announcing an award, and hopefully winning one. Dez couldn't wait to share the news

of her pregnancy with Ginger. She and Bentley would probably get married! It looked like both of them had finally found
true happiness.

"Thanks for my flowers, babe," Dez cooed in Bentley's
ear as she slid into the Hummer next to him.

"No doubt, baby. Ginger told me you like calla lilies," he
replied, grinning.

"Yo yo, listen up!" Sparks yelled over the rowdy entourage,
who were smoking cigars and blasting Dez and Bentley's
single as loud as the volume would go.

"I want to make a toast!" he exclaimed, popping open a
bottle of Cristal with a flourish. He poured everyone a glass.

"This family has been through a lot, but we made it through
in one piece. What else would you expect from Titanium? We
are the toughest. To family!" Sparks held up his glass.

"To family!" they echoed, glasses extended.

"A la familia," Dez said in Spanish. "Salud!" She clinked
her glass with Bentley's, marveling that soon they would be
family in more ways than one.

The trip to the Kodak Theater was short, but the lineup
of limos and chauffeur-driven luxury cars created major
gridlock.

"You ready, Dez?" Sparks asked.

"No doubt!" she answered, full of excitement.

"Good. We believe in you and we got your back, no matter
what happens tonight. You know how to handle the media,
and your performance is tight. I'd say you're as ready as you're
going to get. Good luck, lil' sis. I love you." Sparks looked at
Dez with warm eyes. Dez knew that there was more to his
statement than he let on, but she disregarded it. The past was
the past. Sparks looked at his brother. "I love you too, man!"

"Damn! For a minute I thought you had eyes for my girl!"
Bentley teased.

"Nah, man," Sparks lied, giving his brother a pound and Dez a kiss on the cheek.

Dez swore she could hear the guitar lick from "All Eyez on Me" as she stepped out of the Hummer assisted by a huge bodyguard. All around her, cameras were flashing; the media were in a frenzy. And what was this? They were calling her name! Journalists and fans all vied for her attention. Dez was so overcome with emotion she thought her heart would explode. She posed for the photographers while peeping Bentley out the corner of her eye. He and Sparks were busy taking pictures and fielding questions of their own from the media. Abruptly, Bentley grabbed her arm and pulled her close to speak with Ananda Lewis. Dez had always admired Ananda; not only was she beautiful, she was down-to-earth. Many times Dez had practiced answering questions from Ananda for all of MTV's viewers to see. It was such a rush to finally do it.

And just when Dez thought that this moment had to be the very best moment of her life, chaos erupted. First there were the blinding flashes of light that hurt her eyes. Then there was pain; pain so intense that it was immobilizing. She fell to the red carpet, made even redder by her blood. Her eyes went blurry and out of focus as terrified masses of people attempted to flee the scene. Why wasn't anyone helping her? And where was Bentley?

"Bentley!" she called out weakly to him. Dez held her hand in front of her face and willed her eyes to focus. Her hand was covered in blood.

I've got to get help! Dez thought in a panic. *After all I've been through I ain't going out like a sucker.*

Dez struggled to scream. "Someone please help me! I'm pregnant. *Someone please help my baby!*" And then everything went black.

CHAPTER 24

BENTLEY AND SPARKS RAN ALONGSIDE THE GURNEY AS DEZ was wheeled into the emergency room at Cedars-Sinai Medical Center. There was a journalist who was wheeled in too, hovering between life and death. Throngs of the press were in tow, anxious to get the scoop on not just a celebrity but one of their own as well.

"You can't go in there," a nurse told Bentley as he attempted to follow Dez into an operating room.

"You don't understand. That's my girl," he explained, overcome with tears.

"I'm sorry, sir," she told him, blocking his way. Sparks put his arm around Bentley's shoulder and led him into the ER waiting area.

"What happened, man?" Bentley asked his brother.

"I don't know," Sparks answered, shaking his head. "There was the flash, then gunshots. I saw Dez on the ground, and then you came up."

"Whoever did this is going to pay!" Bentley swore through clenched teeth.

"Yeah, but who did it? We ain't got beef with nobody. We

don't owe anybody any money. We ain't got no gang ties, no mob ties, no drug ties. We busted our asses building this label. I can't believe that someone was just hating. Not enough to try and kill us," Sparks exclaimed. "I mean, who were they aiming at? Was it me? Was it you? Was it Dez?"

"Shit! Was it someone else altogether? Maybe we were in the wrong place at the wrong time," Bentley said.

"I don't know . . . the way it all went down, it was organized. It was like a professional hit, man."

The police interviewed Sparks and Bentley. They repeated the same facts: They had no known enemies. They weren't involved in anything illegal or shady and couldn't think of any reason other than jealousy that someone would want to hurt any of them. Sparks told the police about the case with Dirty Dan, as well as Ysenia's reporting to the tabloids, and the stalking incident with a knife-wielding Leilani. The police gave the standard promise to look into every avenue and follow up on all leads, but both Sparks and Bentley were skeptical that the case would be made a priority. They'd seen what happened in cases like the Notorious B.I.G. and Tupac Shakur murders. The authorities would probably chalk things up to senseless rap violence. The detectives that interviewed them gave them their business cards and assured them that they would contact them if any information became available. Likewise, they asked the brothers to call if they remembered or heard anything.

"If we were white, they'd already have a lineup," Bentley raged.

"Maybe, but talking about race isn't going to help us right now," Sparks told his brother. He knew that Bentley was upset and afraid for Dez. "I need to call Ginger, though. She was supposed to get to L.A. a couple of hours ago with her fiancé."

"I'm going to stay here and wait to hear about my baby," Bentley replied.

GINGER HAD ALREADY HEARD THE NEWS WHEN SPARKS REACHED her by cell phone.

"We just checked in a little while ago. I was getting ready to get dressed when we saw it all on television. Is Dez okay?" Ginger asked, hopeful.

"It doesn't look good," Sparks admitted. "Get down here quick."

"Okay. I'm on my way. Cedars-Sinai, right?"

"Yeah."

"But, Sparks, who did this?" Ginger wanted to know.

"We don't know. We already talked to the police and told them everything we could think of. We told them about Dirty Dan and Leilani, but they gave us the standard 'don't call us, we'll call you' routine," he informed her.

"I'll be there in a flash. I know Dan, and I don't think he has the capacity to kill. And although Leilani is definitely crazy, I don't know if she's *that* crazy. But I may have some information that will help," Ginger told him, then hung up the phone.

In an instant Ginger and her fiancé were at the hospital.

"This is my fiancé, Dr. Jacques Pierre," Ginger said to Sparks and Bentley.

"Nice to meet you," Jacques said, and shook their hands. "I'm going to talk to the doctor and see if I can get a better handle on the situation," he informed them before kissing Ginger on the cheek and disappearing down the corridor.

"How is she?" Ginger asked Sparks as she greeted him and Bentley with comforting hugs and kisses.

"She's still in surgery. She lost a lot of blood. And she was, she was . . . oh my God!" Bentley broke down.

"She was eight weeks pregnant. She lost the baby," Sparks finished. "The doctor just came and told us."

Ginger burst into tears. *Why, God?* she prayed. *Please help me to understand this and trust that you'll make it all better.*

"On the phone you said you might know something." Sparks got down to business, and Ginger quickly composed herself.

"Oh my God yes! There was this guy K.G. Dez used to date him before she met Bentley. When she broke things off with him, he didn't take it so well. She thought he got the picture, but he did have her nervous for a while. He was in some serious denial," Ginger informed them.

"It's a start," Sparks said.

"My baby, my baby," Bentley said over and over softly as he sat in a hard plastic chair with his head buried in his hands.

"Get me Dez's two-way. He paged her a bunch of times. We can give that information to the police," Ginger told Sparks.

Sparks handed her the beaded Judith Leiber bag that Dez had been carrying earlier that night. Then they called the police. The detective seemed a little more optimistic about the lead than he had before. He promised them he'd get right on it.

There had been complications from Dez's surgery. The bullet had gone through her abdomen and lodged against a nerve near her spinal column. Removal had been difficult and highly risky. Dez had lost lots of blood due to hemorrhaging, and having had a transfusion, she was now recovering from the long surgery in intensive care. She was still unconscious, and both her heart rate and blood pressure were unstable.

Cards, flowers, and stuffed animals began pouring into the hospital from hip-hop fans nationwide. MTV and BET had both interrupted their regular programming with updates and a marathon of Titanium Records videos, along with all the videos Dez had ever appeared in. People e-mailed and called the networks to offer their best wishes for her recovery. Naturally, Ysenia took the shooting as an opportunity to talk to the sleazy tabloids and so-called entertainment news programs to milk the tragedy for all she could.

Two days after the shooting, the police contacted Sparks via his cell phone. Both Ginger and Bentley had not left the hospital since the shooting, although Dez was in a coma and was nonresponsive to stimuli.

"Mr. Baker? This is Detective Atkins of the LAPD."

"Detective, have you found out anything about this K.G. character?" Sparks crossed his fingers, and Ginger grabbed his hand and began to pray.

"We followed up on the lead. His name is Kevin Gilliam. He's a high-level drug dealer who is currently being held in a pretrial detention center in Detroit facing a mandatory minimum of twenty-five years to life in a federal penitentiary. He's charged with murder, trafficking, extortion; you name it, he was involved. But he wasn't involved in Dez's shooting. He's been locked up for about three weeks now. And it's highly unlikely that he could have orchestrated this whole thing from behind bars. He's facing his own trial right now. Dez probably isn't his main focus, no matter how smitten he once was. But we're gonna keep digging. It's a long shot, but if he's involved, we're gonna find out.

"As for Leilani Hong Thomas, the young lady that threatened her with a knife, she was working on a soundstage in Miami that night. Several people have vouched for her whereabouts. Meanwhile, there's a lab checking out the footage of the pre-awards show. There has to be something on one of the tapes. Most of the journalists are cooperating with us."

"Most of them?" Sparks questioned.

"Well, some of them are taking their time handing over their footage. They want to be the first to discover anything. They want the scoop," the detective explained. "But don't worry. We're going to find something. Whoever did this wasn't thinking too much. There were a million cameras out there. There's bound to be something. Just try and be patient. We're going to get to the bottom of this."

Sparks disconnected the call.

"I don't understand," he told Ginger. "K.G.'s been locked up for three weeks. He couldn't have been involved. He's about to go on trial facing a major bid. He's probably focusing on how to save his own ass, not causing more trouble for himself right now."

"Think, Sparks!" Ginger begged. "I mean, is there anyone? Who would want to see *you* dead?"

"I keep telling you, we don't have beef. Me and B used to be petty thieves when we were younger, boosters. But we never fucked around with the big boys. I started DJ'ing before we could get too caught up in the streets. We've been all about our music ever since. That's on everything."

"This is so crazy," Ginger said. "K.G. is out. Ysenia wouldn't do it because Dez is her meal ticket. Dan isn't a killer. I know him. He was probably mad as hell that he had to pay her all that money from the settlement of the tape, but killing Dez wouldn't have changed anything. He already paid her, it's not like he can get his money back. He's probably just glad that he's not in jail. But I got to ask you, Sparks. Does Leilani know what went down between you and my sister?"

Sparks looked surprised.

"Yeah, Dez told me," Ginger explained. "But don't worry, your secret is safe with me. I'm just asking because Leilani is nuts. There was that whole incident with the knife. And now that I'm thinking about it, it seems to make sense."

"Leilani was just being dramatic," Sparks replied.

"Stop defending her. She held us at knifepoint. Do the police know that?"

"Yes, I told them. If it was her, the police would know something. Besides, if Leilani is behind this, it's not because of what happened with me and Dez. I never said anything, and I don't plan to," Sparks swore.

"Well, I don't know. But what's more important anyway is that Dez make it through this. She's got to pull through. She can't die!" Ginger began to cry.

"Come on." Sparks hugged her. "Let's go talk to Bentley and see if anything has improved."

BENTLEY SAT AT DEZ'S BEDSIDE, HOLDING HER HAND. HE HAD A blank expression on his face.

"Is she getting any better?" Ginger asked.

"No. Nothing has changed," Bentley replied somberly.

"Well, let's all pray. That's all that's left to do," Ginger suggested, and they did just that.

CHAPTER 25

Four days later

"JONATHAN BAKER?" IT WAS DETECTIVE ATKINS ON THE other end of the phone. "I need you to come into the police station immediately."

"Has there been a crack in the case?" he asked eagerly.

"I won't go into it over the phone. Just get here," he instructed before ending the call.

Sparks and Ginger headed to the police headquarters in Inglewood. Bentley refused to leave Dez's side, but promised to alert them of any change in her condition. He made them swear to page him as soon as they knew something.

"Have you found the shooter?" Ginger asked immediately as Detective Atkins joined them.

"Yes and no," he replied.

"Please just tell us what's going on," Sparks interrupted.

"Well, we've found the perpetrator on film." Detective Atkins popped in a videotape. "This footage came from *Access Entertainment Weekly*. Their cameras were directed at Dez, but from behind her. Take a look into the upper left-hand corner of the TV screen as I play this. Now, I'm warning you, this is graphic. You're going to see Dez go down. But you're also going to see who did it," the detective explained. He played the tape in slow motion. Ginger began to cry as she watched the footage, but tried to keep her eyes focused on where the shots were being fired from. The detective stopped the tape.

"See, right there." He pointed a ballpoint pen at a shadowy man in the upper left-hand corner of the screen. He was holding a giant strobe flash with one hand and a nine-millimeter revolver in the other. Simultaneously, the man illuminated the extra-bright flash and squeezed the trigger on the gun.

"Who is it?" Ginger asked, averting her eyes.

"We don't know yet. We were hoping that maybe you would recognize him," Detective Atkins stated.

"I can barely see him. From what I can see, he looks Chinese or something," Ginger replied. She gave Sparks a meaningful look. Sparks raised an eyebrow.

Chinese! Nah, it couldn't be, Sparks thought. *Could Leilani somehow be behind all of this? Fuck her alibi! I owe it to Dez to find out. But I don't trust the LAPD. We still don't know who killed Tupac or Biggie! They probably don't even care about who did this or why. They're probably only hoping to solve this crime so they can be on Court TV and write a book or get a promotion. But I think I have a way to get to the bottom of this.*

"His picture is being blown up and enhanced and is going out on every station as we speak. Someone somewhere knows who this guy is, and they're going to tell us," Atkins said with confidence.

"Someone knows who did this, all right, and whoever did will get caught," Sparks said. "Have the media alert the public that I'm offering a reward of a million dollars to anyone who can lead us to the identity of this man, his motives, and his connections. The pieces have all got to fit together, but if they do, the million is theirs."

"You do realize that our department is going to get flooded with calls from all kinds of people who just want the reward money, don't you?" Atkins asked.

"What's your point?" Sparks said.

"My point is that we need real leads. I'm not sending my men on some wild-goose chase."

"Well, do what you gotta do."

I know I *will, Detective,* Sparks thought. If his instincts were right and Leilani was connected to Dez's shooting, he was going to catch her himself and he wasn't going to have to come off of a dime.

"Are you thinking what I'm thinking?" Ginger asked Sparks once they had left the police station.

"Leilani?" Sparks replied.

"What are the odds? The crazy girl shows up at the house, holds us at knifepoint, and then Dez is shot by an Asian man? Leilani's the only Asian that's got beef with any of you," Ginger said.

"I just want to know why the police haven't made the connection. I told them about Leilani . . . Maybe if I would have pressed charges, Dez wouldn't—"

Ginger cut him off. "There's no sense in wondering what might have been. And beating yourself up isn't going to help us catch Leilani." Ginger patted Sparks on the shoulder.

"Ginger, I love Dez."

"I know. We all do."

"No. I *love* her. You know this. I would have gladly taken the bullet for her if I could have." Sparks got choked up.

"Come on, Sparks. Let's go to the hospital and check on Dez. We need to let Bentley know what's going on," Ginger suggested, and they headed back to Cedars-Sinai.

BREAKING NEWS REGARDING THE AWARDS SHOW SHOOTING OF
rapper Dez and journalist Sheila Rubin: A suspect has been caught
on tape. The perpetrator is described as an Asian man, five seven to
five ten, slight to medium build. What you're looking at now are
digitally enhanced images of this man. Titanium Records has offered
a one-million-dollar reward to any person with information leading
to the arrest and conviction of the shooter.

Leilani sat transfixed in front of the television smoking
an L.

"Good luck, Sparky boy!" she sneered at the screen. "It
serves the bitch right, you know." Leilani sucked her teeth
and grinned mercilessly.

"She just had to go and ruin everything, didn't she? She
had to be greedy. It wasn't enough for her to be a model. She
had to go and be a rapper too. Dez always had to have all of
the attention. And she couldn't just stick with Bentley. Oh
no! She had to go and try and sink her hooks into my man.
I know she's the reason behind our breakup. She poisoned
his mind against me." Leilani had taken to talking out loud
to herself more and more. If she could distinguish the difference between an internal monologue and an external one,
she was far beyond caring.

"Bitch, bitch, she's such a bitch. She left me hanging at the
party. She put her hands on me. She starred in that awful
Dirty Dan tape. And still, everyone loves Dez. Well, I've
fixed that. Let's see how much the world loves a ghost. How
long will they mourn you, Dez?" Leilani inhaled deeply,
coughed a bit, and then blew a thick haze of smoke into the
atmosphere.

"I told her she didn't want to see me! I was her friend even when everyone talked about her like she had a tail. And how did she repay me? With betrayal. And everyone knows what the punishment for betrayal is. It's death. Benedict Arnold, Brutus, and all of Caesar's homeys, they paid for their treason with their lives. It's the law of the streets, always has been, always will be. Dez had to die." Leilani laughed and laughed until her sides hurt.

"But, God, someone needs to squash that roach already. She's hanging on, I'll give her that. But she can't hang on forever. Not with her injuries. And even if she lives, the reporters said she'll probably never walk again. Who's gonna love that body when it's stuck in a wheelchair? Huh? Who's gonna take care of you when you can't fuck for a living? Huh? Nobody, that's who!" Leilani got off the couch and danced around the room.

"Ding-dong, the bitch is almost dead," she sang as she skipped about. "I've directed my first masterpiece!" she screamed.

"I would like to thank God, the Academy, and, of course, you, all the fans, for making this possible." Leilani blew kisses to an invisible audience seated in her living room.

"I mean, honestly, this is a classic! I had the perfect sound track, thanks to Titanium Records. I had an A-list cast. The set was beautiful. And, of course, there was my vision. This couldn't help but be a classic. No one believes in quality anymore. No one has any creativity. Everyone wants to sample or remake something. There's no originality. Everyone wants to get paid off of what someone else made. They want the story to end in ninety minutes or less, with everything neatly wrapped in a bow. But this is real life. Real life is messy. Real life isn't fair. Real life is a young starlet gunned down on the biggest night of her life. Real life keeps right on going and going and going . . ."

Leilani watched intently as the reporter told of the reward and showed footage of the shooter, the man she hired, setting off a blinding flash and shooting into the crowd. The journalist had been an accident, but Leilani always reasoned that accidents happened. She wasn't worried, though. All Asians looked alike, didn't they? Besides, Ling Bai, her hired assassin, had boarded a plane to another job the night of the shooting. Who knew where he was by now?

Hiring Ling Bai hadn't been easy or cheap. Leilani had to procure his services through her cousin Mike Hong, a member of a deadly and feared Asian gang in Los Angeles. But it was well worth the effort and the expense; soon Dez would be out of the way permanently, and Leilani was going to get away with murder.

Soon she'd contact Sparks and offer her sympathy. If she didn't, she might look suspicious. There had been the incident with the knife, which she truly regretted. She hadn't been thinking clearly and had lost her cool. But everything would turn out just fine. Sparks had been a fool to let her go without pressing charges. Did he actually think she would just forget about it? He could have gotten a restraining order, and then she would have gotten in trouble for contacting him. But he just wanted to make the incident and her disappear, so she got off with a warning. His haste had made it easier for her to manipulate her way back into his heart and his life. He'd be weak and vulnerable and consumed with grief. It would take a while to make him come around. But Leilani was confident that she could manage it. It would be the perfect ending . . .

"BENTLEY, HAVE YOU SEEN THE NEWS?" GINGER ASKED HIM. Bentley was holding Dez's hand, talking to her softly, as he had been doing during the entire ordeal.

"Yeah, I saw it. I was just telling my baby that we were gonna find the person who did this to her. Then we're going to get married and have a family. So you've got to pull through, Dez. I want to marry you." Bentley remained optimistic that if he continued to communicate with her, she would respond.

"Bro, I know you don't want to leave her side, but can we talk to you? Ginger and I have a theory of our own," Sparks said.

"You can say it in front of my baby. I'm not leaving her. Anything could happen," Bentley said adamantly.

"Okay. It's fine." Ginger felt for Bentley. It was obvious through his devotion that he truly loved Dez. "We can talk here."

Sparks cut right to the chase. "We think Leilani is behind the shooting."

"Why? We already know she's crazy. But is she *that* crazy?" Bentley was doubtful.

"Hell hath no fury like a woman scorned. Leilani seemed to believe that Dez was the cause of her and Sparks's breakup."

"That's crazy!" Bentley roared.

"We know," Ginger replied before Sparks had a chance to say anything. "But what are the odds that she's Chinese and the shooter was Asian? Y'all said it yourselves: y'all ain't got beef with nobody. Who else would want to see any of you dead?"

Bentley sat in thought momentarily, then said, "So what are we going to do? Shouldn't the police have figured this out?"

"Shoulda, coulda, woulda. The LAPD ain't never had love for black folks. They ain't managed to find who popped Big,

Pac, or Nicole Brown Simpson. We gotta handle this our way." Sparks pounded his palm with his fist for emphasis.

"Are you cool with this, Ginger?" Bentley asked. "You're a Christian. And what we might have to do ain't very Christian-like."

"I've got my issues. But I believe that God will take care of this before anyone else gets hurt. I'm praying on it. Face it. You all have so much at stake to lose. Bentley, Sparks, you could lose your careers, the label, if you act on your emotions and you hurt that girl. Death is too easy for her psychotic behind. She should suffer. But part of me knows that she needs help. Either way, she should pay for her actions, but don't blow your lives on her."

"She doesn't deserve to live!" Bentley yelled.

"Look. I've got an idea," Ginger said. "It's simple really. If you can trick her into confessing, she'll pay. She killed that journalist. Dez is on the brink of life and death. Whether Leilani goes to the nuthouse or jail, she will suffer."

"Yeah, but how are we gonna do that?" Sparks asked.

"Leilani is sick. We saw that when she pulled a knife on us at your house. All you have to do is act like you want her back. It always works in those psycho chick movies. Tell her how relieved you are that Dez is out of the way or something like that. That's what she really wants. She wants you, and she was willing to kill Dez, since she thought that Dez stood in her way. Flip it on her. Act like Dez has caused you nothing but trouble. Put it on real extra. You'll be able to tell by her reaction. She'll probably tell on herself. What do we have to lose?"

Sparks and Bentley looked at each other.

"Fuck that! I say we smoke that bitch!" Bentley spat.

"Right, and when Dez pulls through and sees you're in jail,

it will kill her. How you gonna marry her and make babies from a cell?" Ginger snapped.

Bentley dropped his shoulders in defeat. "Okay. We'll try this your way. I have to admit, it sounds like a good plan. But if that doesn't work, we're gonna do things the Harlem way!"

"Baby, I need you," was how Sparks greeted Leilani over the phone.

Leilani nearly wet herself. *This is working better than I planned,* she thought.

"Oh, honey! I wanted to call, but I didn't think you wanted to hear from me," Leilani gushed.

"Can you make a flight tonight? I need you. I have to see you."

"You name the time and airline, and I'm on the flight," she promised.

"Go to the airport now. I've got a ticket waiting for you on Delta. Don't worry about packing. We'll go shopping when you get here," Sparks forced himself to say.

Roughly eight hours later, Sparks picked Leilani up from LAX.

"Sparky! I'm so sorry. You must be a wreck," she told him as she greeted him with a big hug. Leilani made sure to rub her body against his to get him going.

"Not exactly, but we can't talk here. I've got a suite booked for us to get some privacy at the Standard. Let's go, baby. We've got a lot to talk about," Sparks said before they hopped in a cab and headed to Hollywood.

GINGER'S HANDS SHOOK AS SHE HOOKED UP THE NANNY CAM in the hotel room. She never thought she would have to put her technical skills to the test in such a manner, but now her sister's life depended on it. She'd already hooked up discreet long-range, high-frequency microphones on the lampshade next to the bed, in the sitting area, and in the bathroom just in case. It was amazing what one could purchase at the local spy shop.

All Sparks had to do was get Leilani to fess up without killing her. As a precautionary measure, Ginger checked into the room next door, and would be monitoring the action the entire time. Hopefully, Sparks would be able to get Leilani to talk without it taking too long or having to go too far.

Ginger and Sparks had gone over the plan what seemed like a million times. To get her warmed up, he'd kiss Leilani a little, caress her a bit, and tell her how much he missed her. If he just had to, he'd make love to her, but Sparks hoped it wouldn't come to that. He'd tell her how Dez had made a fool of him, how she'd nearly destroyed his label. He'd tell Leilani that he wanted Dez gone but that she'd threatened to sue him blind if he dropped her. He'd tell her that he was feeling trapped and that whoever shot her actually deserved the reward because they were doing him a huge favor. It had to work. Leilani would be all buttered up, and since being a hater was her nature, she'd more than likely fess up. Or so they hoped. Otherwise, the LAPD and a snitch would be their only chance to get to the bottom of the shooting.

Ginger's cell phone rang twice. That was her cue to slip next door. The games were about to begin . . .

"JOHNNY, I MISSED YOU SO MUCH. I'M SO SORRY ABOUT EVERY-thing that's happened," Leilani began.

"No need to apologize, Lani." Sparks gritted his teeth and kissed her with feigned passion. "I was blind. You tried to tell me about Dez, but I wouldn't listen. Can you ever forgive me? I've been such a fool."

"Oh, baby. It's not your fault. Dez has a way of making people lose sight of what's really important. It's because she has no priorities herself." Leilani stroked Sparks's face. It was all he could do not to slap her hand away.

"She's so self-centered. It was always me, me, me. Dez didn't care what was best for us. She was only about self," Sparks said.

"But what are you going to do? All that money you in-vested in her," Leilani said, showing her true colors. It was always about the almighty dollar to her, no matter how much she fronted otherwise.

"Baby girl, I'm glad you're here. I haven't had anyone that I could talk to about this. Bentley's heartbroken over that whore. He cared about her more than the label or me," he continued. Leilani shook her head in disgust. "The truth of the matter is, after the incident with you and the knife—"

Leilani cut him off. "That was a huge mistake."

"I'm not so sure," Sparks said, baiting her.

"What do you mean?" Leilani couldn't believe her ears.

"I mean, I wanted her gone. After I thought about every-thing that went down, I realized that having her around wasn't worth what it was doing to you emotionally. I knew that wasn't the real you doing that. Her presence was causing you so much pain. It made you irrational. And not just saying I wanted her gone from the label, but gone from my life, from my brother's life." Sparks paused to gauge her reaction. Leilani looked as if she were about to burst. Sparks continued with the ruse.

"She threatened to sue me if I dropped her. And can you believe the lawyers said she had a case? She was going to bankrupt me," he stated, faking shock.

"She's the proverbial gold digger," Leilani joined in.

"With her dead, I don't have to drop her. Plus, think of all the money her album is going to make. People will buy out of curiosity. And she has no real family. There's no one to split the profits with; she has no estate. Whoever shot her practically did me a favor! I should give them the reward. Hell, the only bad thing about this shooting is that she isn't dead yet. That and the million dollars I'll have to give to the snitch who rats out the shooter. I swear that bitch hasn't stopped costing me money! I hate her! I wish she would drop dead already." Sparks kicked a chair for drama's sake and to keep from kicking Leilani. It was killing him to say those things about the woman he loved so much.

"Baby, you're going to love me even more when I tell you what I have to tell you." Leilani grinned.

"I don't see how I could love you more than I already do," he told her, cupping her chin in his hand and kissing her lightly.

"Oh, I have a feeling that you can and you will. You're not going to have to give up a copper penny for that skank," she announced.

"Why do you say that?" Sparks looked confused.

"I know who shot her. I can guarantee you that the police will never catch him."

"How?"

"Don't be mad . . ." Leilani gave him a sweet smile.

"I could never be mad at you. We've wasted enough time being mad, haven't we?" he said soothingly. Outwardly, he appeared collected, but inside he was raging.

"I'm glad to hear you say that, because *I* had her shot. The journalist was an accident," she said. "As much as I paid for the hit man, there should have been no mistakes. The bullet should have gone through her black heart," Leilani recounted angrily. "But that bitch is about to check out any minute. It all worked out."

"But how did you find a professional hit man?" Sparks wanted her to tell it all, so there would be no questions from the police.

"My cousin Mike, on my mother's side, belongs to the Dragon Triad. It's a gang here that straight up terrorizes motherfuckers. They ain't no joke. He put me in touch with this Chinese dude Ling Bai. It cost me fifteen thousand, and that's with the family discount! But Ling Bai is unstoppable. He knows how to kill anything that breathes, and he does it perfectly. At least he usually does. He doesn't even really exist on paper. He's like a ninja, except only Chinese, not Japanese."

"You're kidding, right?"

"No, not at all. No one is going to tell. Anyone who knows that Ling Bai is the shooter knows that they don't want to fuck with him or the Dragon Triad. Besides, how many people out there know one Asian from another? We all look alike, remember?" Leilani laughed out loud at her joke.

"That was pretty smart, Leilani," Sparks told her.

"That's why you love me. Because I'm smart!"

"Well, this calls for a celebration! I'm gonna order a magnum of Cristal from room service. How does caviar sound?"

Leilani had no idea that the ax was about to fall, and it was her neck on the chopping block.

"Fabulous," she responded. "Mind if I freshen up a little while we wait?"

"Be my guest."

Thirty minutes later there was a knock on the door. Sparks laughed to himself at the irony of it all. He'd been in the shower waiting for room service when the police came and took him away for the bogus assault. Now Leilani was going to jail, possibly for the rest of her life, and she was none the wiser.

"Will you get that, honey? I want to take a quick shower myself," he said after barging into the bathroom. Leilani was wrapping herself in a towel.

"Awww, you should have joined me. We would have had lots more fun!"

"Oh, I have a feeling the fun has just begun," Sparks replied.

Leilani flung the door open to see Detective Atkins standing before her.

"Well, you aren't room service," she told him. Just then, the room service attendant appeared with a cart containing the magnum of champagne, a bowl of caviar, and fresh strawberries.

"Right this way," Sparks told him.

Leilani was surprised to hear Sparks behind her. "Honey, I thought you were taking a shower."

"Oh, I wouldn't miss this for the world—the shower can wait," Sparks answered her. "By the way, have you met Detective Atkins?" Detective Atkins entered the room, followed by Ginger.

"What the hell is she doing here?" Leilani screamed.

"Watching you go down, bitch," Ginger told her, popping the cork on the Cristal.

"What? I don't understand." Leilani spun about, disoriented.

"Leilani Hong Thomas, you are under arrest for the attempted murder of Desiree Mirabella Torres Jackson and the murder of Sheila Rubin," Detective Atkins informed her as he pulled a pair of shiny handcuffs from his back pocket.

"Did you understand that?" Ginger asked as she poured her and Sparks glasses of champagne.

"This is entrapment! It'll never hold up in court!" Leilani screeched as she struggled in a futile attempt to free herself from the handcuffs.

"See, Leilani, the thing about you is that you're not half as smart as you think you are. It would be entrapment if I were a cop, or if the police had been involved beforehand," Sparks explained.

"That's right, Leilani," Ginger said. "This is all our doing. I just called the police. Detective Atkins here just watched your taped confession in my suite next door. So, honey child, you weren't entrapped. You were just plain old-fashioned set up to play yourself."

"This will never hold up in court. You have nothing," Leilani spat.

"Get a good lawyer. Adiós, mami!" Ginger shook her head. She almost felt sorry for Leilani. It was true that they might have a hard time admitting the tape in court. But she knew it was now only a matter of time before the police found more than enough information to nail Leilani.

"*Salud!*" Ginger toasted Sparks with a raised glass.

"*Salud,*" he replied before clinking his glass with hers.

EPILOGUE

The Last Word?

NOW Y'ALL KNOW I'M NOT GOING OUT LIKE THAT. I'VE BEEN through too much and come too far to go out like a sucker. It's a trip that I can hear almost everything that is going on around me, but I can't respond. There's so much I want to say to Bentley, to Sparks, and to Ginger. There's so much I want to thank them for. But I'll have my chance soon enough. I feel myself getting stronger; I know I'm on my way back to life. And although I've always had my theories, I'm not ready to find out if my boy Tupac is really dead or not. I don't wonder if heaven got a ghetto. I know it does, and it's called hell! I was on my way there in a handbasket with gasoline drawers on.

Somewhere along the way I lost my faith; faith in a higher power and faith in myself. But I won't be seeing any parts of hell anytime soon. I'm going to live. And even if I don't live, thanks to Ginger, I know that my salvation is already taken care of. It's by God's grace that I'm still here. And when I come out of this coma, because I will, I'm going to make sure that I spend the rest of my life showing him just how grateful I am for all the chances I've had.

I did a lot of dirt in my day, and for that I'm truly sorry. I used so many people to get what I wanted in the name of survival when what I really needed to live was love. No designer fashion, no pocket full of cash, no trip ever gave me the satisfaction of how it felt to be really and truly loved; loved by my dad and grandparents, by Ginger, by Sparks, and especially by Bentley.

I don't know how I could begin to make up for the wrong that I've done; I can barely remember all the men's faces, let alone their names. But I think that if I give to those in need, give without being asked and without expecting anything in return, maybe that will be a start. Maybe if I help others instead of always being out for self, I can make a difference in someone's life, and not just their wallet.

I still want to rap, but I can't say that my lyrics are going to focus on the same old same old. How much can one person talk about money, cars, clothes, thugging, fucking, and balling? We've had enough of that. It's time for something new, something that will really change the world. I know that as an entertainer I have to give the people what they want, but maybe they don't realize that they want and deserve so much more than what they're getting. I didn't.

I know Sparks isn't going to scrap the album, and I don't really want him to. I worked hard on it, and it is a reflection of who I was at the time. I'm not going to start fronting now. Plus, I'm going to need all the money I can get to pay this hospital bill.

I don't want my fans to get the wrong idea and think that I'm still all about the streets, because I've learned that there's so much more out there. There's a world of good things just waiting to be claimed, even for the girls in the hood. I'm going to show them that there's a way to get it but that they don't have to do what I did. I don't know exactly how I'll handle that, but I guess it's a bridge I'll cross when I get to it. I know that God will give me the courage and the wisdom to do what I need to do, so I'll just be still, put it in his hands, and do what the Spirit guides me to do.

I didn't have the best start in life, and for a long time I let that stand in my way. I used it as an excuse as to why I couldn't do *something, and I even thought that because I grew up poor and with-out a family, I didn't deserve for anything good to happen to me. And because of the rape and how I was raised, I thought I was dirty and tainted and didn't deserve love. But now I understand that it is my birthright and my destiny to inherit all the riches of God's kingdom. I don't have to buy into the whole "all women are bitches and bitches ain't shit" mentality. And I'm going to make sure that no little girl within the sound of my voice buys that garbage either. Women are queens; we just have to realize that we wear the crown.*

I always thought that if I had a better upbringing, I would have had a better life, and maybe that's true. But I'm all grown-up now, even if I grew up way too fast, and now I can't continue to blame my family or my environment. I have the responsibility and the capabil-ity to be "the master of my fate and the captain of my soul," as one of my favorite poems, called "Invictus," says.

I don't profess to have all the answers. Not even by a long shot. But I know that I'm going to get there, God willing. Bentley hasn't left my side, and now there is no doubt that he really loves me. Bent-ley told me that Ginger and Sparks were busy trying to find who did this to me, and I know that if anyone can figure it out, it's those two. They are the smartest people I know, and they love me. The way I see it, they're my best shot, because the LAPD ain't got no love for a black person or a Latino.

Bentley also says we're going to get married and try for another baby; he told me that I lost this one. I know he would have been an excellent father, and I would have been a pretty fantastic mother myself. But maybe it wasn't meant to be right now. But what's defi-nitely not meant to be is me taking a dirt nap. I'm a Leo baby, the biggest of all the cats. The way I see it, I've got at least seven more lives left.

ABOUT THE AUTHOR

Méta Smith was born in Philadelphia and raised on the south side of Chicago. She attended Clark Atlanta University, where she majored in mass communications, and later transferred to Spelman College in Atlanta, where she received a bachelor's degree in English.

Her adventurous spirit took her to Miami on a vacation that turned into a six-year residency. In Miami she fell in love with the South Beach club scene and worked a myriad of jobs to support her nightlife addiction, including waitress, promotions coordinator for the local UPN affiliate, middle-school English teacher, nightclub promoter, exotic dancer, and music video model. The latter two positions inspired her to pen her debut novel, *The Rolexxx Club*.

Méta has also worked extensively in the field of fundraising for philanthropic causes, using her social skills and her gift for writing to raise millions of dollars for a variety of non-profit organizations, including the United Way and the Benedictine Sisters of Chicago, an order of monastic nuns. She lives in Conneaut, Ohio, with her fiancé and son.